You have rescheduled your appointment with her six times in the last three weeks. She asked me to advise you that at this time, yours is the only interview she still requires in order to complete her report."

"Right," Kathryn Janeway remembered. It wasn't that she was avoiding the captain, or Project Full Circle. But being an admiral was about prioritizing. "See if Captain Eden would be available to meet at 0600 tomorrow. If so, I can give her two hours."

"I will transmit your request and forward her response to you this evening," Decan replied.

"And the rest will simply have to wait," she decided. "For the next few hours I don't wish to be disturbed over anything less than the arrival of a Borg armada in Earth's orbit," she said.

"If you'd like, I could contact the Borg directly and ask that they postpone any imminent actions so as not to spoil your evening," Decan said deadpan.

Janeway paused for a moment as his words sunk in. Finally, her face broke into a wide grin.

"Humor, Ensign?" she asked.

The Vulcan acknowledged her with a slight nod. "Often it provides a welcome release of tension."

"That it does." She smiled. "Well done."

STAR TREK VOYAGER®
FULL CIRCLE

KIRSTEN BEYER

Based on *Star Trek*®
created by Gene Roddenberry
and *Star Trek: Voyager*
created by Rick Berman & Michael Piller & Jeri Taylor

POCKET BOOKS
New York London Toronto Sydney Boreth

Pocket Books
A Division of Simon & Schuster, Inc.
1230 Avenue of the Americas
New York, NY 10020

This book is a work of fiction. Names, characters, places, and incidents either are products of the author's imagination or are used fictitiously. Any resemblance to actual events or locales or persons, living or dead, is entirely coincidental.

First Pocket Books paperback edition April 2009

POCKET and colophon are registered trademarks of Simon & Schuster, Inc.

Cover art by Mojo

For information about special discounts for bulk purchases, please contact Simon & Schuster Special Sales at 1-800-456-6798 or business@simonandschuster.com.

The Simon & Schuster Speakers Bureau can bring authors to your live event. For more information or to book an event, contact the Simon & Schuster Speakers Bureau at 866-248-3049 or visit our website at www.simonspeakers.com.

Manufactured in the United States of America

10 9 8 7 6 5 4 3 2 .1

ISBN-13: 978-1-4165-9496-3
ISBN-10:   1-4165-9496-5

For W. Fred Beyer

"Destiny . . . is a fickle bitch."
—BENJAMIN LINUS

PART ONE

WHAT FATES IMPOSE

JUNE 2380

PROLOGUE

Venice was everything Chakotay imagined it would be; perhaps more. Though the simulated version created by Tom Paris on *Voyager*'s holodeck many years earlier had its charms, it bore the same relation to the real thing as replicated eggplant Parmesan did to . . . well, food.

If one could be struck by serenity, such was the cumulative effect of the water of the Grand Canal lapping gently beneath the Ponte degli Scalzi, the faintly pungent yet sweet taste of the air, the dim luminescence of the crescent moon hanging above, complimented by its dimmer counterparts in the small votive candles sitting atop the café's scattered outdoor tables, and the light blanket of damp warmth that nature had tossed over the city on this summer night.

La Zucca, the fifteenth restaurant to bear the name on the site since its establishment in the mid-nineteenth century, was close enough to the most heavily trafficked of Santa Croce's streets that it should have been buzzing with life on a night such as this. The closest public transporter station was two blocks away, having long ago replaced the ancient Santa Lucia railway station. The "bridge of bare feet" arched over the canal less than a hundred meters in the distance. And by all reports, the food was authentic

Northern Italian, and absolutely delicious. Still, the café was all but deserted.

And Chakotay honestly wouldn't have wanted it any other way. It stood to reason that only days after an attack by a monstrous Borg cube, residents might still be skittish about returning to their normal lives or venturing too far from home. But having faced the Borg down more than once, Chakotay could not share their pessimism. At least La Zucca had been open, unlike many other local businesses.

If Kathryn didn't arrive soon, he might have to go ahead and at least sample the cuisine without her. He'd already opened the first of what he hoped would be at least a couple of bottles of red wine. There would be no synthehol on the menu this evening. He didn't think she'd mind if he started them off with a small antipasto appetizer from the menu he'd already had time to memorize. With luck, if he ordered it now, it would arrive at the same time as the admiral.

Admiral Janeway.

Chakotay had to smile to himself. It wasn't that Kathryn didn't deserve to be a vice admiral. She'd been a Starfleet captain for years before taking command of *Voyager* and bringing her safely through the Delta quadrant. Her record was unassailable. What Chakotay still found hard to believe, even two and a half years since *Voyager*'s return from its seven-year journey, was that Kathryn had so readily accepted the promotion upon their return to Earth.

Of course, it would have been bad form to turn down the offer from Starfleet Command. And if the history of this timeline bore any resemblance to that of the "Admiral Janeway" who had assisted her younger counterpart in bringing *Voyager* home, it did suggest that Kathryn would continue to climb steadily through the ranks.

But she had been his captain when they met, and for the first seven years of their life together. Though technically also a captain in his own right, Chakotay had chosen to accept the position of her first officer when his Maquis vessel was sacrificed to save *Voyager* in their first battle with the Kazon. He still vividly remembered the sight of Kathryn, standing on *Voyager*'s bridge with her chin held high but her heart clearly torn as she struggled briefly with her decision to destroy the array that had brought them to the Delta quadrant and was their best chance for a timely return home. When she had finally given the order to Ensign Kim to fire tricobalt payloads at the array, B'Elanna Torres had demanded furiously to know what gave her the right to make that decision for all of them. Even Chakotay had been surprised at the time by how quickly a response had formed on his lips.

"She's the captain," he had said, settling the matter once and for all.

Even now it was hard not to see Kathryn in the light of her most compelling and inspiring role: the center seat of a Starfleet vessel. As his captain she had earned his respect and loyalty. Harder to pinpoint was the exact moment along the way when she had also won his heart.

Still, the damage was done. In nearly ten years of discovery and exploration, success and bitter loss on the field of battle, and ultimately, the tedious demands of duty, he had never wavered in his commitment to her. Finally the time had come to make that commitment more real and permanent than fate had allowed until this night.

In the past, he might have felt a certain amount of anxiety at the prospect. But now, the idea that he and Kathryn would move side by side into their future brought only a sense of peace and relief. It was simple. It was right. It felt like destiny.

The only thing troubling him even slightly was the fact that Kathryn was now over a full hour late. Most likely, Chakotay assured himself, she and the rest of the admiralty were still working long hours in the aftermath of the attack. He hadn't spoken to her, as he'd hoped to, when *Voyager* was finally allowed to enter the Sol system, following their deep-space mission to the Yaris Nebula. The area had been restricted after the appearance of what, by the brief reports he'd heard, had been a massive cube and traffic in and around Earth was only now returning to normal.

They had agreed to meet for this dinner almost a year earlier. Only three weeks ago Kathryn had reminded him of their date, as if he needed a reminder, and half-teasingly described the cruel fate that would befall him should he stand her up. He knew that in the interim she had undertaken a classified mission, but surely she was back by now. Chakotay refused to doubt that wherever she was at this moment, it was here, with him, that she wanted to be, and would be as soon as possible.

Opposite him at her empty place was a gift he had long wished to return to her. He had first given it to her almost five years earlier, on the occasion of a slightly mortifying misunderstanding that had nonetheless been the catalyst for them finally to openly discuss their deep feelings for one another, and the duty that made those feelings irrelevant until *Voyager* was safely back in the Alpha quadrant.

Somehow, Chakotay had managed to set his feelings aside and even halfheartedly pursue other romantic relationships, but he had survived on the hope that one day he would find himself exactly where he was now, in Venice, ready to give back the gift she could not accept when it was first presented to her.

It was a circular mirror, edged with polished stones collected from planets *Voyager* had visited in the Delta quadrant. On the back Chakotay had inscribed the words *When in doubt, look here*.

Struggling with his growing impatience, Chakotay adjusted the mirror ever so slightly in its place, then toyed briefly with the silver ribbon he had tied around its center. He'd seen no need to wrap it completely. Kathryn would remember. In his fidget, he managed to pull the bow off center, so he was forced to grab the mirror and begin to readjust the perfect presentation he had just ruined.

Of course, it was at this moment that he heard soft footfalls behind him. Arriving from the transport station, Kathryn would have come from the south. Chakotay had suspected this would be the case and had chosen a table from the many that were free which would both highlight the dramatic view of the canal and the bridge, but also make it easy for her to spot him.

An unanticipated shot of nervous adrenaline coursed through him and he fumbled the bow again. Finally he decided to toss it aside altogether and simply rose and turned to greet her, now holding the precious gift in his hand.

Somewhere in the back of his consciousness he registered that the footsteps slowed and came to a stop as he turned. He didn't know why this made his heart beat just a bit faster. Perhaps he was spoiling her entrance, but, mid-turn, it was too late to change course.

Only when he had come fully around did he realize that what faint light the moon was casting fell behind the individual now standing before him, a figure he real-ized immediately, even in the obscuring shadows, was not Kathryn.

"Good evening, Captain," a deep male voice said softly.

Fear, like ice, shot through Chakotay.

The man stepped closer, just enough for the soft illumi-nation of one of the café's exterior lights to match the face to the voice Chakotay already recognized.

"Hello, Mark," Chakotay managed through an ever-tightening throat.

"I'm sorry to . . ." Mark began, but failed to find words to continue.

He didn't need to say a thing. His eyes bore the weary, haunted expression of a man whose darkest demon has just stopped by for a good, long visit.

"Kathryn told me weeks ago she was meeting you here tonight," Mark finally offered, as if in apology. "I tried to reach you the moment *Voyager* returned, but things have been . . . well, I'm sure you know. I promised Gretchen I would . . ."

Chakotay raised a shaking hand to silence him. Years ago, Mark Johnson and Kathryn Janeway had been en-gaged. He had married someone else after *Voyager* was lost in the Delta quadrant and its crew pronounced dead. When word had finally reached Earth that *Voyager*'s crew was in fact alive and still on course for home, Mark had told Kathryn honestly what had happened and the friend-ship that had been theirs long before their courtship had reasserted itself. Even now, Kathryn often enjoyed off-duty time with Mark, his wife, Carla, and their young son, Kevin.

Chakotay needed to ask why Mark was standing here now in Kathryn's place.

He needed to. But he couldn't.

Mark was having just as hard a time saying anything more.

Finally, in a barely audible whisper Chakotay found the strength to say, "She's not coming, is she?"

For a moment, Mark stood frozen before him as if knowing that to move into the next second would make the awful truth he carried with him suddenly real.

But it was already real.

Though Chakotay had allowed himself to be distracted by the beauty of the setting and the anticipation of her arrival, as the minutes had passed and she had failed to appear, a gnawing doubt had begun to fester. It had only taken a glance at Mark's face for that doubt to become something more closely resembling dread.

The truth Chakotay's heart had known but stubbornly refused to acknowledge even now was that there was only one thing that would have kept Kathryn from meeting him on time this night.

Finally, Mark shook his head ever so slightly and fresh tears glinted in his eyes.

Somewhere deep in the center of Chakotay's being a distant roar began to build. But it was still possible to keep it at bay, connected as it was to a reality that Chakotay's heart would not accept.

"Just tell me she's not dead," Chakotay said flatly. It wasn't much, this faint possible hope, but it was enough to keep the worst from descending upon him in its full, final force.

Mark inhaled sharply, then composed himself.

"She is," he replied in a grim attempt at stoicism.

The next sound Chakotay heard was that of breaking glass as the mirror he held in his hand fell to the cobbled street, shattering.

SEPTEMBER 2378

CHAPTER ONE

You and the Kuvah'magh are in danger.

For weeks, B'Elanna Torres had been able to think of little else.

The warning had come to her anonymously, a scrawled hard-copy message shoved under the heavy wooden door that separated her private living space from the rest of the monastery on Boreth. Here she had spent the past eight months studying ancient Klingon scrolls in an effort to learn all she could of what fate might have in store for her beloved daughter, Miral.

She had come to Boreth to find her mother. Though their reunion had been brief, it had helped B'Elanna come to grips with the Klingon part of her heritage, which she had vigorously tried to ignore for most of her life. Once that was done, it had been her husband, Tom's, suggestion that they look deeper into her Klingon past in order to banish once and for all the disturbing notion that their daughter might be the *Kuvah'magh*, or Klingon savior.

B'Elanna had initially decided to humor Tom. As he had yet to find a posting on a Starfleet vessel that suited him, it had seemed a harmless enough diversion. Of course, the chance to spend countless hours in only his company and that of their infant daughter had been even more compelling. As much as they both thrived in the world of Starfleet service, after seven years spent facing the very real possibility that each day in the Delta quadrant might be their last, the quiet, contemplative hours spent sheltered on Boreth had brought both of them much-needed space in which to deepen the bonds between them.

Too soon, duty had called. Admiral Janeway had requested Tom's assistance on a diplomatic mission, and within weeks his spectacular service had earned him the only job in Starfleet that Tom Paris couldn't possibly turn down, first officer aboard *Voyager*.

Being separated from Tom was difficult. But it would have been much easier to bear had B'Elanna not begun to seriously believe, shortly after he had left, that there might be more to connect the prophecies about the *Kuvah'magh* and their daughter than either of them had believed they would find.

It had been easy enough to dismiss the many parallels between Miral and this fated "savior" when the notion first reared its ugly head back in the Delta quadrant. *Voyager* had encountered an old Klingon vessel filled with hundreds of warriors whose parents and grandparents had long ago left Qo'noS, in search of the *Kuvah'magh*. Some believed that Miral, though unborn, was the end of their search. And when Miral's hybrid blood cells had managed to cure those same Klingons of a fatal virus, *nehret*, that they had contracted on their journey, it was hard to argue the point, at least in this case, that Miral *had* been their "savior."

The scrolls that had led Kohlar's people to the Delta quadrant were only the tip of the prophetic Klingon iceberg. Those had been written a thousand years ago by a warrior named Amar. On Boreth, B'Elanna had discovered the scrolls of a Klingon ascetic, a man named Ghargh, whose writings preceded the founding of the Klingon Empire by another eight centuries. Ghargh was the one who had said that the *Kuvah'magh* would be a "voyager." His words had sent an unpleasant chill coursing down B'Elanna's spine when she'd first read them. Further, he had inexplicably gone on to say that the true purpose of the *Kuvah'magh* was to restore the Klingon gods—a patently ridiculous notion—even if B'Elanna were a believer—as the Klingons supposedly had slain their gods ages ago for being more trouble than they were worth.

Despite the smatterings of coincidence that could be found in the writings of both Amar and Ghargh, B'Elanna was a long way from accepting that any of this was real, much less relevant to her daughter. Clearly others, however, weren't having as hard a time as she making that leap of faith, and she had no idea to what lengths they might go to see their beliefs made real.

Miral slept peacefully in her arms, her breath slow and deep. Though Tom had helped B'Elanna construct a make-shift crib from straw and animal skins, the only items the monastery seemed to have in plentiful supply, B'Elanna was finding it harder and harder to let Miral out of her arms, never mind her sight. This had forced B'Elanna to rig a private comm station for her quarters. The only other station that provided access to the outside universe was located in a secluded room deep in the bowels of the monastery, and Boreth's residents were granted access to it only sparingly.

Any moment now, Tom's face would appear before her on the small screen. Despite the distance between them, they had managed to speak at least once a week since his departure, but even this, the event that should have been the high point of B'Elanna's day, was now tinged with discomfort.

For weeks now, B'Elanna had struggled with the fear that whoever had warned her that her life and Miral's were in danger might not have been exaggerating. And for weeks, B'Elanna had beaten that fear into brief submission so as not to reveal even the faintest hint of alarm when she spoke with Tom. B'Elanna didn't want to leave Boreth until she was confident she knew everything there was to know about these cursed prophecies. But she wasn't a fool either. If Tom knew about the warning, he would take immediate leave and drag both B'Elanna and Miral from the monastery, kicking and screaming if necessary, to keep them safe.

B'Elanna had lied to Tom repeatedly. She hated doing it. But for now, it seemed necessary. Her final justification had been the brilliant rationalization that she could not be certain how secure her "private" comm transmission was. Were she to reveal her fears to Tom, she might simultaneously be revealing them to those who wished her harm. And that might be all they would need to set whatever plans they had in motion. It was simply too great a risk to take.

Just one more week. Maybe two.

Surely in that time she would be able to find the flaw in the logic suggesting that Miral might be the *Kuvah'magh*. As soon as she did, they would return to Earth, perhaps even to *Voyager,* and Tom would never need to know what she was hiding from him.

It sounded good in theory.

And then the face of the man she adored, the sandy blond hair cut regulation-short, the piercing blue eyes, and the smile that promised such wonderful mischief appeared before her, and B'Elanna's heart leapt even as the practiced mask of utter calm descended on her features.

"And how's my little Kuvah'magh *this evening?"* Tom cooed.

B'Elanna couldn't help but smile. When Tom used his favorite endearment, her fears seemed almost laughable.

"She's trying something new tonight," B'Elanna replied warmly.

"What's that?" Tom asked.

"Sleeping."

"Ah." Tom nodded sagely. *"I wondered when she would figure that one out."*

"A couple of nights ago she managed almost six hours straight," B'Elanna went on. Talking to Tom these days was much easier when they stayed in innocuous territory.

"That's got to be a record, right?"

"Mmm-hmm." B'Elanna nodded. "I'm hoping she sets a new one tonight."

"Has she been wearing you out?" Tom asked, a hint of concern creeping into his voice. B'Elanna knew he would never willingly imply that there was anything in the universe his wife couldn't conquer. Even with a half-Klingon wife it was such a fine and dangerous line between supportive and condescending.

"She has been more active. I swear she'll be walking any minute now, and then we're both doomed," B'Elanna said.

"How's Kularg doing?"

"I honestly never thought I would use the words *Klingon* and *doting* in the same sentence, but the truth is, he adores her. I don't know what he'll do with himself when our stay on Boreth ends."

This was mostly true, though B'Elanna had refused to leave Miral with Kularg even once since she'd received the cryptic message. Daily, however, Kularg managed to find an almost reasonable excuse to stop by B'Elanna's chamber and ask after Miral. The grizzled old man was positively smitten. The fact that he had no grandchildren of his own was a crime against nature.

"Funny you should bring that up," Tom segued.

"What?" B'Elanna asked.

"Leaving Boreth," Tom replied in an attempt at nonchalance.

B'Elanna's heart fluttered, but she managed to keep her game face in place.

"Has something happened?" B'Elanna asked, not really sure if she wanted the answer to be "yes" or "no."

"No, no." Tom shook his head immediately, then sighed with feigned weariness. *"It's my mom."*

"Is she okay?"

"She's terrific. In fact, she just completed the arrangements for a party at the family ranch three weeks from now that'll make your average annual Federation Day celebration look like a small, intimate gathering."

"What are we celebrating?" B'Elanna chuckled.

Tom couldn't hide his embarrassment.

"My promotion to first officer," he replied.

"You were promoted two months ago," B'Elanna pointed out.

"You've met my mom, right?" Tom asked. *"Petite, blonde, and fiercer than a breeding Horta when it comes to anything at all to do with her son?"*

B'Elanna remembered all too well. Julia Paris had been something of a revelation. Her slight figure belied an intensity that was truly something to behold. B'Elanna had always believed that meeting Tom's father, the famous Admiral Owen Paris, would be the more daunting introduction to her new in-laws, but she'd been pleasantly surprised to learn that Tom's single-minded, stubborn persistence had been a gift from his mother.

"Besides, it takes at least eight weeks to schedule an event when you're inviting half the quadrant. Busy schedules and all that," Tom added, clearly mortified at the thought.

"Sounds like it should be awful." B'Elanna couldn't help grinning at his discomfort.

"Right," Tom nodded, *"and of course she's adamant that the whole affair will be a disaster if her daughter-in-law and granddaughter aren't there to be shown off to all of her friends."*

Yeah, that hadn't been hard to see coming.

"Tom . . ." B'Elanna sighed.

"There's still plenty of time for you and Miral to hop a quick transport. And I promise, as soon as it's done, I'll escort you both back to Boreth myself, if that's what you want."

In a way, it was exactly what B'Elanna wanted.

And maybe there really isn't anything more for me to learn here.

"Is this going to be a 'resistance is futile' kind of thing?" B'Elanna quipped.

"Now that you mention it, it's actually kind of terrifying to imagine what the Borg might become if my mother's 'distinctiveness' were ever added to theirs," Tom mused.

Unexpected relief warred with concern within B'Elanna. Her gut told her that whatever forces were allying against her and her daughter, they weren't going to be dissuaded by a party. And she couldn't be certain that by leaving

Boreth, she wouldn't be playing directly into their hands. Still, strong as she was alone, that strength was increased by an order of magnitude when she was with Tom. She missed him. But more than that, she *needed* him.

"Then I guess we can't disappoint her, can we?" B'Elanna replied.

The utter love and gratitude that beamed from Tom's eyes in response made further words irrelevant.

"What did she say?"

Tom was glad his back was to his father so Admiral Owen Paris couldn't see the reflexive eye-rolling that occurred the moment Tom realized his father had been lurking in the doorway while he spoke with B'Elanna.

Tom couldn't blame his father. One of the nice things about being both older and married since he'd last spent any considerable amount of time with his dad was that actions that would have once driven Tom to heated, angry distraction were now eminently understandable and easy to forgive.

Owen didn't mean to pry. But as Tom now knew all too well, if Owen returned to Julia's presence without being able to tell her that her daughter-in-law and granddaughter were now en route to Earth, there would be ten kinds of hell to pay, and Tom wouldn't have wished that on an enemy, let alone the father he had come to respect and love since *Voyager* had returned home.

"Why are you even asking?" Tom asked good-naturedly as he switched off the comm station and turned to face his father's delighted face. "You were listening the whole time, weren't you?"

"I wanted to . . . well . . . er . . ." Owen fumbled for a moment.

Though Tom sort of liked seeing his father stammer about for an acceptable excuse—he couldn't even count the number of times this particular scenario had been reversed between them—he didn't like to see his father in unnecessary distress. Tom had been responsible for more than his fair share of that over the years.

Thankfully, those years were behind them.

"It's all right, Dad." Tom finally smiled. "They're coming. Now go tell Mom so she can alert the Federation News Service."

Owen nodded swiftly in relief, but made no immediate move to hasten to share the good news.

Tom gave his father a few moments before asking, "Something else on your mind?"

Owen took a few steps into the room and answered as innocently as possible, "Did they mention how long they might be staying?"

To be fair, Owen Paris wasn't the only person who really wanted an answer to that question. Tom knew that pushing B'Elanna was fruitless. Progress with his wife on any issue came only in slow fits and starts and was almost always on B'Elanna's schedule. He counted it a major victory that she had agreed to leave Boreth at all. The "how long do you plan to stay" question would come only once she was safely home and hopefully enjoying herself immensely.

"We really didn't have a chance to discuss it," Tom finally replied, and watched as the wheels in his father's head instantly shifted to a higher gear.

Owen nodded and took himself for a short walk, a few paces back and forth, then stopped, pulling himself up to his full height, in preparation to begin "the speech." Whenever there was anything particularly serious on Owen's mind, he usually completed this little ritual before beginning his orations. Tom could always see "the speech" coming from miles away.

"The thing is, son," Owen began. "And please tell me if I'm overstepping my bounds here . . . ," he offered.

Tom nodded graciously for him to continue and tried unsuccessfully to hide the smirk that was forming on his lips. He sometimes couldn't believe how well he now felt he knew his father.

"Both your mother and I were so relieved to learn that you were alive long after we thought, well, the worst. And when you came back to us, you and B'Elanna and Miral, it was almost too good to be true. Of course, you're both young and still anxious to serve Starfleet, and that's wonderful. But if there's anything I regret in my own life, it's the time I didn't make for my family, especially when you and your sisters were young."

There were moments in the past when Tom would have made his father suffer greatly for making such a statement. But the young, injured, insecure Tom Paris who had run as far from his family as possible in an attempt to escape his own failings was now a man at peace. Where once he would have accused his father of worse than the negligence Owen was admitting, now Tom only wanted to offer what comfort he could.

"I understand, Dad," Tom quickly interjected, "now more than ever. It's hard to balance a career and a family. There's no way to get it right all the time."

Owen nodded, wordlessly accepting his son's implied forgiveness.

"I never want you to feel the regrets I've felt," Owen finally went on. "I know B'Elanna needs to understand her heritage, and of course it's your job to support her. But don't you think it would be possible for her to continue her studies or research or whatever the hell she's doing on that Klingon rock a little closer to home? Before you know it, Miral will be walking and then speaking, and . . ." Owen trailed off, at a loss to put into words the various miracles that accompanied the raising of a child, or being a grandfather for the first time. Finally he settled for, "I just don't want you to miss it, son."

Tom rose from his seat and crossed to face his father. "I have no intention of missing *any* of it, Dad," he assured him.

Owen smiled faintly, his eyes alight with some of the mischief Tom had managed to turn into an art form.

"Then you agree that when B'Elanna and Miral return, we should find a way to make their stay more permanent?" Owen asked.

Tom extended his right hand to his father. Owen took it and shook it firmly.

"Absolutely," Tom replied.

"Good man," Owen said, clapping his son on the shoulder amiably.

Owen was clearly now armed with all he needed to face his wife, and he was halfway out the door when Tom suddenly remembered a question he'd been meaning to ask Owen since he reported back to Earth a few hours earlier for his leave from *Voyager*.

"Dad, do you know a Captain Eden?"

Owen seemed to search his memory. "She's part of Project Full Circle, isn't she?"

Tom nodded. "She's requested a meeting with me. I was just wondering if you had any idea what it might be about."

Both Owen and Tom were aware that Project Full Circle was the task force designated by Starfleet Command to analyze *Voyager* one relay and circuit at a time when it had returned from the Delta quadrant. Nine months later, however, and with *Voyager* now fully refitted and back on active duty, it seemed odd that the project was still going and that Eden was still in search of new information.

"I honestly don't," Owen replied. "Eden does have a reputation for being pretty thorough in her research and reports. She can bury a man in analysis quicker than most. She's probably just trying to tie up a few loose ends," Owen finally decided.

"I'm sure that's it." Tom nodded.

"When do you report to her?"

"Tomorrow morning, bright and early."

"Will you still be home for dinner tomorrow night?" Owen asked.

This time Tom failed to hide the rolling of the eyes.

"Yes, Dad," he replied, feigning impatience.

"Don't you 'Yes, Dad' me, Commander," Owen snapped.

For a split second, Tom jumped to attention.

Then both of them shared a hearty laugh as they made their way to the kitchen to let Julia Paris know that all would soon be right with their world.

CHAPTER TWO

Captain Afsarah Eden was a morning person. Her ex-husband, Admiral Willem Batiste, had accused her more than once of being an incurable midnight-oil junkie, but the truth was she simply didn't seem to need as much sleep as most people she knew. She often worked late into the night, wrestling with whatever problem was currently caught in her teeth before catching three to four hours of rest and rising early to attack the next problem on her list.

For the past nine months, that problem had been the *U.S.S. Voyager*—the ship, its crew, and the countless details of their seven years spent in the Delta quadrant.

Initially she had been tasked with a minute analysis of the "modifications" that had been made to *Voyager*'s many systems while the ship was out of range of any Starfleet repair facility. The most interesting were the ablative hull armor and transphasic torpedoes; they had been gifts—or contaminants, according to the Department of Temporal Affairs—from a future Admiral Janeway for use in *Voyager*'s final confrontation with the Borg before the ship had returned home, and had been stripped from *Voyager* immediately. Despite their effectiveness and the potential tactical advantages they provided, they had to be balanced against Starfleet's necessary caution toward such advanced technology as well as the repercussions to the timestream.

Some of the other modifications, the shipboard dilithium refining unit designed by Chief Engineer B'Elanna Torres and the regenerative circuits and relays provided by Seven of Nine—a former Borg that Captain Janeway had somehow managed to repatriate into individuality—merited closer consideration. These modifications had been truly inspired, though brought about by necessity. The *Intrepid*-class explorers had never been designed with such long-range excursions in mind; however, many other starships were, and Eden felt strongly that many of *Voyager*'s innovations should be safely adopted fleetwide.

She'd already spent months arguing this point with Admiral Kenneth Montgomery, Project Full Circle's ranking officer. Though the decision had been made to restore *Voyager* to *Intrepid*-class standard prior to its return to active duty, Eden remained hopeful that she was making headway with Montgomery and that soon, many of the modifications she'd proposed would find their way back onto *Voyager*, as well as other Starfleet vessels.

It had been a whiplash-inducing change of pace a few weeks ago when Montgomery had advised Eden that she was now considered "off" the study of *Voyager*'s technological alterations and assigned instead to spearhead a thorough analysis of all discoveries, both scientific and cultural, made by *Voyager* while in the Delta quadrant. Eden couldn't be sure if this change in her orders was meant to be a compliment. Secretly she suspected that Montgomery might have grown weary of her constant pressure and had simply been looking for a new subject to keep her busy until Starfleet was ready to formally respond to her proposals.

However, once Eden had begun to dig into the existing reports on her new subject, including personnel logs and transcripts of the initial debriefing sessions of all of *Voyager*'s crew, she realized that Project Full Circle's work in this area had, thus far, been cursory at best.

Captain Kathryn Janeway's session—a meeting which Eden would optimistically have scheduled to cover at least a week—had only been half an hour. The rest of the senior officers hadn't fared any better. The fifteen minutes granted to Seven of Nine, surely one of the most extraordinary and potentially invaluable sentient beings currently alive, had bordered on criminally negligent, at least in Eden's estimation.

The "official" rationale—welcoming home a heroic vessel—meant sacrificing thoroughness on the altar of necessity. Hostilities with the Dominion were still fresh in everyone's mind when *Voyager* had made its unexpected return to Earth. Starfleet's focus had been on recovering from the losses it had suffered. It was almost as if the brass believed a complete restoration of Starfleet's numbers to levels prior to the war was the only thing that could assure everyone, Federation citizen or not, that the cost of victory over the shape-shifters bent on galactic domination had been well calculated and had done no permanent harm. *Voyager* added to their tally.

Eden understood the value of quantity, especially when you were showing the enemy your teeth. Personally, however, she was also a fan of quality. To her thinking, *Voyager* had just spent seven years collecting data that, if analyzed and implemented properly, might give the Federation tactical advantages to make the next inevitable conflict with one of those species who had just never learned to work and play well with others much easier to conclude quickly and relatively painlessly.

The Dominion conflict had been one of attrition. Starfleet had managed time and again to keep most of the Dominion's resources on the Gamma quadrant side of their territories, while working to overcome their formidable but fragmented constituency in the Alpha quadrant. Starfleet's losses in this conflict had been the largest in memory. Eden understood why Command had made their choice; she just didn't happen to agree with it, as there was little chance that the only solution to another such conflict was simply *more* ships.

Eden already knew that there wasn't a superweapon buried anywhere in *Voyager*'s logs. But there were other remarkable discoveries: a civilization that used space-time folding technology to cover distances so vast that they made warp drive look like a baby's first steps in comparison, quantum slipstream drives, transwarp drives, never mind their discovery of entire new dimensions like fluidic space. The intelligence *Voyager*'s crew had collected about the Borg alone could fill much-needed volumes.

Establishing Project Full Circle had been a step in the right direction, though it was terribly understaffed. Still, Eden was determined not to waste the opportunity presented by *Voyager*'s unique experiences.

Her first step had been to request permission to conduct new debriefing sessions with as many of *Voyager*'s former crew as she deemed necessary. That request had been granted. The only caveat was that her sessions could not interfere with the crew's other scheduled assignments. Admiral Montgomery had promised Eden privately to try and keep the ship and its crew relatively close to Earth to help facilitate her work, and thus far, he'd been as good as his word.

She was anxiously anticipating the arrival of her first "victim," Lieutenant Commander Thomas Eugene Paris.

Tom managed to arrive at Eden's office a few minutes early despite his mother's insistence that he finish the obscenely large breakfast she'd placed in front of him before she would consent to his leaving the house. He knew she was just making up for lost time. But he'd also managed to put on a few extra pounds in his last couple of years in the Delta quadrant, and had determined to get his body back into "fighting shape" now that the stress of being stranded in the Delta quadrant, a new husband, and an expectant father were behind him. He'd made great strides on Boreth. Though, to his surprise, he'd developed a taste for live *gagh*, the rest of Klingon cuisine was nowhere near as appetizing, and he'd managed to drop back down to his Academy weight before returning to active duty. Much as he loved his mother, he wasn't about to let her undo all the good he'd done.

Captain Eden's aide was a petite Deltan ensign. Tom hadn't seriously looked twice at another woman since well before he'd finally married B'Elanna, but he soon decided that the effect of a Deltan's pheromones had not been exaggerated and was relieved when he was ushered into Eden's office only a few minutes after his arrival.

"Good morning, Mister Paris," Captain Eden said

warmly, extending her hand to Tom as he entered. She was a tall woman, ebony skinned, with large, pitch-black eyes and dark, tightly curled hair trimmed almost to the scalp. She looked to be in her early thirties. Tom had reviewed what he could of her service record before their meeting, however, and knew that regardless of her appearance, she was probably closer to fifty.

"Have a seat and make yourself comfortable." Eden smiled, gesturing to a small conference table with a spectacular view of San Francisco Bay.

"Thank you, sir." Tom nodded.

"Please." She raised a hand gently. "Call me captain."

"Yes, Captain," Tom replied dutifully, wondering how many female officers shared Admiral Janeway's distaste for formal modes of address. He blithely considered throwing a "ma'am" into their conversation, just for fun, but quickly decided that though she seemed congenial enough, he didn't want to press his luck.

Eden situated herself, padd in hand, in a single low chair across the table, while he struggled to find a position of attention on a couch that seemed designed to suck its occupants into deep relaxation.

"I know you're pressed for time, so we'll just get started," Eden said, transitioning to a more businesslike mode.

"Thank you, Captain," Tom replied, wondering if she was aware that he still had five full days of leave at his disposal before reporting back to *Voyager*. The quicker he got this meeting over with, the quicker his mother could continue driving him crazy with party preparations. Or maybe he could just take a brief, unscheduled jaunt to Marseilles, if time allowed.

After a moment of silence Tom felt it was his obligation

to fill, he said, "The truth is, Captain, I'm not really sure what you wanted to discuss."

Eden looked up from her padd sharply. "I'm sorry. I thought that was made clear in the request you received."

"Not really." Tom shrugged.

"I apologize again," Eden said. "My aide, Tamarras, is new."

"It's not a problem, Captain," Tom assured her. "What can I help you with?"

"Well," Eden said, clearing her throat, "it will probably be best if we simply start at the beginning."

"The beginning of what?" Tom asked.

"Your time in the Delta quadrant," Eden replied. "Your initial debriefing session by Starfleet Command on this subject was a little . . ." Eden paused before settling for ". . . sparse. It's time to remedy that."

"Okay," Tom replied dubiously.

"The ship's log indicated that you suffered mild concussive injuries in transit and came to consciousness on the bridge to find it in disarray. What were your first thoughts when you realized that you had been brought to the Delta quadrant?"

That we were monumentally screwed, Tom managed to refrain from saying.

"Well," Tom began, pausing to clear his throat. "It's been a while," he said, struggling to find a clear and more appropriate answer to her question.

"Take your time," she insisted.

Tom sighed deeply. Both his mother and Marseilles were apparently out of luck, because this was obviously going to be a very long conversation.

B'Elanna couldn't believe what she had just heard.

She had come to the emperor's audience chamber determined to make her case quickly. No matter how loudly she had protested, she was forbidden to bring Miral with her to this meeting with Kahless. Kularg had been only too happy to take Miral for what B'Elanna had promised would be only a few minutes, but B'Elanna's gut tensed with nausea every second that passed with Miral out of her sight.

B'Elanna had hurried from the nursery, up the winding staircase that separated the living quarters from the Great Hall, and straight to the anteroom located just behind the emperor's throne. She had been surprised to find not Kahless, but one of his personal guards, Commander Logt, waiting to receive her.

Logt was the woman who had invited B'Elanna to Boreth in the first place. Though she was no taller than your average Klingon female, she still managed to do "imposing" like very few people B'Elanna had ever known. She had a capacity for utter stillness that many warriors lacked. Most were tightly coiled springs ready to snap at a moment's notice. Logt, however, carried within her a deep, slow power. B'Elanna had never doubted the woman's strength. Her position as a member of the emperor's personal guard testified to her abilities and accomplishments on the field of battle. In fact, the only cause for confusion Logt had ever given B'Elanna was over the nature of their relationship. From time to time it seemed clear that Logt truly wished to help B'Elanna in her quest. More often, however, Logt remained cool and aloof, her features as inscrutable as her motives.

This was one of those inscrutable times.

B'Elanna had quickly made her request, that she and Miral be allowed to leave Boreth for a short time due to a family requirement and return in a few weeks. Logt had heard her out in silence.

The part B'Elanna couldn't believe was Logt's ultimate answer to her request.

"No."

"I beg your pardon?" B'Elanna stammered.

"You may leave, B'Elanna Torres," Logt said slowly enough to sprinkle many layers of condescension into her tone, "and you may take Miral with you. But if you do so now, you will not be allowed to return."

"Why not?" B'Elanna demanded.

"Only those whose motives are pure are granted sanctuary on Boreth," Logt replied evenly.

"And what makes you think mine aren't?" B'Elanna asked, appalled.

"A *family requirement?*" Logt said with unmistakable irony.

Had B'Elanna not been ready to crawl out of her own skin, she would have had to admit that Logt had her there.

She opted for as close to rational as she could under the circumstances.

"Miral and I have been separated from our family for months," B'Elanna said. "Their request that we join them to celebrate my husband's promotion is a *requirement*, whether you believe it to be so or not."

"I do not question your devotion, B'Elanna," Logt said a little less imperiously. "Only your motives."

"My *motives*?" B'Elanna bellowed.

Logt's mouth twitched with what looked like amusement.

"You were granted access to our monastery only because of the emperor's interest in your mother. Your stay has been extended because your intention to immerse yourself in your Klingon heritage is honorable. But this is not a recreational facility. Pilgrims to Boreth do not come and go as they please. You are here at the emperor's pleasure, and your request to leave simply because your mother-in-law is throwing a feast hardly rises to the level of requirement."

B'Elanna knew she wasn't going to get anywhere with Logt. She opted to switch tactics.

"Where is the emperor now?" she asked.

"That is not your concern."

"Has he been apprised of my request?"

Logt's voice dropped menacingly.

"He will be," she replied, "but I do not doubt his answer, nor should you question my ability to speak now with his authority."

B'Elanna's fists were clenched so tightly at her sides that the nails of her fingers were now drawing blood in small half-moon indentations on the heels of her palms.

In another lifetime, the only release she would have found in such a moment would be to hit something very hard. But Kathryn Janeway's patient mentoring had tempered the steel at the center of B'Elanna's being. Violence had its place. Here and now, it would accomplish nothing.

B'Elanna took a deep, ragged breath.

Maybe it was for the best. She wanted the option to

return to Boreth. But she and Miral would be leaving in the morning, with or without Logt's permission.

B'Elanna dropped her head in defeat. Almost just as quickly, it snapped back up when the unmistakable clang of metal on metal reached her ears.

Logt's eyes met hers briefly. B'Elanna saw in their momentary widening the same fear that now clawed at her chest.

Without another word, both women rushed from the chamber.

As they ran down the interminable winding staircase, the sounds of battle grew louder, joined by the lusty wails of Miral.

The nursery!

B'Elanna broke off her full-out sprint just long enough to duck into her private chamber and retrieve the *bat'leth* she had brought with her to Boreth. It had been a gift from Kohlar, an ancient weapon patterned after the original Sword of Kahless. B'Elanna hadn't practiced as much with it as she would have liked. But at this moment, that hardly mattered.

Logt stood at the entrance to the nursery, her *mek'leth* already drawn. Had she not stepped to her right, presumably to join the fight, B'Elanna would have run headlong into the woman when she reached the open doorway.

It took B'Elanna only a few seconds to assess the situation. Kularg lay nearest her, a *qutluch* buried in his chest. His blood pooled on the floor and from the look of it, he was already in Sto-Vo-Kor. Logt and three male warriors were battling five females, all of whom wielded *bat'leth*s. A sixth woman stood behind them, holding Miral. B'Elanna was about to join Logt when she realized that one of the men struggling to reach Miral was Emperor Kahless himself.

Another loud cry from Miral reminded B'Elanna that there would be time for explanations later. Now, all that mattered was saving her daughter.

B'Elanna knew well enough the bloodlust that overtook a Klingon in battle. She had never known, however, that the rage could be so focused when that lust was paired with a mother's instinctive need to protect her child.

B'Elanna glided forward, ducking to avoid a wide sweep of Logt's blade. The warrior fighting Logt managed to parry, but she was not prepared for the undercut from B'Elanna's *bat'leth*, which buried itself in her abdomen. With a grunt B'Elanna quickly freed her weapon from the woman, who was now bleeding to death, and turned to face her next assailant. Miral would have been close enough to touch, were it not for the woman and the blade now blocking B'Elanna's path.

This warrior, B'Elanna would fight alone. The sides were now evenly matched. As she brought her *bat'leth* up to block her foe's first strike, B'Elanna realized that whoever this warrior was, she possessed strength and balance that were truly alarming. She was not much larger than B'Elanna, but she fought with fluid grace, as if she were meditating while wielding her lethal blade.

Blow for blow, she easily blocked each of B'Elanna's thrusts. B'Elanna was soon gasping with the exertion, but she gave no thought to herself. Miral was so close, B'Elanna could taste the victory.

Suddenly, B'Elanna was aware of a new sound. As the line of fierce women protected her, the warrior holding Miral had drawn a disruptor from her belt and turned toward the back wall of the nursery where she was cornered. In a matter of a few blasts, she had managed to create a small opening in the wall. A couple more and she would have opened an escape route for herself and Miral.

Oh, hell, no! B'Elanna thought.

Her first move was to take her *bat'leth* in both hands, raising it above her head to defend against a downward swipe. She then twisted the blade to the right, taking some of her opponent's momentum with her and pulling the warrior slightly off balance. With a painful, crunching turn of her wrist, B'Elanna then jerked her *bat'leth* free, forcing the woman over to her left. Before she could recover, B'Elanna continued the turn she had begun, bringing her blade low and level as she spun around. The warrior had almost righted herself when B'Elanna's sword sliced through first one leg, then its mate, just below the knee.

To her credit, the warrior did not cry out despite the agony she must now be suffering as she fell to the floor. B'Elanna didn't take time to wonder, however, as she had just created the only breach in the line separating herself from her daughter.

But by the time she had cleared her fallen foe, Miral's captor had clambered through the hole in the wall and disappeared.

B'Elanna stepped through the opening to find herself in a dark, empty hallway. Miral's cries bounced off the walls around her, and for a disorienting moment, B'Elanna could not find the direction to follow. Within seconds, however, someone else was pushing her way through the wall behind her. It was Logt. The commander paused for a split second, gestured for B'Elanna to go to the left, and took off running full speed down the hallway to the right.

Blade still in hand, B'Elanna ran as if her life depended on it. After about two hundred twisting meters, she realized that she had been sent down the wrong hall. She doubled back, her legs flying beneath her.

The hallway ended in an open door that led to the exterior of the monastery, where the current temperature was well below freezing. Another hundred paces, and she found herself wading through a deep snowbank. Just ahead of her, Kahless, Logt, and their two companions stood motionless in the snow.

B'Elanna reached them, panting so hard it was almost impossible to speak.

"Where?" she gasped helplessly.

Kahless exchanged a look with Logt, who drew the others aside as the emperor moved to B'Elanna, grasping her firmly by the shoulders.

"They are gone," he said simply, willing her to accept the unacceptable. "They must have had a ship in orbit. We saw them transport away."

B'Elanna felt her knees jerk beneath her and finally give way. At the same moment, a feral cry rose from her belly and soon her frustrated rage was bounding off the snowy landscape, assaulting the ears of men and beasts for miles around.

When she was spent, there was nothing left but tears. They choked their way up her windpipe and scalded her eyes.

It was Kahless who finally pulled her to her feet, shaking her fiercely.

"B'Elanna Torres, daughter of Miral!" he shouted.

She stared briefly into his face, her vision distorted by tears that continued to fall.

B'Elanna had honestly never given much thought to the emperor. Kahless was a legendary figure, almost a creature of myth. But now, standing in the presence of the clone grown from Kahless's blood and imprinted with every tale and teaching attributed to the long-dead original, she instinctively understood some of the power of that legend. She understood it, because in some way, he was sharing it with her now, when without it, she would not have been able to stand.

A few deep breaths and the tears stopped. She stood before him and managed a faint nod.

"Better," Kahless said, his long white hair whipping in the wind that danced around them.

"Come," he finally said.

"Where?" B'Elanna found voice to ask.

"To find your daughter," he replied.

CHAPTER THREE

Admiral Janeway was running late. These days, that was not unusual. Thankfully, her new aide, a stern, fair-skinned young Vulcan ensign named Decan, had no trouble at all maintaining his sublimely composed countenance, especially when Kathryn's was fraying. Decan would never replace her dear friend Tuvok, but she found his mere presence a comforting reminder that finding the calm in the center of a storm was preferable to being tossed about on the winds.

"You have another incoming transmission from Admiral Paris," Decan advised her evenly as Kathryn searched through a stack of padds, in desperate need of the one that contained her schedule for tomorrow.

"Please inform the admiral that I'll be transporting over in less than five minutes," she replied.

"But that would be a lie," Decan said without a hint of accusation in his voice. "Given the state of your desk and the number of items we have left to discuss, I would estimate you will be unable to leave this office in less than seven point five minutes."

Kathryn favored him with a smirk. Odds were he was right.

"Then tell him it is my *intention* to transport over in the next ten minutes."

"Very well." Decan nodded before stepping back to his desk outside her office as she turned her attention to a new stack.

No, no, not this one either—but I need to remember to forward that to Admiral Upton, Kathryn said to herself, hoping the mental note would find a place to stick as she tossed aside another set of padds. "Oh, Decan," she called out, still searching her desk vainly.

Within seconds the ensign appeared, almost startling her. The young man had catlike reflexes, but that hardly explained how he often seemed to simply materialize right in front of her when she needed him most. It was certainly the hallmark of an excellent aide. But it was also the littlest bit creepy. Kathryn found herself wondering whether or not he might have some kind of personal transporter embedded beneath his skin that helped him to create this illusion.

"Contact Reg Barclay and let him know that I've reviewed his syllabus for next quarter's Borg seminar, but I want Seven to take a look before I approve it. I'll be seeing her tonight, so he'll probably have her notes before midnight."

"Yes, Admiral," Decan replied, reaching for a padd buried beneath the stack she had just created and handing it to her.

Of course, it was the one she had been seeking.

"Thank you, Ensign," she sighed with relief.

"Do you want me to reschedule your appearance on *Illuminating the City of Light*?" he asked tactfully.

Janeway realized that the interview, which had been on her agenda for weeks now, conflicted with two other briefings set for the following afternoon.

She nodded. "With my deepest apologies."

Despite the fact that she could spend another hour working and still not clear her desk, she was more than ready to put this day behind her.

"Which only leaves the request from Captain Eden," Decan said.

Almost ready.

"What does she want again?"

"Captain Eden has requested a minimum of four hours at your earliest possible convenience. You have rescheduled your appointment with her six times in the last three weeks. She asked me to advise you that at this time, yours is the only interview she still requires in order to complete her report."

"Right," Janeway remembered. It wasn't that she was avoiding the captain, or Project Full Circle. But being an admiral was about prioritizing. And right now her life was only slightly more hectic than running *Voyager*'s bridge had been the day they had first entered the Delta quadrant.

"See if Captain Eden would be available to meet at 0600 tomorrow. If so, I can give her two hours."

"I will transmit your proposal and forward her response to you this evening," Decan replied.

"And the rest will simply have to wait," she decided. "For the next few hours I don't wish to be disturbed over anything less than the arrival of a Borg armada in Earth orbit."

"If you'd like, I could contact the Borg directly and ask that they postpone any imminent actions so as not to spoil your evening," Decan said deadpan.

Janeway paused for a moment as his words sunk in. Finally, her face broke into a wide grin.

"Humor, Ensign?"

The Vulcan acknowledged the question with a slight nod. "Often it provides a welcome release of tension."

"That it does." She smiled. "Well done."

"Enjoy your evening, Admiral," Decan said.

"I intend to," she replied. "Thank you."

"You are welcome, Admiral."

Tom didn't usually think of himself as a worrier. But right now, he couldn't help it. B'Elanna and Miral should have transported in over an hour ago. He had already put three calls in to Earth Orbital Control and all they could tell him was that B'Elanna's shuttle had yet to arrive.

The friends who had assembled at the Paris ranch to greet his wife and child for a small "family" reunion prior to the next day's festivities were all doing their best to keep his spirits up by trying to pretend that nothing was really wrong. Captain Chakotay and Lieutenant Harry Kim were listening amiably to *Voyager*'s former EMH as he recounted his most recent clash with one of the Federation Research Institute's geneticists, a Tellarite named Deegle. Seven of Nine and Tuvok stood nearby, pretending to give the Doctor their full attention but clearly not terribly interested. Poor Seven, who worked with the Doctor at the institute on a daily basis, had probably already heard this particular rant at least a dozen times before.

Tom's father was in his office, no doubt making someone at Orbital Control's ears bleed. When Tom hadn't gotten far in determining just where B'Elanna might be, his father had placed a gentle hand on his arm and told his son, in a voice that could have frozen magma, "Leave this to me," before disappearing into his private sanctuary.

His mother flitted in and out of the room, checking everyone's beverages and reminding her guests that a variety of appetizers had been positioned strategically about the living room. A four-course dinner was drying out in the kitchen, but Julia Paris, ever the optimist, smiled warmly at her son each time she caught his eye as if to assure him that any minute now, everything would be fine.

"At which point I tried to tell Deegle that the Oaxacatian genome, while undoubtedly more complex than the Nekrestian, had several shared markers which were worth further study," the Doctor said plaintively to his captive audience. "And can you imagine what he replied?"

"I can," Seven of Nine deadpanned.

Both Harry and Chakotay had a hard time biting back their laughter.

"Of course you can, Seven. You were there," the Doctor replied imperiously.

But before he could continue, Tom's heart leapt at the sound of the front door chiming.

Tom hurried past his friends, but he was no match for his mother, who, to Tom's disappointment, was ushering Admiral Janeway into the room, rather than B'Elanna and Miral.

"My apologies, friends," Janeway said warmly to all before greeting each of those present individually.

Moments later, Owen returned, his face failing miserably to mask his concern.

Tom hurried to his side.

"Well?"

"This is intolerable." Owen shook his head.

Janeway, ever alert to a sea change in any room's temperature, turned immediately to her former mentor the moment he entered. She had served with Admiral Paris back when he was a captain and she was a junior science officer.

"Admiral Paris," Janeway said with a nod as she interrupted.

Owen's face broke into a rare grin as he opened his arms to Janeway and she shared a brief embrace with him.

"I didn't think you'd ever get here," he said warmly.

"I was unavoidably detained." She smiled in return, then turned more serious as she asked, "What's wrong?"

Tom and Owen exchanged a look before Owen said, "B'Elanna hasn't arrived. And now no one can even confirm that her shuttle left Boreth."

Janeway's jaw tensed as her mind began to whir.

"You've already spoken to the station?" she asked Owen.

He nodded. "Time was, you asked a simple question and you received a simple answer. Honestly, sometimes I wonder what's happening at Starfleet Academy if these are the cadets they're graduating. B'Elanna's shuttle should have departed four days ago, but Earth Orbital Control has no record of the departure or flight plan. They assure me they've tried repeatedly to contact Boreth, but have yet to receive a response."

"So we don't even know if B'Elanna ever left Boreth?" Janeway asked.

Owen nodded grimly.

"Why somebody didn't think to contact me . . ." Tom began.

"You mean, why didn't B'Elanna contact you?" Janeway asked gently.

"It doesn't make any sense." Tom shook his head in frustration.

"Well, there's only one thing to do," Janeway said, patting Tom gently on the back.

"What's that?" Owen asked.

"We need to contact the ambassador."

"Which ambassador?" Tom asked.

"Worf, the Federation ambassador to the Klingon Empire," Janeway replied. "He'll get to the bottom of this quicker than anyone."

"I don't know why I didn't think of that," Owen mused as he directed Janeway toward his office.

"Because we're talking about your daughter and granddaughter, Admiral," Janeway replied knowingly as she followed him out.

Turning back to the others, Tom noted that Chakotay was now missing as well.

"Where's the captain?" he asked Harry, who was absentmindedly moving some cheese and crackers around on his cocktail plate.

"He stepped out. Call from Admiral Montgomery. He'll be right back," Harry assured him.

Tom could tell that something was troubling his best friend, probably something more than B'Elanna's tardiness, but at the moment he was simply too distracted to press further. Knowing Harry, Tom would be the first person he'd confide in when he was ready.

"That is unfair." Seven's voice rose above the other murmured conversations.

"It is not," the Doctor replied.

"To conclude that all Tellarites are 'pig-headed' when your interactions with the species have been limited to Doctor Deegle is to prejudge them. It is not worthy of you or them," Seven insisted.

"Their physical characteristics notwithstanding," Tuvok added softly.

"Why you insist on defending the man—" the Doctor began, but was interrupted by Chakotay, who strode briskly into the room and made his way straight to Tom.

"What is it, Captain?" Harry asked before Chakotay could speak.

"We've received new orders," Chakotay replied, obviously disconcerted.

"What happened?" Tom demanded, his gut churning with worry that this might be news about his wife and daughter.

"It's the Changeling," Chakotay said, defusing one worry while simultaneously creating a new one.

Neither Harry nor Tom needed to ask *which* Changeling Chakotay was referring to. A few months earlier, Chakotay had been kidnapped and impersonated by a Founder who, in concert with the Cardassian scientist Crell Moset, had almost managed to kill Chakotay and his sister. Moset and the Changeling had been experimenting on a group of colonists on Loran II in hopes of finding a cure for the disease that limited the Changeling's shape-shifting abilities, and they would have succeeded without *Voyager*'s intervention.

Before Chakotay could continue, Janeway and Owen returned to the room, trailed by Julia. Everyone gathered around as Janeway announced that she and Admiral Paris had just made contact with Ambassador Worf, who had promised to find out what had happened to B'Elanna's shuttle and report back to her as soon as possible.

"I'm sorry, Tom," she added kindly. "There's really nothing more we can do right now."

"Perhaps we should all sit down to dinner, then?" Julia said, trying to make this sound like a pleasant suggestion.

"I'm sorry, Mrs. Paris," Chakotay replied, "but I'm afraid that Tom, Harry, and I will have to disappoint you." When everyone in the room had given him their full attention, he quickly briefed his listeners about their new problem. "Apparently, after he escaped from Loran II, the Changeling made straight for Kerovi. He had been impersonating a Kerovian aide for some time, but when he arrived, he murdered the diplomat affiliated with that aide and assumed her identity."

"I thought he could only impersonate male humanoids," Harry interrupted.

"We all did." Chakotay nodded.

"Who was the Kerovian diplomat?" Janeway asked softly.

"Merin Kol," Chakotay replied.

In response, Janeway raised a hand to massage her forehead and temples.

"Merin Kol is dead?" she asked, her voice heavy.

"I'm sorry, Admiral, she is," Chakotay replied, briefly placing a gentle hand on her shoulder. Chakotay was well aware that for several months prior to their misadventures on Loran II, Janeway had been in serious diplomatic negotiations with Kol. Kerovi was debating leaving the Federation. In fact, they had ultimately decided to secede altogether shortly after the Changeling had escaped. Janeway had felt this failure keenly, and to learn that it might have been instigated by this Changeling was even more disturbing.

"The good news is the Kerovians discovered the deception and were able to capture the Changeling. He is in custody now, and they are putting him on trial for the murder of Merin Kol and her aide."

"What are your orders?" Janeway asked.

"*Voyager* is to report to Kerovi as soon as possible. Though they're no longer members of the Federation, the Kerovians understand that the Changeling compromised our security as well as theirs and are willing to allow us to interrogate him before the trial. They've postponed the trial for two weeks to allow us time to get there and debrief him, but in order to maximize our time with him, we need to depart immediately."

Tom's heart sank. His duty was clear. He would report to *Voyager* immediately and begin preparations for their departure. How he would do that while worrying about B'Elanna and Miral was another matter, one he was not at all sure he had the ability to manage.

"Tom, Harry," Chakotay said intently, "I need both of you back on the ship as soon as you're packed."

"Aye, sir," Harry said automatically as Tom nodded mutely.

Chakotay then turned to Tom's mother. "Julia, I can't tell you how sorry I am to take Tom away from you tonight. I know the celebration you have planned would have been lovely."

Julia smiled faintly. "It's no problem, Captain," she

assured him. "I've been a Starfleet wife for over forty years. You get used to sudden changes of plan."

Owen straightened a little at that, clearly proud of his wife, and put an arm around her tiny waist.

"We'll still go ahead with the party," he assured her softly.

She smiled, patting him gently on the chest, then said, "Well, if you gentlemen can't stay to eat, can I at least send you off with some of tonight's dinner?"

"I would really appreciate that." Chakotay nodded.

"Yes, ma'am," Harry added with forced cheerfulness.

─────────

As everyone hustled about saying quick farewells, Kathryn took a moment to assure Tom that she would keep him apprised of any news from Ambassador Worf, which did a little to calm him. She then pulled Chakotay aside.

"I'd like to ask a favor, Captain," she said softly.

"Name it," he replied automatically.

"Merin Kol was more than an associate. I considered her a friend," Kathryn said tensely.

Chakotay nodded. "I understand."

"I'm going to contact Admiral Montgomery immediately," she continued. "The favor is this: please don't depart McKinley Station until you've heard from me."

"Done," Chakotay assured her. "Do you mind if I ask what you have planned?"

Kathryn raised her determined face to his.

"I'm going with you," she replied, her voice stone cold.

─────────

Harry Kim had been dreading this night for weeks—not this night, exactly, but the last night of his leave. And it had just been cut unceremoniously short, almost making what was to come easier. At least the waiting was done.

After several weeks of indecision, Harry had finally come to a realization. Now, he simply had to share it with the other person whom that revelation affected. No matter how many times he had rehearsed the conversation in his head, it never seemed to end well—hence, the dread.

He was half packed when the doorbell of his small apartment in San Francisco chimed.

"Come in," he called, stuffing an extra pair of boots into his Starfleet-issue duffel bag before zipping it closed.

The door slid open and Libby Webber entered.

As usual, she took his breath away. Most of her dark, curled hair had been swept up, leaving only a few tendrils draping down the back of her neck and perfectly framing her face. Her lightly tanned skin was set off beautifully by the deep green tunic she wore over what she always referred to as her "comfy" black pants.

Libby crossed to him immediately and Harry automatically took her in his arms, hugging her close.

She pulled back just enough to say with hopeful eyes, "You said it was urgent."

Harry's eyes remained glued on hers as he took a deep breath.

"Thanks for coming on such short notice."

Libby smiled warmly.

"It was you or rehearsing for next week's Ktarian Festival. Not really a hard choice," she assured him.

Harry nodded as he gently took her arms, which were still draped over his shoulders, and released himself from her embrace.

Concern flashed briefly over Libby's face, and for a moment her gaze shifted over the room until it came to rest on Harry's duffel bag.

"You're leaving again, aren't you?" she asked patiently.

"I am," he replied, taking a few steps back. "I have to report to *Voyager* immediately."

"How long will you be gone?"

"At least a month," he sighed.

Harry saw her fleeting disappointment and how quickly she conquered it.

"Well, it could be worse." She smiled gamely.

"Actually, Libby, it kind of is."

Now the concern came to stay on Libby's face. She sat down on the edge of the bed, next to Harry's bag.

Libby had been the one true love of Harry's life for more than ten years. Despite the fact that seven of those years had been spent apart, they had resumed their relationship almost immediately upon *Voyager*'s return to the Alpha quadrant. For Harry, it had been a romantic fantasy come true, until a couple of months ago when he had finally proposed to her and Libby had done the unthinkable: she had turned him down.

She insisted then that she simply needed more time. What Harry had discovered when he thought about it, which was much too often for his liking, was that whatever the problem was, more time wasn't going to solve it.

Harry wanted to sit beside her. But he also knew that if he was going to get this out, he'd better stay on his feet.

Libby looked up at him warily, her breath coming in short, rapid bursts.

She knows what's coming.

"I've given this a lot of thought, Libby," Harry began as kindly as he could. "I love you. I always have, and part of me probably always will."

"I love you too," she said softly.

"I know. Just not enough to marry me."

"Harry—" she began.

"Hang on," he said, raising a hand to stop her. "I know you said you weren't ready; that the timing was the problem. The thing is, timing is probably never going to be our strong suit. I'm a Starfleet officer. I'm always at the mercy of the next mission. Your performance schedule only makes that more complicated." Harry paused and sighed deeply. "I just think we both need to face reality. Marriage isn't something you have to think about, not at this stage in a relationship. If you're not sure now, you're never going to be. I think we both need to accept that, and move on."

Libby was fighting back tears. Whether they were of disappointment or anger, Harry couldn't tell. She rose and crossed to face him. For a moment she struggled, unable to find words. Finally, she nodded.

"You're sure this is what you want?"

Of course it's not what I want, part of Harry insisted.

"I think it's what's best," he said instead.

Libby sighed, then raised her right hand and briefly caressed Harry's cheek.

"I wish this wasn't one of those times when I knew there was nothing I could say to change your mind," she said sadly.

"I appreciate that," Harry replied.

"Okay," she said, dropping her hand. After one last look and a shake of her head, she turned to go. When she reached the door, she turned back, silhouetted in the bright hall light streaming in through the open door.

"Promise me something?" she asked.

"If I can," Harry replied.

"Take care of yourself," Libby said. "And let me know when you get back. I understand things can't be the way they were," she went on, her voice shaking, "but I can't imagine a universe in which you and I aren't at least friends."

"Neither can I," Harry lied.

Libby nodded, and was gone.

The moment the door slid shut behind her, Harry released a huge sigh and sat for a moment on the bed where just moments before she'd been. The smell of her perfume lingered. It was a light floral scent, never cloying.

Harry would miss it.

But he also knew that there were worse things than missing someone. Overstaying your welcome was one of them, second only to beating your head against a brick wall.

Seven years in the Delta quadrant had taught Harry a lot. And they had changed him. As he snapped his suitcase shut, the vastness of those changes began to sink in.

Libby was his past, and the past was over. He would try to be hopeful about the future.

In time, he knew he'd get there. The journey would begin the moment he stepped out his front door.

CHAPTER FOUR

B'Elanna didn't know how long they'd been walking. Had she been able to think straight, she could probably have hazarded a reasonable guess based on their distance from the monastery or the coldness of her extremities. But there was only one thought she could hold in her mind long enough to make any kind of lasting impression.

She's gone.

At first it had been a deep wound, gnawing its way outward from the center of her being. Now it was something else: a truth that would strike like a harsh blow, setting her heart racing, and then immediately recede into the distance of her mind. Just when it seemed far enough away that it might be nothing more than a nightmare, it would assault her again. In the brief space that separated the end of this disturbing cycle from its renewal, B'Elanna found neither the strength nor the ability to focus on anything else.

Her steps ceased, along with her companion's, when they at last reached a clearing at the edge of the forest, which B'Elanna knew began a few kilometers south of the monastery's walls.

Wordlessly B'Elanna watched as the two warriors who had fought at Kahless's side in the nursery began to gather wood to build a fire. Only now did she recognize them.

Grapk and D'Kang.

Several weeks earlier, her studies in the library had been interrupted by these two new arrivals. They usually kept to themselves, though they seemed to be interested in the same ancient scrolls B'Elanna was translating. She had always had the uneasy feeling that they were watching her. It was little comfort now to know that they must have been, but with the best of intentions.

"Rise!" Kahless's voice demanded.

B'Elanna tore her gaze from Grapk and D'Kang to see Commander Logt lying prostrate in the snow before the emperor.

Logt's initial reply was too muted for B'Elanna to hear. Curiosity more than anything carried her toward the pair. Finally she caught a few words.

". . . beg only for a quick death, though I do not deserve it."

"I said, rise!" the emperor repeated more ferociously, and Logt obliged him by pulling herself to her knees.

"It is not me you have failed," Kahless said harshly.

"I and the other guardians swore to protect the life of Miral Paris with our own," Logt said in a matter-of-fact tone. "I have failed. My life is forfeit."

"Miral Paris is not dead," Kahless replied.

Something new sliced through B'Elanna's gut. It might have been hope.

"But, Emperor . . ." Logt stammered.

"How do you know that?" B'Elanna demanded, stepping between them.

Kahless held one hand up to silence her as he removed his *d'k tahg* from his belt. For a moment the edge of the blade pointed toward Logt's throat. Then the emperor tossed it into the air, catching the blade in his hand and presenting the hilt to Logt.

"Should the day ever come that we find Miral dead, I will indeed send you to Gre'thor. Until then, your life belongs to B'Elanna Torres."

Something close to hatred flashed briefly in Logt's eyes. B'Elanna easily understood. To go from serving as the emperor's personal guard to the service of a half-Klingon commoner would have been a hard choice for any warrior. Most would rightly have preferred death.

But Logt's anger quickly passed. With a sigh she accepted the blade and drew it lengthwise along the flesh of her left palm. As fresh blood dripped onto the snow at her knees, she offered the blade to B'Elanna, saying, "I hereby swear to serve you faithfully until we have found your daughter, Miral. Should I fail in this task, my life is yours to claim."

B'Elanna didn't understand why this was so important. But if Kahless wished it, she felt she should play along. Mere practicality suggested that at this point, she could use all the help she could get.

She accepted the blade and used it to cut her own palm. Allowing the blade to fall, she watched as her blood mingled with Logt's.

"I accept your oath," B'Elanna said softly, "and will release you from it when my daughter is once again safely in my arms."

"Now that that is settled," Kahless said approvingly, "let us move closer to the fire. There is much to discuss, and little time."

B'Elanna turned to see a cheerless blaze roaring in the center of the clearing. Grapk and D'Kang were standing before it, warming their hands.

Kahless took his place opposite them and motioned for B'Elanna to sit beside him. Logt rose and began to slowly walk the perimeter. Soon, Grapk and D'Kang stomped toward her and after brief, muted discussion, took up positions on either side of their "camp."

B'Elanna found this protection somewhat comforting. Kahless seemed to accept it as a matter of course.

"How do you know that Miral is still alive?" she asked again.

"Because I know who took her," Kahless replied, "and why."

"Who?" B'Elanna demanded.

"Are you aware that on your mother's side, you are descended from a Klingon warrior named Amar?" Kahless asked.

B'Elanna was in no mood for a history lesson, but given the fact that the scrolls that had started this nightmare had been written by someone named Amar, she bit back her impatience and simply shook her head.

"Amar lived fifteen hundred years ago and was a companion of the original Kahless. He fought at Kahless's side against Molor when the empire was founded. Amar died driving our enemies from our lands. But his sacrifice was not in vain. His death and that of his brother warriors secured the fledgling Klingon Empire."

"Is he the same Amar who wrote the scrolls of prophecy that sent Kohlar and his people on their quest to find the *Kuvah'magh*?" B'Elanna asked.

"He was." Kahless nodded. "But prophecy is a rare gift. -

Visionary Klingons have been few and far between in our history."

"What did he see?" B'Elanna asked.

"You have read the scrolls. You know as much as I do," Kahless replied.

"The prophecies of Amar were vague," B'Elanna argued. "They could have referred to any child."

"Any child descended from a noble house, whose mother was not raised on Qo'noS? Any child found after two warring houses had made peace? Any child who was recognized as the *Kuvah'magh* before she was born?" Kahless asked kindly.

"Okay," B'Elanna allowed, "but what about the scrolls of Ghargh? They're filled with the nonsense about the *Kuvah'magh* being destined to bring back the Klingon gods. And don't they predate Amar's by almost another thousand years?"

"Your scholarship does you credit," Kahless replied.

At this, B'Elanna had to forcibly restrain herself from shouting. This wasn't an assignment at the Academy. She wasn't looking for a passing grade. This was the life of her daughter.

"All I want to know," B'Elanna said through clenched teeth, "is what any of this has to do with Miral."

"I, too, was once a skeptic," Kahless went on, as if oblivious to her tone. "Though Amar was a fierce and beloved companion, he was long dead. And Ghargh's words seemed to mean nothing to a race which had long ago abandoned faith in any omnipotent beings in favor of the warrior ethic which now binds us all."

"What changed your mind?" B'Elanna asked.

"I met your mother," Kahless said, smiling faintly. "She

came to Boreth, determined to undertake the Challenge of the Spirit. She told me of her vision of you and she on the Barge of the Dead—a vision which I have come to learn that you shared with her."

B'Elanna nodded for him to continue.

"I traced her lineage and learned that she was descended from Amar. I began to wonder if she had inherited more than his warrior's strength; if she had also been granted the gift of prophecy. That is why I was so pleased when you followed her here, and gratified to see that you now seem determined to embrace your heritage."

"I did what I did for my mother and my daughter," B'Elanna said.

"And your actions have brought honor to both of them."

"Did my mother have further visions?" B'Elanna asked, wondering if in the brief time they had spent together reunited on Boreth, Miral had forgotten to mention something so significant to her daughter.

"She did not," Kahless replied. "But her words were enough to send me searching our past through deeper mysteries which might now be unfolding before us all."

"I don't understand," B'Elanna interrupted.

"I do not believe that Amar was ever familiar with the prophecies of Ghargh. But you and I have now studied them both. What do you see when you look at them?"

"Ghargh's writings are filled with speculation about gods, and Amar doesn't mention them at all," B'Elanna replied. "They seem to contradict one another."

"Not as much as you might think. Both are products of the men who wrote them and the times in which those men lived. Ghargh's preoccupation with the Klingon gods is simply a reflection of the reality that when he was alive, there were still many Klingons who believed in gods and prayed to them for various boons. Amar did not share those beliefs, but he still understood the role of the *Kuvah'magh* as that of a savior to the Klingon people."

"What is Miral supposed to save us from?" B'Elanna asked.

"Then, you did not complete your study of Ghargh's writings?"

"I intended to," B'Elanna replied a little defensively. *But then my mother-in-law decided to throw a party.*

"According to Ghargh, the *Kuvah'magh* is destined to save the Klingon people from the *joH'a mu'qaD*," Kahless replied.

B'Elanna struggled to translate. "The Curse of the Gods?" she attempted.

Kahless nodded.

"I do not pretend to know the nature of this curse. All I can tell you is that there are Klingons still living today who believe that it is real and that it will signal the end of the Klingon Empire."

"Are they the ones who have taken Miral?"

"I believe so," Kahless went on. "They are called the *qawHaq'hoch*—those who 'remember all that they know.' They were founded during the First Dynasty to gather and keep the most accurate records of the lineages of various Klingon families. They continue to do so to this day, though they were driven underground at the end of the Second Dynasty."

"Why?" B'Elanna was now truly curious.

"Their leader at the time was a master bladesmith named Hal'korin. She served in the court of the Emperor

Reclaw. When K'Trelan slaughtered the imperial family, Hal'korin disappeared, taking the *qawHaq'hoch* with her. Legend says that she constructed a sanctuary for them, and that only those who join the order are privy to the location of this sanctuary."

"Hal'korin was a woman?" B'Elanna asked, unable to hide her surprise.

Kahless nodded. "A remarkable one. She learned sword-craft from her father, and unless I'm much mistaken, she had a hand in forging the *bat'leth* you now wield."

B'Elanna knew the weapon Kohlar had given her was ancient, but she hadn't realized until that moment just how old it really was.

"To this day the *qawHaq'hoch* believe that the Curse of the Gods is real. They have watched for the coming of the *Kuvah'magh*, knowing that it is the only way to avert this apocalypse. But there is another sign of impending doom, one that predates the birth of the *Kuvah'magh*."

This was news to B'Elanna.

"The scrolls of Ghargh say that before the *Kuvah'magh* returns, *Fek'lhr* will be reborn."

Just as the notion that the savior would bring back the Klingon gods, this idea struck B'Elanna as somewhat absurd.

"I thought *Fek'lhr* was a mythological creature, the one that guards the gates of Gre'thor."

"He is," Kahless replied. "But I am now certain that our adversaries believe this first sign has already come to pass, and that this is the reason that the *qawHaq'hoch* have chosen to act now. If they have taken her, it is to protect her until she can play the role which fate has de-creed for her. She is alive, B'Elanna, because they would never harm her. Their only interest would be in keeping her safe."

While this was somewhat comforting, it was equally infuriating. B'Elanna couldn't believe she was now made to suffer for the backward beliefs of fringe religious lunatics.

"How do we find them?" was B'Elanna's next question.

Kahless paused briefly before continuing. "The *qawHaq'hoch* are not the only Klingons still alive who believe that the prophecies of the *Kuvah'magh* are real. When Hal'korin escaped K'Trelan's wrath, the new emperor sent several of his most faithful warriors to find and kill Hal'korin and the *qawHaq'hoch*. The descendants of those warriors are still trying to complete this task. They are called the Warriors of Gre'thor."

Great. More fanatics.

"They have been searching for the *qawHaq'hoch* for hundreds of years and still haven't found them all?" B'Elanna had to ask.

Kahless nodded. "I have already contacted them, and they should be in orbit within the hour. They will lead us to the *qawHaq'hoch* and to Miral."

Suddenly B'Elanna was aware of Logt standing beside her. Her eyes blazed with barely repressed fury.

"Pardon, Emperor, but I cannot believe you would entrust your safety and hers to those mongrels."

Kahless rose. The tingle of restrained energy tickled B'Elanna's skin as he faced his former personal guardian.

"I would never lead a warrior into battle unaware," he reproached her.

Standing to face Kahless, B'Elanna asked, "What is she talking about?"

With a final icy glance at Logt, Kahless returned his attention to B'Elanna.

"The Warriors of Gre'thor believe in the prophecies of the *Kuvah'magh*. Where the *qawHaq'hoch* would protect Miral with their last breath, the Warriors would prevent the coming apocalypse by simply killing the *Kuvah'magh* on sight," he replied.

B'Elanna took a second to make sure she had this right in all of its appalling implications.

"So you've contacted the Warriors of Gre'thor to help us find the *qawHaq'hoch* who have taken Miral, and when we find her, the Warriors are going to kill her?"

Kahless placed a huge hand on B'Elanna's shoulder. "We fight one battle at a time," he replied.

It was all B'Elanna could do to keep from screaming.

"Lieutenant Campbell to the captain."

Seated in his ready room aboard *Voyager*, Chakotay replied, "Go ahead, Lieutenant."

"I am transmitting our updated operations report to you now."

"Very good."

"Once all personnel are accounted for, we will have clearance to launch."

"Keep me advised, Lyssa."

"Aye, sir. Campbell out."

Chakotay had always thought that the amount of "paperwork" required of a Starfleet vessel's first officer was cumbersome. He had thought that right up until he had assumed command of *Voyager*. It still amazed and slightly galled him that Kathryn had always managed to make this part look so easy.

As he signed off on the most recent engineering report, he found himself missing B'Elanna more than usual. Though she lacked Vorik's affinity for detail, her reports had always been colorful and more interesting to read. He said a quick silent prayer that word of her safety would arrive soon.

A chiming at his door interrupted his thoughts.

"Come in," he called.

He looked up to see Tom Paris ushering in an officer Chakotay had never met.

"Captain Chakotay," Tom said formally, "allow me to introduce you to our new counselor, Lieutenant Cambridge." Tom then placed a padd, undoubtedly containing Cambridge's orders, on Chakotay's desk.

The man in question said nothing, but stood at a vague approximation of attention before his desk. In a glance Chakotay took his measure. He was human, probably in his mid-fifties, which was interesting only in that by that age, most Starfleet personnel had achieved ranks well above lieutenant unless they were "problematic" or had chosen to start their career with Starfleet late. He wore a short full beard that was a medium brown streaked generously with white, as was his slightly too-long curly hair. His uniform, though regulation black and blue, hung loosely on him and was in serious need of pressing or recycling. His boots looked comfortable, and hadn't been polished in some time.

Chakotay knew it was inappropriate for him to dislike Cambridge at first sight. But at the moment, he was having a hard time helping himself. The man's initial impression suggested a propensity for insubordination.

Chakotay dismissed Tom with a nod and rose, moving around his desk to extend a hand to Cambridge.

"Welcome aboard, Lieutenant," Chakotay said briskly as Tom exited the room perhaps a little too hastily.

Faint surprise and amusement flickered across Cambridge's face as he took Chakotay's hand.

"Thank you."

Chakotay had never really stood on ceremony, but he was pretty sure there should have been a "sir" at the end of that sentence.

Opting to keep things congenial for now, Chakotay went on, "I wasn't aware that Commander Paris had already managed to secure a replacement for Counselor Astall." Much to Chakotay's regret, his first counselor had advised him shortly after their return from Loran II that a family emergency had arisen and she required an indefinite leave of absence. Chakotay had approved her request, and delegated to Tom the task of submitting the request for a new counselor to Starfleet Command.

Cambridge said nothing, but instead of staring straight ahead as protocol would have dictated, he met Chakotay's eyes with polite disinterest.

Sensing that it was time to take control of the situation, Chakotay gestured to a long, low sofa that ran along the far wall. "Please, take a seat, Lieutenant."

With a slight shrug that suggested he'd rather not, Cambridge ambled up the steps dividing the room's two distinct areas and sat down, crossing his long legs and placing his hands in his lap. To all intents and purposes, he looked as if he owned the room.

Chakotay sat opposite him, across the small table, trying and failing to match Cambridge for relaxation.

Finally Chakotay said, "I'm sure I'll be able to learn a lot about you from your service record there, but probably not as much as you can tell me."

"How much time do you have, Captain?" Cambridge replied drolly.

"Enough," Chakotay said firmly. "What was your last posting?"

Cambridge heaved a weary sigh and said, "The last starship I served on was the *Melbourne.*"

Chakotay paused to think. The ship didn't sound familiar.

In answer to his unspoken question Cambridge went on, "Which was destroyed at Wolf 359."

Chakotay knew the battle well, just as he knew that there had been very few survivors. Though Starfleet's first major confrontation with the Borg had taken place years ago, it could easily have scarred a sensitive soul deeply, and most counselors were known for their sensitivity.

"I'm sorry," Chakotay said sincerely. "How did you manage to survive?"

"The first thing I always do when I report to a new starship is make damn sure I know where the escape pods are."

"Why is that?" Chakotay asked, his voice hardening.

"Practicality and experience," Cambridge said breezily. "Though Starfleet purports to exist under the auspices of peaceful exploration, every vessel I've ever served on has done more than its fair share of fighting."

Doing the math in his head, Chakotay realized it had been eleven years since Cambridge had served on a ship.

"May I ask what you've been doing since then?"

"You may," Cambridge replied. "After the *Melbourne* was destroyed, I requested a transfer to Starfleet Medical."

This was a relief of sorts. If Cambridge had been working at Starfleet Medical all these years, he had to be at least competent in his job.

"And why did you decide to return to duty aboard a starship?" Chakotay asked.

"I didn't," Cambridge answered.

"Then what are you doing here?" Chakotay asked, at something of a loss.

"I honestly don't know." Cambridge shrugged. "But I would have to guess that either someone up there thinks highly of you, or they don't think highly enough of me."

Chakotay had heard more than enough. He rose to indicate that the conversation was at an end, and after a long pause Cambridge finally uncrossed his legs and got to his feet. It was unfortunate that there wasn't time to get the counselor off his ship before they departed for Kerovi, but Chakotay had already decided that this would be his first order of business the moment *Voyager* returned to Earth.

"Dismissed, Lieutenant," Chakotay said coolly.

"Thank you." Cambridge nodded and turned to go.

"Thank you, *sir*," Chakotay corrected him.

Cambridge paused and turned, opening his hands in apology. "Thank you, sir," he repeated.

Chakotay crossed the room in two steps and met Cambridge's mocking eyes with his most stern look.

"Despite what you may believe, Lieutenant Cambridge,

Voyager is a unique ship with an exemplary crew. We give a hundred and fifty percent to our jobs on a slow day. I won't settle for anything less from you. And the next time I see you, I expect your personal grooming to be regulation, your uniform to be pressed, and I'll be looking for my reflection in your boots."

"Really?" Cambridge asked in genuine surprise.

"Really, *sir*," Chakotay corrected him again.

"Yes, sir," Cambridge obliged him, this time with a little more respect.

They stared at each other just long enough for Chakotay to realize that his initial dislike had, in a few short minutes, become something closer to contempt. The look in Cambridge's eyes suggested that he wasn't alone in his antipathy. Finally the lieutenant nodded slightly and moved away.

When he'd almost reached the door, he turned and said, "Would it be possible for one of your ensigns to direct me toward whatever walk-in closet I'll be calling home for the foreseeable future?"

"There are ship directories in every main hall," Chakotay barked. "Learn how to use them."

"Excellent," Cambridge replied, then just managed to add, "sir."

When the door had finally slid shut behind him, Chakotay took a few deep, measured breaths. It had been a long time since he'd met anyone as adept as Cambridge at bringing out his inner hard-ass. The only rival that came immediately to mind was the young Tom Paris.

Chakotay moved to his desk and picked up Cambridge's orders. They had been signed by Admiral Montgomery. Chakotay took a moment to review Cambridge's attached service record. He had been born in Bristol, England, and studied at Oxford before gaining admission to Starfleet Academy thirty years earlier. Surprisingly, there were absolutely glowing reports attached to each and every one of his postings, including that of his superior at Starfleet Medical. In addition, he had published dozens of articles in psychological and anthropological journals.

It was easy for Chakotay to see why anyone with Cambridge's qualifications would be singled out for service aboard *Voyager*. Had Chakotay never met him, he would have no doubt approved the transfer without a second thought. But somewhere between the deeds and the man was a chasm Chakotay believed he had no interest in crossing.

It was a shame. Glancing at the most recent of Cambridge's scholarly articles, a piece comparing the mythological beliefs of four species Chakotay had never even heard of and their psychological relevance, he realized that in any other context, he would have found the man fascinating.

His musings were interrupted by a familiar voice.

"Permission to come aboard, Captain?"

Looking up, Chakotay saw Admiral Janeway standing in the doorway. Her face fell a bit when she saw the concern clouding his.

"I'm sorry, should I have knocked?"

"Not at all, Admiral," Chakotay said, looking in vain for his smile. "I gather Starfleet Command granted your request?"

Janeway crossed to him and nodded. "They've authorized me to evaluate the situation on Kerovi once we arrive to determine whether or not there might be room for diplomatic rapprochement. After everything Merin Kol and I went through, I sincerely hope there will be."

"You shouldn't doubt your abilities, Kathryn," Chakotay said with genuine warmth. "Heaven knows I never do."

She smiled in thanks as Tom Paris's voice came over the comm system.

"Bridge to the captain."

"Go ahead," Chakotay replied, noting that Kathryn had to bite her lip not to answer for him out of sheer habit.

"We've just received clearance to depart."

"I'm on my way," Chakotay said. As Chakotay moved toward the door that led directly to the bridge, he asked, "Would you care to join me?"

"No, thanks." Janeway smiled. "I'll just catch the turbolift and go right to my cabin. I've got a lot of material to review before we get to Kerovi. And I'm hoping to hear from Ambassador Worf sooner rather than later."

"Nothing yet?"

"No." Janeway shook her head, obviously disappointed. Chakotay nodded, sharing the sentiment.

"Dinner, my cabin, nineteen-hundred hours?" he asked.

"Is that an order, Captain?" she teased.

"Yes," he replied, well aware that as she still outranked him he didn't actually have the ability to do any such thing.

"Then I'll be there."

Only after Chakotay had made his way onto the bridge and settled in to watch as Tom guided the pilot, Lieutenant Tare, through their departure did he allow himself to realize how glad he was to have Kathryn aboard again, if only for a short time. He loved leading *Voyager* and her crew. The ship felt more like home than any place he had ever known. He knew that despite its frustrations and tedium, Kathryn truly enjoyed her work as an admiral. But part of him believed that both of them had been at their best when they had served together. For the next few weeks, it would be nice to revisit that.

I've missed her, he realized, acknowledging a simple fact he rarely allowed to surface. Chakotay's next thought was to wonder whether or not she ever felt the same.

CHAPTER FIVE

Kahless had first contacted Captain T'Krek several weeks earlier, right around the time he had made a connection between a meeting he'd had years ago and Ghargh's contention that the rebirth of *Fek'lhr* would signal the fated apocalypse. He had always made it a point to keep an eye on the Warriors of Gre'thor and their captain. Renegade Klingons both fascinated and troubled him. More often than not, they did more harm than good.

The emperor did not believe T'Krek was aware of the reports of *Fek'lhr*'s rebirth. Given that this knowledge had come to Kahless in a completely unrelated matter, he doubted that anyone, at least up to this point, had made the connection. But the *qawHaq'hoch* had demonstrated this night that they knew and were several moves ahead of everyone else currently playing this particular round in the *komerex zha*. T'Krek's ignorance, however, would undoubtedly serve Kahless and B'Elanna well when they ultimately found themselves at cross purposes with the Warriors of Gre'thor, which the emperor did not doubt they eventually would be.

For the time being, T'Krek and his men remained Miral's best hope.

When the transporter effect finally cleared, Kahless

found himself facing not only T'Krek but also a dozen of the fiercest warriors he had ever had the pleasure of laying eyes on. Their outdated uniforms harkened back to a much earlier era, and punctuated their status as privateers.

"My emperor," T'Krek said with obvious respect as he made a low bow. Those behind him likewise bowed. "Welcome aboard the *Kortar*. You honor us with your presence. The Warriors of Gre'thor are at your service."

Pretty words, Kahless thought. *But they are only words. The second our interests diverge, T'Krek will remember that he serves no one but himself and a millennium-old grudge.*

Once this little formality was complete, T'Krek turned his attention to Grapk and D'Kang, who stepped down off the transport platform and were each embraced by T'Krek as if they were family members long ago given up for dead.

"Welcome home, brothers," T'Krek said heartily. "You have done well." Grapk and D'Kang then moved to embrace the other assembled warriors in a similar fashion.

He glanced briefly at B'Elanna, who was watching the proceedings like a patrolling sabre bear. Doubt flickered furtively across her face when Grapk and D'Kang's allegiance was revealed. Kahless had known that T'Krek had sent these two to Boreth, undoubtedly to watch B'Elanna and Miral. They had both fought with honor at his side, and he trusted them as far as he trusted any of T'Krek's men.

Just as he was about to step aside to introduce B'Elanna, she whispered in his ear, "Remind me to ask you something later."

Kahless nodded, then turned again to T'Krek, who was now staring at B'Elanna with disdain.

"Captain T'Krek," Kahless said, "this is my companion, B'Elanna Torres, daughter of Miral."

"She is the one you spoke of, the *thing*'s mother?" T'Krek said, not bothering to hide his contempt.

B'Elanna tensed at Kahless's side. To her credit, she took a deep breath and refused to rise to T'Krek's bait. Unfortunately, he didn't take this for the gift it truly was.

"You are a mongrel," he spat at B'Elanna.

"I'm half human and half Klingon," B'Elanna replied with dignity worthy of the Lady Lukara.

T'Krek moved to stand directly across from B'Elanna. Only the extra height she gained by remaining on the transporter pad allowed them to see eye to eye.

"The emperor may ask of me what he wishes. By what right do you dare board my vessel and seek my assistance?" T'Krek growled.

In a flash, Logt, who had been behind Kahless the entire time, moved between B'Elanna and T'Krek and punched him squarely in the jaw.

"Hold your tongue, old man," she shouted, "and take care before you again address the mother of the *Kuvah'magh*."

T'Krek recovered from the blow, laughing heartily. His men joined him, clearly itching for a fight. T'Krek then drew his *bat'leth* from a leather strap wound across his back as Logt simultaneously drew her *mek'leth*.

"Logt!" B'Elanna shouted.

As every eye in the room turned to her, B'Elanna drew her own *bat'leth* and stepped forward.

"I'm the one he's challenging," B'Elanna said clearly to Logt.

"Anyone who challenges you must first get through me," Logt replied, not taking her eyes from T'Krek.

"Not today," B'Elanna replied.

It clearly took every ounce of self-restraint Logt possessed for her to nod and move aside.

T'Krek stepped away from the pad toward the center of the room as the others quickly formed a circle around him and B'Elanna, grunting and growling in approval.

B'Elanna was the first to strike. T'Krek, who had a head and a half on her in height, blocked it easily, but was clearly surprised a little by the strength behind the blow. Kahless wondered if T'Krek had any idea how dangerous a foe he currently faced. B'Elanna had too much to lose at the moment.

B'Elanna then raised her weapon again in a series of blows that T'Krek had a harder time dodging and parrying. She moved quickly, almost frantically, as if all of the frustrations of the last few hours had finally been given the release they needed. Still, there was little tactical skill in B'Elanna's maneuvers, and Kahless worried that nerve and adrenaline were going to get her only so far.

The room, which had until now been filled with shouts of encouragement for T'Krek, grew suddenly silent. With B'Elanna's last charge she had managed to graze T'Krek's forearm with her blade, drawing blood.

The emperor didn't understand this mistake. It should have been an easy enough blow for T'Krek to block, but his attention seemed somehow divided.

As B'Elanna backed off to regroup, T'Krek surprised everyone by raising one hand to signal his forfeit and dropping his own *bat'leth* to the floor.

"I concede the victory to B'Elanna Torres, on one condition," T'Krek said sternly.

B'Elanna looked as if she wouldn't be satisfied by anything less than T'Krek's head on the end of her *bat'leth*, but her breath was now coming in great heaves, and she only nodded in assent, even as she continued to shoot *d'k tahg*s at him with her eyes.

"May I see that *bat'leth*?" T'Krek asked.

B'Elanna held it up where she stood, its sharp side leveled at T'Krek's neck. It was a petulant gesture, but T'Krek deserved it.

T'Krek approached her fearlessly and examined its surface area as she held it aloft. Suddenly he gasped and focused intently on an indentation, a decorative trefoil in the center of the blade. Then a wide grin of triumph spread across his face.

"My brothers," T'Krek declared to all, "behold the end of our search."

To Kahless's amazement, T'Krek and all of his men knelt down and bowed their heads before B'Elanna.

B'Elanna shot a worried glance at the emperor, who simply nodded to suggest she just go with it.

After a somber moment, T'Krek rose.

"You are most welcome among us, B'Elanna Torres, daughter of Miral," he said as reverently as he had first greeted the emperor.

"Fine," B'Elanna replied warily. "You want to explain to me why?"

"The *bat'leth* you are holding," T'Krek said, "where did it come from?"

B'Elanna seemed disconcerted by the ease with which T'Krek had moved from foe to friend, but she was wise enough to prefer talking to fighting.

"A warrior named Kohlar, whose people traveled tens of thousands of light-years from Qo'noS, gave it to me when I encountered him in the Delta quadrant."

"Are you aware of its history?" T'Krek asked.

"It was his father's," B'Elanna replied, "and his grandfather's before that."

"May I?" T'Krek asked.

Despite her obvious misgivings, B'Elanna handed the blade to T'Krek. He then pointed to the trefoil.

"Do you see this?"

"I have eyes," B'Elanna replied harshly.

"But do you know *what* you are seeing?"

From the look on her face, she clearly had to concede that she did not.

"This is the mark of Hal'korin," T'Krek said patiently. "And this *bat'leth* is the final piece to a puzzle the Warriors of Gre'thor have been trying to solve for a thousand years."

At that, a raucous cheer was raised by the others. As B'Elanna turned to face Kahless, he could see in her eyes that she now shared his thoughts.

Neither of them was sure that this was a good thing.

"Of course I told Admiral Montgomery that if the Borg ever do make another assault on the Alpha quadrant, transphasic torpedoes are going to be our best defense, Temporal Investigations be damned."

"Uh-huh." Chakotay nodded politely.

Kathryn knew he wasn't really listening. By her estimation, he hadn't heard a word she'd said for at least five minutes.

"And I know Admiral Nechayev agrees," Janeway went on, "though frankly I was incredibly shocked when she arrived at our meeting stark naked."

"Right."

"Admiral Montgomery didn't seem to notice," she went on. "I guess things at Starfleet Command have changed quite a bit since we left . . ."

"Mm-hmm," Chakotay murmured, then paused as her words finally pierced his internal musings. "What?"

Kathryn smiled.

"Not a pretty mental picture, is it?"

"Sorry. My mind was wandering," Chakotay admitted.

"That much I gathered."

They had already recycled their dinner plates but lingered at the table in Chakotay's quarters, he nursing a glass of Antarean cider and she working on a cup of cappuccino.

"You want to tell me what's bothering you?" Kathryn offered. "Or maybe just what's bothering you the *most* right now?"

Janeway had always known that Chakotay would make an excellent captain, and she had lobbied for him to be assigned to *Voyager*. But she also knew just how lonely command could be. She had looked to him or to Tuvok when she needed counsel. He had Tom, and if memory served, *Voyager* had been provided with a full-time ship's counselor since Chakotay had assumed command. But Janeway knew all too well that Chakotay was a deeply private person. The admiral couldn't imagine how bad things would have to get before he chose to open up to either of those two options.

"I'm wondering if we're really the best people for this particular mission," Chakotay said.

"The mission to Kerovi?"

Chakotay nodded. "Yes, we've already interacted with the Changeling, and our experience should serve us well. But we were also his victims, and that's going to be pretty hard to compartmentalize when we're face-to-face again."

"We've talked about this before, Chakotay," Kathryn said, her voice full of sympathy. "I know what you suffered, not just for yourself and Doctor Kaz, but for Sekaya."

"Watching my sister die, or *almost* die, was certainly the worst of it."

"I understand you've been assigned a new ship's counselor," Janeway said. "I think you should make sure he's fully briefed on your experiences at Loran II and insist that he accompany your team when it comes time to interrogate the Changeling. He should be able to provide you with a healthy perspective."

"And I would, if I weren't planning to have him transferred the moment we return to Earth."

Kathryn was taken aback. "He's that bad?"

Chakotay nodded. "Remember the complaints we got when the Doctor was first activated about his bedside manner?"

Kathryn smiled wistfully. The ship's former Emergency Medical Hologram had grown into such a supportive and compassionate physician during their time in the Delta quadrant that it was hard to reconcile what he was now with what he had been in those early months.

"Counselor Cambridge has only completed one full duty shift today and three of the five crewmen he met with have already written complaints."

"Really?" Kathryn grimaced.

"The best reports found him mildly dismissive and a little hostile."

"Have you had a chance to speak with him?"

"Oh, yes."

"And what did you think?"

"I think *dismissive* and *hostile* are a little generous."

"Well, I can hardly wait to meet him."

"Indeed." Chakotay nodded. "You'd just better hope you don't end up needing his services on this trip. What I can't understand is why everyone at Starfleet Medical is so taken with him. His record is filled with glowing recommendations."

"What species is he?" Kathryn asked.

"British," Chakotay replied.

Kathryn chuckled lightly in response before adding, "Maybe he takes some time to get to know."

"I hope you're right," Chakotay said skeptically.

"Ops to Admiral Janeway," Lyssa Campbell's voice rang out over the comm system.

"Janeway here."

"You have a priority transmission from Starfleet Command."

"Route it to the captain's quarters," Janeway replied, rising to cross to Chakotay's comm station at his desk and activating the interface.

A few seconds later, Decan's ever-composed face appeared before her.

"Good evening, Admiral," he greeted her. *"I have Ambassador Worf for you."*

"Put him through," Kathryn said briskly as Chakotay rose to stand opposite her while she received Worf's report.

"*Before I do so, Admiral, I wanted to let you know that Captain Eden has requested you contact her from* Voyager *as soon as your schedule allows.*"

Kathryn sighed.

"Did I cancel that appointment this morning?" she asked, knowing full well she had forgotten to do so before boarding *Voyager*.

"*No, Admiral,*" Decan said evenly. "*I took the liberty of contacting Captain Eden first thing when I arrived, but by then you were already several hours overdue for your meeting with her.*"

"I'm sorry, Decan."

"*I did pass your apologies along to her.*"

Kathryn looked up to see Chakotay doing his best to hide a smile at her embarrassment.

"Tell Eden I'll be in touch as soon as possible," Kathryn replied. "Now let's not keep the ambassador waiting any longer."

"*Yes, Admiral.*"

After a brief interlude in which Decan's face was replaced by the blue and white seal of the Federation, Ambassador Worf's face suddenly glowered before her.

Janeway knew Worf by reputation and a few brief conversations. She also knew that most Klingons wore a semipermanent scowl that often belied a well-hidden but slightly warmer spirit. Worf's expression now gave no hint of that warmth, only cold frustration.

"Good evening, Mister Ambassador," Kathryn said sternly. "You have news?"

"*I do, Admiral,*" Worf replied, "*and I wish it were better.*"

Kathryn's gut tensed, but she nodded for him to continue.

"Five days ago, there was an attack on the monastery at Boreth."

"What kind of attack?" Janeway demanded.

"Three warriors were found dead in the monastery's nursery. The child, Miral Paris, is missing, as is her mother, Emperor Kahless, and a member of his personal guard, Commander Logt," Worf reported.

"Do you have any idea who was responsible for the attack?" Kathryn asked, doing her best to keep her fears tightly reined.

"Not at this time," Worf replied. *"As Lieutenant Commander Torres was a guest of the empire during her stay on Boreth, this is still considered an internal Klingon matter. Unfortunately, the Federation cannot interfere with the ongoing investigation by the Klingon authorities unless we are formally asked to do so."*

"But they *are* investigating?"

"Of course," Worf replied. *"Chancellor Martok has taken a personal interest in these developments and has demanded hourly updates on the progress of the investigation. He is, however, unwilling to entertain any action at this time by the Federation, though I have offered it repeatedly."*

"The chancellor is worried because Kahless is missing," Kathryn surmised. She could see in Worf's subtle nod that she had guessed right. "But there is no way to know at this time whether or not B'Elanna and Miral are with him."

"That is correct."

"That is unacceptable, Ambassador."

"I concur, Admiral," Worf said. *"Which is why I have made the Federation's position regarding the safety of its citizens in Klingon space abundantly clear to the chancellor. He has assured me he takes this matter very seriously, but for*

now, there is nothing more that you or I can do. I will update you the moment I have further news."

It took all of Janeway's diplomatic training to make the "Thank you, Mister Ambassador" with which she signed off sound moderately congenial.

Once the connection was terminated, she looked immediately to Chakotay. His hand was at his brow, slowly massaging the deep worry lines formed along his tattooed forehead.

"What do you think?" she asked.

A heavy sigh escaped Chakotay's lips as he began to pace the room.

"I think we have to hope that Martok gets to the bottom of this before both of us lose our minds worrying about B'Elanna and Miral," he replied.

"And in the interim?"

Chakotay looked at her, questioning. Finally he answered, "In the interim we continue on our current mission."

Kathryn had expected that this would be his response. Despite his Maquis background, of the two of them, he had always tended to play things much safer than she.

"Without your first officer?" Kathryn asked.

"What do you mean?"

"I mean the moment you tell Tom Paris that his wife and child are missing from Boreth, the only way to keep him on this ship will be to put him in stasis," Kathryn replied.

Come to think of it, even that might not do the trick. Kathryn recalled vividly that Tom had a particular aversion to stasis chambers and an uncanny ability to escape them, even when supposedly sedated.

Chakotay stopped pacing and drew himself up to his full height, hands clasped behind his back. "I think you underestimate him," he replied.

"Let's find out, shall we?" Kathryn challenged.

A few minutes later, Tom arrived in Chakotay's quarters and received a full briefing on what limited information was currently at the captain's disposal. He took the news relatively well. The moment Chakotay had finished speaking, he said, "Thank you, Captain. Of course, I'd like to request an immediate leave."

Chakotay blinked back his surprise.

"To do what?"

"The *Delta Flyer* was brought back aboard just before we departed McKinley Station. With your permission I'll take it and begin my search at Boreth," Tom replied evenly.

"Request denied," Chakotay said softly. Before Tom could protest, he continued, "Ambassador Worf made it very clear that no Federation intervention was required nor would be welcomed at this time."

"That's supposed to stop me?" Tom asked in amazement.

"No," Chakotay answered. "Your duty to this ship is supposed to do that."

Tom stared briefly at Chakotay in wonder, then raised his right hand to the collar of his uniform, tugging firmly at one of the three pips that were pinned there.

"Gentlemen," Kathryn interrupted, sensing where this was going, "let's think about this."

"There's nothing to think about!" Tom shouted. "We're talking about my wife and my daughter."

"I know that," Chakotay replied angrily. Tom might

arguably have loved B'Elanna more than Chakotay did, but the captain had loved her longer. And Miral was as dear to him as his own child.

Kathryn stepped between them. "I realize the situation is delicate, but there has to be another option."

"What would you suggest, Admiral?" Chakotay asked, barely concealing his distaste for being second-guessed at this moment.

"Were it up to me, I'd alter course right now for Boreth," she replied calmly.

"We have our orders," Chakotay insisted.

"To hell with our orders," Tom interjected.

"*Commander,*" Chakotay said harshly, reminding Tom in one word that this was not the time or the place to push too far. He then looked back to Janeway, who stood with her arms crossed at her chest.

"If you're worried about the fallout from Starfleet Command, I could pull rank and take the heat for you," Kathryn suggested.

Chakotay shook his head warily. "You wouldn't."

Kathryn gave it a few seconds' thought, then dropped her arms to her sides in defeat.

"No, I wouldn't," she replied, "and I apologize for even suggesting it. This is your ship. I'm a guest here. And I would never do anything to imply that you don't have my full faith and confidence."

"I appreciate that."

"But I still think we need a better option," she added.

Chakotay looked to Tom, then back at Janeway. She knew all too well the many pressures that were being weighed and measured: his duty to Starfleet, his love for B'Elanna and Miral, his concern for Tom, and his certainty that to intercede at this point could well set off an interstellar incident.

Command is a wonderful challenge, except when it isn't, she thought bitterly.

Finally Chakotay tapped his combadge.

"Captain to the bridge."

"Go ahead, Captain," Harry Kim's voice replied.

"Alter course and proceed at maximum warp to Qo'noS."

After a brief pause of surprise, Kim replied, *"Aye, Captain."*

Tom looked at Chakotay with gratitude. Kathryn knew that her face betrayed that as well, mingled with respect.

Now why didn't I think of that?

"We have two weeks to reach Kerovi," Chakotay said in a tone that brooked no discussion. "A detour to Qo'noS will only take a few days. We'll contact Martok directly and ask to be allowed to assist with his investigation. If he approves our request, we'll notify Starfleet Command. If not, we'll resume course for Kerovi."

Tom's gratitude faded somewhat. It wasn't everything he wanted, but it was a start.

"Thank you, Captain," Tom said.

"Is there anything you can tell us about what B'Elanna was doing on Boreth since you left, or who might wish Miral any harm?" Chakotay asked Tom.

Tom eased a frustrated sigh. "Not really," he replied. "We were translating and studying ancient texts, looking for more information about the *Kuvah'magh*. B'Elanna wanted to learn more about her Klingon heritage, for Miral's sake, and it seemed as interesting a place as any to start."

"Did she find anything to add to what you already learned about these prophecies from our encounter with Kohlar?" Kathryn asked.

"Not while I was there." Tom shook his head. "But . . ."

"But what?" Chakotay asked.

"I don't know," Tom replied. "I've talked to B'Elanna every week since we've been apart, but lately, I hate to say this, something's felt a little off."

"What do you suspect?" Kathryn asked as kindly as she could.

"I think she's hiding something from me," Tom finally admitted. "I wanted to ask, but then when she agreed to come home . . ."

Chakotay placed a hand on Tom's shoulder.

"Don't worry. We'll find them."

Tom nodded, though his agreement didn't betray much hope.

"But by the time we get to Qo'noS, we need to know more than we do now about anyone who might have done this," Chakotay added.

"What are you going to do?" Kathryn asked.

"I think it's time we asked the smartest people we know for a little help," Chakotay replied.

Kathryn smiled for the first time since she'd heard from Worf.

I should have thought of that too.

CHAPTER SIX

Captain Eden had read and reread the paragraph in question three times before she realized that Tamarras was standing at her desk.

As she looked up, her aide said, "Please pardon the interruption, Captain, but Admiral Batiste asked me to advise you that he is transporting over."

"Let me know when he arrives," Eden replied, dismissing her.

It was nice that she could look forward to her ex-husband's arrival with only mild annoyance. Clearly this indicated a healthy level of personal growth on her part. Eighteen months ago, just after the separation, which she had briefly allowed herself to believe would only be temporary, being in Willem's presence for either personal or professional reasons had been significantly more troubling. *Devastating* was probably closer to the truth.

Eden didn't know how it worked for other people, but she was constitutionally incapable of shifting emotional gears with Willem's seeming ease and grace. It was not okay with her that one moment they had been partners, lovers, and, most important, friends who had built a life together and the next they were no longer any of those things. It had not been okay for months. It had remained not okay until her good friend Ken Montgomery had gently suggested she might avail herself of the services of a counselor.

Luckily, she had seen the wisdom in Ken's suggestion. She had reported to Starfleet Medical and been assigned to Doctor Hugh Cambridge. They had met regularly since then for very productive sessions, and over time she had come to see that what she had called a marriage had been nothing of the kind. Strangers who regularly found themselves seated together on a morning transport might have found that they had more in common than she and Willem. They would certainly have been more polite to one another. In reasonably short order, rather than grieving over the loss of a relationship that she had once believed was all she could have hoped for, she had realized that what she and Willem had once shared had been born of need rather than love and both of them were definitely better off alone than they had ever been together.

Things had further improved when she had been transferred to Project Full Circle. Though the project fell under Willem's authority, he rarely interfered with the team's nominal leader, Admiral Montgomery. Come to think of it, Eden had to wonder why Willem wanted to see her today. It had been over a month since they had last spoken.

She returned her attention to the report she was writing, resolved to continue working rather than waste time speculating. Soon enough she'd know why Willem was darkening her door.

. . . inhabited by a loosely affiliated group known as the Mikhal Travelers, encountered on Stardate 50396.

Reports indicate that the planet in question had been settled more than ten thousand years earlier. Artifacts of this ancient civilization were discovered by the Mikhal and revered as objects of beauty. There is no indication that the Mikhal were aware of any deeper meaning to the artifacts. References to the artifacts also found briefly in the personal logs of Crewman Kes. Further analysis recommended based upon . . .

But this was where it got tricky.

Further analysis and study of these artifacts was actually critical as far as Eden was concerned. But her knowledge of that fact could not be supported by anything in *Voyager's* logs; it could only be supported by evidence buried in Eden's subconscious mind. At least she assumed it was her subconscious. Nothing in her conscious mind suggested there was anything of interest or value in the artifacts discovered on this remote planet almost seventy thousand light-years from Earth. Until she had seen a holo-image of one of the carvings—taken by Kes, an Ocampan female who had accompanied *Voyager* on her journey for only three years—Eden had read nothing terribly interesting about the artifacts and certainly would not have referenced them in her analysis.

After Eden had seen the image, it had stirred something within her—something that felt strangely like a memory.

She needed to know more. Her gut told her that this was important, but until she could prove it, her instinct would never be taken seriously.

Afsarah Eden despised not being taken seriously.

She had learned that from her time with Willem.

As a result, Eden tended to overcompensate. Since she was aware of this proclivity, she chose to think of it as a personality quirk rather than an annoying fault. She was not sure that her superior officers, particularly Admiral Montgomery, agreed with this assessment, but that was not her problem at the moment.

Right now she simply needed to decide how important it was to include this paragraph and its implied recommendation in her initial report.

A chime sounded, and after she called out, "Come in," the door of her office hissed open.

Willem Batiste noted that when he entered Afsarah's office, she didn't bother to look up from her computer. She would keep him waiting as long as it suited her. As he was technically her superior officer, this might be construed as insubordination. But he had also broken her heart, and this meant that rank or no, there would always be a fair number of delicate eggshells strewn between them and he would do well to tread lightly. Their relationship had become decidedly amicable in the last year, and it served his interests to keep it that way.

He could wait. A little passive aggression never killed anyone.

"What can I do for you, Admiral?" she finally asked, still refusing to tear her eyes away from whatever she was working on.

"Good afternoon to you too, Afsarah."

This earned him a glance of interest from her dark, almond-shaped eyes.

"I'm sorry," she said lightly. "Was I being rude?"

"I prefer to think of you as highly motivated and commendably focused," he replied cordially.

This was enough for her to stop working altogether and turn to face him with her full attention.

"Now I know I'm in trouble," she said flatly.

"Why would you say that?"

"You're being nice."

"I've always been nice," he said with mock defensiveness.

"It's your story. You can tell it any way you like."

"You're looking well, Afsarah," he went on, ignoring the barb.

"Thank you, Willem," she said appreciatively. "You look exactly the same."

He didn't ask her to clarify. What she thought of how he looked was really of no concern to him one way or the other.

"Would you like something to drink?" she offered. "Iced tea with mint, perhaps?"

"I would." He smiled. She had always been so eager to please him, and usually succeeded, knowing exactly what he would prefer to drink on this unseasonably warm afternoon. That constant comforting attention had been hardest to lose when they separated. Fortunately, this small reminder of that loss barely stung anymore.

It stung even less when she tossed her head toward her office's replicator and said, "Feel free to help yourself."

Willem crossed dutifully to the replicator and ordered two iced teas. Once they had materialized before him, he returned to her desk, taking the seat opposite her and placing her glass well within her reach.

"How is your report coming?" he asked casually.

"It would be coming much better if I could nail Kathryn Janeway down for more than a few minutes at a time," Eden replied.

"Then you're not finished?"

She paused, giving him a hard stare. Eden wasn't a telepath, but when she looked at him like that he always felt underdressed, if not completely exposed.

"What's your interest, if I may ask?" she finally countered.

"For the moment, that's none of your concern," he answered, hoping to imply professional necessity without being too cagey.

The right side of her mouth curled upward. She seemed equally amused and intrigued.

"Admiral Montgomery indicated that I should take all the time I needed to complete this analysis," she said. "Admiral Janeway has been unavailable for the last several weeks, though I'm assured she'll remedy that when she returns from her current mission. The only other senior member of *Voyager*'s crew that I've been unable to interview is their chief engineer, B'Elanna Torres. Admiral Janeway informed me this morning that her current whereabouts are unknown. Assuming she's not dead, I'll interview her the moment she returns to Earth. Until then, I'm afraid you and Admiral Montgomery are just going to have to wait."

Willem nodded politely. He had expected as much. Ken had been copying him on all of Eden's status reports, so he already knew that her final analysis would probably not be complete for several more weeks.

He just wasn't sure he could wait that long. Though Eden was unaware of this fact, he had been the one to suggest that she be transferred from technical analysis to her current assignment. Batiste had never met a more tenacious individual, and her kind of research was exactly what he needed if he was going to get enough evidence to support his proposal in a timely manner.

He wasn't sure if taking her into his confidence at this point would help to grease the wheels. If Eden disagreed with him, Vulcans would dance naked in the streets before she would aid his cause.

But if she could be made to see reason . . .

There was no one in the universe he would rather have at his right hand in a fight.

Batiste rose and returned his glass to the replicator to be recycled. He remembered all too well that cleaning up after him had been a pet peeve.

"I would appreciate it if you would keep me apprised of your progress," he said simply. "In the meantime, I'd like a copy of whatever you have completed up to this point."

Eden's eyes betrayed her deep desire to understand why, but to her credit, she only nodded in the affirmative.

He was almost at the door before she said, "You're really not going to tell me why you're so interested all of a sudden?"

His interest wasn't sudden. It was exactly nine months old at this point.

"I really can't," he replied, as if it pained him more than her.

"Have a good evening, Admiral," she acquiesced, returning her attention to her computer. "I'll forward you a draft file before I leave tonight."

He nodded and left her alone with her curiosity.

The admiral hated playing these games. But soon enough, they would no longer be necessary.

<hr>

Once he was gone, Eden allowed herself only a few moments of consideration before deleting the questionable paragraph. Now that she knew her analysis would be scrutinized by Willem, rather than just Ken Montgomery, she absolutely couldn't risk including it.

At least not until he tells me exactly what he's planning, she decided.

If her history with Willem was any guide, she might very well be the last to know.

<hr>

The scene that met B'Elanna's eyes was disorienting. She knew she was deep in the bowels of the *Kortar,* an old but well-maintained warship of a class she didn't recognize. She assumed that the space where she now stood with Kahless, Logt, T'Krek, and dozens of his brethren had originally been a cargo hold. But she could have sworn she was standing outside on Qo'noS at night. Only the deep, musky odor she associated with too many Klingons in too close quarters and the absence of a breeze seriously distorted the illusion.

The moment they had entered the vast space, Kahless had smiled in recognition. On Qo'noS, this place was called *Qa'Hov.* B'Elanna had distant memories of touring it as a child. She had long ago banished the memories of her first visit to her mother's homeworld because her most vivid recollections of those times were of the many Klingons who stared at her with contempt. Now that she understood that most Klingons stared at any stranger the same way, she took it less personally, but at the time it had only reinforced her desire to be anything but half Klingon.

The shrine reproduced here was part of a public sector of the Kartad Forest. The monument at the shrine's center, a stone obelisk less than six meters tall and roughly a meter square at its base, hadn't been terribly impressive when she was a child. Had she fully comprehended when she was a little girl that the obelisk was twelve hundred years old, she might have mustered a little awe. Staring at the perfect re-creation of the monument that the Warriors had constructed aboard their ship, she discovered some of the wonder she had been unable to summon in her younger days. B'Elanna didn't understand why it was necessary to keep it in a cargo hold when a holodeck would have done just as well, but everything about the Warriors she had observed up to this point, especially their antiquated uniforms, suggested that they didn't do anything the easy way, or the modern way.

The deck was split-level; a deep circular trench surrounded the obelisk, approximately four meters in diameter. But the sky above, an exact replica of the stars orbiting Qo'noS, was the most breathtaking part of the illusion, and the piece that necessitated a vast volume of space within the ship.

B'Elanna remembered the shrine as one of many on Qo'noS dedicated to Kahless. She couldn't recall what particular deed worthy of epic song he might have performed at this site, and she felt a little bad about that. The wide gaping holes in her knowledge of Klingon history had been perturbing enough while she wandered among the other pilgrims on Boreth. Standing in the emperor's presence, it was downright embarrassing. She felt certain that in the actual shrine there were at least a few plaques that would have filled in the missing pieces for her. T'Krek had apparently not felt it necessary to add these details for this re-creation.

The assembled warriors began to arrange themselves in a circle around the trench. Only when she reached the lip of the indentation did B'Elanna notice the glints of light reflecting off metal below. The trench was filled with *bat'leth*s, lying end to end in a perfect but incomplete circle. Now that she was a little closer to the obelisk, she also noticed for the first time that it was not simply smooth, polished stone. It was actually quite rough, and was pitted throughout with long gouges that scarred its surface.

Finally, her curiosity exceeded her humiliation and she turned to Kahless.

"What is this place?" she asked softly.

"It used to be called the 'home of the stars of the gods,'" Kahless whispered. "Now, of course, they are the stars of Kahless," he added, "but that was never the intention of its builder."

"Who built it?" B'Elanna asked, uncomfortably aware that no one else was speaking.

"I do not know," Kahless replied, and B'Elanna instantly felt a little less ignorant.

T'Krek stood at the base of the obelisk. He turned his attention to B'Elanna and approached before the emperor could say anything further.

"Twelve centuries ago, the *pe'taQ* Hal'korin designed this shrine as a gathering place for the *qawHaq'hoch*. The order was divided into twelve corps, each led by the fiercest warrior among them. The leaders of the twelve could only be identified to one another by the weapons they carried. Hal'korin, may she writhe in agony in Gre'thor, forged twelve *bat'leth*s and marked them as her own. Only when the twelve were assembled could the secrets of her cursed order be revealed."

From a purely tactical point of view, B'Elanna could see the wisdom in this; passwords, codes, handsigns, and the like were all time-honored traditions among those for whom subterfuge was a way of life. At the same time, the machinations of this ancient society also reinforced her certainty that all of these people, *qawHaq'hoch* and Warriors of Gre'thor alike, were barking lunatics.

"What secret do you seek?" Kahless asked. B'Elanna had the sense that he asked the question for her benefit and was silently grateful.

"When brought together in this place, the twelve *bat'leth*s will reveal to us the location of the *qawHaq'hoch* sanctuary. We know that the sanctuary was created by Hal'korin, to hide these heretics and their dark work should they ever fall from favor, as they ultimately did."

"The Warriors of Gre'thor have, to date, found and slaughtered eleven of the twelve leaders, and the descendants who claimed their place," T'Krek went on, his chest swelling at the fond memory. "Their weapons now rest here.

"The blade you carry, B'Elanna Torres, is the twelfth sword of Hal'korin." T'Krek held his hand out to B'Elanna. "With your permission."

Kahless nodded, and B'Elanna passed her *bat'leth* to T'Krek. He then knelt before her and placed the sword in the trench, its ends clanging softly as they were locked into place between the two on either side. The *bat'leth*s now formed a perfect, unbroken circle.

B'Elanna wasn't sure what she expected to happen. At first she decided that the unimaginable stress of the past several hours might finally be taking its toll when she felt her gorge rising and her stomach began to churn. She took a few halting steps to ward off the dizziness as the stars above her head began to spin. She was suddenly aware of two strong hands on each of her arms, holding her firmly, those of Kahless and Logt. With a heavy, metallic clank, the sensation passed and B'Elanna realized that it hadn't been her head that was swimming. Whatever mechanism controlled the projections of the stars above her had actually moved, reorienting itself to a new alignment, probably of a particular time and date necessary for the ritual she was now unwillingly sharing.

She enjoyed a momentary sense of calm, until the ground at her feet began to glow. Soon enough she realized that the *bat'leth*s in the trench were actually floating on a substance that was now the consistency of molten lava. Somewhere in the back of her mind she remembered that the original shrine had been constructed at the base of a long-dormant volcano, common enough on Qo'noS.

Those around her knelt at the sight. At first B'Elanna assumed it was more quasi-religious nonsense, until she realized that the now luminous *bat'leth*s had begun to cast laserlike points of light toward the obelisk. The tallest of the Warriors standing right at the lip of the magma-well blocked some of the spectacle by their position. Without reverence, B'Elanna, Kahless, and Logt likewise knelt and watched as T'Krek moved about the obelisk, studying and measuring the points on the monument illuminated by the refracted light of the weapons. He then turned his attention to the sky above, comparing the patterns in the stone to those fixed overhead.

Finally T'Krek grunted, "Bridge."

"What are your orders, Captain?" a disembodied voice growled.

"Set a new course," T'Krek said haughtily. "The sanctuary is located on Davlos."

"At once, Captain," the voice replied.

As those around her rose and began to congratulate themselves with hearty cries and pounding of chests and shoulders, B'Elanna's eyes remained glued to the obelisk. She promised herself that later she would return and examine every atom of the monument with a scanning device more sensitive than her eyes. She gazed at the *bat'leth*s floating in the trench. A thought gnawed at the back of her mind.

For all of its elegance, Hal'korin's crude mapping system is ripe with potential for minute variations that would undoubtedly alter the location indicated by the obelisk. T'Krek seems certain that he's found what he was seeking, but without further analysis, I'm not ready to bet my life or Miral's on his calculations.

It was a journey of at least four days to Davlos, even at maximum warp. For now, B'Elanna had nothing but time, and she was determined to use it well.

She was suddenly aware of Kahless, helping her to her feet. When she rose and looked up at him, he said softly, "There was something you wanted to ask me earlier."

With so many thoughts racing through her mind, B'Elanna had to search for a moment to recall her question. Finally it came back to her.

"On Boreth, did you try to warn me of the danger we now face?"

He shook his head.

"Perhaps I should have," he admitted sadly. "I was confident in my ability to protect you, and I apologize for not sharing my concerns with you sooner."

B'Elanna felt her ire rising. Part of her wondered if all of this might have been avoided had Kahless chosen long ago to bring her into his confidence. She bit back the first response that came to her as, despite her oath, Logt would probably snap her neck for even the slightest display of impudence toward the emperor.

"I see," B'Elanna managed to reply. Of course, if Kahless hadn't written her the cryptic message, that begged the question: *Who had?*

B'Elanna was suddenly conscious of her extreme fatigue. Every bone in her body was racked with the pain of either stress or injury. Her stomach began to growl, though the thought of food was sickening. A low, tingling buzz washing over her suggested she'd do well to find a bed soon.

It was almost a pleasant thought. To curl up beneath the animal skins she'd grown accustomed to on Boreth, Miral tucked into one arm, and . . . *oh, dear gods* . . .

Tom, she thought, her heart splintering anew in her breast.

She hadn't given him a moment of consideration since she had stood before Logt in the audience chamber, making her request. In real time it had been less than twelve hours earlier, but those hours had been so full of fighting and fleeing and desperate worry. Since Tom had left her on Boreth and returned to active duty, she had grown too accustomed to thinking of her problems as only hers, and taking solitary measures to solve them. But now, when the weight of her loneliness was palpable and the ache to feel his arms around her so pressing, B'Elanna saw how well she had deceived herself.

Her need for her husband was not an idea. Nor was it something she could turn on and off at will. Like the life of her daughter, it breathed within her. For too long she had only been able to glimpse that soft tender place in her dreams, when in flashes she could smell the sweet tang of his flesh, or feel his imagined hands caress her gently. These dreams had done little to comfort her in the harsh light of day, and so she had buried them, as if she could will them to dissipate and with them, the bond that was so inconvenient when they were separated.

Tom would never have done the same; of that much she was certain. Now she had days ahead to wonder if, when she shared this horrible lapse with him, he would ever forgive her.

CHAPTER SEVEN

"To what do I owe the honor of this visit?" Chancellor Martok asked.

His question was directed at Chakotay. Though Janeway was the ranking officer, this was, as she had reminded Chakotay when they entered the Great Hall and were ushered into Martok's private chamber, "His idea and, therefore, his hoverball match."

The admiral and Paris stood just behind Chakotay, waiting with palpable impatience. It was only due to the influence of Ambassador Worf that Martok had agreed to the audience at all. Worf stood ominously behind their group near the ornately carved doors of the suite.

Starfleet captains weren't in the habit of requesting audiences with the chancellor of the Klingon Empire. Chakotay seriously doubted that his request would even have been considered were it not for their personal connection to B'Elanna and the fact that she had gone missing at the same time as Kahless.

In the brief exchange they had shared with Ambassador Worf—who doled out words with the same care that a Ferengi took when parting with latinum—they had been told that Martok had agreed to the meeting as a courtesy to the ambassador, but insisted that it take place "quietly," so as not to raise questions among the rest of the High Council, now in session. Martok had apparently chosen not to alert the council to the emperor's disappearance until he could provide them with Kahless's new whereabouts, which still remained a stubborn mystery.

Chakotay knew Martok by reputation only. His renown as a leader of men in battle preceded him. Martok had come to power during the Dominion War. The very day he arrived on Qo'noS, his position as chancellor had been challenged by a usurper who had managed to lay waste to the Great Hall and much of the monastery on Boreth before that coup had come to its violent and bloody end. Martok bore livid scars, each one a testament to the battles he had fought. He had no need for pretense or a need to show his power. He wore it as easily as the massive cloak denoting his office.

Several years earlier, he had lost his left eye at the hands of the Jem'Hadar, but his remaining one rested unnervingly on Chakotay. The captain returned the hard stare with assurance. He knew Martok had no patience for weakness, or politics.

"Thank you for agreeing to meet with us, Chancellor," Chakotay began politely. "You do us a great honor."

Martok nodded, as if that much was obvious. Chakotay decided that there was no way to wade comfortably into these waters; best just to dive in and get it over with.

"I've come to offer my assistance, and that of my crew, in the search for B'Elanna Torres, her child, and the Emperor Kahless. As I am sure you are aware, B'Elanna is the wife of my first officer, Lieutenant Commander Tom Paris, and Miral is his daughter. B'Elanna served honorably aboard *Voyager* during our years in the Delta quadrant. She is family."

"Your concern is appropriate, Captain, and does you credit," Martok replied sternly, "but surely Ambassador Worf has already advised you that our investigation of their disappearance is already under way. We do not require *your* assistance at this time."

Chakotay knew a dismissal when he heard one. He had come too far, however, to accept it quite so quickly.

"But perhaps the more resources we are able to apply to the problem, the more quickly we might expect to arrive at a solution," Chakotay offered.

"I assure you, Captain," Martok glowered, "it is not a question of resources. I have assigned the finest warriors at my disposal to this task. I know you do not mean to suggest that the Klingon Empire *requires* the interference of Starfleet in this matter."

"Of course not," Chakotay responded immediately. "I wish only to make you aware that should you decide that our assistance might be of use to you, we stand ready to provide it."

Insulting the leader of the Klingon Empire had not been at the top of Chakotay's list of things to do that morning, though from the decidedly chilly reception he was receiving, he felt he might have.

"Then you may consider me so advised," Martok said, waving his hand to one of the two guards who flanked Worf by the door.

"I appreciate your—"

But Chakotay never had a chance to finish that statement.

In a flash of movement, Chakotay barely glimpsed Paris out of the corner of his eye moving toward the wall on his left. A heartbeat later, Tom was holding a huge *bat'leth* that had been resting in ceremonial elegance on the wall, displayed nobly along with several others that decorated the room. With a cry, Tom rushed toward Martok, raising the sword overhead, but before Chakotay could move to restrain him, that mission was deftly accomplished by the two *Yan-Isleth* whose job it was to protect Martok's life with their own.

Paris put up quite a fight, but the behemoths on either side of him made that struggle fruitless. One guard wrenched the *bat'leth* from him, almost tearing his right arm out of its socket in the process, while the other forced Tom to the floor.

It ended as quickly as it had begun, with Paris lying at Martok's feet, pinned down by both of the guards. Worf had moved instantly to Martok's side and now stood there, seething with fury. The only two people in the room with a modicum of composure left were Janeway, who stood by Chakotay's side stoically, and Martok, who hadn't moved a muscle during the attack or its aftermath.

"I must tell you, Commander Paris," Martok said with a smirk, "your diplomatic skills leave something to be desired."

Chakotay decided that the fact that Martok hadn't ordered Paris to be dismembered on the spot was probably a good sign, though Worf looked ready to do just that at the chancellor's request.

Tom was still struggling beneath his captors' feet as Chakotay quickly ordered, "Stand down, Commander!"

"I . . . will . . . not," Paris managed, continuing to grapple helplessly against the two behemoths, whom he could not have hoped to better on his best day.

With something like amusement playing across his face, Martok said, "Let him speak."

Though it clearly went against their wishes, the two guards unceremoniously lifted Tom to his feet, while continuing to hold him relatively steady in their viselike hands.

"I don't have time for this!" Tom bellowed, now that he once again had full access to his lungs. "Conversation, diplomacy—we're wasting time! My wife and my daughter are missing, and I won't stand here and play games while you gamble with the life of my family out of pride!"

Chakotay understood that this was partly his fault. By reining Paris in, even for the short time it had taken them to reach Qo'noS, he had only given him a chance to stoke the fires of his rage. Though he had matured greatly in the last several years, Tom was still a wild and headstrong creature, never more dangerous than when threatened. The captain probably shouldn't have allowed him to be on the away team.

"I couldn't agree more, Chancellor," Janeway added, putting Chakotay in an unenviable spot.

The captain didn't know whether Martok was driven by necessity or ego. At any rate, an unbroken front was usually strongest, so Chakotay said with all the restraint he could muster, "I apologize for Commander Paris's rashness. But not Tom Paris's actions. She is his mate. We are offering our ship. *Iteb Qob qaD jup 'e' chaw'be Suvwl'.*"

Martok glanced at Worf, who met his inscrutable gaze. Chakotay knew that this little scene was not going to be received well by Command. But when negotiating with any culture, it was usually beneficial to find common ground. The Klingons were a people of few words, preferring to allow their actions to speak for them. Tom had done no more than communicate his wishes in a language that Martok would understand.

Martok nodded slightly to Worf and then returned his gaze to Tom. With grudging respect he said simply, "Very well, boy, let's see what we can do *together* to find your family."

"But you must agree that this attack is much more likely to be the work of the Warriors of Gre'thor," Doctor Harees said for the fifth time in the last ten minutes.

"I do not," Seven replied as patiently as she could. She didn't know if it was Harees's stubbornness she found most annoying at the moment or the fact that to accommodate the Elaysian's physiology she and the Doctor had agreed to have this meeting with the Institute's resident Klingon expert in her zero-g office. No matter what Seven did to focus on a stationary point or simply remember to take slow, regular breaths, floating freely about the room was a nauseating sensation. Naturally this unsettling requirement didn't bother the Doctor at all. He had no actual stomach to upset, and was able to stabilize his mobile holographic emitter to keep him still in a position several meters above the floor. As a result, he could chat for hours with Harees in complete comfort. To further emphasize the fact, he was actually floating now with his hands in the pockets of the loose dark trousers he "wore," paired with a vividly patterned shirt whose design she felt certain he must have gotten from Neelix's old replicator files. His garish attire and self-composure only irked Seven further because she was currently sweltering in one of her light gray bodysuits, which rarely felt so restrictive.

"But, Miss Seven . . ." Harees began again in a high-pitched nasal whine, an attempt at politeness that only succeeded in hitting Seven's last available nerve. Even the Doctor was no match for Harees in the condescension department.

"Simply repeating a false assumption does not make it any less false, nor does it strengthen a weak argument," Seven interjected petulantly.

The first few months Seven had spent in the company of the most adept and facile minds in the quadrant had been a fascinating change of pace from her life aboard *Voyager*. She and the Doctor had been welcomed warmly and immediately made to feel that their contributions were both unique and valued. Over time, Seven had begun to realize that these wonderful minds were unfortunately housed in the bodies of individuals who usually possessed the emotional intelligence of the average five-year-old human. As a result, they tended to defend their positions with vehemence, which Seven found inappropriate on a good day and downright annoying on most others.

The Doctor had explained patiently that often individuals such as these, whose mental gifts so far outpaced their contemporaries, tended to lack the social graces commensurate with their other accomplishments. Seven secretly enjoyed the fact that the Doctor's tolerance had finally met its limits when the Tellarite Deegle had joined the group a month earlier.

The moment Seven had received Chakotay's message, she had alerted the others to what little they knew of the events on Boreth, and everyone had agreed that Harees was the best resource the group possessed when it came to all things Klingon. Harees had obliged them with a lengthy recitation on the legends of the *Kuvah'magh* and the various prophecies relating to that mythical figure. Harees possessed an eidetic memory and had already shared with them several passages contained in dozens of ancient manuscripts, many of which suggested that Miral Paris's unique circumstances had much in common with the promised savior.

Things got muddier when it came to the issue of what exactly the *Kuvah'magh* was supposed to save the Klingon people from. The so-called "Curse of the Gods" was a troublingly vague designation for an apocalypse, particularly since it had been over a thousand years since Klingon gods had been substantively referenced by any notable scholars. Still, the signs of the pending apocalypse seemed clear enough; the birth of *Fek'lhr* and the subsequent birth of the *Kuvah'magh*.

Harees had gone on to present the short list of known believers in these prophecies, and as the only group who was known to still exist were the Warriors of Gre'thor, she had settled on them—much too quickly, in Seven's estimation—as the most likely to have committed the attack on Boreth.

"I do not accept your premise," Harees responded.

"Of course you don't," Seven shot back. "If you did, your argument would collapse under the weight of its—"

"Seven, please," the Doctor said briskly, obviously hoping to temper Seven's frustration.

"The Warriors of Gre'thor are the only viable candidates for this attack," Harees insisted again. "Their antipathy for the *Kuvah'magh* is well documented, as are numerous reports of their activities over the last millennium."

"The Warriors of Gre'thor were formed to destroy the *qawHaq'hoch*, were they not?" Seven asked.

"Yes, but—"

"They exist only to stamp out every last vestige of these ancient heretics."

"As you say, but—"

"Then if they are still active, it is logical to assume that the *qawHaq'hoch* are also still in existence," Seven went on.

"There is no evidence to suggest—" Harees began.

"Seven's right," the Doctor interjected. "The fact that the Warriors of Gre'thor have not yet abandoned their quest must mean that to the best of their knowledge, their work remains unfinished."

Seven was the tiniest bit relieved that he had been the one to finish her argument for her. Compartmentalizing came as naturally to her as breathing. But from the moment Chakotay had apprised them of B'Elanna's disappearance, she had been unable to separate her fears for B'Elanna and Miral from her need to take constructive action. Debating the obvious with an Elaysian who had serious superiority issues wasn't constructive. The truth was, she needed to be right about this, because if she was wrong, B'Elanna and Miral were probably already dead.

Seven found that thought completely unacceptable. During the four years she spent aboard *Voyager,* prior to its return to the Alpha quadrant, Seven and B'Elanna had clashed regularly on almost every topic. In truth, the two women had never really warmed to one another, though they had developed a healthy mutual respect. Captain Janeway had always insisted that *Voyager*'s crew was a family, one in whose company Seven would find solace that far outweighed the experience of being a drone in the Borg collective. The sad truth was that Seven hadn't fully begun to accept this notion until that family had parted ways upon their return to Earth.

Seven had immediately become reacquainted with her only living biological family on Earth, her father's sister, Irene Hansen. Aunt Irene was a steady, comforting presence. Silently she communicated her utter devotion to her niece, but also refused to smother her in it. Seven was encouraged to pursue any professional or personal activity that interested her, but always found herself looking forward to Sunday mornings, when she would transport to her aunt's home in the Midwest for brunch and lazy afternoon walks. There Irene had proved most adept at a skill that often eluded Seven's former shipmates; her aunt was an excellent listener.

Irene was a gift Seven was extremely grateful for. Once she realized there was no way for her to interact daily with her first *real* family—Admiral Janeway, Captain Chakotay, Tom and B'Elanna, Harry Kim, Commander Tuvok, Icheb, and Naomi Wildman—Seven had found their absence unsettling. True, she remained close to the Doctor; they worked together every day. And events seemed to conspire to bring her together with her former crew at least from time to time. Admiral Janeway made excuses to check in with her regularly, and Seven kept a watchful eye on Icheb's progress at the Academy.

But the absence, which had begun as a dull ache, had, over time, transmuted itself into a more constant discomfort. The Doctor suggested that she needed to try harder to make new friends. The idea of doing so among the members of the Institute was unappealing at best, and he hadn't blamed her for that.

Finally she had come to accept that the discomfort existed because she truly *felt* something for the *Voyager* crew. Feelings, once an object of study, had unwittingly become part of Seven's internal makeup. This realization and her aunt's gentle insistence that it was a normal part of her humanity had caused the pain, along with the corresponding loneliness. But that pain had reared a new and very ugly head when Seven was asked to confront the possibility that B'Elanna was dead, and that hurt was magnified when she considered the anguish it would also cause Tom Paris. She had read it clearly on his face the night she had spent at his parents' home waiting in vain for B'Elanna to arrive with their daughter.

As death was an unacceptable outcome, Seven felt it was her duty to find another, more palatable one. But Doctor Harees, it seemed, had other ideas, and Seven was quickly losing what little patience she possessed.

"Further," the Doctor added, "if the Warriors of Gre'thor were responsible for the attack, it is much more likely that the bodies of B'Elanna and Miral would have been found at the monastery."

"Also true," Seven finished for him. "Historically, the Warriors make no secret of their victories and usually display the bodies of their victims as a warning to those who continue to stand against them."

"Be that as it may—" Harees said, but was interrupted by the sight of Deegle, rising to join their ranks.

"I have discovered something which I believe may be pertinent to your discussion," Deegle announced.

The Doctor rolled his eyes.

"By all means," he said too gallantly to be taken seriously.

The Tellarite went on, unperturbed. "While in the process of committing our files to memory I found that several years ago, this group was asked to verify the findings of an anonymous petitioner regarding a peculiar genetic anomaly. A *Klingon* anomaly. I have the results here," he said, presenting a padd to the Doctor with a flourish.

"Are you sure you wouldn't rather just recite them for us?" the Doctor asked peevishly.

"If you'd prefer . . ."

The Doctor snapped the padd from Deegle's hand. Seven guessed that even had the padd now in his hand contained the precise coordinates where B'Elanna and Miral could be found, the Doctor would probably debate it for several hours with Deegle just to save face. The only thing he seemed to dislike more than Deegle was admitting Deegle was right.

"As I was saying," Harees continued, anxious to return to the argument at hand, "I believe that to purport that the *qawHaq'hoch* could have committed such an attack in the absence of any other verification of their continued existence is to grasp at the most flimsy of straws. Perhaps B'Elanna and her daughter were, in fact, the final members of the *qawHaq'hoch* . . ."

But Seven wasn't listening to Harees anymore. Instead, she watched as the Doctor's expression moved from exasperation to curiosity to genuine concern.

"What is it?" Seven demanded.

"It may be nothing," Deegle began.

"Nothing but the first sign of the Klingon apocalypse," the Doctor finished, tossing the padd to Seven.

Unfortunately this caused Seven a frustrated moment of gracelessness as she struggled to catch it. After taking only a few minutes more to absorb Deegle's discovery, she and the Doctor nodded to one another, their thoughts obviously running along the same disquieting path. The only comforting certainty Seven could find in Deegle's revelation was that the time for theoretical discussions had ended.

B'Elanna would have sold her soul for a Starfleet-issue tricorder. The Klingon version Logt had managed to procure for her was both slower and less precise than the counterpart B'Elanna was used to relying upon. Still, it was the best she could hope for under the circumstances.

She had managed a few hours of fitful sleep after the ceremony at the obelisk. When B'Elanna had finally given up on further efforts, despite the fact that her arms and legs felt as if she'd spent the previous day scaling a rock face, she has risen weary but determined to begin her studies of the monument.

Kahless had yet to materialize. B'Elanna assumed he was either resting or making nice with T'Krek. Either was preferable to having him stand over her shoulder while she worked. Logt was already fulfilling that duty admirably. B'Elanna had half heartedly suggested to the woman that she should try and get some rest as well. Logt had been hovering over her at full attention when B'Elanna had awakened in the dank quarters T'Krek had provided them. B'Elanna seriously doubted that Logt had closed her eyes since they left Boreth. Klingons were well known for their resilience, and Logt could probably go at least another day before fatigue would become an obstacle. Still, Logt had dismissed B'Elanna's suggestion with a scoff and only suggested that B'Elanna cease to worry about her physical needs and instead concentrate on her own.

B'Elanna needed something to occupy her mind. Without it, she would go mad before they reached Davlos. Natural curiosity had guided her back to the monument, and she had begun by analyzing the obelisk itself. It had taken hours for her to precisely coordinate the markings rendered in the stone with their stellar counterparts. Once the pattern had become clear, however, it was almost childish in its simplicity. Thousands of stars were actually referenced on the monument's surface. A thorough search of every system would have been impossible even for the vaunted Warriors of Gre'thor, irregardless of the years. Without the coded *hat'leths*, the map inscribed on the obelisk was useless.

Next she next turned her attention to the swords. B'Elanna had always believed that hers was impressive, if a little ornate for pure practicality. Unlike most *bat'leths*, which had two sharpened edges that came to points at either end of the weapon, the blade Kohlar had given her—modeled on the original sword of Kahless, as were all of the *hat'leths* resting in the trench—contained a third pointed edge in the center of the blade. This third edge was also carved with the intricate Imperial trefoil design in which was embedded the mark of Hal'korin.

The metallurgic analysis was equally fascinating. Most *bat'leths* were forged from baakonite. The swords Hal'korin had created were largely comprised of this metal, but also contained trace elements of another substance, which the tricorder could not identify. In all likelihood it was some rare metal that Hal'korin had worked into her weapons but that, a thousand years later, might be much harder to come by. B'Elanna knew nothing of the craft of sword-making. But a cursory comparison of her blade with the more modern *bat'leth* that Logt had obtained for her showed clearly that the ancient *bat'leth*s were significantly more robust than those in common use today. The analysis suggested that the ancient blades had been formed by a folding technique that reduced impurities, thereby strengthening the swords and allowing them to maintain their sharpness long past the time when most others would dull.

B'Elanna circled the trench, conducting a painstaking scan of every blade. She then darkened the room to study the ways in which the swords cast light upon the monument. Her initial analysis showed that T'Krek had been correct in calculating that the *bat'leth*s pointed to Davlos as the location of the sanctuary. What was most interesting was the fact that it was the impurities within the blades that allowed this effect to be created. The blades should have blocked all light, casting nothing but shadows upon the monument. Miraculously, however, light did penetrate the *bat'leth*s, but only in points where the tricorder indicated were heavy with specific concentrations of baakonite and the other trace metal.

Backtracking, B'Elanna compared the metallurgic variations within each blade. She could not imagine the patience or mastery of forging that would have been required to produce impure variances so specifically. Likely as not the *bat'leth*s were forged and then the monument was constructed based upon the respective impurities, but even if that was the case, the precision was still staggering. In every instance, B'Elanna found a variance of less than .00027.

The tricorder emitted a shrill bleat as it completed its latest set of calculations. She glanced at them, already certain of the result. B'Elanna stared at it for a long moment, then actually rubbed her eyes to make sure she wasn't imagining things.

Every instance but one.

B'Elanna paused.

There was no question that she had reached her mental and physical limits. Hope and desperation might account for the error she now saw before her. She checked her findings again, then rechecked them two more times just to be certain.

Only then did the knot in her stomach loosen just a bit.

"Logt," she called softly as she set her tricorder at the lip of the trench and gently removed the *bat'leth* in question from its place. It sat three places away from hers in the circle.

"What is it?" Logt asked as she approached.

Without taking her eyes from the weapon, B'Elanna said, "How hard would it be to find out exactly where the Warriors of Gre'thor acquired each of these *bat'leth*s?"

Logt considered the question, then replied, "I do not know how thorough their records are. Most likely they retain their history in songs and stories."

Oh, let's hope not.

"I need to find Kahless," B'Elanna said, replacing the sword in the trench and rising to face Logt.

"I shall accompany you."

"No," B'Elanna replied briskly. "You are going to break into their database and see if there is any written record of these lunatics' exploits. Download whatever you find into this tricorder."

The woman looked at B'Elanna as if she had finally abandoned what few senses Logt had ever given her credit for possessing.

"Where you go, I go," Logt replied evenly.

"We're not going to argue about this," B'Elanna said fiercely. "In a matter of days, this ship is going to reach Davlos. It will take them less than twenty-four more hours to thoroughly scan the planet."

Logt's right eyebrow twitched. She was either tired or impressed.

"By the time they do that, we need to be gone," B'Elanna continued. "And if we haven't figured out where that *bat'leth* came from and made a discreet escape, we'll never find Miral before they do."

"And what will you be doing while I conduct this research?" Logt asked.

"After I speak to Kahless about stealing a shuttle, I'm going to spend some quality time with the replicator nearest our quarters."

Logt favored her with a hard stare. B'Elanna knew that she had not provided the warrior with sufficient details of the plan that was forming in her mind, but perhaps B'Elanna's certainty was all Logt needed for now.

"As you wish," she said with a slight nod.

B'Elanna hurried from the chamber. It would have been exaggeration to say that she was hopeful, but she was suddenly infused with a heady sense of cautious optimism. For the first time since this nightmare had begun, B'Elanna believed she knew how to find Miral on her own, and she had the beginnings of a plan. Its success hinged on too many variables for her to stomach at the moment, but it was enough to keep her feet hurrying along as she made her way through the *Kortar*.

All she needed was one very important piece of information, and a little luck. With that, they could be off this cursed ship and reunited with those she actually trusted to get this job done—most important, Tom.

The only remaining question was how long it would take the Warriors of Gre'thor to realize their error, and B'Elanna's subterfuge.

B'Elanna didn't believe in signs, especially now that she was surrounded by people who consciously chose to live and die by them. But if fate had a hand in any of this, it had finally given her a slim advantage over the Warriors of Gre'thor, and, as she knew all too well, the smallest advantage often meant the difference between life and death.

One thought spurred her onward.

They're heading for the wrong planet.

CHAPTER EIGHT

Admiral Kenneth Montgomery was playing golf.

He hated golf.

Willem Batiste had introduced him to the game almost five years earlier, and in all that time, Montgomery's game had yet to improve. Batiste's, on the other hand, was coming along quite nicely. When they'd begun their regularly scheduled monthly "meetings" in Desert Springs, they'd both agreed to abandon the game within a year if neither of their handicaps improved. Over time, however, the tranquillity, the dry warmth, and the way in which the activity forced them out of their routine became more of a draw than their respective skills.

Very few humans or aliens were really taken with the game these days. Like baseball, for many it seemed to be a quaint anachronism. For Batiste, that had quickly become part of the appeal. He considered it a rare opportunity to "get back to nature." An avid camper, Montgomery wondered if Batiste truly understood how ridiculous he sounded when he said things like that. He also wondered why so few aspects of the game, particularly the clubs or the balls, had continued to be adapted with modern technology in the last few thousand years, apart from a few cosmetic alterations to the shape of the putter and wedges. Of course, such adaptations would have made the game easier, but that was apparently not the point.

Further, Montgomery had become convinced over the last few years that Batiste must be cheating. *That bastard's practicing in his off hours,* he thought bitterly as Willem executed a perfect three-hundred-meter drive that landed just off the green of the sixteenth hole. The hole was a par three, but Montgomery doubted he'd reach the green in four strokes, especially the way he was chopping up the course today.

The admiral stepped up to the tee and did his best to quiet his mind. Unlike most of his regular duties, multi-tasking was not a skill that was helpful when applied to golf. Instead, the game required a balance of focus and calm, an ability to get out of one's own way and simply allow the body to execute a single, swift graceful motion in which the club was responsible for the majority of the work.

"Looks like that slice is coming along beautifully," Batiste joked as Montgomery's shot flew dramatically toward the tree line banking the right side of the fairway.

Montgomery replaced his driver in his bag and hefted it onto his shoulder in preparation for the death march to retrieve his ball. Another of Batiste's little quirks was that he insisted they walk the course rather than use hovercarts. This usually added at least an hour or two to their game, but as these "meetings" were meant to be part recreation, part work, Montgomery rarely found reason to dispute this request until right around the eleventh hole, when he found himself wishing that his combadge would sound, alerting both of them to an interstellar disaster that would make finishing the game impossible.

"See you on the green," Montgomery said optimistically as he began his weary trek.

"I'll walk with you," Batiste replied amiably. "There's actually something I've been meaning to ask you about."

"What's that?"

It took most of the few minutes required for them to reach the tree line and actually find Montgomery's ball, wedged between the gnarled roots of a jacaranda, for Batiste to outline the proposal he was preparing to make to Starfleet Command regarding *Voyager*.

Montgomery almost tripped at about the same time Batiste relayed the mission's most startling feature.

"You want them to *what*?" Montgomery demanded, worried that the heat, the frustration, and the exhaustion might finally be getting to him.

"You heard me," Batiste replied placidly.

Montgomery stepped back gingerly to avoid touching the ball and adding yet another stroke to the game as he considered his friend.

He looks serious, Montgomery had to allow. *And he sure sounds serious.*

This could mean only one thing.

"Have you lost your mind?" Montgomery asked.

Batiste chuckled, stepping aside to allow him as unobstructed a path to the fairway as his dismal shot would permit.

"I have not." Batiste smiled.

"And have you, by any chance, run this absurd notion by Admiral Janeway yet?" was Montgomery's next question.

"You're the first person I've told," Batiste said casually. "I was hoping to get your input, as well as Eden's final report, before I discuss it with the rest of the admiralty."

"A Ferengi would have an easier time selling hot water in hell than you'll have getting this past Kathryn," Montgomery replied. Most starship captains developed a sense of proprietary regard for their crews, even their former ones, but Kathryn Janeway had taken that propensity to entirely new dimensions when she had been promoted to vice admiral. True, the circumstances of her ship and crew had been unique, and that alone granted her a certain amount of latitude among her peers. But Kathryn's crew was dearer to her than colleagues or friends. To her, they were family. And she watched over them with the keen eye of a mother hen, even from the distance her new position required.

"Setting that aside for the moment, what are your thoughts, Ken?" Batiste asked patiently.

Montgomery shook his head, realizing that he'd just pulled his sand wedge from his bag rather than his pitching wedge.

At this point, what the hell difference does it make? he thought, lining up his shot with his back braced uncomfortably against the tree.

He was half considering his response and halfway into his backswing when his combadge chirped. Amid the desert stillness it sounded like the firing of a phaser, and he brought the club down sharply, digging into the hard soil and barely tapping the ball over the tree root before it dribbled a few feet farther, coming to rest several meters short of the fairway but at least in the relative clear.

"If you'd like to try that again?" Batiste offered graciously.

Montgomery waved him off, equal parts disgusted and relieved, and stepped a few paces farther into the trees before he opened his side of the comlink.

"What is it?" he barked in frustration.

"I'm sorry to disturb you, Admiral, but I have a priority communication for you from Captain Chakotay."

"Put it throught," Montgomery ordered.

After a brief pause, Chakotay's voice greeted him. *"I hope this isn't a bad time, Admiral."*

"Oh, it's an excellent time," Montgomery assured him, grateful at least that whatever Chakotay wanted to discuss with him had brought him a few moments' reprieve from the dismal game.

Of course, when Chakotay had finished relaying his message, Montgomery was less inclined toward gratitude. Emerging from the tree line, he found Batiste standing beside his bag, sipping from his water bottle. The hover-cart he had called after closing the communication with Chakotay could be heard buzzing toward them from the direction of the clubhouse.

"Sorry to cut this short, Willem, but I have to get back to San Francisco right away. Captain Chakotay is testing out his improvisational skills, and we'll probably be at war with the Klingons before the day is out."

"I thought *Voyager* was on its way to Kerovi."

"They *were*," Montgomery shot back bitterly.

Batiste nodded. "Understood. I think I'll play through."

"Good idea." Montgomery nodded. "Give you some time to reconsider."

"Then you don't approve of my idea?" Batiste asked.

"I don't," Montgomery replied honestly. "Of course, I can see the value in what you're proposing, from a purely exploratory point of view. But I also believe that sometimes you can ask too much of a person. *Voyager*'s time in the Delta quadrant wasn't your average deep-space mission. Those people went through hell. I'm not saying they wouldn't be up to it. *Voyager's* crew is one of the best Starfleet has ever produced. But I would never ask it of them, and neither should you, my friend."

Batiste nodded. Montgomery didn't honestly know if he was agreeing with him or simply mustering a new argument.

Either way, Kathryn will set him straight.

And that would be a conversation worth watching, Montgomery decided, if only to see Batiste struggle as futilely as he had all afternoon.

Paris barely noticed Chakotay return to the embassy conference suite Ambassador Worf had provided them for their work. Spread before him on a table lay the fruits of the Klingons' investigation to date, and they were a sparse meal at best.

One of the Klingons discovered dead on Boreth had been Kularg. Tom found that one image of the man kept playing over and over in his mind, once he had wiped away the vision of Kularg lying on the nursery floor, his blood pouring forth from the dagger driven into his heart.

Often when Miral had refused to stop fussing, particularly around nap time, Kularg would say, "The time has come for blood pie." The first time he'd heard this, Tom had worried that his daughter had finally become too infuriating for Kularg to handle and had just been relegated to the dinner menu. But before Tom could step in, Kularg had deposited the crying child on her back on a pile of tanned *targ* skins and softly started to assemble the imaginary blood pie on Miral's tummy. He would announce each ingredient, then pantomime placing it on her stomach. Of course, the stirring motion that accompanied each addition was the part that usually calmed Miral the most. This gentle massage, combined with the fascination that would often overtake Miral as she diligently watched the movement of his hands, usually meant that well before the "pie" was done, Miral was either laughing from the tickles or fighting to keep her eyes open as sleep overtook her.

Tom had never known a Klingon like Kularg, and believed he probably never would again. Klingon society still had rigid ideas about the roles of men and women. Kularg's nurturing instincts might have been construed by some as a form of weakness. Tom saw only honor and strength in the old warrior and someone he would miss.

The only other bodies discovered at the scene were those of two females who had yet to be identified. They were not of a noble house, nor were they commoners. As best anyone could tell, they had never before set foot on Boreth, nor on any other Klingon colony. Until they had been found dead, it seemed they had never existed.

For the time being, the Klingons investigating the matter seemed to believe that the attack had been directed against Kahless. The concurrent disappearance of Commander Logt, one of his personal guardians, only reinforced this notion. It was no secret that there were still many Klingons who had difficulty accepting Kahless as their emperor, symbolic though that title was. Clone or not, the man had already provided such valuable service to the empire that Tom saw this point as completely moot. But Paris worried that Martok's only interest in the events on Boreth was to make certain that this was not the prelude to another attack on his position as chancellor.

Usually, Tom didn't suffer from delusions of grandeur or the belief that the universe revolved around him or his small cares. But he firmly believed that the attack had been directed at Miral. The problem was he couldn't prove it, and until he could, he wasn't going to change the focus of the investigation.

He wished Tuvok was here now. The Vulcan who had once been *Voyager*'s tactical officer was now teaching at Starfleet Academy. But during their time in the Delta quadrant, Tuvok had demonstrated on numerous occasions that he possessed a keen investigative sense, beginning with an encounter with two warring cultures during which Tom had been falsely accused and convicted of murder. Tuvok's tenacity had saved his life. Paris couldn't help but think that if Tuvok and his tenacity could be brought to bear, it would aid his efforts immeasurably. Depending upon how things developed in the next few hours, Tom decided he should make this recommendation to Chakotay and Janeway to see if there might be any strings that could be pulled.

One of Worf's aides, an efficient human named Giancarlo Wu who had gone out of his way to be helpful, entered the conference room carrying a rather large box. He placed it before Tom and said gently, "Commander, these just arrived. They are all of the personal items that were left in your family's quarters on Boreth."

Paris thanked him with a nod, then steadied himself to begin going through them.

"Have they been thoroughly analyzed by the investigative team?"

The young man cleared his throat and replied, "If by *analyzed* you mean tossed carelessly in a box and labeled for storage, then yes."

Paris had to swallow hard before he could reply, "Thank you," his voice thick with emotion.

At the far end of the table, Chakotay was conferring with Admiral Janeway. Tom caught bits and pieces, including Chakotay's remark that Admiral Montgomery had been apprised of their situation and would provide them with new orders shortly. As long as those orders didn't include continuing on their former course to Kerovi, Paris couldn't have cared less. In the meantime, he knew that both of them were studying recent starship traffic around Boreth along with the lists of all those who had been in residence at the monastery at the time of the attack.

Forcing himself to keep in mind that the items in the box before him were simply objects and not the last pieces of the wife and child he would never hold again, Tom began to sort through them. The first thing he discovered was the civilian clothes B'Elanna had worn when she first came to Boreth, as well as a number of robes and hide cloaks she had accumulated. Several soft pieces of cloth, the Klingon analog of diapers, were also present, and though Paris knew well that they had been scoured by rough Klingon hands after each use, he still believed he could smell Miral, or at least the scent he had last associated with her, on every one of them.

It was more than he could bear.

Tom's heart heaved within his chest as the hot tears he had forbidden to fall rose to his eyes.

Setting the cloths aside, he struggled to focus. He recognized all of the box's contents thus far, but noted that a few important things were missing; among them, Miral's favorite blanket and B'Elanna's *bat'leth*.

The only two things B'Elanna wouldn't leave behind if she'd been forced to leave Boreth in a hurry.

This thought was at least almost comforting.

At the bottom of the box was a light cloak B'Elanna usually wore at bedtime. Tom knew that it would be covered with her scent and for a moment felt his legs shudder beneath him. He gathered the folds of fabric in his hands, kneading them gently for a moment, trying to find the strength not to wallow, when a faint crackling sound met his ears.

Paris played the fabric over again in his hands and discovered the source of the sound: a small piece of parchment crumpled in one of the pockets.

He removed it and laid it carefully on the table, assuming it would be a scrap of text B'Elanna might have made note of in her studies. Much as he dreaded the thought of another visceral reminder of her absence, the sight of her handwriting, Tom forced himself to open it carefully so as not to damage the delicate page.

It was written in Klingon. And it was not written by B'Elanna's hand. The only word he could make sense of at first almost dropped him to his chair.

Kuvah'magh.

He knew that with some effort he could translate the rest. He just wasn't sure if he wanted to. Like as not, this was part of B'Elanna's research, nothing more, part of his mind insisted.

Tom studied the other words. The next one he recognized made his heart beat even faster.

Danger.

Finally Tom abandoned his attempt and simply scanned the words into his tricorder. A moment later, the horrific translation glowed out from the tiny screen.

You and the Kuvah'magh *are in danger.*

The pain that had been strangling his heart only moments before was immediately replaced by rage.

She knew.

Where or when B'Elanna might have received this message was unclear. But suddenly the faint misgivings he'd had every time they spoke for the last several weeks became both crystal clear and horrifying.

You and the Kuvah'magh *are in danger.*

B'Elanna had lied to him.

True, it was a lie of omission, but he wasn't ready to grant her anything.

She knew. She knew and she didn't tell me.

Had he been able to think more clearly, he might have found some solace in the fact that here at last was tangible proof that his gut had not been mistaken. Finally he could present the Klingons with evidence that they were sniffing the wrong dung heap.

His thoughts were interrupted by a sharp intake of breath from the other side of the table.

He looked up to see Admiral Janeway rising to her feet as a relieved smile spread across her face.

Turning, he found the reason.

Standing at the door to the conference room were B'Elanna, Logt, and the Emperor Kahless.

All three of them looked like hell.

Hovering behind them was Ambassador Worf. He nodded briefly to Tom, then backed from the doorway to allow them privacy.

Kahless and Logt moved toward the far side of the room. Though they had never met Chakotay or the admiral, they, too seemed painfully aware that Tom and B'Elanna both needed a moment before whatever else was to come could begin.

B'Elanna's face held its fierce determination for the first few moments her eyes locked with Tom's. But soon it started to crumple as pain and fear met the desperate need she seemed to be trying to communicate.

Tom's heart answered hers with a brief mutual longing and relief. But it was replaced almost instantly with the knowledge of her betrayal and how much that betrayal might have cost them both.

Tom wanted to go to her.

She wasn't rushing to him though, and he thought ungenerously that her guilt must be holding her back.

Finally, however, he realized that there would be time for arguments and recriminations later. For now at least, she was here, and that was something.

Tom started forward on trembling legs and crossed the small space separating him from his wife.

He just didn't know if the first thing he should do was to kiss her or kill her.

───────

The *Kortar* had been in orbit above Davlos for seventeen hours. Ten hours ago, their initial scans had revealed no indication that the sanctuary might be found there. But T'Krek was too keen a hunter to be dismayed by such a setback. The *qawHaq'hoch* had mastered the ability to hide themselves. Obviously some sort of energy field or natural anomaly was interfering with the ship's sensors.

The only solution, therefore, was to look closer.

Twenty teams had been dispatched to the planet in shuttles to facilitate the search. Thus far, none had reported any anomalous findings that might point to their quarry's hiding place.

But T'Krek had learned patience.

As an added precaution, he had decided to keep their honored "guests" secured within quarters until their search was complete. He knew that once they found the infernal child and ended her life, B'Elanna would either kill him or, much more likely, die trying. He had tried repeatedly while en route to Davlos to make the emperor see that this was the only way. The *qawHaq'hoch* had survived this long only because they had a clear purpose, a destiny. From what Grapk and D'Kang had learned on Boreth, T'Krek no longer doubted that Miral Paris was the *Kuvah'magh*. Had they completed their appointed task, T'Krek would have been able to kill the child himself on Boreth. But at least his brother Warriors had done part of their job right. This meant that each man had lost only an arm by T'Krek's hand when they had made their final report to him and offered him their lives for their failure.

But the emperor had refused to acknowledge T'Krek's reasoning. This had been troubling, but not altogether unexpected. The emperor would say only that *his* interests were those of the empire. How the birth of a child who would call only destruction down upon them was meant to serve the empire, T'Krek could not understand, but Kahless had only looked at him with a benign sense of superiority when he made this point.

Perhaps T'Krek should try again.

Though he was unwilling to abandon the idea that they would eventually find the *Kuvah'magh* on Davlos, their victory would be that much sweeter should the emperor stand beside him when he cut the child's throat.

T'Krek opened a comm channel.

"T'Krek to Emperor Kahless."

There was no answer.

"Emperor Kahless, respond," T'Krek ordered.

Again, silence.

T'Krek turned to the warrior manning operations.

"Ligerh, locate the emperor."

Ligerh nodded and performed a quick scan.

"The emperor is in his quarters."

"Is he alone?"

"No, Captain. B'Elanna Paris and Commander Logt are with him."

T'Krek wasn't going to grovel. Kahless might be the emperor, but this was *his* ship.

"Bring him to me," T'Krek ordered.

Two minutes later a frantic voice came over the comm channel.

"Captain, this is M'Rent."

"Report," T'Krek said calmly.

"The emperor's quarters are empty. A tricorder was adapted to display false life signs."

T'Krek's tone made the price of subsequent failure on M'Rent's part painfully clear.

"Find them!"

CHAPTER NINE

B'Elanna's first request, once she and Tom had shared an awkward embrace that promised a much longer conversation later, had been that the group adjourn to *Voyager* before discussing anything in detail.

She and Kahless had spent twenty minutes with Ambassador Worf before being escorted to the embassy conference room, briefly recounting the events of the last week. Logt had been busy at the time overseeing the transfer of the shuttle they had stolen from the *Kortar* to the custody of the Defense Force officer on duty at the orbital docking station above Qo'noS.

Both Janeway and Chakotay had greeted B'Elanna more warmly than Tom, and both had agreed immediately to her request. As Chakotay and Wu were finalizing the details, Worf reentered the conference room and headed straight for Kahless.

"The chancellor has asked me to advise you that you will have the full support of the Klingon Defense Force at your disposal in your continuing efforts to recover Miral Paris," Worf announced.

Before Kahless could respond, B'Elanna cut him off. "Thank you, Mister Ambassador, but this is a *family* matter and I would prefer to handle it with *Voyager's* help."

Worf turned his grim visage to B'Elanna. "I apologize, Commander, but I was under the impression that *Voyager* would be returning to its previous mission. Of course, I can contact Starfleet Command and request other Federation support if you would prefer."

"That won't be necessary," Chakotay intervened. "I've kept Starfleet apprised of our situation."

Worf nodded.

"But you should know this, Mister Ambassador," B'Elanna went on. "The Warriors of Gre'thor intend to find and murder my child. Should I cross paths with them again, I won't hesitate to kill every last one of them to prevent that."

To her surprise, Worf almost cracked a smile.

"Then you will need to act quickly if you intend to beat Martok to it," he replied dryly.

The shock on B'Elanna's face was apparently all the encouragement he needed to continue. "Until this afternoon, the chancellor was not aware that the Warriors of Gre'thor were still active. They have, from time to time, provided admirable service to the empire in the past, but only, it seems, when the mood strikes them. The chancellor intends to bring them to heel. They will fall in line, or they will be disbanded."

Good luck with that, B'Elanna thought, catching Kahless's eye and noting the subtle shake of his head, suggesting he also believed this would prove a difficult nut for the chancellor to crack.

Fifteen minutes later, Logt had rejoined them in *Voyager*'s main conference room. Also in attendance was the ship's senior staff, including Harry Kim, who had almost wept with relief when he first laid eyes on B'Elanna,

Operations Officer Lyssa Campbell, and the new ship's doctor, a Trill named Jarem Kaz.

B'Elanna had heard a great deal about Kaz from Tom. Apparently his symbiont had shared a troubled personal history with the Changeling they had confronted at Loran II, and Kaz had almost died in their efforts to stop him. He had also been of great service when *Voyager* had first returned to Earth and become embroiled in a covert plot by a deranged admiral to form a new Borg collective. This, it seemed, had been the impetus for Chakotay to request his assignment to *Voyager* on a permanent basis.

Both Tom and Chakotay thought highly of Doctor Kaz, though frankly B'Elanna wondered how he could ever replace the only doctor she had ever truly felt comfortable with, the ship's former EMH.

The only other officer in the room whom B'Elanna had never met was the ship's new counselor, Lieutenant Hugh Cambridge. He barely nodded to her when they were introduced and studiously kept his own counsel as B'Elanna and Kahless in turns brought everyone in the room up to speed regarding the events on Boreth and what they had discovered aboard the *Kortar*. Only when Kahless shared his belief that the *qawHaq'hoch* were responsible for Miral's kidnapping did a faint "Interesting" escape Cambridge's lips involuntarily. A sharp glance from Chakotay was met with a withering nod, and Cambridge retreated into silence.

Kahless glossed over their escape from the *Kortar,* as if it had been a mere inconvenience. B'Elanna's recollection of barely managing to rig her tricorder to fool the ship's sensors and the subsequent hours she, Kahless, and Logt had spent crawling through the ship's maintenance tubes to reach the shuttlebay undetected was more colorful than Kahless's version, but she was happy to banish it, along with Logt's quick dispatch of the guards who had been assigned to the cloak-equipped shuttle they ultimately stole, to the realm of bad memories.

Tom seethed quietly by her side. The only two people in the room who seemed to be even cognizant of the tension flaring between them were B'Elanna and Cambridge, who glanced at Tom several times with a bemused expression. He appeared to be attempting to calculate just how long it would take before Tom's patience with the proceedings came to an end. When it finally did, Cambridge actually checked his chronometer and nodded to himself, suggesting that his estimate had been accurate.

"So if the sanctuary isn't on Davlos, then where the hell is it?" Tom said, once Kahless had finished describing their escape from T'Krek's vessel.

"And how long before the Warriors of Gre'thor realize they're looking in the wrong place?" Harry added, clearly trying to assess the dangers *Voyager* might face now that they had become part of the equation.

"While we were on the *Kortar*, I was able to do a thorough analysis of the Hal'korin *bat'leths*," B'Elanna said, picking up her part of the story.

"And one of them was a forgery," Cambridge interjected.

"That's right," B'Elanna said, unable to hide her surprise.

"How did you know that?" Chakotay asked sharply.

"There have been numerous accounts over the years of weapons designed by Hal'korin that later turned out to be fogeries," Cambridge replied. "Unless I'm much mistaken, Hal'korin's weapons still fetch considerable sums in any illegal weapons market. Her swords, in particular, are highly prized, hence the the proliferation of fakes. *Bat'leths* like the ones she's describing would be considered museum pieces today, and definitely priceless."

"So how does that help us find Miral?" Tom said pointedly to B'Elanna.

"Since the impurities in the swords provide the key to decoding the markings on the monument, only the true *bat'leths* can give you the right answer," B'Elanna replied evenly. "T'Krek's calculations could be off by hundreds of light-years. The forged *bat'leth* was acquired only thirty years ago from a man named Kopek."

"Do we know where he is?" Tom demanded.

"He is now a member of the Klingon High Council," Kahless replied, "and as soon as we are done here I will contact him to discuss his dealings with the Warriors of Gre'thor." There was no mistaking the ominous tone in Kahless's voice.

As B'Elanna briefly considered how glad she was not to be Kopek right now, a voice sounded over the comm system.

"Bridge to Captain Chakotay."

"Go ahead."

"We are being hailed by the Klingon Ambassador to the Federation. His personal ship had just entered orbit and he had two representatives from the Federation Research Institute on board who are requesting immediate transport to Voyager."

Chakotay and Janeway immediately exchanged a knowing smile. Janeway rose from her place and said, "If you'll excuse me for a moment, I'll meet them in the transporter room and bring them up to speed."

B'Elanna was briefly puzzled until she remembered that Seven and the Doctor had joined the institute several months earlier. Though part of her felt she should wait for their arrival before continuing, the expectant faces of the others convinced her to continue.

"I brought the eleven true *bat'leth*s with me," B'Elanna said, "leaving T'Krek with replicated fakes. All we have to do is find the final sword of Hal'korin and take them all to the actual sanctuary on Qo'noS."

"That is, of course . . ." Cambridge began, then with a deferential glance at Chakotay, asked, "May I?" Chakotay nodded, and Cambride went on, "Assuming that the *qawHaq'hoch* are in fact responsible for Miral's abduction."

"They are," B'Elanna shot back automatically.

"That remains to be seen," Cambridge replied.

"What makes you think they aren't?" Tom asked harshly.

B'Elanna reached for his hand, and he just as quickly pulled it away.

Cambridge shot an appraising glance at Kahless before continuing, "Forgive me, Emperor, but the last tangible proof that the *qawHaq'hoch* even exist is over eight hundred years old. There was a dispute over the rightful inheritance in two ancient Houses, and the *qawHaq'hoch* were contacted to mediate because at the time, it was common knowledge that their records of all Klingon lineages were the most accurate in the empire, and the least tainted by any political intrigues. Their data files of the Houses were produced and the dispute was settled, but not before there was an attack, undoubtedly by the Warriors of Gre'thor, and all representatives of the order present at the mediation were killed. Since that time, no verifiable record acknowledging any activity by the *qawHaq'hoch* has been discovered."

"Is this true?" B'Elanna asked Kahless.

"It is," he replied. "However, they remain, in my estimation, the most likely to have committed this crime."

"Your *estimation*?" Tom asked with evident frustration.

"The emperor is right about one thing," Cambridge said in a more conciliatory tone. "Of all the various sects known throughout Klingon history to have taken the prophecies about the *Kuvah'magh* seriously, the *qawHaq'hoch* were the most adamant in their faith. It's difficult to imagine that they could have existed, undetected all these years, but not impossible. The hypothesis would be more sustainable if we also possessed evidence that the first sign of the *joH'a mu'qaD* had come to pass. I find it hard to believe that anything else might have caused the *qawHaq'hoch* to act so precipitously and thereby risk revealing themselves after all this time."

"The first sign has come to pass," Kahless assured Cambridge.

"Really, sir?" he asked, clearly intrigued. "Can you prove this?"

"What is he talking about?" Tom interjected.

"I'll explain later," B'Elanna said.

"Or I could explain now," an imperious voice from the doorway said.

B'Elanna turned.

"Don't you mean *we* could explain?" the Doctor corrected Seven of Nine, who stood beside him in the entryway. Admiral Janeway ushered them into the room as the Doctor went on, "The Klingon ambassador was kind enough to give us a lift when he was apprised of our mission and its *sensitive* nature," the Doctor added.

"We were reluctant to transmit our findings to you, even over encrypted channels," Seven went on, "as we could not be certain that they would not be intercepted. The ambassador's was the first and quickest transport we were able to obtain."

"Yes, Ambassador Lantar was quite accommodating," the Doctor replied too ironically to be taken seriously.

"If you hadn't insisted upon trying to bend his ear every five minutes of our journey," Seven began to chide him.

"Thank you both," Chakotay interrupted, ending further discussion of this unhelpful topic. "I'm sure I speak for everyone here when I say welcome aboard and thank you for coming. Any information you can provide will certainly be most helpful."

As the Doctor took a moment to greet his old comarades and to introduce himself to Cambridge and the emperor, Seven addressed herself to B'Elanna.

"I am pleased to find you unharmed," she said with compassion, which almost startled B'Elanna.

"Thank you, Seven."

"I can assure you that I have no intention of regenerating until we are able to locate Miral."

B'Elanna was so moved by this sentiment that she was unable to find words. She nodded gratefully, after which Seven moved to the room's display monitor, where she quickly downloaded a data padd.

Once everyone present had quieted, Seven began, "Several years ago the institute where the Doctor and I are currently working was asked to analyze the genomes of three Klingon children who were born with a birth defect which until that point had never before been seen."

Images of the childen appeared on the screen behind her. The collective intake of breath from most of those around the table assured her that she had everyone's complete attention.

"As you can see, these children appear to be severely deformed. Their cranial ridges are overdeveloped, distorting the facial structure, and the teeth, particularly these paired incisors which protrude through the upper and lower jaws, are overly elongated and pronounced."

Doctor Kaz rose quietly from the table and moved closer to the screen to study the display more carefully.

"Of course, the more serious defects are not obvious," the Doctor said, crossing to stand beside Seven. "Malformations in the brain and hormonal imbalances resulted in the absence of all higher reasoning functions, while elevating their natural aggression. Had these children survived, they would have developed into creatures driven purely by instinct—quite ferocious and extremely dangerous."

"What happened to them?" Doctor Kaz asked.

"The individual who requested our group's assistance did so anonymously," Seven replied. "But we were advised that all three of the children died prior to the inquiry."

B'Elanna had been unable to tear her eyes from the screen from the moment Seven had brought up the image of the children. Though she had never been one to take Klingon mythology too seriously, particularly before their encounter with Kohlar in the Delta quadrant, she had to admit that had she seen this image in any other context, only one thought would have entered her mind.

"*Fek'lhr*," she said softly.

Paris rose from the table, unable to contain himself any longer.

"Would someone for the love of all that's holy please tell me what this has to do with my daughter?"

"Tom, please," B'Elanna said, turning her fear-filled eyes to his.

"It's quite simple, Mister Paris," Cambridge said. "Klingon apocrypha say that the empire will only be destroyed by the *joH'a mu'qaD*, or 'Curse of the Gods.' Two signs precede this curse: the rebirth of *Fek'lhr*, a creature well known in Klingon mythology as the beast that guards the gates of Gre'thor, followed by the birth of the *Kuvah'magh*. The only Klingons known who still take these prophecies seriously are the *qawHaq'hoch* and their historic enemies, the Warriors of Gre'thor. Given the fact that both signs have arguably now come to pass, it seems only likely that both groups would believe that the pending apocalypse will follow briskly on their heels." Turning to Kahless, he went on, "Your reasoning about the identity of Miral's kidnappers is indeed most sound, sir. Only one question remains."

"What is that?" Kahless asked.

"Who betrayed the identity of B'Elanna's child to the *qawHaq'hoch*?" Cambridge asked.

"I don't understand," B'Elanna said.

"Who, besides you, your husband, the emperor, and your former crewmates, had any idea that your child might be the *Kuvah'magh*?"

Paris and B'Elanna both turned to each other, searching for the same answer.

"No one," Tom said, at a loss.

"Then I suggest you look for the culprit here," Cambridge tossed back.

"That's enough," Chakotay barked, silencing Cambridge. "Sir, I believe you have a meeting on Qo'noS," he said.

Kahless nodded. "I will make contact as soon as I have further news." As he strode from the room, he paused to grasp B'Elanna and Tom firmly by the shoulders. "Your daughter needs you now more than ever," he said intently. "See that you do not fail her."

B'Elanna nodded as she saw the blood rushing to Tom's cheeks. Finally, he grasped her hand. It was a small gesture, but it almost brought tears of relief to B'Elanna's eyes.

"We will remain in orbit until we receive word from the emperor," Chakotay advised the room. "In the meantime, Lieutenant Kim, you should begin preparations for a potential attack by the Warriors of Gre'thor. Once they discover B'Elanna's ruse, they probably won't have a hard time figuring out where she would have gone next."

"Captain," Doctor Kaz interjected, "I'd like to spend some time reviewing Seven and the Doctor's analysis."

"We would be happy to assist any way we can," the Doctor assured him.

"Keep me apprised of any new developments." Chakotay nodded. "Dismissed."

He then rose and crossed to Paris and B'Elanna, who were sitting in loaded silence as the rest of those assembled moved from the room, the only exception being Admiral Janeway, who followed closely behind Chakotay.

"I know this isn't the reunion you were both hoping for," Chakotay said gently, "but I'm sure you could both use a little time alone."

Paris started to contradict him, but Chakotay raised a hand to silence him. "You're off duty until further notice, Commander." Then he added, "Get some rest. You're both going to need it."

Janeway stepped closer to take B'Elanna's free hand and to place another on Tom's shoulder. "I don't want either of you to worry," she said in her most determined voice. "We're going to find Miral, even if we have to rain down fire on the entire Klingon Empire to do it."

B'Elanna managed a mute nod as Tom replied, "Thank you, Admiral."

<hr />

As everyone made their exits, Chakotay caught Cambridge's eye and with a nod directed him to join him in the hallway.

Once Cambridge had obliged him and the others were well out of earshot, Chakotay said, "That was an impressive display, Lieutenant. I had no idea your knowledge of Klingon mythology was so sound, or so deep."

"Then I can only presume you gave my service record the most cursory of glances before contacting Starfleet personnel to request my immediate transfer," Cambridge replied.

"I beg your pardon?" Chakotay snapped back.

"As well you should, sir," Cambridge said. "For what it's worth, I have no objection to serving aboard *Voyager* for as long as you're willing to have me. To be honest, I've never seen a group of people so thoroughly in need of my services."

Chakotay had only a few seconds to stand in shock before his combadge chirped.

"Ops to the captain."

"We'll continue this discussion later, Counselor," he said coolly.

With a soft "Of course, sir," Cambridge executed a slight bow and stalked off toward the turbolift.

Chakotay took a deep breath before tapping his combadge.

"Go ahead."

"You have a priority transmission from Starfleet Command."

"Route it to my ready room," Chakotay replied.

A few minutes later he was seated at his desk, and the face of Admiral Montgomery appeared on the screen before him.

"What is your current status, Captain?" Montgomery inquired.

"The emperor, his personal guard, and B'Elanna are all alive and well and have rendezvoused with *Voyager*," Chakotay replied.

"That's good to hear," Montgomery said with genuine relief. *"Then I presume you have resumed course for Kerovi?"*

Chakotay took a deep breath. "No, sir. Miral Paris is still missing, but we believe we have a solid lead and will discover her whereabouts shortly. I've been assured that Chancellor Martok has been advised of our activities and is in constant communication with the emperor, who is still assisting us with the search. Until Miral has been found, we must continue in our efforts."

Montgomery stared back at Chakotay appraisingly.

"I'm sorry, Chakotay, but I can't allow that. As it stands now, you will barely have time to reach Kerovi before the trial begins."

"Would it be possible to contact the Kerovians?" Chakotay asked. "Perhaps if we explained the nature of the problem . . ."

Montgomery shook his head. "We're barely on speaking terms with the Kerovians as it is. They want to know why we failed to capture or kill the Changeling at Loran II. The two weeks' grace period they allowed before beginning the trial was all the courtesy they can be expected to extend us."

"Why can't we simply interrogate the Changeling once the trial is over?" Chakotay asked.

"Prior to joining the Federation, the Kerovian justice system offered only one penalty for a convicted murderer: execution," Montgomery said sternly.

"Their membership status only changed a few months ago," Chakotay said. "Have they completely overhauled their legal system in that short time?"

"Not yet," Montgomery replied, "but the public is exerting considerable pressure on the government to reinstate capital punishment, especially given the nature of the Changeling's transgressions. The Kerovi were our allies when we fought the Dominion. They know how to kill a Changeling, and I wouldn't be surprised if they found that it was a tidier way to deal with this problem and the public outcry than figuring out how to keep him locked up for the rest of his very long life."

"When did abandoning moral principles become tidy, sir?" Chakotay asked.

"You missed the war, Captain," Montgomery replied gravely. "It was, without a doubt, one of the darkest periods *in Federation history. Our principles took a beating, and the losses sustained, combined with the potential devastation of our way of life, forced everyone involved to make difficult decisions. I'm not convinced that the Kerovian government will cave to the pressure, but I'm also not certain that's a risk we should take right now."*

Chakotay paused to give the admiral's words the consideration they deserved.

"Then perhaps you should dispatch another ship to Kerovi as soon as possible," Chakotay finally replied.

"Are you refusing a direct order, Captain?"

"I'm sorry, Admiral, but at no point in this conversation do I recall hearing you order me to resume course for Kerovi."

Montgomery faced Chakotay in steely silence.

"Now that I have been fully briefed on the events on Boreth and the forces involved, I believe that without our assistance the odds of safely recovering Miral will be slim to none."

"The needs of the many, Captain," Montgomery began.

"Are being considered," Chakotay finished for him. "More is at stake here than Miral's life. We've already discovered evidence to suggest that this is simply the prelude to a more serious crisis for the Klingon Empire. This issue is not many or one, Admiral. The issue is which 'many' are we most concerned about right now. I honestly believe that it is right here that *Voyager* and her crew can do the most good."

Montgomery could clearly see he wasn't getting anywhere. Finally he replied, *"I'll see if we have any other ships that could be dispatched in time for Kerovi. In the mean-*

time, I want hourly updates on your status, and at the first opportunity, I expect you to resume your former course."

"Understood, Admiral." Chakotay nodded. "Thank you."

Montgomery closed the channel.

Chakotay did not doubt that his instincts in this matter were correct, though he paused to wonder if his personal misgivings about the mission to Kerovi might be clouding his judgment. He agreed that it was vital for Starfleet to interrogate the Changeling, sooner rather than later. But that was one demon he was in no particular hurry to face. And he couldn't imagine what it would do to his crew's morale were he to inform them that the search for Miral was being abandoned. As Kathryn had suggested, the best person to discuss this with was probably his ship's counselor.

Of course, that thought was only slightly more unappealing than confronting the Changeling. It was small comfort to realize that there was one person on board who would certainly relate to his dilemma, and whose counsel he would welcome.

"Chakotay to Doctor Kaz."

"Kaz here, Captain."

"Please report to my ready room."

"Actually, Captain, would you consider joining us in sick-bay? We've just stumbled upon something you should probably see right away."

"I'm on my way," Chakotay replied, making a mental note to stop by engineering first. It seemed likely that Seven and the Doctor would be staying awhile, and though the Doctor didn't actually require a living area, Chakotay would do him the courtesy of providing one, if only to give

Doctor Kaz a break from time to time. Seven's needs were more challenging. The regeneration alcove she'd used in the cargo bay when she lived on *Voyager* had been dismantled months ago, but the specs were still in *Voyager's* database. Vorik would need to assign a team to construct one as soon as possible.

From the sound of Jarem's voice, Chakotay seriously doubted that whatever he, Seven, and the Doctor had found was going to be good news.

CHAPTER TEN

Kahless watched as Councillor Kopek entered his private office in the Great Hall and immediately called for increased illumination. The *varHuS* candle wall sconces were probably a nice touch when he was tossing one of his all too eager bedmates across the hand-carved *ledka* wood desk for a quick dalliance between council sessions. But they would be hell to read by.

Kahless had been waiting in the office for only a few minutes, having dispatched Kopek's aide with orders to bring the councillor to him immediately. Those minutes had been sufficient to further damn the man in the emperor's eyes. For a warrior to surround himself with objects of honor and victory was one thing. For him to revel so garishly in decadence and luxury was a clear sign that the man had completely lost his way, *if the true way was ever shown to him,* Kahless thought, quietly simmering.

No, he answered his own question. The true path of a warrior was the birthright of every Klingon, whether base or noble born. This *petaQ* had turned his back on the ideals that made a Klingon worthy of honor; of that much, Kahless was certain.

Kopek seemed surprised to see the emperor standing in the center of the room. Perhaps he believed that his aide would never have allowed the emperor into his private office alone, *as if the sniveling* yIntagh *had a choice,* Kahless thought with satisfaction. Whether Kopek and his men truly believed in the restored emperor, they would never cross him openly in the Great Hall without exposing themselves to Martok's wrath.

"Emperor Kahless," Kopek greeted him with a scowl. "You honor me with your presence."

"Just as you dishonor me with yours," Kahless replied.

Any pretense of cordiality dropped from Kopek's mien. "What do you want?" Kopek demanded.

Kahless wanted to make him suffer more, but time was his fiercest enemy at the moment.

"Thirty years ago, you conducted a transaction with the Warriors of Gre'thor," Kahless said simply. "You provided them with a forged *bat'leth*, supposedly created by Hal'korin. Where is the real one?"

"Thirty years is a long time, Emperor," Kopek said warily. "I cannot honestly say I remember the exchange you refer to."

Kahless's blood cried out for an appropriate response to this insolence. He did not doubt he could best Kopek in combat. But victory over a man with no honor tasted bitter as sour *warnog*.

"Kneel, Kopek," Kahless said softly.

Kahless was demanding no more than he deserved, and much more than Kopek would ever willingly pay. But the man hadn't survived through so many years of political subterfuge by not knowing which battles to fight. With forced humility, Kopek grudgingly knelt.

Kahless closed the distance between them in two steps and placed his *d'k tahg* at Kopek's throat.

"Has your memory improved?" Kahless asked.

Kopek remained motionless, but his hateful expression betrayed the violent action he clearly wanted to take.

In truth, the knife Kahless held was the dullest weapon at his disposal. He was almost pleased that Kopek hadn't forced him to use it by rising to the bait.

"I will never understand why Gowron agreed to make you emperor," Kopek snarled.

"I expect nothing less of you," Kahless replied, sheathing his blade. Kopek started to rise, but with a glance, Kahless kept him on his knees. "Some years ago, a common woman came to me, as hundreds have since, to lay her cares at my feet and beg for guidance."

"What has this to do with me?" Kopek demanded.

"This woman had been seduced by a great warrior, or so she thought. She had borne him a child out of wedlock—the warrior's first-born son."

Grim recognition flickered across Kopek's face.

"She had feared for the life of the child. She looked on it only with a mother's love, but even she could see that the child had been born cursed. Still, she presented him proudly to his father, and he repaid her trust by taking the child to the top of Mount Vor and dashing its brains out with a rock."

Kopek met the emperor's unflinching gaze.

"The woman sought only wisdom, to understand how she had failed. Had the child's birth been a sign that taking the warrior to her bed had been wrong? He was already promised to another in marriage. And had the warrior done right in destroying the evidence of their affair?"

After a long pause, Kahless went on. "I told her that the only error she had made was to trust you, Kopek."

"You cannot prove any of this," Kopek hissed.

"But I can," Kahless replied. "Once you had murdered your child, you set fire to its body. But the woman could not bear to watch it burn. When you departed, leaving her to her misery, she doused the flames and buried the child's remains in an unmarked grave in her parents' field. She still visits it, once a year, to remind herself of her youthful folly and rededicate herself to the path of honor. Analysis of the remains, coupled with her testimony, would surely provide all the evidence the chancellor would need to make your shame a matter of public record, to dishonor you before the council and strip your House of its name and considerable wealth."

"You did not see the child!" Kopek raged. "It was a deformed monster."

"Then he took after his father," Kahless replied.

Finally, Kopek bowed his head.

"The *bat'leth* you spoke of earlier," Kopek said, "is no longer among the holdings of my House."

"Where is it?" Kahless demanded.

"It was sold to a private collector on Naliah IV."

"A name, Kopek."

"Fistrebril," Kopek replied. "But I warn you, she will never part with it willingly."

"That is not your concern," Kahless assured him as he strode past Kopek toward the doors.

Kopek rose and called to Kahless. "Am I to assume our business is concluded?"

Kahless turned. "Do you honestly believe that the Klingon emperor would trade in shame and dishonor?" he bellowed. Kopek involuntarily took a step back in response. "Your guilt is yours to bear. It will remain yours for as long as the woman who came to me lives. Should I ever learn that she has died anywhere but peacefully in her bed many years from now, I will reveal your dishonor to all. Her life is all that I have risked in coming to you now, and all that I demand for my silence."

Kopek had the temerity to look relieved.

"But fear not," Kahless went on. "I doubt that your many sins since that day on Mount Vor will be as easy to expiate. You will fall, Kopek, because you live only to hold on to your power and to accumulate more. Martok works daily to restore the empire to the path of honor, and there is no place for you on that path. You will learn the true way, or you will reap the seeds of self-destruction you have so carefully sown."

With that, Kahless left Kopek to his thoughts. Though it was most likely a futile gesture, Kahless had knowingly chosen to give Kopek an opportunity to reclaim his honor. He doubted the *petQ* would take it. Once a road was as well worn as the one Kopek currently walked, it was no mean feat for any man to willingly choose another. But Kahless believed that no Klingon was beyond saving. Even Kopek.

Paris's new quarters on *Voyager* were those that had once belonged to Chakotay. One of his promotion's perks, the suite was much larger than either Tom's or B'Elanna's previous one and easily accommodated both of them.

They had retreated in tense silence following the briefing. The moment they entered, B'Elanna went immediately to the suite's 'fresher. She knew that the sonic shower would effectively eliminate the many unpleasant smells that had been her constant companion since departing Boreth. But what she really needed was the longest, hottest bath ever.

While she showered, Tom had been thoughtful enough to provide her with a replicated tank top and pants. This could only mean that before they slept, which both preferred to do without clothing, they were going to talk, B'Elanna thought ruefully.

When she finally emerged from the bathroom, Tom was seated in the suite's dining area. He had replicated several servings of snack foods, none of which tempted B'Elanna in the least.

"Feel better?" he asked.

"Not really," she replied honestly.

The only thing that might accomplish that would be for him to take her in his arms and hold her. But he seemed in no hurry to do that.

"Tom, I—" she began.

He turned on her, his eyes alight with brittle anger. "How could you?" he demanded.

"How could I what?" she asked, genuinely at a loss. She knew he must be devastated by Miral's absence, but whatever was devouring him from the inside out was more than that.

In response, he tossed a crumpled piece of parchment onto the floor between them.

B'Elanna recognized it at once, and was a little relieved to at least be able to name the monster now sharing the room with them.

"I wanted to tell you," B'Elanna said softly.

"But it slipped your mind?" Tom asked, rising from his seat.

"No, I . . . it just . . ."

"You decided to put your life and Miral's at risk without even so much as mentioning it to me?" Tom shouted.

Finally, B'Elanna found her own rage.

"And what were you going to do about it?" she demanded hotly.

"Made damn sure you both left Boreth, for starters," Tom shot back.

"Your life was here, Tom. And from here, there was nothing you could have done to help us," B'Elanna insisted.

"My life?" Tom said, aghast. "*You're* my life, B'Elanna. *Miral* is my life. None of this means anything without you."

B'Elanna was struck more by the force of his words than the substance.

Before she could summon a response, he spat, "And if you didn't want me to return to active duty, you should have just said so."

"That's not fair," B'Elanna cried. "You were miserable on Boreth, and we both knew it. You were practically climbing the walls. And the first chance you had to leave, you did it so fast I'm surprised you didn't leave a warp trail."

Tom closed the space between them. His breath was coming in quick spasms and his face was flushed. In better days this might have been all the impetus B'Elanna would have required to forcibly throw him to the floor before ripping his uniform off him.

"This isn't my fault, B'Elanna," he warned. "*It's yours.* And we might not even be here right now if you had decided to tell me what was going on. But you didn't. You lied to me. Several times. And now we might never see Miral again, thanks to your stupid pride."

The soft, brutalized center of B'Elanna's being began to wail. This was the place that she had guarded from everyone she had ever known, until Tom. This was the part of her he had promised to cherish and protect when he made her his wife. B'Elanna could have gladly closed her eyes and willed herself to die, so devastating was the thought that he would ever intentionally hurt her like this.

Especially now.

"You're right," she said coldly. "This is all my fault. I should have come running to you at the first sign of trouble. I should have remembered that I am nothing but a woman, a delicate flower to be admired but not respected. I apologize for forgetting my place in this marriage. Do you *feel better* now?"

This wasn't going at all as B'Elanna had anticipated. She knew he would be angry with her for not contacting him the moment Miral was taken. And she honestly believed he had a right to that anger. Further, she did believe that the lion's share of responsibility for this tragedy should reside permanently on her shoulders. But she didn't think a little compassion from her husband would have been out of line either. Tom couldn't think for a second that his suffering at this moment could possibly eclipse hers.

The truth was, she could only fight alone against so many fronts, and she had neither the patience nor the strength for this one.

Tom had the good sense to at least appear to be abashed by her words. But B'Elanna's rage, once kindled, was never so easily slaked.

"I came back to *Voyager* because I believed you would help me, Tom. But this isn't helping. And if you can't find it in yourself to stand beside me right now, then I suggest you get the hell out of my way."

B'Elanna turned on her heel and started toward the door. She didn't know where she was running to, only that she could no longer bear to be in the same room with Tom.

"B'Elanna, get back here," he shouted after her.

But the moment she reached the door and activated its sensor, she found herself facing Counselor Cambridge.

"Is this a bad time?" he asked.

"Actually, it is," Tom said.

"Excellent," Cambridge said, stepping inside.

Before the door slid shut, B'Elanna noted the face of Commander Logt, standing stoically outside their quarters, obviously still "on duty."

Tom seemed to sense that his anger might have just found a more appropriate target. Stepping toward Cambridge, he said, "What I meant was, you shouldn't be here right now. If my wife or I require your assistance, we'll make an appointment."

"Everyone on this deck knows that you both require my assistance, Commander," Cambridge said sharply. "None of them are getting any sleep right now, that's certain."

B'Elanna found herself staring open-mouthed at the counselor. Very few people, even professional therapists, would so easily wander into a *kos'karii* pit.

"Sit down, both of you," Cambridge ordered.

Some deeply embedded Pavlovian response to authority kicked in. Or maybe they both simply recognized a stone wall when they saw one. Regardless, both of them perched side by side on the long end of the desk nearest the door.

"Now apologize to each other."

Tom's mouth joined B'Elanna's in the open and shocked position.

"Time is precious," Cambridge added, encouraging them to get on with it. "I won't even insist that you *mean* it for now."

"Look, I don't know who you think you are, *Lieutenant*," Tom said, "but this is completely out of line."

"I couldn't agree more," Cambridge said evenly. "Both of you are behaving like children."

"I don't think—" Tom began.

"Do either of you give a damn about your daughter?" Cambridge interjected. "Because if you don't, you'd be sparing the rest of us a great deal of hazard if you'd just acknowledge that fact right now."

B'Elanna felt a rush of fresh, hot tears rising to her eyes. She turned to Tom, and saw that he too was struggling to hold back an onslaught.

Cambridge studied them in silence before continuing.

"I see. Then might I suggest that rather than setting aflame the few tattered shreds of accord that are holding your marriage together, you focus only on Miral right now. These other quibbles, who did or did not do what to whom and when, should definitely be discussed at some length when this crisis has passed, but for now they're a waste of precious energy and will only serve to further divide you. How you've managed to remain a couple this long without learning to disagree constructively will surely top our future sessions. But allow me to redirect your attention to the ball on which the eyes of both of you should be glued. The life of your daughter and, most likely, the fate of the Klingon Empire is now hanging in the balance, and keener wits and calmer heads than these are going to be required if all this is to have the slightest chance of ending well. Those who have taken your child are not going to part with her willingly. Save your strength for them. And in the meantime, get some bloody rest."

The counselor's diatribe effectively drained the heat and tension from both of them.

"He's right," B'Elanna said, turning to face Tom.

Tom nodded, mutely.

"I'm sorry," B'Elanna offered.

This time, Tom did reach for her, and for the first time since she'd seen the anonymous warning, she remembered what it was to feel safe as his arms pulled her close. The sensation was fleeting, but it grounded B'Elanna long enough for her to realize that there was truly nothing she could not forgive Tom, especially careless words spoken in anger.

"Let's get some sleep," Tom murmured softly into her neck.

"I don't know if I can," she nuzzled back.

"Ahem," Cambridge cleared his throat. "I'm sure sickbay has something that might help with that."

Tom kept a firm hand around B'Elanna's waist as they followed Cambridge out of their quarters and made their way to sickbay. B'Elanna would have wrapped him around her like a blanket if she could have, so desperate was she to never again feel such a palpable distance between them as she had until this moment.

Logt automatically fell in step behind them.

As they walked, B'Elanna said softly to Tom, "Why do I like him?"

"I can't imagine," Logt replied tonelessly.

Admiral Janeway intentionally took the longest route possible from the mess hall back to her quarters. Immediately following the meeting she'd stopped by Neelix's old kitchen, driven there by nostalgia as much as the need for a quick snack. Though the food preparation area—at one time the captain's personal dining area before *Voyager* had been flung across the galaxy—had been replaced by several new replicators, she could easily imagine the Talaxian who had become dear to her as any member of her crew, humming softly as he bustled about in the small space, struggling to make the dining room as close to home as possible for the crew. Though she and Neelix still kept in touch, the time between communications was now calculated in months, a fact she genuinely regretted.

As it happened, nothing the replicator could produce really tempted her, so she settled for a fresh cup of hot coffee before turning her steps back toward her cabin.

Prior to this mission, she had boarded *Voyager* only once since its return from the Delta quadrant, and at the time, the ship had been in pieces and she had been leading an assault team whose primary mission was to return Seven of Nine to the cargo bay and give her adequate time to regenerate.

As she walked, Janeway realized she was unconsciously heading toward sickbay. She knew Seven and the Doctor would be busy with Doctor Kaz, digging deeper into the genetic defect they had discovered, but privately she hoped she might steal a few moments alone with Seven. They hadn't had a long chat in a while, and Janeway wanted to make sure that Seven was all right. She'd sensed more than a little tension between Seven and the Doctor in their recent briefing and could tell that Seven was straining a bit under the pressure they were all experiencing. No doubt Seven was determined to solve this problem for all of them, but Janeway didn't want to see her taking too much on herself.

She passed a few new faces along the way, as well as plenty of old ones. Most seemed genuinely pleased to see her and stopped briefly to chat. It was gratifying to see that so many who had served with her in the Delta quadrant had remained on board when the ship returned to active duty. She doubted that anyone who had requested reassignment would have been denied. But it seemed that the bonds they had forged over those tumultuous seven years remained strong, and their presence was a testament to that, as well as to their faith in Captain Chakotay.

Janeway didn't regret her choice to accept promotion. But she would have been lying if she'd said that a part of her didn't miss walking these halls and knowing that she belonged to them.

She stopped in her tracks at the sight of Harry Kim dispatching a security team throughout the deck for what was probably a drill. She remembered how mercilessly Tuvok had ridden his security staff when he had held Harry's position. She had rarely, if ever, found cause to question Tuvok's mastery of combat tactics and knew that Harry's ability to move seamlessly from operations to head of security was in no small part due to the vast experience he had gained while serving with the Vulcan. On paper it might have looked like an abrupt duty change, and a challenge that Kim was ill prepared to meet. But Harry was as bright, dedicated, and well rounded a young officer as she had ever met. He thrived on a challenge, and for someone who was certainly destined to assume command of his own ship one day, he would benefit immeasurably by spending as much time at tactical as Starfleet would permit before assigning him to his next logical post, as some very lucky captain's first officer.

Once Harry had dismissed his team, he looked up to see Janeway standing nearby. His face broke into a wide, boyish grin, and Janeway couldn't help but remember the way he'd stood in her ready room so alert she worried he might strain himself, when he had first reported to duty aboard *Voyager*.

It can't be eight years ago. It feels like yesterday.

"Admiral," Harry greeted her cheerfully.

"Carry on, Lieutenant." She smiled. "I'm sure you're very busy right now."

Kim's smile dissipated.

"Has the emperor made contact yet?"

"No, but I'm sure Chakotay will inform you when he does."

Harry nodded before adding, "It's good to have you here, Admiral."

"It's good to be here," she replied, "though I wish it was under happier circumstances."

"Of course."

"How are your parents?" she asked.

"Oh, they're wonderful," he replied. "I spent a few days with them just last week. At the rate they're going, they'll probably outlive us all."

Janeway smiled. In a softer, more conspiratorial tone she added, "And what about that charming young woman, Ms. Webber, isn't it?"

Harry's face fell. "She's fine, but she and I, well . . ."

Janeway's heart broke for him as he went on.

"We've decided to part company. I think it's for the best."

"Oh, Harry, I'm sorry to hear that."

"It's all right. It happens."

"That it does," Janeway said, nodding. It was an unfortunate reality that often relationships between Starfleet officers and civilians were difficult to maintain. For a long time, hers and Mark's had been a pleasant exception to that rule. She would have thought that if anyone was capable of making it work, Harry would have found a way, but she didn't know Ms. Webber all that well and trusted that if he thought this was the best course for them, it probably was.

"Be sure and give my best to your parents the next time you speak to them," Janeway said warmly.

"I will, Ma'am," Harry said automatically before correcting himself, "I mean, Admiral."

"It's all right, Harry." Janeway smiled. "This certainly feels like crunch time to me."

Over Harry's shoulder, Janeway saw Counselor Cambridge, Tom, B'Elanna, and Commander Logt walking hastily through the hall. They seemed intent on their destination, and Janeway hesitated to derail them. At least it seemed that Tom and B'Elanna had resolved some of their differences. You could have cut the tension between them in the conference room with a laser scalpel, but now they walked arm in arm.

Janeway stepped aside to allow them to pass when B'Elanna's borrowed combadge chirped.

"Bridge to Commander Torres," Lyssa Campbell's voice called.

"Go ahead," B'Elanna said.

"Incoming transmission for you from Qo'noS."

B'Elanna looked to Tom before replying, "Route it to sickbay. I'll be there in just a minute."

Kim joined the group immediately as they continued down the hall. Janeway debated only a few moments. She knew that in her quarters, dozens of communiqués were awaiting her attention. Decan had advised her just after she had returned from the embassy that the list of messages waiting for her review was growing longer by the second.

But none of that could vie with any credibility for the top spot on her list of concerns right now. Whatever Kahless had discovered could hold a vital clue to Miral's location, and though her presence wasn't necessarily required, Janeway couldn't bear the thought of rustling through red tape while everyone else worked on this problem without her.

It had always been the most difficult part of her nature with which to contend. She was a capable leader, but she was also never more at peace than when her sleeves were rolled up and she was actually working on a tangible problem. Unfortunately, the days when Janeway could simply join B'Elanna in engineering for hours at a stretch realigning magnetic constrictors or tinkering with the dilithium matrix were long gone.

For whatever reason, fate had placed her here and now, and the only clear course she could see ahead ended with Miral safely back in her parents' arms.

The rest would simply have to wait.

Janeway chose to leave the communiqués unread for now and redirected her steps to join the others going to sickbay.

CHAPTER ELEVEN

Chakotay had already received Jarem's report, peppered with interruptions from Seven and the Doctor. To his credit, Doctor Kaz was unruffled by their constant "clarifications." He might have been relatively new to *Voyager,* but Kaz had quickly become a presence Chakotay felt he could trust and lean upon, and he'd more than proven his worth. His grace in dealing with Seven's imperious presence and the Doctor's tendency toward condescension, which it seemed had been nurtured during the Doctor's time at the Institute, only enhanced Chakotay's regard for Kaz.

The captain was surprised when the doors whisked open and Cambridge entered, followed quickly by Tom, B'Elanna, Harry, Kathryn, and Commander Logt.

"Kahless has found something," B'Elanna said immediately. "Doctor, may I use your office?" she asked.

"Of course," Kaz replied.

Paris and B'Elanna hurried into the small office, separated from the rest of sickbay by a transparent wall.

"The rest of you should hear this," Chakotay said, inviting the others to crowd around the display station near biobed one. "Doctor Kaz, Seven, and the Doctor have made significant progress in their analysis of the aberrant Klingon genome."

"It appears that the mutation which resulted in the birth of these children is not, as we first suspected, a random anomaly," Kaz advised the group.

"Fascinating," Cambridge intoned, staring at the findings on the display.

"As you can see," Seven continued, "the mutation is the result of an expression of this recessive base pair combination."

"Starfleet's classified database contains a significantly larger control group of Klingon genomes available for comparison than those at the disposal of the Institute, so we were able to compare our findings against a much larger population," the Doctor added, not to be outdone.

"The bottom line is," Kaz went on, "this isn't a mutation at all."

"It's evolution," Cambridge said softly.

"What does that mean?" Harry chimed in.

"It suggests that over time, significantly larger numbers of Klingons will be born expressing these characteristics," Kaz said. "What we're seeing might actually be the next step in the development of the Klingon species."

"But don't populations typically evolve traits that are beneficial to the species?" Kim asked. "This looks more like some kind of devolution."

"While we have no idea how successful," Kaz said, "or what the longevity of these Klingons would be, it is clear enough that they will possess strength and ferocity that far outstrip their present-day counterparts. All we can say for sure is that more Klingons like these will be born, and if their birth rate ever surpasses those of the Klingons living today . . ."

"The Curse of the Gods, indeed," Cambridge finished.

"Is it some sort of programmed DNA molecule?" Harry asked.

"It's possible," Kaz replied. "Otherwise, it's difficult to understand why it has remained dormant for so long."

"It's also possible, as the sequence is recessive, that random—" the Doctor began.

Their musings were interrupted, however, by B'Elanna and Paris, emerging from Kaz's office.

"Kahless knows where the twelfth *bat'leth* is. He wants me to join him on Qo'noS. He can have a ship ready to depart within the hour," B'Elanna reported.

Chakotay didn't doubt for a moment that while B'Elanna might see this as the most useful course she could take right now, it wasn't the smartest.

"I'll go," Tom said, as if reading Chakotay's mind.

"Captain, with your permission, I'd like to join Commander Paris," Harry added.

"A moment, please," Janeway interrupted. "B'Elanna, where is the *bat'leth*?"

"Naliah IV," she replied.

"In that case, I have an alternate suggestion," Janeway said.

"Admiral?" Chakotay asked.

"Naliah IV is less than a day from Earth. And it's at least two days by shuttle from here," she said. "I'll contact Tuvok. I'm sure he'd be willing to take a few days' leave to retrieve it for us. He could rendezvous with *Voyager* more quickly than any of you could get there and back."

No one seemed inclined to question her.

"You think he'd do it?" B'Elanna asked.

"Of course he would," Janeway assured her.

"I agree," Chakotay said, effectively ending further discussion.

"If you'll excuse me," Janeway said, hurrying from the room.

Tom gently guided B'Elanna toward Doctor Kaz. "Was there something else?" he asked pleasantly.

B'Elanna sighed, resigned. "I was actually hoping you might have something to help me sleep."

Kaz nodded. "This way," he said, and directed her toward a biobed.

"I'll contact Kahless and inform him of the change in plans," Tom said softly to B'Elanna, moving back to Kaz's inner sanctum.

"Harry?" Chakotay asked.

"Yes, Captain."

"Would you check with Lyssa and make sure she's arranged for quarters for our guests. And check with Lieutenant Vorik to see how the temporary regeneration alcove I requested is coming along."

"Right away, sir."

These would normally have been duties for his first officer to perform, but Chakotay was determined to keep such things off Tom's plate for the next few days. B'Elanna needed her husband more than *Voyager* did right now.

"Doctor Kaz, I'd be willing to stay and continue our research," the Doctor said hopefully.

"Doctor Kaz was due to end his duty shift several hours ago," Seven said pointedly.

"Oh, I don't mind," Kaz said, loading a hypospray for B'Elanna.

"Get some rest, Jarem," Chakotay ordered Kaz. "You

are, of course, welcome to continue working, Doctor," he assured the EMH.

"Perhaps our time would be better spent preparing our report to the Klingon High Council," Seven suggested to the Doctor.

"Why don't we see how Vorik's work is coming along first," Harry offered diplomatically.

"Very well," the Doctor sighed. "I should definitely take a look at any temporary regenerative device he constructs for Seven to make sure it is compatible with her needs."

The captain had to suppress a grin at the look of disdain on Seven's face.

How have these two managed to work together day in and day out? Chakotay wondered. They had been an incredibly efficient and helpful pair while serving on *Voyager*, and he knew that their mutual affection and regard for one another were well entrenched. But familiarity had a way of breeding discontent at times, and Chakotay secretly worried that both of them might need to broaden their social horizons to avoid putting too much strain on their friendship. He had noted in the few times they'd met over the last several months that the pair seemed to spar more forcefully than he could remember.

Seven and the Doctor dutifully followed Harry from sickbay, while Kaz conferred quietly with B'Elanna before administering a portion of the hypospray and providing her instructions for further use, should she require it.

Chakotay was about to depart when he noted Counselor Cambridge staring fixedly at Commander Logt, who was hovering as near to B'Elanna as decorum would allow while she spoke with Kaz.

What happened next took everyone left in the room, Chakotay most of all, by total surprise. With a grace and dexterity Chakotay would never have suspected, Cambridge passed by Commander Logt nonchalantly, as if he were merely heading for the exit, and as soon as he had passed her line of peripheral vision, turned quickly and kicked the woman's legs out from under her.

"Counselor Cambridge!" Chakotay shouted as Logt attempted to recover, but before she could, Cambridge struck her repeatedly in the gut and face, momentarily subduing her. He then grabbed both of her arms and pinned them behind her back, locking her into a kneeling position.

"A moment, Captain," Cambridge gasped as he tightened his grip to ensure that Logt was truly under his control.

"Explain yourself, Counselor," Chakotay demanded, as B'Elanna and Kaz moved cautiously toward the pair.

"What the hell are you doing?" B'Elanna asked, already a little groggy.

"If you want to know where the *qawHaq'hoch* have taken your daughter, Commander," Cambridge replied, "you can either wait for your friend to retrieve the final *bat'leth*, or you can simply ask this woman. I'm sure she can tell you. She's one of them."

B'Elanna seemed as stunned by this as Chakotay.

"Can you prove this, Counselor?" the captain asked sharply.

"Absolutely," Cambridge insisted, "with a little help."

Logt seethed and hissed as she struggled in his grasp.

Chakotay stepped forward. He didn't trust Cambridge, but then, Logt wasn't shouting out any denials either, which he certainly would have been doing in her position.

"This is absurd," B'Elanna stammered. "Release her."

"Gladly," Cambridge replied cheerfully, "just as soon as someone pulls back her baldric and tunic so that her thoracic spine can be clearly seen. There you will find a brand, the mark of *Hal'korin*, which all members of the order sear into their flesh when they are initiated."

Chakotay threw a questioning glance at B'Elanna and could see that she was every bit as confused as he.

"That's not possible," B'Elanna said, doubt creeping into her voice.

"Bloody hell, just do it," Cambridge retorted.

"I'll do it," Chakotay said, moving closer. As quickly as possible he pulled down the back of Logt's tunic and there, just as Cambridge said, was a scarred mound of flesh in a shape too precise to have been a simple birthmark or battle wound.

"He's right," Chakotay said in disbelief.

"What's going on?" Paris asked, emerging from the Doctor's office.

Before anyone could reply, Chakotay heard a loud cartilaginous snap as Logt threw her body forward, lifting Cambridge from the ground and rolling him over the back of her head. Whatever damage she might have done to her shoulders in the process didn't seem to be a problem as she quickly climbed over the counselor, thrusting a hard elbow into his upper back, rendering him unconscious.

Chakotay immediately dove for Logt but missed, landing instead atop the inert Cambridge while Kaz had the good sense to call for a security team.

Righting himself, Chakotay saw Paris moving to confront Logt, who quickly drew a small blade from her belt and sent it whirring into Tom's leg.

Paris crumpled to the floor as B'Elanna cried out his name and Chakotay struggled to find a piece of floor to stand on.

Kaz was the next to take a run at Logt, but she dispatched him quickly, turning the only weapon at his disposal—the half-empty hypo of the sedative he'd given B'Elanna—against him, and he, too, stumbled back as soon as the medicine hit his system.

B'Elanna was struggling to remain alert as she threw herself at Logt. In her weakened state, Logt quickly subdued her and by the time Chakotay was on his feet Logt was standing with her back to the biobed, B'Elanna's body held in front, a larger Klingon blade held precariously at B'Elanna's throat.

"Let her go," Chakotay said, hoping against hope that the woman could be reasoned with.

"I cannot," Logt replied, as if this saddened her almost as much as Chakotay.

She then shouted a command to the computer, and she and B'Elanna disappeared in the glistening beam of a transporter.

The doors to sickbay slid open and a half-dozen security officers poured in.

Chakotay didn't have to think too hard to imagine where Logt would have taken B'Elanna.

"Red Alert!" he called out. "Computer, lock down the shuttlebay immediately!"

Two of the officers were lifting Tom to the nearest biobed as another tried to revive Doctor Kaz, while the rest of the group hurried out of the room.

"Chakotay to the Doctor, medical emergency."

Within seconds the Doctor materialized before him and after a quick, "What happened?" followed Chakotay's abrupt gesture toward Tom. The Doctor cleared a path through the remaining security team and activated the biobed's surgical arch.

The captain then rushed for the door but was halted as the deck jerked beneath him, almost sending him sprawling.

"Kim to Chakotay," Harry's voice called.

"Go ahead," Chakotay replied, stumbling into the corridor.

"The Delta Flyer *has just blown its way out of the shuttlebay,"* Harry advised.

"Tractor them!" Chakotay ordered, "And transport me immediately to the bridge."

Seconds later, Chakotay materialized next to the tactical station where Kim was struggling to get a lock on the hijacked shuttle.

Chakotay watched as Logt executed a dive roll to evade the blue beam meant to tether her irrevocably to *Voyager.* Soft bluish wisps began to stream from the shuttle nacelles and Chakotay smiled, sensing they'd just caught a break. From the look of it, the *Delta Flyer's* warp engines might be malfunctioning.

"Stay with her," Chakotay ordered Lieutenant Tare at the helm.

Tare did her best to turn the ship's bulk even as Logt reversed the course of the *Delta Flyer* and flew straight toward *Voyager.* For a breathless moment, Chakotay feared collision, but as the *Flyer* filled the main viewscreen, Logt finally succeeded in bringing the shuttle's warp engines online. In a blinding flash, the small craft disappeared.

"Follow them!" Chakotay ordered.

"Acquiring warp trail," Campbell called from ops.

After a few frustrating seconds of silence, Chakotay barked, "Where are they headed, Lieutenant?"

"I'm sorry, sir, I don't know," Campbell replied.

Kim crossed the few feet separating tactical controls from ops and studied her readouts.

"She ghosted the trail," Harry finally announced, slamming his fist down hard on the console.

"She what?" Lieutenant Tare asked.

"Just before she went to warp she dumped enough warp plasma into the area to fool the ship's sensors. We can't acquire her heading, Captain. She's gone," Harry said, shaking his head in frustration.

The captain took a few deep breaths, until the adrenaline that had been coursing through him for the last several minutes dispelled and his heart slowed to match the pulse of the blinking red lights illuminating the otherwise darkened bridge.

"Stand down Red Alert," he ordered. "Chakotay to sickbay."

"*I'm a little busy at the moment, Captain,*" the Doctor's voice replied.

"Is Counselor Cambridge recovered?" Chakotay asked.

After a short pause the Doctor said, "*He's conscious, if that's what you're asking.*"

"Have him report to my ready room," Chakotay said menacingly. "Carry him if you have to."

<hr />

The events in sickbay were a blur to B'Elanna. One moment she'd felt the pleasant wash of relaxation as Doctor Kaz's sedative entered her system, and in the next, all hell was breaking loose. Logt had been on her knees. Then she'd thrown a dagger at Tom. Someone had screamed.

Was that me?

The next thing B'Elanna remembered, she'd been dumped into a soft leather chair. As she struggled to remain conscious, she'd seen Logt, powering up a shuttle control panel.

What am I doing on the Delta Flyer?

Then an explosion, and B'Elanna had been forced to dig her hands into the seat to avoid being tossed out of it.

When the rocking and bucking had finally stopped, B'Elanna found herself wanting either to vomit or to sleep. A face appeared before her, much too close, and a cold, rough hand was probing her neck.

B'Elanna forced words through her parched throat, a side effect, no doubt, of the sedative. "Tom . . ."

"Will survive," Logt assured her. "I intended only to disable him, and my aim was true."

"You swore to protect me . . ." B'Elanna barely managed.

"That is exactly what I am trying to do," Logt said calmly as B'Elanna fell into a chasm of darkness.

Janeway strode briskly into Chakotay's ready room to find him pacing like a caged tiger before his desk.

"What happened?" she asked.

"Commander Logt is a member of the *qawHaq'hoch*. She's taken B'Elanna and the *Delta Flyer*, and I haven't a clue where they've gone. Oh, and she almost killed Paris in the process."

"Almost?"

"The Doctor is performing surgery right now. The blade missed his femoral artery by a hair. The Doctor says he'll make a complete recovery."

"At least that's good news," Janeway said. "Isn't it likely that wherever Logt's gone, it's probably the same place they took Miral?" she added.

Chakotay shook his head.

"Maybe. That's assuming Miral is still alive."

"She has to be," Janeway said, as if willing it to be so.

"Kathryn, she's been missing for over a week," Chakotay replied. "And I don't think anyone knows what the *qawHaq'hoch*'s agenda is, or the lengths to which they'll go. We didn't even know one of them was among us. Logt knows what we're planning, and who's to say they won't kill Miral just to keep her from us, especially if we're on the right track."

"So we're damned if we do and damned if we don't?" Janeway asked. "Where's your optimism, Captain?"

"I suppose it's taken a beating over the last few days."

"That's understandable, but the law of large numbers says we have to catch a break soon, right?" Janeway moved to halt Chakotay in his steps and stared into his troubled eyes. "You've done everything possible to fix this, Chakotay. You've bucked Command, risked insulting the chancellor of the Klingon Empire, helped to uncover evidence of a more serious threat now facing the Klingon people."

"Not bad for a week's work," he said wryly.

Janeway smiled. "Did I ever, in the seven years we served together, do anything that led you to believe that being captain was easy?"

He shook his head. "No. You just made it look that way . . . most days."

Janeway nodded, acknowledging the compliment. "I spoke with Tuvok. He'll be on his way to Naliah IV within the hour."

"Then with any luck we'll be on our way in a couple of days." With a shake of his head Chakotay added, "Ken Montgomery will probably have me demoted to crewman and scrubbing plasma conduits by that time, right?"

"Not if I have anything to say about it," she replied firmly.

They were interrupted by a chiming at the door.

"Come in," Chakotay called.

Counselor Cambridge entered, looking more than a little the worse for wear.

"You wished to see me, Captain?" he asked.

Chakotay turned to face him, his weary misgivings replaced by righteous anger.

"What were you thinking?" he asked harshly.

Cambridge stood his ground

"It occurred to me that the sooner Commander Logt was revealed for the traitor she is, the sooner we might find Miral Paris," he said evenly.

"And it never crossed your mind that it wasn't your call to make?"

Cambridge paused for a moment to consider this.

"You mean, why didn't I come to you first to express my concern?" he asked.

"Exactly."

"I was taking the initiative?" Cambridge suggested.

Chakotay looked ready to strangle the counselor.

"If you'll recall, at our last staff meeting, I did advise you and everyone present of the likelihood that someone close had betrayed B'Elanna on Boreth," Cambridge added.

"It's a pretty big leap to go from there to attacking the woman in sickbay."

"Not really," Cambridge replied. "I'd observed the commander throughout the meeting and for some time after. Her body language alone was practically screaming that she was hiding something. In addition, she never let B'Elanna out of her sight except to argue with her husband. I admit it was a good, though not terribly difficult, leap of logic."

"The next time you decide to take a leap," Chakotay said, his jaw clenched, "you will run it by me first. Your precipitous actions resulted in the capture of B'Elanna and almost killed Tom Paris."

"Not to mention a nasty bump on the head," Cambridge offered.

"Had you told me what you were thinking," Chakotay went on, "we could have had a security team present when we confronted her. Your instincts were right, but every other choice you made was absolutely wrong."

Janeway wondered if she was going to have to physically restrain Chakotay. The results were unfortunate, but she honestly believed that had Chakotay been the one to discover Logt's subterfuge, he would have probably acted on it as recklessly as Cambridge had.

I wonder if he realizes how much he and Cambridge have in common, or if, given that, these two will ever get along?

Cambridge had the good grace to look humbled.

"I apologize, Captain," he said seriously.

"Dismissed," Chakotay hissed.

CHAPTER TWELVE

Given how little intelligence he had for this mission, Tuvok believed he was making excellent progress. Naturally, he took no joy in this. He was Vulcan. But he allowed himself to feel satisfied by his work.

He had reached Naliah IV and entered orbit in just twelve-point-five hours after leaving Earth. At Admiral Janeway's request, Starfleet Command had provided him with a Type-9 shuttlecraft, which he was most comfortable piloting, as these small, sleek vessels had been part of *Voyager*'s standard complement. Tom Paris and B'Elanna Torres had done no end of tinkering with the Type-9's over the years, and Tuvok had learned from them how to tweak the dilithium matrix and push the warp engines, rated for warp 4 and below, to almost warp 6 without compromising the ship's integrity. He had been forced to override several of the safety systems. Given the constraints of time, Tuvok felt the choice was both logical and appropriate to the situation at hand.

Naliah IV was sparsely populated, a backwater planet favored by those who wished to unobtrusively carry on activities of dubious legality, or to simply disappear. There was nothing in the Starfleet Intelligence files relating to anyone named Fistrebril. Tuvok's sensor sweeps of the planet had revealed only two compounds likely to be hiding the artifact he sought—the two that appeared the most innocuous to his initial scans.

The first was registered as the home of a Ferengi merchant. Tuvok did not doubt that the interior would be the height of gauche, but the exterior of the structure was actually quite shabby. A well-concealed sensor net ringed the property, and the majority of its discernible defenses appeared to be automated.

The second was an architectural masterpiece, a dwelling embedded within a cliff overlooking one of the planet's four largest bodies of water. Its opulence would have been more appropriate to Risa; everything about it, from the lushly landscaped gardens and sculpted fountains to the graceful lines of the stone façade and bays of ten-meter-high windows that no doubt offered staggering views of the ocean, suggested a luxurious retreat.

What caught the Vulcan's attention was not the two armed guards who patrolled the mansion's front entrance, but the sixteen others who were equipped with sensor-resistant armor that made them nearly invisible to Tuvok's orbital scans.

Either the occupants of the mansion had made far too many enemies in their lifetime, or they were intent on protecting something with deadly force. This site also had dozens of sensor dead zones, which had initially read as natural formations beneath the dwelling but upon closer examination were clearly shrouded to fool scanners.

Logic suggested that the occupants of this palatial home were most likely either to possess the item he was seeking or to know enough about the planet's other residents to best direct his efforts.

Tuvok transported into a ravine a half kilometer from the property's perimeter. After a brief hike through the dense brush that covered the hillside, he found a natural rock outcropping to reconnoiter the compound.

Visual survey of the armored guards suggested that they were incredibly diligent and precise. They paced their assigned perimeters with a steady gait, leaving no expanse wide enough for an intruder to compromise their patrol for more than two seconds at a time. Tuvok's tricorder also detected several power sources buried at regular intervals in the rocks a hundred meters beneath his feet, which were probably evidence of an energy field of some kind that would activate in the event of a breach.

If he'd had a security team at his disposal, it might have been possible to quietly disable enough of both the field generators and the guards before the occupants of the residence could retaliate. As Tuvok was alone, he decided that a solo stealth approach, no matter how well executed, was probably little more than a suicide attempt.

That left only one decidedly unpalatable option.

Rising from the rocks, he evaluated the security of the compound. Tuvok dusted off his uniform and keyed his tricorder to interlink directly with his shuttle's transport system. Seconds later, he engaged the transporter and appeared, just as he had calculated, at the front door of the mansion, where the two armed guards positioned there, obviously startled by his abrupt appearance, immediately trained their weapons on him.

"Good afternoon," Tuvok greeted them cordially.

"What do you want?" one of them growled.

"I wish to speak to the owner of this residence," he replied.

"The owner isn't here," the other grunted.

Tuvok took a fraction of a second to center himself before quickly grabbing the business ends of both weapons and jerking them from the guards before they had a chance to fire. He then dropped low, digging the butt of one of them into the first guard's abdomen before swinging wide with the second, smashing it into the second guard's head. A few blows later, both guards were sitting in an unconscious heap beside the door, and both of their weapons had been disabled.

Tuvok then proceeded to tidy his jacket and pants from the scuffle. He stepped over the guards and knocked upon the heavy wooden door.

A few moments later, he heard a muted series of clicks and the door swung open, revealing a petite woman of indeterminate age, with fine golden hair falling just past the waist of a midnight blue beaded gown, the cut of which perfectly accentuated her well-toned and equally well-proportioned figure. The woman's obsidian eyes, set beneath precisely arched brows, met Tuvok's without flinching. With a graceful gesture she swept the tresses framing her right cheek behind a delicate ear, revealing that the pinna contained two openings to the auditory canal, one in the center, and a smaller one near the upper edge. The flesh at her temple was raised by several delicate involutions. He was instantly intrigued. He had never met a Ullian before.

"How rude," were her first dismissive words.

"I apologize for any inconvenience my arrival may have caused," Tuvok said, "but it is imperative that I speak with the owner of this residence as soon as possible."

"You might have simply asked," the woman replied, gazing at her unconscious guards.

"In fairness, I did."

The woman's face cracked around the edges of her mouth in a hint of a smile. "Come in," she said.

The Vulcan followed her through a high atrium that was filled with dozens of varieties of fragrant flowering plants. Among them Tuvok noted a few species of rare orchids. A wide arch opened at the end of the hall, leading to a sunken living area with exquisitely carved furniture and a bay of high windows. Centered on the room's main wall was a painting Tuvok could not immediately place, but it appeared to be in the impressionistic style favored on Betazed during the Cultural Renewal five centuries ago. A few tasteful sculptures, writhing nudes in a rare crystalline stone that suggested they had originated on Deneva, were strategically placed. However, the item that stopped Tuvok in his tracks was a small lamp encrusted with amber gemstones set on a pedestal behind an opaque force field.

Tuvok stepped closer to make sure his eyes were not deceiving him. The low flame emanating from the lamp was said to be eternal. Its color was the rarest blue-green, and it could only have originated in one place.

"May I ask how you acquired the Light of Amonak?" Tuvok asked. Legend reported it had been stolen from a Vulcan temple two thousand years earlier.

"You may ask," the woman replied, approaching Tuvok with a clear glass of greenish liquid and offering it to him as she sipped from her own, "if you will tell me what brings a Starfleet instructor to Naliah, Commander Tuvok."

Tuvok considered his response. Clearly in the few moments it had taken him to disable her men, she had managed to learn more about him than he would have thought possible.

"You have me at a disadvantage," Tuvok said, accepting the glass but forbearing to drink from it.

"You have no idea," she replied.

"I have come seeking someone named Fistrebril," Tuvok said, opting for honesty. At the moment it seemed the best defense.

Again, her face cracked into a subtle, wistful smile. "I haven't heard that name in years."

"But you have heard it?" Tuvok asked.

"Why are you here, Tuvok?" she asked a little more insistently.

Tuvok felt his senses tingle uncomfortably. It was nothing more than a faint dizziness, but he was instantly aware that she was somehow attempting to probe his mind.

A thief, and a highly adept telepath, Tuvok thought calmly. He was aware that many Ullians possessed a unique type of telepathy. Their special gift was the ability to probe and bring forth long-forgotten memories in others. Centuries ago, this skill had been used toward destructive and violent ends. To the best of his knowledge, most Ullians currently working within the Federation focused their abilities on retrieving memories which would allow them to create a vast repository of historical data.

Instantly the violating sensation passed.

"I seem to be getting a little rusty," she replied, clearly more embarrassed by her failure to hide her actions rather than the fact that she had tried in the first place.

Interesting as this woman was, Tuvok was ever mindful of time's inexorable forward motion.

"I was led to believe that a trader named Fistrebril acquired an ancient *bat'leth* crafted by the Klingon master Hal'korin approximately thirty years ago from a warrior named Kopek," Tuvok advised her, "and that Fistrebril now resides on Naliah IV."

"Not *much* of a warrior," she said with what seemed like bemused regret.

"Then you know the object of which I speak?" Tuvok inquired.

The woman paused, her eyes boring into Tuvok's, before she answered with a slight nod.

"I am prepared to offer any consideration you might request in return for borrowing the sword for a short time," Tuvok said.

"The sword is priceless," the woman replied. "But then, you know that, don't you?"

"It is without any measurable market price," Tuvok acknowledged. "But as with most things, I am certain that we might agree to a remuneration you would find acceptable."

"Why did you not attempt to take it by force?" the woman asked.

"It seemed a futile gesture," Tuvok replied, "as this compound is eminently well defended."

"Halk and Vrenton's efforts suggest otherwise," she said, visibly chagrined.

"They were taken by surprise," Tuvok assured her.

"I am sorry, Tuvok," the woman said, "but there is nothing you could offer me which would convince me to part with the *bat'leth*. It was most challenging to acquire, and though you seem honest enough, I seriously doubt that if I allowed you to depart with it I would ever see you again."

"On the contrary, madam, I give you my word that I only require its use for a brief period of time, after which I will personally see that it is restored to you."

"Your logic is flawed, Tuvok," she said evenly.

"Which part?"

"Your assumption that you will be leaving here at all," she replied.

Tuvok tensed, setting the untasted beverage on a near table.

"And why is that?"

"I receive so few visitors anymore," she said almost playfully. "And I have no intention of parting with the most intriguing one to cross my path in some time."

Instantly, a force field snapped into existence, blocking the room's only exit. The only consolation Tuvok could immediately find was that for the moment, she was trapped behind it along with him.

Tuvok did not doubt that she believed she had the power to hold him indefinitely. But he also realized that she had just revealed what might very well be her only weakness.

"You require companionship," he stated flatly.

"That's one word for it."

Tuvok actually recoiled at the thought of physical contact with the woman. Her obvious beauty aside, it would be akin to caressing a live grenade.

Before he could formulate a response, he saw himself clearly standing in a cavern lit by the dancing flames of a welcoming fire. He had visited this place many times, both in life and in his thoughts. It was the temple his father had sent him to as a young man to learn to overcome an inappropriate emotional attachment he had developed for one of his classmates. Though he usually reflected with gratitude upon this memory there was no comfort in it now. He stood as he had the day he'd arrived, filled with righteous anger at his father and trembling with rage at the thought of being separated from Jara.

She released him from this memory and Tuvok found himself gasping for breath. The respite, however, was too brief.

She began to hunt like a scavenger through his mind. Images he had long repressed were forced to the surface.

He sat opposite Kes in his quarters on *Voyager*. She was attempting to visualize the subatomic structure of a cup of tea. As she mentally excited the particles, she lost control and Tuvok's mind began to burn with the heat intended for the tea. He briefly tasted the blood pouring from his nose.

He stood in a detention cell, his mind locked in a meld with Lon Suder. Violence he had only imagined coursed through him. He touched upon an unknown desire to find pleasure in the infliction of pain, even as he watched Suder raise his hand to crush the skull of Crewman Darwin.

Then, the memories rushed forward in a torrent he was unable to still. A Hirogen hunter struck him in the face. He gasped for air as a cargo bay was filled with blinding smoke. The last shreds of his identity trickled through his fingers as the Borg Queen made her horrifying presence known, welcoming him into the Collective.

In the distance, someone was shouting.

He returned to the present moment to find himself lying on the floor, choking on his screams.

She stood over him, her face alight with something close to joy.

"My goodness," she said. "I didn't realize how lucky it is that you've come. We should be able to enjoy ourselves like this for days."

Tuvok felt no fear as she said this. He did, however, realize that if he did not find a way to defend himself against her assault, he would probably not last the afternoon, let alone as long as she intended.

He forced himself to look beyond her at the Light of Amonak. The flame danced before him. It took every last ounce of control he still possessed to close his mind to all but the movement of the fire.

He felt her again in his mind, but now, she stood behind a wall which rose higher and higher as his meditation on the light restored the tranquillity he associated with his normal conscious state.

"What have you done?" she demanded, her voice instantly dropping its flirtatious tone.

Tuvok pulled himself up gently, and sat upon the nearest ottoman as he replied, "Perhaps if you told me exactly what you seek, I might be able to accommodate you."

Her incredulousness was apparent. "You would offer yourself to me freely?"

Nothing could have been further from the truth.

"If you will agree to allow me to borrow the sword," he replied.

"It seems I have underestimated you, Tuvok," she whispered.

You have no idea.

She knelt before him in a pose which suggested submission. The air practically crackled with the tension of anticipation.

"Show me," she said.

"Show you what?"

"Your pain."

Placing his fingers over her brows and cheekbones, he gazed directly into her eyes and said softly, "My mind to your mind."

She gasped with what Tuvok sensed was pleasure, as he slowly entered the cavernous depths of her consciousness. The mental barriers he had constructed over the years to protect his psyche from telepathic intrusion had been fortified by the Light of Amonak. He worked with surgical precision, offering her the images he knew she sought, but finally, he controlled what she saw.

She sipped greedily at each violent confrontation he fed her. She saw him fight the Kazon, the Vidiians, the Ilarians, the Mari, and the Borg. She witnessed the havoc he wrought upon his quarters in the dark days following his meld with Suder. She lingered lovingly over the anguish he had known in bidding farewell to Noss.

Even as he occupied her with these images, he probed her mind for the information he required.

He quickly discovered that beneath her enigmatic façade was a mind almost drowning in a vast and tumultuous sea of deception. Her raw strength was palpable, but it paled in comparison to the depths of her need.

He passed over dozens of identities she had assumed over the years of acquiring her massive wealth. Even he could not determine at this point who she truly was or once might have been. He glimpsed multiple attacks upon innocent minds; minds she had ravaged in the name of her unquenchable thirst.

More importantly, Tuvok saw the precise location of the *bat'leth* he was seeking, along with the codes required to deactivate her security grid.

He felt her buck beneath him, attempting to reassert her control over the meld. For all of its intensity, her mind was a crude weapon.

It could never hope to compete with the hundred-plus years he had spent honing his mind to a finely disciplined beam of pure white light.

Though she had not earned his compassion, he felt obligated to offer it, nonetheless.

You suffer needlessly, Tuvok assured her.

It is not my suffering that is of interest, she replied. *It is yours.*

Only then did he truly accept the reality that for her, no amount of mental discipline he might be able to briefly impose upon her could ever heal the wounds that separated her from sanity.

Tuvok knew what he must do. He felt her tremble beneath his hands. The intimacy she so desperately desired was the weakness that would allow him to breach the last of her defenses.

Though Vulcans did not experience pain in the ways that most humanoids did, it was a part of them. Tuvok brought this buried force to bear, the true depth of agony he had experienced in his life, and gave her every bit of it, everything she thought she wanted from him and had already determined to torturously drag from his mind, the moment he had knocked upon her door.

Yes, the part of her mind which was still intact cried out.

Then Tuvok gave her more.

He felt her utterly abandon what little control she still maintained, even as she realized fleetingly what this abandonment would likely cost her.

A few minutes later, he terminated the meld. She crumpled to the floor, her beautiful shell now housing a mind which had been forced to retreat in the wake of the fury he had unleashed upon it.

He carried her gently to a chaise that faced the Light of Amonak. He positioned her so that its flame would be the first thing she would see when she eventually regained consciousness. Its calming force would do much to ease her troubled psyche when she awoke.

He had no difficulty deactivating the room's force field or locating the *bat'leth*. It was housed in one of several storage rooms carved into the cliff beneath the house. Only once he was safely returned to his shuttle and had set his course to rendezvous with *Voyager* at Qo'noS did he allow himself to reflect on his actions.

Though he could never condone the wanton destruction of sentient life, he could rest in the certainty that what he had done to her had been merciful in comparison to what her mind had revealed that she intended to do to him.

His only regret was that at no point in the meld had he actually been able to discover her true name.

The last few hours had been the hardest for Tom. The Doctor had done his typical, exemplary job repairing the damage done by Logt's knife. The knowledge that he had once again lost his wife was a wound that continued to fester, and was beyond the ministrations of anyone. He was teetering on the edge of a place he hadn't visited within himself in a long time: despair.

Assembled in the transporter room were Chakotay, Admiral Janeway, Seven, the Doctor, Harry Kim, Counselor Cambridge, and the Emperor Kahless.

Tuvok's shuttle had just entered the bay, and he was at this moment en route to the transporter room.

As the group stood in tense silence, Tom overheard Kahless say something in a low voice to the Doctor.

"It is an amazing piece of technology," the Doctor replied to the emperor's query.

"And it allows you to travel anywhere you wish?"

"It does." The Doctor nodded proudly. "I will admit that when I was first activated and was confined to either sickbay or the holodeck, it was hard to imagine what I was missing. Now, I simply could not fathom my existence without this mobile emitter."

At last the doors to the transporter room slid open and Tuvok entered carrying the *bat'leth*, which Tom would have sworn was B'Elanna's had he not known otherwise.

"I hope we haven't put you to too much trouble, Tuvok," Chakotay said amiably.

"None that bears discussing at the moment," Tuvok replied. Turning to Paris, Tuvok said, "Admiral Janeway has advised me of the developments here. Any assistance I may provide in locating both B'Elanna and Miral, I am at your disposal."

"It's good to see you too, Tuvok," Paris replied, warmed by the sentiment.

"Well, ladies and gentlemen, shall we?" Janeway asked of the room.

As those assembled arranged themselves on the transporter platform, Kim, Seven, Tuvok, and Chakotay dividing the twelve *bat'leths* between them for their journey to the planet, Chakotay turned to Janeway, saying, "Should we advise Chancellor Martok of our impending arrival and request his permission to access the monument?"

"Why?" Kahless interjected. "It's my shrine."

No one, least of all Paris, seemed inclined to argue with that.

CHAPTER THIRTEEN

B'Elanna stirred from the deepest sleep she had enjoyed in a long time.

The baby.

Miral was crying. *She needs me.*

B'Elanna had become most adept at navigating through Miral's first several months of life. Despite her semiconscious state, she rolled over onto her side, reaching out for her daughter.

Her fingers met cold, hard stone.

B'Elanna forced her eyes to open and found herself lying on a smooth stone shelf in a small cell, hewn from solid rock. The faint buzz of a force field met her ears. Lifting her sluggish body, she turned and saw that the cell's only entrance was blocked by an energy barrier.

The memories returned. Logt had captured her and taken her from *Voyager*. B'Elanna had no idea where she was or how long she'd been unconscious. She had set out to rescue Miral and instead become Logt's prisoner.

Impotent fury washed over her as B'Elanna was forced to accept the fact that she had, once again, failed her daughter.

Then Miral cried out again.

B'Elanna's heart began to run a thready race. She practically flew toward the doorway of her cell, only hesitating to touch the wall of deadly energy that was the last barrier separating her from her child.

Her mind worked the problem. The field's generator had to be buried beneath the rock walls. If she could find a sharp enough edge, she could dig. B'Elanna turned, scanning the room for anything that could be useful. If nothing else, her hands might have to do.

A shadow fell over her from behind as Miral's screams intensified.

Wheeling around, B'Elanna saw Commander Logt standing on the other side of the barrier.

She was holding a very unhappy Miral in her arms.

"Miral!" B'Elanna shouted in mingled joy and frustration. Her arms physically ached to assume Logt's burden.

She started toward the doorway but Logt stopped her with a brisk, "Stand back."

Logt then nodded to someone B'Elanna could not see and within seconds, the force field dropped.

It took every ounce of self-control B'Elanna possessed not to charge forward as Logt calmly entered the cell. Only once the field had blinked back into existence did Logt extend her arms and allow B'Elanna to take her child, who was literally clawing her way out of Logt's embrace to her mother.

The moment her arms were once again wrapped securely around her daughter, B'Elanna sank to the floor, cradling Miral, alternately hugging and kissing her. Though Miral welcomed this at first, soon enough it was clear B'Elanna was practically smothering her, and Miral again began to struggle and cry out.

B'Elanna released her gently, and Miral pushed herself onto the floor. Once she was solidly on her hands and knees, she did something that threatened to tear B'Elanna's still pounding heart from her chest. With only moments of unsteadiness, Miral pushed herself up onto her tiny legs and began to teeter forward and away from her mother.

After only a few seconds, her unsteady gait toppled her forward, but even finding herself again on the floor, Miral only cried out lustily, not in pain, but in frustration with herself.

"Oh, my sweet darling," B'Elanna cooed as she crawled toward Miral. "You're walking!"

With a determined scowl, Miral again pushed herself up, and this time, she giggled at herself before clapping her tiny hands together and reaching out for B'Elanna.

"Your daddy will be so proud!" B'Elanna congratulated her. In reply, Miral barked out a loud "Da!"

There were many sins B'Elanna intended to make Logt answer for at a more appropriate time. Denying her the opportunity to witness her daughter's first steps, and from the sound of it, Miral's first halting attempt at a word, were at the top of that list.

"As you can see, your daughter is unharmed," Logt said evenly.

In a flash, B'Elanna closed the space between them and drove her fist into Logt's gut.

As expected, Logt recovered quickly, throwing B'Elanna to the ground. To B'Elanna's delight, she clutched her abdomen and demanded, "What was that for?"

"Tom," B'Elanna said fiercely.

Logt replied with a weary nod of respectful acknowledgment and said, "You must be starving."

B'Elanna was, but her pride reasserted itself.

"What are you going to do with us?" she demanded.

Logt took a deep breath, considering the question.

"If you will refrain from acting rashly, I have much to show you. I can assure you, any attempt at escape is futile. There is nowhere to run."

I'll be the judge of that, B'Elanna thought.

"Lead the way," B'Elanna said haughtily, scooping Miral up from the floor.

Logt started walking, and B'Elanna followed her out into a dimly lit hallway. It was like stepping into the bowels of an ancient dungeon. Apart from the occasional energy barrier, suggesting the existence of more cells like B'Elanna's, this was as dank and forlorn a place as she had ever seen. She had believed from day one that the qawHaq'hoch were fanatics, blinded by religious obsession. Their prison only solidified her belief that this accursed order was a remnant of the past. B'Elanna tightened her grip on her daughter, swearing she would bury it once and for all.

Miral squirmed in her arms as Logt led them up a short staircase carved into the rock. B'Elanna shushed her, as they emerged into a vast cavern. Like the chamber below, it had been excavated from rough stone, and it reached over a hundred meters above and in all directions. The stone edges protruding from the walls were the only remnant of the room's original nature.

The cavern was a warren of high-tech chambers, from what B'Elanna could see, devoted primarily to scientific research. Embedded in almost every wall of the partitioned space were touch-activated displays. Peeking where she could, B'Elanna glimpsed surgical bays, massive scanners and diagnostic interfaces, and a variety of devices, the purpose of which she could only guess. It reminded her vividly of a Starfleet facility. Every surface was clean, the air had a tinny, recycled quality, and light poured into the chamber courtesy of a ring embedded into the rock over ten meters above her head.

There were Klingons everywhere she looked. None of them were dressed as warriors, but they wore woven tunics in varying colors, which suggested some division of labor.

"Not what you were expecting?" Logt asked, interrupting her thoughts.

"Not exactly," B'Elanna had to admit.

Logt continued on, past this hive of activity. Occasionally someone would look up as they walked and grace B'Elanna and Miral with a reverent nod or slight bow.

B'Elanna found it mildly distasteful, but managed to respond as graciously as possible with a nod of her own.

Finally, they emerged into a larger partitioned space. It was filled with tables, not unlike those in Boreth's library, and the walls were lined with shelves housing scrolls, many of which rested behind energy barriers, no doubt to protect them from the ravages of oxygen exposure. Above these shelves, larger automated drawers had been set into the rock. They stretched all around her and so high into the wall above that B'Elanna could not see where they terminated.

Groups of workers were collected at a few of the tables, poring over manuscripts, making notes on standard padds. Logt led her away from them, toward an empty table that offered a semblance of privacy.

"This is our hall of records," Logt began, once B'Elanna was seated with Miral in her lap. The child seemed exhausted by her earlier exertions and was slowly drifting toward what B'Elanna felt certain would be only a short nap.

"The *qawHaq'hoch* were founded over fifteen centuries ago. Our initial purpose was to keep records of all Klingon births, deaths, and marriages. As the great and noble Houses of the empire began to grow and prosper, our work became more valuable. Very few Klingons of so-called noble birth were anxious to see their bloodlines diluted by mixing with commoners. Emperors rose and fell on our watch, and as their interests often diverged of necessity from truth, we were both a blessing and a curse, depending upon who was in power at any given time."

"And when did you go from being custodians of history to religious fanatics?" B'Elanna demanded.

"The faith of our people is part of our history," Logt chided her. "Very few Klingons still hold that faith in any regard, but it has sustained us for thousands of years. When the prophet Amar was slain at Kahless's side, his mate joined our order. She brought to us the original scrolls of Amar, and reaffirmed our belief, as expressed by Ghargh, that in time the will of the gods would be made known to us."

B'Elanna nodded for her to continue.

"As you already know, the day came when we were forced to continue our work in secret. Hal'korin, one of our most illustrious members, created this sanctuary for us and provided us with the means to exist undetected for all time.

"Throughout the centuries, we have kept abreast of all technological advances and put them to good use. We now possess the most accurate records of the genetic history of the Klingon species ever compiled."

"How thrilling for you," B'Elanna observed dryly.

"You should take care, B'Elanna," Logt said coldly. "Right now we are all that stands between the Klingon Empire and its downfall."

"Because of this curse?" B'Elanna asked disdainfully.

"Our faith has long foretold the two signs of the Curse of the Gods. Understand that when we say 'gods' we are not referring to some noncorporeal entity to be prayed to in times of need or feared in times of peril. It is our belief that long ago, the first Klingons had an interaction with what we presume to be an alien species. These aliens would have been sufficiently advanced at the time of this encounter to appear godlike to our forebears. It is also likely that these aliens were driven out by those they thought to control or abuse. The Klingon heart is now as it has always been, fierce and unbending."

"And so the Klingons killed their gods because they were more trouble than they were worth," B'Elanna said.

"Our research shows, however, that there was some early corruption of the original Klingon genome, possibly as a result of experimentation or interspecies relations with these aliens. It is slight, and it did result in the adaptation of several favorable traits, our redundant organs, for example. We have long suspected that the Curse of the Gods would be an inevitable expression of this taint. As the Federation Research Institute verified at our request, and as your own friends confirmed, this corruption will result in a struggle between two kinds of Klingons which will tear the Empire apart. Only the *Kuvah'magh* can save us now."

B'Elanna interrupted her harshly. "The scrolls say that the *Kuvah'magh* will bring the Klingon gods back and by doing so will avert this curse. Miral is an infant. How is she supposed to fulfill that destiny, living in this cave in the middle of nowhere?"

"Miral cannot escape her fate, and the curse, seemingly fulfilled, will take time to come to fruition. Within thirty generations the Klingon species as it exists now will cease to be. *Fek'lhr* births will gradually outnumber those of normal Klingons, and our destruction will follow. Miral has more than enough time to fulfill the prophecy. But it is of the utmost importance that she be protected until she is old enough to do this.

"It was never our intention to deprive you of your child," Logt assured her. "But we have always been cognizant of the threat posed by the Warriors of Gre'thor—"

"Would the Warriors of Gre'thor have even known about Miral if you hadn't kidnapped her and forced Kahless to contact them?" B'Elanna shot back, her frustration mounting.

"The moment Grapk and D'Kang arrived on Boreth, I knew their brethren would not be far behind," Logt replied.

Realization struck B'Elanna.

You and the Kuvah'magh *are in danger.*

"You were the one who sent me the warning?"

"Of course."

"Then why didn't you just let me take Miral and leave Boreth?" B'Elanna asked.

"You fail to consider the peril you would put her in should you ever return to Starfleet, especially as uninformed as you were at the time," Logt insisted. "Had you applied yourself more diligently to your studies, perhaps—"

"I get it," B'Elanna snapped, unwilling to be lectured like a schoolgirl.

"We are the only ones who can keep Miral safe. And we will die to the last initiate before we will fail in our duty to see that she fulfills the role fate has prescribed for her," Logt said more patiently, diffusing some of B'Elanna's hostility.

B'Elanna sighed deeply. Religious fanaticism was one thing, and quite easy for her to dismiss. But the beliefs of the *qawHaq'hoch*, substantiated as they apparently were by the science, were a little harder to fault. B'Elanna pulled Miral closer, briefly disturbing the child's sleep. At the very least, she could relate to the order's desire to sacrifice themselves, if need be, for Miral's sake. There was nothing B'Elanna would not do from this point forward, to try and spare Miral this fate, even if it meant finding these mysterious gods herself and dragging them back to Qo'noS.

"I understand," B'Elanna grudgingly admitted. "But I'll never leave Miral with you. She's my daughter. She deserves a normal life, no matter what fate might have in store for her."

"I have a suggestion I would ask you to consider," Logt said.

"What?"

"Join us."

B'Elanna took the suggestion like a slap across her face. She had the good sense to realize that Logt seemed to believe she was bestowing a great honor upon her. Pity was, there was no way B'Elanna would ever be able to accept. If Tom had been like a caged *targ* on Boreth, she couldn't imagine what it would do to their marriage to take up residence here.

When B'Elanna didn't answer immediately, Logt rose from the table and said, "Perhaps you should take some time to consider it."

"I will," B'Elanna agreed.

As they made their way back toward the far end of the cavern, B'Elanna was struck by something she hadn't noted at first, so overwhelmed had she been by the many surprising details of the sanctuary.

Before she could ask Logt about it, the overhead lighting dimmed and a soft alarm began to sound.

Logt quickened her pace, B'Elanna rushing behind, until they had cleared the work stations. To the right was the staircase leading down to the holding cells. To the left was a small archway, leading to another tunnel. At the entrance was what looked like a small decorative sculpture, a circular base with a small stone monument extending up from its center. The stone was now pulsing with a bright white light at regular intervals that matched the sound of the alarm.

"What's happening?" B'Elanna asked.

"Something has triggered the planet's orbital security perimeter," Logt replied as shouts and orders erupted around them. Workers poured out of their research spaces and hurried into the tunnel past the miniature version of Hal'korin's obelisk, and from the distant sound of clanging metal, they were arming themselves for battle.

Voyager, B'Elanna thought, hope giving her a new rush of adrenaline.

Logt hurried B'Elanna back to her cell and pushed her inside. There B'Elanna found a plate of fresh bread and dried meat waiting for her beside a large pitcher of water. B'Elanna gingerly set the sleeping Miral down on the stone bench where she had awakened, thinking Logt gone, but just as she had done so, Logt grabbed the child with one hand and leveled a disruptor at B'Elanna with the other.

"What are you doing?" B'Elanna shouted, waking Miral.

Logt backed from the room, and the force field sparkled into place.

"Consider my offer, B'Elanna," Logt said grimly before disappearing from view.

B'Elanna could have wept with rage. Instead, she settled for slapping the force field, and received a healthy shock and singed flesh for her trouble.

She paced back toward the bench and in her anger, tossed the plate of food to the ground. Logt had lulled her into trust and once again betrayed her.

At least she's consistent, the voice of reason managed to pierce the dissonance of B'Elanna's mind. It sounded eerily like the voice of Counselor Cambridge.

B'Elanna stopped to collect herself. Howling at the fates or berating herself for her stupidity was of no use to Miral. If *Voyager* had found them, or worse, if the Warriors of Gre'thor were at the door, B'Elanna would do well to prepare for battle.

She dropped to the floor and collected the food she had discarded. She forced it quickly down her gullet, devouring every last morsel and washing it down with the water.

As she ate she considered her options. Wherever they had taken Miral, it was undoubtedly the most secure location within the compound. Much as she hated to admit it, B'Elanna should at least try and join the fight if the Warriors of Gre'thor were at hand.

As she imagined the battle and saw Logt leading her forces, she remembered the question she had wanted to ask Logt before the perimeter alarms had sounded.

Every face she had seen when they toured the sanctuary was female. She had been trying to imagine Tom there with her and realized how lonely and out of place he would surely feel.

Where are all the men?

"Another big tree . . . some more pretty flowers . . ." Kim said, cataloguing the results of his visual scan of a sector of Cygnet IV.

"Are we boring you, Lieutenant?" Seven asked.

Seven, Harry, Kahless, and Cambridge were standing in *Voyager*'s astrometrics lab, scrutinizing every square millimeter of the planet Hal'korin's obelisk had told them was the location of the hidden *qawHaq'hoch* sanctuary. Everyone present had expressed both awe and relief when the *bat'leths* B'Elanna had provided them had worked exactly as she described, once they were placed at the monument.

The ship's initial sensor sweeps of the surface had revealed nothing to suggest that any humanoid life-forms were present on the planet, but as Harry had mentioned—*perhaps one too many times for Seven's patience,* he decided silently—this verdant, lush world sure was pretty.

"Seven, what am I looking at?" Harry asked, staring at a geothermal scan the sensors had just spat forth in a three-dimensional holographic representation at one of the adjacent terminals.

Seven moved from Kim's side to examine the findings. "I recalibrated the sensors to look for geothermal anomalies. If anyone is operating from a hidden location, it is likely to be buried either within a natural rock formation or perhaps beneath the surface of one of the planet's oceans. As there are no obvious power sources present, I concluded that they are most likely tapping into the planet's core for sustainable resources," Seven advised him.

"Or they've got one hell of a cloaking system," Harry added.

Seven ignored him, studying the display for a moment as Cambridge took the opportunity to better study her lithe and obscenely well-proportioned frame, which was quite gloriously accentuated by her deep red one-piece body suit. For reasons Harry wasn't tempted to analyze too deeply, the counselor's harmless appraisal and obvious appreciation of what he saw sent a tinge of jealousy shooting up from the depths of Harry's psyche.

It's none of your business, Harry's better angels advised him as his cheeks began to redden. It was true that any man with a pulse—and probably some women, come to think of it—couldn't help but admire Seven's physical attributes. Harry had barely been able to speak in complete sentences in her presence for the first several weeks she'd been aboard *Voyager.* But his initial attraction had become brotherly affection over the years. She might look like every man's fantasy, but once you got to know her, Seven was much too complex to simply relegate to the realm of eye candy. In many ways, she was as innocent as a child. She was still learning what it was to be human.

This brought out Harry's protective side, and that seemed to be kicking in with a vengeance as he observed Cambridge.

"Anything worth taking a closer look at, Seven?" Kim asked in a brisk tone, which had the immediate effect of redirecting Cambridge's attention from Seven to him.

"Perhaps," Seven said, altering the display to zoom in on a particular sector. "Bring up the surface scan of sector 347," she said imperiously, moving back to the main screen.

With an inward smile Harry noted that she hadn't even observed Cambridge's interest. Of course, Seven was like that when she was working. She could focus with an intensity unknown to most humans.

Harry then turned his attention to sector 347.

"Pretty rocks and a mountain," he said.

Seven obliged him with a sidelong smirk.

"The thermal scans of this area show anomalous readings. These spikes are higher than other comparable rock formations on the surface," she said, watching carefully as the display panned over the area.

"What exactly are you hoping to see?" Cambridge asked, clearly not wanting to be left out of the conversation.

"I'm not sure," Seven replied.

"Go back," Kahless's voice interrupted.

Harry jumped at the urgency in the emperor's tone. The entire time they'd been standing in this room, he had seemed content to merely observe their progress. Kim didn't think that Kahless had moved a muscle in the last hour; Harry had actually forgotten he was there.

Seven reversed the scan to retread the ground it had just covered.

"There," Kahless said softly, stepping closer and pointing to an outcropping of rocks near the base of the area's highest mountain.

"I don't see anything," Seven said, pausing the display.

"Magnify that section," Kahless commanded.

Harry studied the rocks for anything that might explain the emperor's sudden interest.

This is a waste of time, he thought, frustrated.

"There it is," Cambridge said almost reverently, moving to Kahless's side.

"There *what* is?" Seven asked pointedly.

Harry was relieved to know that he wasn't the only one in the room who couldn't see whatever had caught the emperor's attention.

"Computer, overlay this grid with an image found in my personal archive: file Cambridge, Klingon mythological studies, *qawHaq'hoch*, mark of Hal'korin," the counselor ordered.

The computer complied and a sloping vertical line, intersected by twelve smaller lines, appeared over the rocks.

"Scale to size and look for comparable pattern in the rock face."

A few moments later the computer completed the operation, and the mark of Hal'korin was shown to match perfectly with what looked like a natural scarring of the rocks.

"Wow," Harry said, impressed.

"Computer," Seven requested, "calculate the likelihood that this pattern occurred naturally. Cross-reference all planetary scans."

The computer's cold feminine voice responded, *"Prob-*

ability that the pattern is naturally occurring are forty-six million seven hundred thirty-nine thousand to one."

"We've found them," Kahless said assuredly.

Turning to Kim, he said, "Collect a security team, Lieutenant, and have them ready to transport to the surface immediately. Make sure your team is comprised of your finest warriors."

Despite the fact that Harry didn't actually report to the emperor, he found himself starting directly for the door when Cambridge interrupted, "Pardon me, Emperor, but that would be an incredibly bad idea."

"Why?" Kahless demanded, clearly shocked at the insolence.

"Is it your intention to overwhelm the hundreds of warriors in the sanctuary below with the force of a handful of *Voyager's* finest, or did you have a more subtle attack in mind?"

Kahless simply stared at Cambridge in wonder.

"As we do not possess sufficient numbers to overwhelm them, at some point we must consider entering into negotiations. And for that to succeed, we might not want to offend them right off the bat," Cambridge went on.

"Offend them how?" Seven asked.

"How does it go?" Cambridge mused. After a moment he quoted, " 'Beyond the gate she joins in noble stead, the path where only men must fear to tread.' "

Kahless glared hard at the counselor until his lips broke into a wide, ferocious smile.

"Your studies do you credit, human," Kahless nodded approvingly, "though it is a dubious translation of Brach'Tun's letter."

"I'll admit the Klingon text doesn't rhyme, but the meaning is unaltered. And Brach'Tun was, arguably, the last Klingon to actually speak directly with a member of the *qawHaq'hoch*, and live to tell the tale," Cambridge replied. "His daughter, wasn't it?"

"Excuse me," Harry interrupted. "What's the problem?"

Kahless answered his question with one of his own.

"Who among your crew are the fiercest women warriors?" the emperor asked.

CHAPTER FOURTEEN

Lyssa Campbell had barely closed her eyes when Kim's voice came blaring over the comm system, ordering her to the transporter room. She'd completed two full duty shifts on the bridge before turning over ops to Ensign Lasren, a Betazoid who was far too young and eager to please for Lyssa's tastes.

Unfortunately, as soon as he had assumed his station, Lasren had discovered a strange energy reading, a subtle gravimetric displacement, which Lyssa had first noted some nine hours earlier and quickly relegated to the realm of "odd things often encountered while scanning space." Lasren had insisted on running a full spectral analysis, which had, as Lyssa anticipated, yielded no new information. But given the fact that the anomaly had first appeared on her watch, she'd felt duty bound to see the quest through to its end. After advising Lasren not to take the disappointing results of his snipe hunt too hard, and grabbing a quick dinner in the mess, she'd hurried to her quarters more than ready for the three hours of sleep she now desperately needed before alpha shift began.

She'd arrived in the transporter room to find Admiral Janeway already briefing Lieutenants Samantha Maplethorpe and Vanessa Waters. Seven of Nine was conferring with the transporter operator on duty, a soft-spoken, burly man, Ensign Donner, suggesting that she was already apprised of the mission's specs.

Lyssa was quick to grasp the broad strokes. They had located what they believed was the entry to the *qawHaq'hoch* sanctuary, and theirs was the first team being sent to breach the perimeter.

Only after they had beamed down to the surface and begun the short hike to the plateau that they believed concealed the entrance did it dawn on Lyssa that she was surrounded by only female officers.

Sure, it happened from time to time. But it was a little odd, especially considering the fact that Commander Paris should have been leading the charge to recover his wife and child.

"Is it me, or are we a little estrogen heavy this trip?" Lyssa quietly remarked to Waters.

"Weren't you listening?" Waters asked a little petulantly. The trim, white-haired security officer seemed to be having a little more trouble with the climb than Lyssa, who was a passionate and frequent hiker.

"I'm running on about fifteen minutes of sleep, Waters. Want to cut me a little slack?"

"The *qawHaq'hoch* are supposedly all female," Waters advised her between heavy breaths. "Kahless says if we send men to the sanctuary, it adds insult to injury. Any man who enters is killed on sight. Women, they might at least talk to. It's like a rule or something."

"Sounds like a dumb rule to me," Lyssa replied. "I mean, how do they . . . or what do they do when . . . I mean . . . that's just no fun at all."

Before Waters could reply, Admiral Janeway had reached the crest of the plateau and signaled for the team to halt. After a quick scan and a brief conference with Seven, the message was relayed down the short line for everyone to stay put while Janeway and Seven approached the entrance alone.

Lyssa's phaser was already in her hand, and for good measure she scouted the terrain. At first blush, it looked like an excellent spot for an ambush. And given the fact that sunrise on this part of the planet was about a half hour away, the dim twilight only enhanced her sense that they were being watched by one or many, who had them at a considerable disadvantage. Still, *Voyager*'s sensors were no doubt trained on the away team, and should be able to alert them to any imminent threat.

At the entrance, which appeared to be nothing but a wall of solid rock, Janeway and Seven were arguing. It wasn't the first time Lyssa had seen these two butt heads over the years, and depending on the circumstances, they could be entertaining to watch. Back in the Delta quadrant, Seven of Nine had always been the person on *Voyager* who didn't seem the least bit awed by their formidable leader. Right now, between her exhaustion and the uncomfortable squatting on the side of a mountain, Lyssa just wished they'd get on with it.

They seemed to reach a consensus, and Janeway tapped her combadge quickly and spoke into it so low that Lyssa couldn't make out the words. Lyssa then heard the hum of a transporter beam, and a *bat'leth* appeared on the ground at Janeway's feet.

The admiral claimed it and attempted to wedge it into

the rock face. As Lyssa found herself wondering if the admiral hadn't gone round the bend, the solid wall actually vanished, revealing a small opening.

I'll be damned, Lyssa thought, remembering that Starfleet didn't just give those extra pips away.

Janeway signaled for the rest of the team to join them.

"All right," she said, once they were gathered. "I'm going to take point. Seven, you'll bring up the rear, weapons at the ready. Our tricorders can't penetrate this rock. There's either a natural or technological barrier scattering our signals, so we really don't know what we're going to find in there."

A lot of really frustrated Klingon women, Lyssa surmised, but refrained from saying it aloud. Actually, the thought was more than a little disconcerting. Klingons, male or female, could be formidable adversaries, and none of them could afford to forget that.

Lyssa fell into line directly behind Janeway as they entered the tunnel. Almost immediately her nostrils were assaulted by a gust of rank air. Janeway switched on her palm beacon. They cleared the tunnel, which led the team into a much larger space.

Maplethorpe had already exited the tunnel and Waters was huffing behind her. *Seven was probably irritated no end,* Lyssa thought with a grin.

As Lyssa took a few steps farther into the cavern, she was searching for the switch to her own beacon. She realized that the sound of heavy breathing she'd first thought was Waters, was actually coming from the wrong direction.

As a whip of adrenaline rushed up Lyssa's spine, she turned to Janeway, who was playing her light slowly over the cavern in the direction of the disconcerting sound, which was now mingled with a metallic clank Lyssa couldn't place.

Finally, Lyssa found her beacon's switch, though she almost dropped her phaser in the process. Her beam of light momentarily transected with Janeway's, then moved farther to the left, illuminating a face that Lyssa's worst nightmares couldn't have coughed up on their best day.

A sharp intake of breath from Janeway alerted Lyssa to the fact that the admiral might be paralyzed with fright. It certainly seemed like a viable option.

The creature, or at least what she could see of it, was covered in grayish white fur streaked with what Lyssa could only assume was blood. The shape of its massive face was reminiscent of a polar bear's, but where that animal had always had a benign and regal appearance to Lyssa, this creature's gaping maw was filled with rows of jagged teeth, and its fierce orange eyes were tainted with feral desperation. Around its neck was a heavy iron chain. Lyssa followed the chain and found its end embedded in the wall of the cliff. The leash was clearly meant to limit the creature's movement.

The creature let out a deafening roar that should have brought the cavern down on top of them.

Without further thought, Lyssa thumbed her phaser to maximum stun, took two quick steps to place herself in front of Janeway, and fired.

Her beam struck the creature's right shoulder, and Lyssa watched in horror as the energy discharge was dispersed over the animal's fur, doing no damage whatsoever. Then she understood: the creature's oily coating, undoubtedly applied by its keepers, somehow acted as a scattering field diffusing her phaser fire.

The next ear-splitting roar first caused Lyssa to take an immediate step back, even as she thought she heard Janeway shouting for her to hold fire. Then, the creature fixed her solidly with a cockeyed grin and shook its head rapidly. Lyssa realized with growing alarm that she had unintentionally just become the most interesting thing in the room.

Suddenly, she felt the wind knocked out of her as something very large and sharp came swiping into her midsection from the right. The next thing she knew, the foulest stench she'd ever smelled was upon her, as she found herself staring at nothing but crusted, yellow teeth.

"Hold your fire!" Janeway commanded as she hurried Lieutenant Maplethorpe back toward the tunnel. The others had just emerged and were quickly moving toward the right of the cavern, as far from the terrifying noise as the space would allow.

Janeway's first instinct had been to rush to Campbell and try to pull her clear of the creature's range of motion, but the razor-tipped claw that had felled her, then dragged her to the mouth of the creature, had made that choice impossible. Before Janeway could move, the creature had ripped Campbell's head from her body. The several crunches that followed suggested that Lyssa's misery was over, while simultaneously causing Janeway's gorge to rise.

Once the creature seemed satisfied that it had dealt with the threat, it roared again and loped forward, but was quickly straining against its leash. The rest of the team had at least ten meters of space in which to maneuver, but the only real option left to them was to retreat the way they had come.

As long as that chain holds, Janeway thought grimly.

"What the hell is that?" Waters whispered frantically.

"A *targot*," Seven replied calmly.

"Geez, Seven, I didn't really want to know," Waters said.

"It is a bearlike predator, native to—" Seven began.

"We'll put it in the report, Seven," Janeway hissed to silence her.

The *targot* continued to eye them hungrily.

"So, back the way we came then?" Maplethorpe urged.

"Not yet," Janeway said. "Seven, focus your light just past the creature's head."

Seven did as she was told and quickly illuminated what Janeway was sure she'd already seen: another tunnel leading farther into the mountain.

The only way to get there was to somehow get past the *targot*.

Janeway knew they only had a few minutes at the most to make a decision. She considered the notion that their four remaining phasers might succeed where Lyssa's solitary one had failed, but it didn't seem likely. Clearly the *yuwHaq'hoch* had tools up their sleeves that were completely unknown to Federation science.

While it was possible that there were several other entrances to the cavern, given the fact that one of Hal'korin's *bat'leths* had opened the door, it seemed likely that this was meant to be the road to the sanctuary. This also meant that there had to be a way to get past the *targot*.

But how?

Perhaps the beast had been trained to recognize members of the order.

Or maybe something simpler.

If brute force wasn't going to get the job done, what were the other options?

An idea flickered briefly into Janeway's mind, courtesy of a Doberman pinscher who had once taken a liking to Molly, her Irish setter.

As the only other choice was retreat, and Janeway hadn't come this far to be defeated by fear, she turned to the others.

"I'm going to try something. If it doesn't work out, you're to return to *Voyager* immediately," she said quickly.

"What are you going to try?" Seven asked.

"What do you mean '*work out*'?" Waters demanded frantically.

The admiral faced both of them with her sternest gaze. They both clearly recognized from her expression that she was impervious to argument, and nodded without further questions.

Janeway then turned and squared her shoulders. She took a few halting steps into the darkness toward the *targot.*

Nice bear, she thought grimly.

The creature rocked its head in her direction. The cavern was now faintly illuminated by the others' wrist beacons, but there wasn't enough direct light on the animal's face for Janeway to get a sense of its intentions.

She stepped forward again, and the beast raised itself up and lumbered toward her.

Well aware that this might be the worst choice she'd made in a long list of questionable calls over her lifetime, Janeway took another step forward and extended her right hand, palm up. From this distance the beast could easily take off her arm, probably up to the shoulder.

The creature emitted a quick huff of air and growled menacingly.

Janeway stood her ground, her heart pounding so hard it felt like it was looking for a way out of her chest, whether the rest of her body intended to come along or not.

A heavy, wet, noxious tongue landed on Janeway's palm. Grimacing, she forced herself to remain still.

Once the creature had had a good taste of her sweat, it lost interest in Janeway and retreated back to its corner. It left just enough space for her to move past it toward the far tunnel, which she could clearly see sloped downward.

When she was several meters down the tunnel, Janeway turned back to see the wide-eyed faces of the away team. She nodded, encouragingly, and Seven was the next to step up, mimicking Janeway's movements precisely.

Waters and Maplethorpe were harder to sell, but to their credit, followed Janeway's lead and a few moments later, all four were moving cautiously down the tunnel.

"That was a foolhardy choice, Admiral," Seven admonished her softly.

"Are you arguing with the results?" Janeway asked.

"No," she said, "though I don't understand why the creature allowed us to pass."

"We need to get you a pet, Seven," Janeway replied.

"Admiral?"

"If the *qawHaq'hoch* have to use this entrance . . . There had to be a way past the creature that didn't include killing it, much as I would have liked to for Lyssa's sake," Janeway said wearily. "It's used to the company of those who interact with it regularly, which means the *qawHaq'hoch* are also probably comfortable around it. You had to be willing to set aside your fear and let it get to know you a little. Many animals, no matter how ferocious they may appear, can be quite gentle and accommodating to their masters. By standing up to it in a nonthreatening way, you let it know that you are part of its pack."

"While I find your reasoning sound, it was still a huge risk to take," Seven said.

"Not when you consider what we stand to lose if we fail," Janeway replied.

***

Voyager's bridge was shrouded in tense silence. At Chakotay's left, Tom Paris sat with concentrated intensity. He had raged privately to Chakotay when he learned of Logt's treachery, and Chakotay had allowed him to blow off steam. He still didn't know if Tom was angrier with himself or with B'Elanna for their current predicament. Since then, he had alternated between barely repressed fury and a darker despondence. If they didn't succeed in finding and safely returning B'Elanna and Miral to him, Chakotay worried that his old friend and trusted first officer might never recover.

Come to think of it, that wasn't a scenario Chakotay had any interest in exploring either.

"Status, Ensign Lasren," Chakotay said.

"Sensors show no sign of the away team, Captain. We lost them the moment they entered the mountain," Lasren replied.

It wasn't surprising, and actually gave credence to Kahless's belief that the *qawHaq'hoch* were hiding within, though Chakotay couldn't imagine what technology they were using to flummox the ship's sensors.

A brisk sigh escaped Paris's lips. Chakotay knew that if he didn't provide Tom with an outlet for his aggression soon, the waiting would drive him over the edge. Problem was, there was simply nothing any of them could do until the admiral reported in, or missed her first scheduled check.

Kim suddenly called out, "Captain, I'm picking up a vessel decloaking to starboard."

"On screen," Chakotay ordered, rising to his feet. "Who the hell is that?" he asked as the ungainly ship came into view.

"It's the *Kortar*, sir," Lasren's voice replied.

Chakotay had feared for days that T'Krek's vessel wouldn't be far behind his. Had Chakotay been in his place, he would have begun tracking B'Elanna and Kahless as soon as they'd escaped. As it stood now, Chakotay had no idea how long the *Kortar* had had *Voyager* in its sights.

"Red Alert," Chakotay ordered. "Harry?"

"Shields are at maximum, Captain," Harry replied. "Arming phasers."

"Hail them, Lasren," Chakotay said.

After a brief pause Lasren replied, "No response, sir."

Chakotay watched as the *Kortar* moved at low impulse past *Voyager* and assumed a slightly lower orbit of the planet. Within a few moments, bright bursts of orange phaser fire erupted from it and began bombarding the planet below.

"What are they targeting?" Chakotay asked, more for confirmation, because he already knew the answer.

"Sector 347," Harry replied. "They're bombarding the area surrounding the mountain presumed to be hiding the sanctuary."

"They're trying to flush them out," Paris said sternly.

"Or, from this distance, they can't be more accurate," Chakotay suggested.

"Captain, I'm detecting transporter activity," Lasren interrupted.

"How many?" Chakotay asked.

"A hundred Klingon life signs are now on the surface, moving toward the entrance our team discovered."

"Open a channel," Chakotay called.

"They can hear you, sir," Lasren replied.

"This is Captain Chakotay of the Federation Starship Voyager. We are on a rescue mission, and your actions are putting our people at risk."

"You think they don't know that?" Tom asked softly.

"Cease fire and transport immediately or we will take action," Chakotay finished. Personally, he didn't feel that T'Krek deserved the warning, but protocol demanded it.

"They've completed another transport," Lasren advised. In the time Chakotay had given them, the strength of their forces on the surface had just doubled.

"Harry, target their weapons systems and fire," Chakotay ordered.

T'Krek clearly anticipated the move. Voyager's phasers barely grazed the target as the Kortar's helmsman began evasive maneuvers.

The turbolift doors slid open, and Kahless and Tuvok stepped onto the bridge as Harry called out, "They are returning fire."

Voyager shuddered under the impact.

"Shields are holding," Harry advised.

"Attack pattern omega pi," Chakotay ordered in response.

"Captain," Kahless called, as Tare and Harry executed the maneuver, positioning *Voyager* between the *Kortar* and the planet, "I will lead a team to the surface to engage the Warriors of Gre'thor."

"Do it." Chakotay nodded as the ship took another hit.

"Permission to join the away team?" Paris asked immediately.

Chakotay stared hard at Tom, but it wasn't really a tough decision.

"Bring them back to us," Chakotay said firmly.

"I will, Captain," Tom replied.

As Tom followed Kahless to the turbolift, Harry said, "Six teams are assembling in the transporter rooms, but we'll still be outnumbered three to one, assuming the *Kortar* doesn't send more troops."

Chakotay didn't like the math, but given the size of his crew, there wasn't much he could do about it.

"Captain, I'd like to join the away team. As their commanding officer—" Harry asked.

Chakotay cut him off. "I need you on the bridge right now, Lieutenant."

"I will assume Lieutenant Kim's post, Captain," Tuvok offered.

"Very well." Chakotay nodded.

Chakotay appreciated Harry's request. The *Kortar* was engaging defensively. Their true goal seemed to be to keep *Voyager* busy while their men attacked the sanctuary. T'Krek wasn't doing any serious damage to Chakotay's ship, and probably wouldn't until the captain forced his hand.

"Tare, we need a little distance so we can drop shields and transport our teams down."

"Aye, Captain."

Within moments she had maneuvered the ship at one quarter impulse just clear of the *Kortar*'s weapons.

Chakotay followed her actions from the command console embedded in the arm of his chair.

The captain ordered Lasren to drop shields and authorize the transports.

They barely had time to restore their shields before the *Kortar* moved into position behind them.

Almost seventy of Chakotay's crew were now on the planet, about to engage the Warriors of Gre'thor in battle. Chakotay didn't honestly know if it was a battle they could win; the odds were definitely against them. But he knew for certain that defeat wasn't on their minds as they rushed headlong to the aid of their companions.

"*Voyager*'s personnel have engaged the Warriors on the surface," Tuvok called out from tactical.

Gods of my fathers, give them strength, Chakotay silently prayed.

CHAPTER FIFTEEN

Seven of Nine had never had a *bat'leth* held at her throat. There was, unfortunately, nothing she could do about it for the time being. The away team had been ambushed in the tunnels by a dozen Klingon warriors armed to the teeth, and Janeway had given them unequivocal orders to surrender. Seven agreed with the admiral's choice, but she remained unhappy with the immediate results.

Seven had been agitated from the moment they entered the *targot*'s cavern. Her pent-up worry for B'Elanna and Miral aside, watching the creature dismember Lieutenant Campbell had been a horrific and wasteful spectacle. She had maintained her composure, yet an unfamiliar voice had stirred, demanding action. The *qawHaq'hoch* had caused considerable pain and disruption in the lives of those she cared about, and it had to end.

Sacrificing her life in a futile gesture against the superior force that had captured them, Seven realized, would not bring her any nearer her goal.

The *qawHaq'hoch* led the away team through a series of winding, downward-sloping tunnels. The shaft they chose had been invisible to her tricorder until they entered it. It was clearly a shortcut known only to the order.

The route Janeway's team had followed after confronting the *targot* had been significantly more hazardous. The first obstacle they had encountered had been a series of swinging bridges suspended over a long chasm. Constructed of brittle wooden slats, the bridges had creaked ominously under their weight, and the team had been forced to cross them one uneasy member at a time. Waters had been the one to discover that crouching low while walking, a difficult balancing act that was most painful to the thighs, kept the bridges steady and allowed for quicker passage.

Next they had encountered a junction where thirteen shafts led in varying directions. Their tricorders were useless at aiding them in a choice, and checking each one individually was definitely a worst-case scenario. Maplethorpe had noticed that above each shaft was an engraved marking. The tricorder had successfully translated them as Klingon pictographs, precursors of the written Klingon language, with very simple meanings, like *birth, honor, glory, battle,* and *death.* Initially this hadn't made their selection process any easier, until Janeway had observed that the orientation of the symbols suggested the path of one's life. Beginning with *birth,* one moved through *battle* to *honor, glory*, and ultimately *death.* Beyond *death* was a symbol the tricorder translated as *memory* or *history.* Seven had intuited that given the *qawHaq'hoch* obsession with the past, this might be the right road. Because the *qawHaq'hoch* were Klingon, Maplethorpe had urged them toward *battle*, while Waters thought *honor* more appropriate. Finally, Janeway had pointed out that there was only one pictogram that represented a part of life that was solely the purview of women.

A few hundred meters into the tunnel marked *birth*, they found themselves surrounded by the warriors who had taken them captive.

They had reached a terminus, and each had been silently assigned two women to guard them while the leaders of the warriors had inserted a *bat'leth* into the wall and triggered an entrance into a larger chamber. In the brief glimpse she'd had before the door had slid shut, Seven had noted a flurry of activity in the vast space beyond. She surmised the activity was connected to the distant but regular blare of what sounded like an alarm, and wondered if their presence had activated the warning system.

After a few moments, the door slid open again and Commander Logt moved quickly toward them. Before she reached them, the ground shook and particles of loose dust filled the air.

"What was that?" Janeway demanded.

"Undoubtedly your people are losing patience with your efforts, Admiral," Logt said briskly.

"That's not *Voyager*," Janeway corrected her. "We're not due to check in for a few more minutes, but even if we missed that contact, they would never fire directly on this place without ascertaining that we were already dead."

"We should oblige them," the warrior holding Seven suggested unhelpfully.

Another warrior rushed to Logt's side and whispered something in her ear. The only word Seven could make out of the hasty communication was "Gre'thor."

"Take them to the holding cells," Logt ordered, and immediately the guard behind Seven dug the blunt end of her weapon into Seven's back to urge her forward.

"We would prefer to fight at your side," Janeway said calmly.

Logt looked back, clearly surprised by the admiral's offer.

"The Warriors of Gre'thor have arrived," Janeway said evenly. "They have come to kill Miral Paris, and no one here will sit idly by while that happens."

"We have betrayed you and those you hold most dear," Logt countered. "You cannot be trusted."

Janeway abruptly grabbed the blade of the weapon leveled at her throat, drawing blood from her palm. She then raised her dripping hand to Logt and said, "I swear to you now that we will stand with you against those who have come to kill us all. Once they are defeated, we can discuss the fate of Miral Paris."

Logt favored Janeway with a hard stare, then drew a short sword from her belt and unflinchingly opened a gash into her left hand. Raising it, she clasped Janeway's and said, "I accept your oath."

Janeway nodded grimly, and Logt turned, saying, "Follow me."

———

Kim thought he had been well prepared for conflict. He and his security staff had drilled repeatedly on the holodeck in various combat scenarios. As Klingons made some of the most challenging opponents, they were often chosen as opponents in training simulations—exclusively, since Harry had learned of the threat posed by the Warriors of Gre'thor.

Unfortunately, the reality of this situation bore little resemblance to any of the simulations.

The Warriors of Gre'thor were vicious. They seemed to take pleasure in the gory chaos surrounding them. Their weapons of choice were variations on Klingon *bat'leths*, *mek'leths*, and shorter blades they sent whizzing through the air with alarming accuracy—though they were also armed with disruptors.

It also didn't help that they were engaging them on a hillside, and for now, the warriors held the higher ground.

There was little usable cover. The hillside was dotted with scrub brush, and the loose soil made keeping one's feet and balance almost impossible.

Harry had led his team to a rocky outcrop that offered a semblance of protection. From there, they fanned out through the brush on their bellies, looking for clear shots in an attempt to pick off as many of their foes as possible with their phaser rifles.

It seemed that no matter how many they felled, there were always more. The Warriors had successfully formed an impenetrable line along the ridge that led to the sanctuary's entrance.

The other two *Voyager* teams, one led by Kahless and the other by Tom, were spread out along the hillside. Their cover was equally sparse, and for every shot they managed to get off, four came answering back from the Warriors' disruptors.

In the first few minutes of battle Harry had lost Peterson and Pallizolo, and he could see the bodies of at least five more security personnel lying dead on the hillside.

What they needed was a way to breach the line. Settled behind a rock, and stinging from dozens of small burrs that had punctured his uniform as he crawled through the brush, Kim signaled for Ensign Ward to lay down cover fire.

Ward rose and fired his volley and Harry turned quickly, stabilized his elbows on the rock, and fired five clean shots, successfully picking off one of the Warriors above.

"This is getting us nowhere fast," Ward said grimly as he crouched, narrowly avoiding a disruptor blast that pinged off the rocks above and started a small downpour of loose grit onto Harry's head.

"Harry, can you hear me?" Tom's voice shouted through Harry's combadge.

"We're pinned down about twenty meters from your position," Harry replied.

"Kahless is going to swing his men wide to the left and charge that flank. Prepare to lay down cover fire."

"Understood," Harry said, motioning to his team to collect themselves and hurriedly advising them of their new target.

Moments later, they rose and sent a barrage of fire toward the Warriors collected at the farthest left edge of the ridge as Kahless cried out, leading twelve of Harry's best men and women up the hill. Reager and Uzan fell instantly, but the others managed to reach the line, where they immediately engaged the Warriors in hand-to-hand combat.

In the subsequent chaos an opening appeared in the center of the line as the Warriors nearest the fray turned to aid their comrades. Kim ordered his team to concentrate their fire to the right of the breach, hoping to widen it while avoiding firing too close to the Starfleet officers who had charged the line.

Paris's team clearly had the same idea, and within minutes the line had been successfully divided.

"*Are you thinking what I'm thinking?*" Tom called over the combadge.

It was time for his team to assault the line. Given their position, Tom's team would have to go first, but Harry would be on his heels.

"We're right behind you," Harry replied.

Kim motioned to his team to lay down cover fire. Tom's team had barely begun their ascent, when a fresh group of Warriors poured through the breach in their line and charged down the hillside directly toward Tom's position.

"Oh, hell," Ward said in disbelief.

Harry didn't have to order his men to do the obvious. They immediately turned their rifles toward the onslaught, taking down as many Warriors as possible before they reached Tom's officers.

And still, more were coming.

━━━━━━━

Janeway stood between Seven and Waters. The dozens of women waiting at the main entrance to the sanctuary chamber had been arranged in columns, preparing to meet the Warriors of Gre'thor, should they find their way through the maze of caverns above. An eerie calm had descended upon them. Overhead, the cry of a Warrior or the clash of metal would reach their ears, but few among the ranks even flinched at the ominous sounds.

With a nod, Logt, who stood at the head of the line next to B'Elanna, dispatched twenty warriors, who went rushing into the tunnels above. Janeway hadn't been allowed to greet B'Elanna when she had been brought to join the ranks. But she had caught sight of Janeway and Seven, and clearly her spirits had been buoyed by their presence. Janeway was pleased that Logt had accepted her suggestion to allow B'Elanna to join their fight.

Soon, the pings of disruptor blasts came echoing down, along with what sounded like a distant steady march.

It's only a matter of time, now, Janeway thought, steeling her nerves with a deep breath.

"Stay with them!" Chakotay shouted to Tare. "Tuvok, keep targeting those disruptors."

Bursts of angry energy flew from *Voyager*'s phaser array as Tare maneuvered into position off the *Kortar*'s aft bow to give Tuvok a clear shot.

Unfortunately, whoever was piloting T'Krek's ship just as quickly compensated, effectively evading, once again, the potentially disabling shot.

For what had seemed like hours, but in reality had only been a little over ten minutes, *Voyager* and the *Kortar* had done this hostile dance, each unable to inflict any serious damage on the other.

The only good news, apart from the fact that their shields were holding, was that *Voyager* had eliminated T'Krek's ability to send further reinforcements to the planet's surface.

Chakotay held tight to his chair as Tare dropped *Voyager*'s nose in a short dive, while Tuvok unleashed another barrage of phaser fire.

This time, one of the *Kortar*'s many aft-mounted cannons erupted in a ball of orange flame.

"Good shot," Chakotay congratulated Tuvok. "Tare, bring us around—"

"Captain, another vessel is approaching at full impulse," Lasren called out, interrupting him.

"Can you identify it?"

But before Lasren could reply, another Klingon warship, bigger and meaner than the *Kortar*, appeared on the viewscreen and immediately opened fire upon the *Kortar*.

"It is the Chancellor Martok's flagship, the *Sword of Kahless*," Tuvok's maddeningly placid voice advised Chakotay.

Before Chakotay could smile in relief, Tare had adjusted their course, and *Voyager* joined the flagship in another barrage, which did serious damage to the *Kortar*'s port weapons array.

"The *Kortar*'s shields are failing," Tuvok called out.

Clearly outgunned, the *Kortar* quickly turned tail and began to maneuver out of orbit.

The *Sword of Kahless* let loose another volley, but before it could reach the *Kortar*, the renegade ship had jumped to warp.

"Analyze their warp trail," Chakotay ordered. "Helm, prepare to lay in a pursuit course."

"Aye, sir," Tare replied.

"Captain, we are being hailed," Lasren called.

"Onscreen."

The face of Martok appeared before Chakotay, grinning broadly.

"*Greetings, Captain Chakotay,*" Martok said.

"A pleasure, as always, Chancellor," Chakotay replied.

"*While I appreciate your assistance up to this point in subduing the* Kortar," Martok said pointedly, "*it is no longer required.*"

"Understood." Chakotay nodded.

"It appears you have dispatched ground forces as well," Martok said.

"We have."

"At the moment they appear to be outnumbered. We should remedy that."

"By all means."

"Once my troops have been deployed," Martok said, "I will pursue the Kortar."

Much as Chakotay would have liked to be the one to bring the Warriors of Gre'thor to their end, he knew better than to deny the chancellor his prize.

"Good hunting, Chancellor," Chakotay nodded, "and thank you."

"Qapla'," Martok replied, signing off.

Seconds after Tuvok confirmed transport of a hundred soldiers to the battlefield below, the Sword of Kahless jumped to warp, in pursuit of its quarry.

Knowing Martok, it would be to the ends of the known universe.

———

"Fall back!" Paris shouted.

Every meter of ground he gave up was one more meter Paris knew he would eventually have to conquer if he was ever going to see his family alive again, but it would be pointless to die standing his ground.

Disruptor blasts pounded into the ground and pulverized the solid rocks dotting the hillside. Tom threw his right hand over his shoulder and wildly fired his hand phaser to discourage pursuit. The lusty cries coming from behind him had Tom doubting it was making any difference.

Suddenly his right foot sank into a deep crevice, and Tom went flying facedown into the dust. Despite the angry, hot pain now gripping his leg, Paris forced himself to curl onto his side to keep from skidding on his stomach down the rest of the incline. His head, barely protected by his hands, hit something hard, and he came to rest in a shallow gully. Temporarily blinded by the sun, Tom automatically raised his phaser and fired wildly.

The warrior who had been pursuing him dodged these aimless shots and suddenly blocked the sun, stepping into Tom's line of sight with a *bat'leth* raised above his head, ready to strike.

Tom took better aim and fired again, but the phaser had exhausted its power supply.

With a ferocious grin the warrior began his downward stroke, and Tom pushed off the ground to his left, hoping to avoid the worst of what was coming.

But the strike never came.

Instead, Tom heard another loud cry, and the grisly thump of metal meeting flesh that was not his.

Paris quickly scrambled to his hands and knees and looked up.

The warrior who should have killed him was now teetering toward his left, as if suddenly half of his body had become too heavy for the rest to bear. A long gash ran from his right shoulder to the middle of his belly, and blood was pouring over the long blade embedded in his gut.

Behind this grim spectacle stood another Klingon, who proceeded to pull his blade—a *mek'leth*, now that Tom could see it more clearly—from his victim. The slain warrior fell to his side, mere inches from Tom's head.

With a curt nod to Tom, the victor then turned and hurried back up the hill toward a pair of Starfleet officers who were fighting hand to hand against a single Klingon attacker.

What's happening? Tom wondered dizzily. Either he'd hit his head harder than he realized or something had changed.

Tom tried to rise, but his right ankle wouldn't hold his weight. A sharp pain in his right leg also suggested that his recent surgery might need another look when all was said and done.

He steadied himself on the boulder that rested at the lip of the gully and looked out over the hillside. He could easily pick out the few Starfleet officers still standing in the melee, but now Klingons were also fighting Klingons.

Has there been a mutiny in the last few minutes? Tom wondered. Not that he minded. Any port in this storm would do just fine.

Then he realized that most of the Klingons now rampaging over the hill were wearing the distinctive black and silver of the Klingon Defense Force as opposed to the antiquated uniforms of the Warriors of Gre'thor.

Suddenly, Harry was rushing to his side. He was cradling his right arm in his left, and his uniform was torn in several places, many of which seeped fresh blood, but otherwise his injuries appeared to be superficial.

"Who are these guys?" Harry asked breathlessly when he reached Tom. "They transported in just behind the ridgeline, and I figured we were done for."

"That would be the cavalry, Harry," Paris said with a smile.

Tom had always enjoyed John Ford's movies.

The first two Warriors to reach the entrance of the sanctuary were quickly dispatched by the women on the front line. One was beheaded by a single swipe of a *bat'leth,* and the second struggled valiantly for a few moments before being surrounded by four *qawHaq'hoch* with equally lethal agendas.

As the ranks around her began to disperse, Janeway wondered why they weren't using the disruptors on their belts. Killing was killing, and it didn't seem to be less or more honorable whether done by blade or blast. But watching the *qawHaq'hoch* engage hand to hand, she realized that they had been well trained for hundreds of years in ancient battle techniques. As the next wave of unfortunate Warriors poured into the entrance, braying like wild animals, the women met their force with serene composure, moving fiercely, decidedly, and with great effect.

The admiral clutched her phaser rifle tightly, prepared to fire at the first open shot. Soon enough disruptor blasts began to fly throughout the cavern, and the ranks broke as everyone moved either to engage or to seek cover.

Janeway planted herself behind an overturned desk that had been pulled from a nearby work area and took aim at the sanctuary entrance. Firing well above the heads of the women battling there, she managed to take down one warrior who was rushing into the fray.

She aimed again, only to have her shot spoiled by an insistent tugging on her arm. Turning, she saw Seven, her rifle tossed over her shoulder, gesturing toward an opening in the cavern to her far right. Janeway barely had time to glimpse B'Elanna disappearing into it, alone.

The battle raged around them. To their credit, the *qawHaq'hoch* had things well in hand. Janeway could clearly see Maplethorpe and Waters in the middle of the fracas, teaming up on one disarmed warrior with their fists.

"B'Elanna might need our assistance," Seven said urgently.

Janeway nodded and, following Seven, ducked and dodged her way through the chaos toward the tunnel B'Elanna had disappeared down.

Over the din of battle raging above, B'Elanna strained to hear any sound that might reveal Miral's whereabouts. She doubted seriously that the *qawHaq'hoch* had left her daughter unattended. Gripping the *bat'leth* Logt had armed her with, B'Elanna refused to give her worries full rein.

B'Elanna hurried past the cell she had been held in and followed the darkened hall to a dead end.

Doubling back, she heard footsteps approaching and ducked into the shadows, raising her weapon to strike. She paused when an urgent whisper met her ears.

"B'Elanna?"

It was Admiral Janeway.

B'Elanna quickly stepped into the path of Janeway and Seven of Nine.

"I'm here."

B'Elanna greeted Janeway with a quick hug so intense it might have cracked a rib. "Thank you for coming." She looked at Seven. "Both of you."

"How did you convince Logt to allow you to join the fight?" B'Elanna asked.

"It's a long story," Janeway replied hastily, "but suffice it to say that while it might be a good day to die, I'd much prefer we all get out of here in one piece."

"We have to find Miral," B'Elanna said quickly.

"Do you have any idea where she's being held?" Janeway asked.

B'Elanna shook her head in frustration. "She has to be down here, but the rest of these cells are empty."

Seven had already pulled out her tricorder and was scanning the walls diligently.

"Anything?" Janeway asked.

"These rocks, just as those above, are quite efficient at blocking our scans," Seven replied.

"I know she's here," B'Elanna insisted.

"Admiral," Seven said, pausing at a section of the wall opposite the cell that had been B'Elanna's.

"What is it?"

"I'm not sure," Seven replied, raising her hand and running it gingerly over what looked like solid rock. "There are faint energy readings emanating from this wall. This might be the power source for those force fields."

B'Elanna hurried to her side and mimicked her movements.

When B'Elanna touched the wall, an interface panel that had been shrouded suddenly appeared.

"It must be set to activate only by a Klingon," Seven surmised.

B'Elanna was frantically searching the display for any indication of Miral's whereabouts. Finally, in frustration, she raised her *bat'leth* and drove it into the panel, which immediately spouted forth a hail of sparks.

Seconds later, the solid wall at the end of the cavern vanished to reveal twelve *qawHaq'hoch* warriors standing in an unbroken circle around one warrior who clutched a struggling Miral in her arms.

"Crude, but effective," Seven noted as she and Janeway leveled their rifles at the warriors.

"Give me my daughter!" B'Elanna bellowed.

The women stood in tense, defiant silence.

"She's not going to ask nicely again," Janeway warned.

"B'Elanna Torres!" another voice shouted from the corridor.

Wheeling around, B'Elanna saw Commander Logt rushing toward them.

"Don't make me kill these people," B'Elanna said furiously. "I'm taking my daughter back, and I really don't care anymore who is standing in my way."

Janeway and Seven moved to stand beside B'Elanna, while still keeping their weapons trained on Miral's guardians.

"The Warriors of Gre'thor who discovered the sanctuary are all but defeated," Logt said, "but more will come. We must all leave this place at once."

"If we can reach the surface safely, *Voyager* will be able to transport us out," Janeway suggested.

Logt turned her most intimidating glare upon the admiral.

"You swore to stand with us in battle," Logt cautioned Janeway. "Your life is forfeit if you break that oath."

"Well, you're welcome to try and take it from me," Janeway

replied, "but as far as I'm concerned, we've fulfilled that oath. The only issue now is what will become of Miral."

"And what of the oath you swore to me on Boreth?" B'Elanna demanded of Logt.

"I swore only to serve you faithfully until your daughter was found," Logt replied. "That, too, has been done." She stepped toward B'Elanna, clearly hoping to make her see reason. "B'Elanna, you must listen to me. The scrolls say that only the *qawHaq'hoch* will be able to protect the *Kuvah'magh*. Join us, and there will never again be a need to keep you from Miral."

B'Elanna shook her head in disbelief. Determination was one thing, but it was a fine line between that and the lunacy of Logt's suggestion.

"If you are referring to the scrolls of Ghargh, they say nothing of the kind," Seven interrupted, correcting Logt.

Logt turned fiercely on Seven. "Do not presume to teach me the truths of the faith to which I have dedicated my life!"

"Seven is right," B'Elanna said, her eyes suddenly blazing with relief. "The scrolls never mention the *qawHaq'hoch* at all."

"They refer numerous times to 'those who remember,'" Logt insisted.

"But who is to say that they meant *you*?" B'Elanna replied. "Your order wasn't founded until almost a thousand years after Ghargh wrote those words, and the founders of the order may have chosen the name *qawHaq'hoch* simply because they intended to fulfill the prophecy."

"In my experience, fate doesn't give a damn about our intentions," Janeway added.

"I can't join you, Logt," B'Elanna went on, "but I understand now what awaits Miral when she is grown, and I'll prepare her for it. There is nothing I will not sacrifice to see that she lives long enough to avert this curse, should it come to that."

"It is also possible that by bringing the genetic defect to light, Klingon scientists may discover another solution," Seven suggested. "Perhaps the true purpose of your work has been to reveal this threat long before it might otherwise have been discovered. You may already have protected the *Kuvah'magh*, not from those who wish to kill her, but from the destiny that was foretold."

"Seven has a point," Janeway added. "If you were to share your findings with the Klingon Empire and other Federation scientists, they would certainly be willing to devote whatever resources are necessary to reversing this genetic defect."

"Listen to them, Logt," B'Elanna pleaded. "Didn't Amar say that the only thing more dangerous than a secret was those who keep it?"

"No," Logt replied. "Amar said that a secret's only danger was in the keeping of it."

"I don't see the difference," B'Elanna said, shaking her head.

Logt paused, clearly torn by B'Elanna's words.

"Nor do I," she finally agreed somberly. "In all the months you studied on Boreth, B'Elanna, I never believed you had learned a thing," she went on. "Perhaps I was mistaken."

Paris stood in the transporter room, shaking with a combination of fatigue and relief.

Harry and the emperor were by his side. Kahless had already congratulated them heartily on a battle well fought, but Tom knew that had it not been for the timely appearance of Martok's men, they would all have been torn to shreds on that hillside. He could see from Harry's haunted expression that visions of the battle would probably populate his nightmares for many days to come.

Finally, the familiar whine of the transporter sounded, and the forms of Janeway, Seven, Waters, and Maple-thorpe appeared before them. Tom's heart sank as the group hustled to clear the transporter pad until, moments later, a second transport brought B'Elanna, Miral, and Logt to *Voyager*.

Tom could barely see through the tears that now poured freely from his eyes the heart-rending vision of his daughter, clinging tightly to B'Elanna.

B'Elanna rushed to his arms and Tom quickly embraced them both. Only Miral's cry of discomfort forced him to loosen his hold. Miral began to wail in earnest, and it was the most beautiful sound Tom had ever heard.

"Hello, baby," Tom said softly, gently caressing Miral's head as he kept his other arm wrapped firmly around B'Elanna's waist.

Miral's eyes fixed on his face, and she paused briefly as her cries turned to dismayed hiccups.

"Did you miss your daddy?" Tom asked lovingly.

"We both did," B'Elanna said softly.

Tom turned to B'Elanna and kissed her hungrily.

"Let's never do this again," he whispered the second his lips were free.

B'Elanna was about to reply when Miral demanded

their full attention by shouting at the top of her little lungs, "Da!"

Tom focused on her instantly, unable to believe what he had just heard.

"Da! Da!" Miral said again, opening her arms wide and reaching out to her father.

OCTOBER 2378

CHAPTER SIXTEEN

"How did it go?" Kathryn demanded the moment she opened the door of her San Francisco apartment to Chakotay.

"I could use a drink," Chakotay replied.

"That bad?"

Given the less than optimal series of events of the past two weeks, following directly on the heels of the battle at Cygnet IV, Chakotay thought his hearing with Admirals Montgomery, Upton, and Batiste had gone reasonably well. But the worry lines creasing Kathryn's brow clearly indicated that she had feared the worst.

"All things considered," Chakotay said as she gestured toward the small dining table, which had been set for two, "I think the panel was very understanding."

Kathryn stared in disbelief as she accepted a glass of merlot Chakotay offered before pouring his own.

"Define *understanding*," she requested as she sat on the sofa and fortified herself with a generous sip.

Taking this as a cue that the dinner she had replicated for them would go down better over less serious conversation, Chakotay followed Kathryn's lead and took a seat beside her.

"They were, of course, seriously displeased with my failure to complete the mission to Kerovi."

"You did try," Kathryn said defensively.

"I did," Chakotay nodded, "but apparently I don't get any points for trying."

In fact, the moment his crew had been safely returned to *Voyager*, Chakotay had immediately set course for Kerovi in hope that they would arrive before the Changeling's trial had concluded. There were far too many Klingon Defense Force warriors remaining on the planet for *Voyager* to accommodate, so Kahless had offered to remain on Cygnet IV with them. A brisk communication with the Klingon authorities had assured the captain that a a ship would be dispatched immediately to collect Martok's soldiers. To Chakotay's amazement, Kahless had also agreed to accept Commander Logt back into his service as his personal guard. She had remained on the planet, no doubt doing what she could to assess the damages sustained by the *qawHaq'hoch* at the hands of the Warriors of Gre'thor.

Last Chakotay had heard, the *Kortar* had continued to elude Martok, though several ships in the Klingon fleet had joined the hunt. This loose end troubled Chakotay considerably, because he knew it would cause B'Elanna and Tom no end of worry.

As soon as *Voyager* had entered Kerovian space, they had been met by an armed fleet of vessels and ordered to turn back. Chakotay was advised that the Changeling they had come to interrogate was dead, and their presence was no longer required or welcomed.

Based on his last conversation with Montgomery, Chakotay had feared that the Kerovian government had caved to public pressure and executed their prisoner. Janeway had used some of her back-channel contacts to learn that the Changeling had actually attempted to escape custody just before the trial began, and had been killed.

"Given the fact that you helped uncover a serious threat to the health and well-being of the Klingon Empire, I would have hoped that the panel would at least understand your decision to delay the mission to Kerovi. It's not as if you could have known that the Changeling would be killed before you arrived," Kathryn argued.

"They rightly pointed out that I made my choice to alter course based on my personal relationship with B'Elanna and Miral. I didn't know that by pursuing that course, I would be providing assistance to our allies, so even though the mission was an unqualified success, they're still concerned about my judgment," Chakotay replied.

"That's ridiculous," Janeway said, as if she were the one whose judgment was being called into question. As she had backed Chakotay every step of the way between Earth and Cygnet IV, in a manner of speaking, it was.

"I actually believe I was spared a harsher punishment because Martok sent an official commendation to Starfleet for my meritorious service to the empire, expressing his gratitude for our 'assistance' and noting Tom Paris's diplomatic skills."

Kathryn actually chuckled at this. "How thoughtful of him."

"And I'm also willing to bet that you're in more trouble over this mess than I am."

The admiral rose from the couch and moved to gaze out the window. Finally she replied, "You let me worry about my troubles, all right?"

Chakotay set his wineglass on the table and sat up, studying her face. She was smiling faintly, but there was a glint of steel in her eyes that was usually reserved for battle. "I did advise the admirals that I take full responsibility for the mission, its accomplishments and its failures," he said seriously.

"That's very kind of you, but we both know that's not how it works," she said with a sigh. "I was the ranking officer. I think they expected me to drag you to Kerovi, kicking and screaming, if that's what it took. Failing that, I should have assumed command and followed their orders over your protests."

"It's too bad they don't know you better than that."

"And it's comforting that you do."

After a pause Kathryn was obviously ready to change the subject.

"I understand the Doctor, Seven, and Doctor Kaz presented a joint report to the High Council outlining their findings, and their analysis will be studied further. The Doctor in particular is quite optimistic that with further research, they will be able to find a cure for this so-called Curse of the Gods."

"Are Seven and the Doctor back at the Institute then?" Chakotay asked.

Kathryn nodded. "Though I'm not sure how long that will last."

"You noticed the tension between them too?"

"Hard to miss it. The Institute is lucky to have them, but I think it would be best, in the long term, for both of them to broaden their horizons," she said. "At any rate, I'm not sure that pure theoretical research is the best use of either of their considerable abilities."

"Did you have something else specific in mind?" Chakotay asked.

"Not really." She shook her head ponderously.

Chakotay sensed a weariness in her that was usually reserved for her more introspective moments.

"I owe you my thanks, Kathryn," he said gently, "and not just for backing me up with Command."

"By my count we're a long way from even," she responded enigmatically.

At first Chakotay didn't know how to take this, but she clarified when she saw his puzzled expression.

"You had my back every single day we spent in the Delta quadrant, even when you didn't agree with me," she said thoughtfully.

"That was my job."

Kathryn paused.

"It was more than that."

Chakotay allowed her statement to hang unanswered in the air between them. Beyond this point lay dragons, and both of them knew it. Much as he wanted to open his heart, experience had taught him caution, especially when it came to Kathryn.

"I'm sorry," she said, shaking her head ruefully. "I've spent the last four days with Captain Eden, reliving in gory detail every single thing I could remember, and a lot of things I wanted to forget, about the Delta quadrant."

Chakotay finally understood what had triggered her mood. His sessions with Eden had been equally arduous, but more than a month had passed since then, and he'd been too busy in the interim to dwell on the tangle of emotions those interviews had forced to the surface of his mind. Now more than ever, he was content to leave those things in the past. What mattered was the future.

"Do you have any idea why Starfleet is digging into all of this now?" he asked. "It's been almost a year, and it seems like an abrupt policy change, especially when you consider how cursory their review was when we first got home." It was the first question that had come to mind when he'd met with Eden, and one that she had consistently evaded answering.

Kathryn's eyes met his, and he was immediately concerned by the hint of fear that flickered there.

"I don't know anything for certain," she said, choosing her words carefully. "Let's just say I've heard some decidedly unpleasant rumors."

Chakotay knew better than to ask more, though he was positively dying to do so.

"Have you received new orders yet?" she asked.

"Actually, yes," he replied. "Our next illustrious mission is a diplomatic transport to Cestus III. It's not even an ambassador. We're ferrying key staff members. I'm trying not to take it personally." He went on, "After that hearing today, I can't help but feel they're trying to keep me on a short leash until they're certain they didn't make a mistake by giving me command of *Voyager*. I wouldn't be surprised if our next several missions are equally inspiring."

"Be careful what you wish for," Kathryn tossed back.

Again Chakotay had the sense that there was something really troubling her that she could not or would not share right now.

"How about you?" he asked, knowing full well she

would continue to deflect his interest until she was good and ready.

"After acknowledging my more serious lapses, my fellow admirals gave me a slap on the wrist for failing to read communiqués in a timely manner and for ordering Tuvok to steal that *bat'leth*. I'm pretty sure I'll be chained to my desk for the foreseeable future."

"They'll have to make those chains out of tritanium if they expect to hold you there," Chakotay teased.

"Don't count on it," Kathryn replied seriously. "In fact, I think we'd both do well to lay low and toe the line, at least for a while. Starfleet Command can be patient, but not infinitely so."

Chakotay nodded, before doing his best to bring some levity to the moment.

"Didn't Tuvok return the *bat'leth* to its rightful owner on his way back to Earth?" he asked. "You didn't order him to steal it, so much as borrow it, right?"

Kathryn smiled. "He did. He told me he'd given his word, and you know how Tuvok is about promises."

Chakotay knew all too well. *Duty* and *honor* weren't just words to Tuvok. They defined the man.

"Did he ever fully brief you on his mission to retrieve the *bat'leth*?" Chakotay wondered aloud.

"No," she replied. "He seemed almost . . . I guess *embarrassed* isn't the right word, but I believe there's more to the story there than either of us will ever know."

"Has summer session begun at the Academy?"

"In a few days." Janeway smiled. "I'm sure Tuvok is back to doing his usual exceptional job, even if his students don't see it that way right now."

"It was fun having him at tactical again," Chakotay mused.

"I bet it was," Kathryn said nostalgically.

There was a brief lull as Chakotay was struck by the realization that only a few weeks ago, those nearest and dearest to him had once again been united in facing a common foe. It was hard to accept the idea that it was probably the last time that would ever be true again.

The future beckoned.

"I don't know about you, but I'm starved," Chakotay finally said.

"Then you're in luck," Kathryn said, rising and moving toward the table.

Chakotay bit back the response that came immediately to mind. *Luck* probably wasn't the right word when it came to Kathryn's cooking. He would never refuse an invitation, simply for the company. Coffee was the only consumable item Kathryn ever did justice to without a replicator's help, and even then the results were sometimes iffy at best.

He looked up in time to see the admiral glaring at him mischievously. Clearly she'd been reading his mind.

"I was talking with Mother earlier this afternoon—she sends her regards, by the way—and when I told her you were coming for dinner and that I was making her stew, she insisted on preparing it herself and transporting it over. She still doesn't trust me with the replicator at home, let alone anything made from scratch."

Chakotay tried not to let his relief show. "That was very kind of her," he said diplomatically. "Please pass along my thanks."

"Shut up," Kathryn said curtly.

"Yes, ma'am."

Julia and Owen Paris sat in their living room trying to ignore the muted shouting that had been coming from Tom and B'Elanna's upstairs room for the last hour.

Miral was snoring softly in Julia's arms. When Julia had received word that both B'Elanna and Miral were safe and would be returning to Earth with Tom, she had doubted her ears. She had given up her husband for lost on more than one occasion, and spent four long years in limbo, wondering if she would ever learn of her son's fate, only to have him restored to her. Cheating death once again had seemed like too much to ask of fate.

But somehow, her son had performed a miracle and her beloved granddaughter was sleeping peacefully while her parents were turning what should have been a time of grateful celebration into further strife.

Julia shook her head in frustration. *Didn't they realize how precious life was? Didn't they understand that every moment they were given to spend together was a blessing?* Whatever they were disagreeing about amounted to nothing in the face of the alternative.

Perhaps this was a truth one learned only with time. But if youth was wasted on the young, the wisdom of age didn't have to be.

Julia turned to Owen. She saw that his thoughts mirrored hers and wondered at the fact that they didn't need to say a word for her to know this. Their hearts were safe in one another's keeping, and their deepest fears, dreams, and desires were so entwined it was impossible to know where one's began and the other's ended.

Julia moved to gently transfer Miral to her husband's

arms, but he stayed her, placing a soft hand on her knee. He stared into her eyes, offering love and reassurance, kissed her lightly on the cheek, then rose and turned toward the staircase.

"This is getting us nowhere," Tom said wearily.

"That's because you're not listening to me," B'Elanna insisted.

"Just tell me what you want to do," Tom replied, sitting dejectedly on the end of their bed.

"It's not that simple."

It could be, Tom thought.

Tom couldn't believe that after surviving one of the most brutal series of events imaginable, they had emerged unscathed but were now at more deeply entrenched cross-purposes than they had been when Miral was still a prisoner of the *qawHaq'hoch*.

"I can't go back to *Voyager* with you," B'Elanna said.

"I think we've established that," Tom shot back.

He knew Chakotay would be thrilled to have her in engineering, even just in a part-time, advisory capacity, and since Miral was still an infant, they had at least a couple of years together before her education would become a serious concern. It seemed like the perfect and obvious solution, until he had suggested it to his wife as a *fait accompli*.

"And I can't possibly stay here," B'Elanna added unnecessarily.

Tom's parents would have jumped at the chance to have B'Elanna and Miral stay with them, until they'd found other, more permanent lodgings. This was the only suggestion that seemed more unpalatable to B'Elanna than returning to active duty.

"Again, I agree. What do you want to do?" Tom said.

He was exhausted. They'd been trampling over this ground for days and seemed no closer to a compromise. At this point, if she'd said she wanted to join a circus he would have seriously considered the idea.

Anything but this never-ending argument.

They were interrupted by a soft knock at the door. Both turned at the sound, guilt and grief clear on their faces. B'Elanna recovered first and threw Tom a look that said *Get rid of them*. Before Tom could even rise to greet whichever of his parents was on the other side, the door opened and Owen stepped into the room.

"Hi, Dad," Tom said, resigned.

"Is Miral all right?" B'Elanna asked softly.

"She's fine," Owen replied. "It's you two I'm worried about."

"We'll be all right, Dad," Tom said, rising to face his father. "We've just got a few things to work out."

Owen stared hard at his son, then turned an equally disappointed face to B'Elanna.

"You have no idea how lucky you both are," Owen said softly. "You have your health, your family, and your whole lives in front of you. I understand that reasonable people can disagree from time to time, and you've had more than your fair share of challenges to overcome, but this is not the way two people who love and respect one another behave."

"Owen—" B'Elanna began, but he silenced her with a glance.

"You have just been given a second chance at a life together. The threat of losing your daughter should have brought you closer to one another. Instead, it seems to be tearing you apart, and for the life of me I can't understand why you don't see that you're both throwing away happiness with both hands.

"Every single thing I have ever achieved with my life, my work, and my family would feel meaningless without my wife by my side. Powers rise and fall. Leaders come and go. History makes a mockery of our best-laid plans. In the end, you are left with only those things you have shared with one another. The bond you created when you decided to marry is sacred and not to be taken lightly. If you nurture it, it will sustain you through the darkness. But if you treat it carelessly, if you allow the safe haven of your life together to become a battlefield, it will never survive. For the sake of the child you created, and for the sake of the love that brought you together in the first place, you must learn to disagree with one another patiently. There is a solution to whatever obstacle you are facing right now. And I guarantee you it will be easier to find if you work together."

Owen paused to let his words sink in.

"Good night," he said softly, and left the room without a backward glance.

Tom watched him go, then moved toward B'Elanna and took her in his arms.

"I'm sorry," he whispered.

"So am I."

They held one another long enough for their hearts to find the same calm rhythm.

"Let's sleep on it," Tom suggested. "Maybe in the morning—"

B'Elanna silenced him with a gentle kiss.

Three hours later, as Tom slept deeply, B'Elanna rose from their bed and slipped quietly from the room. Miral was sleeping in a crib in Owen and Julia's room. They had suggested this when Tom and B'Elanna had come to stay a week earlier, and it seemed like a good idea at the time, though B'Elanna still slept fitfully when Miral was not nestled beside her. Tom's parents rightly believed that their son and daughter-in-law needed at least a few nights of uninterrupted rest. B'Elanna had agreed at first, but had quickly become impatient, unable to put into words the panic that still choked her when she awakened abruptly in the darkness and Miral was not there.

After pausing briefly at Owen and Julia's bedroom door and peeking her head into the small opening to see Miral sleeping, B'Elanna crept downstairs to Owen's private office and quickly worked the companel.

After a few moments, the face of Kahless appeared on the screen on Owen's desk. When they had parted, he had provided her with a secured frequency on which he assured her he could always be reached. They had spoken almost daily since then.

"Is there any word yet from Martok?" was always B'Elanna's first question.

"*No,*" Kahless replied. "*The chancellor can search from now until the end of days, but he will not find the* Kortar. *Even if he does, as long as one Warrior of Gre'thor still lives, the* d'k'tahg *resting at your throat will remain.*"

"I keep trying to explain that to Tom, but he thinks I'm *being irrational.*"

"Do not fault him, B'Elanna," Kahless chided her. *"He is not Klingon. He does not understand tenacity the way we do. He is a brave man and a valiant warrior, but he is only human."*

B'Elanna's deepest wish since the day she'd realized that she was half Klingon and half human had been to be *only* human. Tonight she would have sacrificed anything to make it so.

"Then you still believe they will come after Miral again."

"The Warriors of Gre'thor have spent a thousand years with a single purpose. They will work daily to fulfill that purpose until the last of the qawHaq'hoch *and the* Kuvah'magh *are dead."*

B'Elanna's heart rose to her throat. Angry tears threatened to pour forth.

"Wherever I go, I am placing the lives of those I love at risk," B'Elanna said, finally putting into simple words the truth she had been trying to make Tom see for days.

"Then we must find a way to make them believe that your child is dead," Kahless said simply.

His words stung like a sharp slap.

"How are we going to do that?"

"It will take time and planning, but it must be done," Kahless assured her.

B'Elanna could not imagine what might be necessary to pull off such a deception, but she had been floating in a dark sea of indecision for so many days, with fear her only constant companion. The emperor's plan, *any plan,* was a lifesaving rope tossed to her only seconds before drowning.

"What do I have to do first?" she asked.

She could not have been more surprised by the emperor's response.

"I want you to tell me everything you know of the mobile emitter that your holographic friend uses to travel independently," Kahless replied.

The explanation would take hours, but it would be more productive than tossing and turning beside her sleeping husband.

With the refreshing reality of a simple question before her to which she knew the answer, B'Elanna began to speak.

CHAPTER SEVENTEEN

The first message the Doctor received upon his return to the Federation Research Institute was a hundred-thousand-word opus from Doctor Deegle. It listed the many faults he had found with the presentation he, Seven, and Doctor Kaz had made to the Klingon High Council. While debating simply trashing Deegle's thesis out of spite, the Doctor noticed a message marked urgent from Lieutenant Barclay. In a matter of seconds he had digested the text and hurriedly contacted the Institute's personnel liaison to advise her that though he had just returned from Qo'noS, he would once again be leaving immediately for Jupiter Station.

En route, he had fretted that the cellular degradation that had threatened his creator, Doctor Lewis Zimmerman, and that the Doctor had successfully treated over a year and a half earlier, might have returned, and he spent most of the trip reviewing his research on the condition along with relevant new journal articles. The Doctor had written frequent updates to Zimmerman since their first real meeting, but he had always intended to reconnect personally with his cantankerous creator and even held out hopes that the tenuous connection they had made might be nurtured and over time grow into a more collegial relationship. But between his work at the Institute and the occasional emergent crisis with his former crew, he had yet to make good on that intention and now worried that he might never have the chance. Reg's message had been typically vague: *"You are urgently needed at Jupiter Station. Dr. Z requires you immediately."*

It was something of a shock when he entered the lab to find Haley, the Doctor's petite blonde holographic assistant of many years, sharing a laugh with Lieutenant Barclay over an adjustment Reg had made to Zimmerman's holograph pet iguana, Leonard, which had caused the creature to begin singing Klingon opera at random intervals.

"What's happened?" the Doctor interrupted to ask.

"Oh, Doctor," Reg said warmly. "You got my message."

"I did. What's wrong with Doctor Zimmerman?"

Haley and Reg shared a look of confusion.

"Nothing," Haley replied, "but it's awfully nice to see you again. How have you been?"

Before the Doctor could respond, the door to Zimmerman's lab swished open and the man emerged without looking up, saying, "I hope you're not planning to get any sleep over the next few days, Lieutenant Barclay, because Leonard has been permanently transferred to your quarters and will remain there until his vocal subroutines have been . . ."

The Doctor found himself involuntarily straightening up and squaring his shoulders at the sight of his designer, a man who was the spitting image of the Doctor, with the exception of the deep worry lines that betrayed the years that had passed since he first introduced the EMH Mark I. The Doctor noted that Zimmerman's hair—unruly and grayer than the last time they'd met—had been restored to its pre-illness dark brown sheen.

Somewhere in the Doctor's subroutines was buried a file that demanded that he always present himself in the best possible light when in Zimmerman's presence, though that file was certainly not part of his original programming. It had undoubtedly evolved, along with many other similar proclivities, as he had grown in his sense of self and his commitment to exceed his and Zimmerman's expectations.

"Hello, Doctor Zimmerman," he said pleasantly.

Zimmerman stopped mid-sentence to glare at the EMH.

"Oh, God," he said, "am I dying again?"

"I certainly hope not," the Doctor replied, "but if you are, you have summoned the right hologram."

"You're not dying, Doctor Z," Reg assured him. "Don't you remember I told you I was going to contact the Doctor about our new project?"

"Reg, we've been working together for years now," Zimmerman replied. "How is it you haven't yet noticed that I rarely listen to anything you tell me?"

"What new project?" the EMH asked.

Zimmerman heaved a weary sigh, then began to walk in a tight circle around the hologram, studying him carefully.

The Doctor had the immediate and uncomfortable thought that he had somehow lost his clothing between here and the door.

"Why are you out of uniform?" Zimmerman demanded. "Did they run you out of Starfleet after that holographic rights nonsense a few months ago?"

The Doctor bristled under Zimmerman's scrutiny.

"No one has run me out of anything," the Doctor replied officiously. "I was invited to work with the Federation Research Institute and have been there in a civilian capacity for the last several months, among the other great minds of this generation."

"I see you haven't lost your sense of self-importance." Zimmerman scowled. "Never forget that I could change that with a few well-placed tweaks to your subroutines."

The Doctor noticed Reg and Haley easing their way out of the room toward the small recreation area. With a nod he encouraged them to keep moving before turning to face his maker.

"Doctor Zimmerman, I came here at Reg's request and was concerned that you might not be well. As there is nothing I can do to improve your sense of etiquette or decorum, and you are clearly in excellent health, I will be happy to leave you in peace and return to my other obligations, which I assure you are most pressing."

Zimmerman chuckled faintly.

"It's good to see you too."

The Doctor paused to accept what passed for warmth from Zimmerman.

"Get in here," Zimmerman ordered, turning toward his holographic research lab.

The Doctor followed him into the inner sanctum, amazed at the number of memory algorithms that immediately began to run, recounting the weeks he had spent struggling desperately to save the life of a man who hadn't respected him, much less believed him capable of such a miracle.

"Why the hell did you allow yourself to get caught up with that idiotic Oliver Baines?" Zimmerman demanded once the doors had hissed shut.

The EMH was about to respond when he realized that for Zimmerman to know about Oliver Baines, he must at least have been reading the Doctor's updates, if not responding to them. The thought brought a smirk to the Doctor's lips.

"While I cannot condone Baines's methods, I do not consider the rights of holograms to be idiotic," he replied evenly.

"Holograms aren't sentient, Mark I," Zimmerman shot back.

"Present company excluded," the Doctor insisted.

Zimmerman rolled his eyes, an unnerving sight as the Doctor hadn't realized until that moment how annoying that gesture must be when he made it himself.

"You're a special case," Zimmerman conceded. "I can count on a couple of fingers the number of times any hologram I have created or read about has demonstrated characteristics which suggest sentience, and until that changes, the thought of you lending your support to a nonissue strikes me as a waste of good programming."

"I am living proof that holograms have the capacity—" the Doctor began to argue.

"The *potential capacity*," Zimmerman corrected him. "And you're not here to debate the issue with the preeminent authority on the subject."

The Doctor found himself smiling again.

Despite his protestations to the contrary, Reg clearly hadn't been acting alone when he summoned the EMH to Jupiter Station, though he knew full well Zimmerman would argue himself hoarse before he would admit it.

"Then why am I here?" the Doctor asked.

"You're here because if left to your own devices you will run completely amok."

"I beg your pardon," the Doctor retorted.

"You disagree? All right, let's take a little stroll through your memory buffers. For seven years your program was forced to evolve and adapt beyond anyone's wildest expectations. And the minute you get home, instead of charting a course which would continue to challenge your limits, you settled for babysitting."

"I was helping a friend," the Doctor interjected hastily. "Interpersonal relationships—"

"Are important, I agree," Zimmerman went on. "But I must admit, after the alterations you made to your physical parameters in the Delta quadrant, I didn't expect you to content yourself with mere platonic friendships. They are not the only arena in which you must continue to expand, especially if you don't want it to shrivel up and fall off."

As the Doctor considered the impossibility of this disturbing image, Zimmerman continued.

"Then, you run off and join the egghead brigade—"

"The Institute contains some of the finest minds—"

"I've met most of them," Zimmerman countered, "and a bigger pack of blowhards I never hope to meet again."

As the EMH agreed, at least in principle, he found it difficult to come up with an instantaneous retort.

"They're about theory," Zimmerman continued. "They'll think a thing to death and then suck on its bones. What they do isn't living, and if you're going to continue to advance, you need to start living again."

The Doctor found himself silenced by the admonishment, primarily because it had not occurred to him that he had not been living until this moment. What had occurred to him, numerous times in the last several months, was the fact that he wasn't nearly as happy as he used to be. The Doctor associated this sense with the loss of daily interaction with his friends aboard *Voyager*, and realized that he had actually felt at his best and most useful when he was working by their sides to aid B'Elanna and Miral.

When he used to imagine his life in the Alpha quadrant, should *Voyager* ever make it that far, his dreams had been varied, but had included every aspect of his personality he had begun to develop while on *Voyager*: continuing his medical work, to be sure, but also the occasional musical recital, completing an exhibit of his holovid record of *Voyager*'s journey, and certainly, the hope that at some point he might meet someone with whom he could continue to explore a deep interpersonal relationship.

It shocked him to realize that he had done none of these things, and though he might have more time than organic life-forms, it was still too precious a commodity to squander.

"You're right," the Doctor said dolefully.

"Of course I'm right," Zimmerman replied. "Now what are you going to do about it?"

The Doctor didn't have a ready answer.

"While your subroutines are twisting themselves into cascade failure, do you mind if I make a suggestion?" Zimmerman asked.

The Doctor nodded. "Please."

By the end of the afternoon the Doctor had submitted a letter to the Federation Research Institute indicating that for the foreseeable future, he would be working in a full-time capacity with Doctor Zimmerman. He would, of course, continue to make himself available to the Institute on a project-by-project basis, should the need arise. When this was done, the Doctor went to work composing a lengthy letter to the only person who he expected to be even a little dismayed by his choice: Seven. Once he had heard the broad strokes of Zimmerman's new research and considered the practical applications, his imagination and enthusiasm had been fired in a way he could never remember experiencing. The Doctor had already suggested to Zimmerman that Seven would be an invaluable addition to their team, and though his creator hadn't argued the fact, he had encouraged the Doctor not to get his hopes up when it came to Seven of Nine.

Experience had already taught the Doctor that lesson all too well. He extended the invitation nonetheless, but wasn't surprised a few days later when he received her brisk refusal.

As Captain Eden had expected, she had been among the very last to learn of Willem's plans.

After finally spending the better part of a week interviewing Admiral Janeway, an experience that left Eden with a profound respect for the challenges Janeway had endured and in awe of her devotion to duty, the captain had finally completed her analysis and forwarded it to Admiral Montgomery. She had expected to hear from Willem within a few hours of transmitting it, but instead there was frustrating silence.

Determined to put it out of her mind, Eden had decided to spend the weekend in Paris, where the Louvre was featuring a spectacular new exhibit of several newly discovered paintings by D'Mack of Vulcan. While staring at the most impressive rendering of a sandstorm she'd ever seen, she'd run into Admiral Upton, who was touring the museum with his wife and young daughter. He'd been gracious enough to compliment Eden on her work and her report, though he admitted he hadn't had a chance to study it as deeply as he intended. He'd then proceeded to inquire as to how Batiste was taking Command's denial of his proposal regarding *Voyager*. She'd been forced to admit that she had no idea, and was further humiliated when she'd had to remind Upton that she and Willem were no longer married.

The admiral had seemed appropriately mortified by his gaffe and apologized profusely. She'd met Upton only a handful of times and wasn't terribly surprised that he wasn't current on the state of her personal life.

As Willem had apparently used her analysis in support of his argument, Upton had assumed that Eden was fully briefed on the proposal. He suggested that if she and Batiste were serious about making better use of *Voyager*'s unique resources, they might start by looking a little closer to home. By silently pretending to know much more than she did, Eden had managed to get the gist of Willem's plan out of Upton before excusing herself politely and hurrying from the exhibit. Propriety suggested it was a good idea not to allow one's head to explode in front of a superior officer in a public place.

Eden had returned to San Francisco determined to confront Willem at once. He lived only three kilometers from her apartment, and she debated walking the brief distance in the cool moonlit air to clear her head and take the edge off the heat her anger was generating. Finally, she decided that Willem had earned that anger honestly and should be spared none of it.

She rang his door chime three times before the doors slid open and she heard a muffled, "Come in," from the direction of Willem's bedroom.

This was the apartment they had shared when they'd been married. Willem had offered to allow her to continue living there when they'd separated, but Eden had found the notion unimaginable. Entering the living room and noting that the honeymoon picture of the two of them sunbathing on one of Delgara's most exclusive private beaches no longer hung over the mantel was enough to stir up dozens of less pleasant memories of their last weeks together.

"Give me just a minute," Willem called from behind the closed bedroom door.

Eden assumed he knew it was her. She couldn't imagine that he opened his front door willingly to strangers.

Then again, he always has been a cocky son of a bitch.

Briefly she wondered if he was alone. Ultimately it didn't matter. She was here on business and she honestly didn't care who heard what she had to say to him.

Eden planted herself, arms crossed, before the large screen that had replaced their honeymoon photo. A quick scan of the rest of the visible living spaces told her that Willem's housekeeping had gone to seed since they'd separated. Unruly stacks of padds littered the coffee table amid several tall glasses, some still half filled with tea. The bookshelf on the far wall was overflowing with dozens of old tomes. Willem was one of the few people she knew who actually liked to read for pleasure from bound manuscripts rather than padds. Isolinear chips were scattered haphazardly about.

The dining table was filled with more used dishes. It looked as if he'd just finished throwing a party, but Eden knew he had not. She could count on one hand the times he had grudgingly agreed to entertain their friends while they'd been married.

A pile of dirty rags and a pungent metallic odor suggested he'd recently cleaned the golf clubs that had been placed in a corner of the dining area; they were arranged fastidiously in their bag. The things he chose to care about never ceased to amaze her.

Not that any of this is my concern any longer, she reminded herself. If Willem wanted to live like a wildebeest, that was his business.

He finally emerged from the bedroom wearing a tattered old robe she'd offered to replace numerous times but to no avail. Like a child's favorite blanket, Willem had insisted on keeping it. It was his attire of choice for sitting around the house.

She almost gasped in alarm when he stepped far enough into the room's dim lighting for her to see the haggard, drawn expression he wore.

"You look like hell," she said involuntarily, and with more compassion than she'd intended.

He offered her a wan smile before setting himself down gingerly on the sofa.

"And you look angrier than one of hell's demons," he replied wearily.

If Afsarah had truly hated him, this might have been all the impetus she would have needed to launch her attack. But she didn't hate him. Eden no longer missed or needed him, but she could never hate him. Even loathing might not have been enough to counter the concern she found welling inside her at the sight of his feverish face and lethargic limbs.

"What's wrong?" she asked, seating herself on the arm of the chair angled to the far side of the sofa.

"Nothing a few days' rest won't cure," he replied dismissively.

"Have you seen a doctor?"

"I have." He nodded.

"And?"

"And he has seen me."

"Willem!"

"And he said I'm going to be fine if I take it easy for a few days," he replied a bit testily.

Eden didn't believe him. But she also knew she could sit here and grow old before he'd tell her more. Willem avoided doctors as though he was allergic to them. If he had gone to Starfleet Medical, it could only mean that whatever ailed him was too frightening or painful to ignore.

"Now why don't you tell me what made you storm over here at this hour," he said.

Eden tried to summon some of her frustration, along with the choice words she'd planned to express it with, but found instead only a resigned sigh.

"Why didn't you tell me what you were planning to propose to Command?" she asked.

"Would it have made a difference in the contents of your report, or the speed with which you completed it?"

Eden considered the question. Finally she uttered her disquieting but honest response.

"It might have."

A sad smile traipsed across Willem's lips.

"I guess I wanted the proposal to be considered on its merits. I felt that the potential for discovery, bolstered by your objective analysis, would be sufficient to win the day," Batiste said.

Eden shook her head. "You didn't make admiral with that much of your naïveté still intact."

"All right," he admitted. "I didn't count on the strenuousness of Admiral Janeway's objections."

"You want to send her former crew *back* to the Delta quadrant," Eden said in exasperation. "She risked everything to bring them home safely. She overcame impossible odds and ridiculous obstacles for seven years straight. More times than I care to count, any sane person would have turned back, found a nice little planet to settle down on, and cut their losses, and every single time she was faced with that choice she flat-out refused. She successfully negotiated safe passage from the Borg, for crying out loud. *And you didn't think she'd mind?*"

"This is different," Willem countered abruptly.

"How?"

"With our recent advances in slipstream technology, there's almost no risk that a new exploratory mission would be stranded again."

"Slipstream is untested."

"For now. Six months from now that won't be true, and it will take at least that long to assemble the fleet we'll need."

"Don't say 'we,'" she corrected him. "This is your pipe dream, not mine."

"I thought you agreed with me."

"Why would you think that?"

"Twenty-nine times in your analysis you recommended that key discoveries made by *Voyager* warranted follow-up."

"From the Alpha quadrant," Eden replied.

"You know that won't happen," he shot back. "And you also know that *Voyager* only scratched the surface of what's there to be discovered. The previously unknown life-forms alone, never mind the weaknesses they discovered and were able to use to their advantage against the Borg—"

"Were largely due to the presence of Seven of Nine," she finished for him. "Just because she's home now, that doesn't mean she's forgotten anything about the Collective. She can tell us everything we might need to know."

"The Borg *adapt*, Afsarah. The next time we meet them, they won't be the same Collective she left behind, and we both know that."

"You're worried about a Borg attack?" Eden asked. "That's why you're so fired up about this?"

"I'm worried about a lot of things."

Eden studied his inscrutable face. Much as she wanted to tell him to let this go, to gracefully accept Starfleet's denial and move on, his obvious disappointment, coupled with her personal curiosity, silenced her. She would never in a million years have concocted Willem's proposal, nor would she have had the gall to submit it to Starfleet, but she had to admit that in some ways, Willem was right.

No one knew the current status of the Borg, or their transwarp network, which obviously had at some point extended to the Alpha quadrant. *Voyager* had destroyed one hub before they had returned home, but clearly the Borg possessed the technology to re-create it. It might take a while, but all the Borg needed was a reason, and who was to say that they might not set their sights on the Federation, or the ship that had bested them time and again.

Come to think of it, the Borg don't even need a reason.

All they needed was time.

The thought made Eden's blood run cold.

She had been prepared to read him the riot act for using her work to support an argument she would never have made. A few minutes later, she was left wondering why she hadn't seen all along that as difficult and dangerous as this mission might be, the Federation's continued existence could depend upon it.

"Why does it have to be *Voyager*?" she asked.

"Who would you send—a crew that's actually been there or one that has read about it in somebody else's logs?"

"Janeway will never approve the mission."

"It's not entirely her call to make. Obviously Command is going to weigh her recommendations heavily, and for now they agree that there is no 'pressing need' for the mission. But I for one don't want to be sitting around here with my pants down when that 'pressing need' shows up looking to assimilate me."

Suddenly Willem caught his breath. He strained for a moment in obvious pain before shuddering into a more relaxed posture.

Eden rose.

"You should get some rest," she said softly, turning to go.

"Afsarah," he called after her.

"What?"

"I'm sorry. I should have told you my intentions."

She didn't turn back. "Damn straight you should have."

Instead of transporting home, she entered her office a little after midnight and began to revise her analysis, focusing considerable attention on those things *Voyager* had discovered about the Borg, but more importantly, on the many remaining unanswered questions about the Collective.

JUNE 2379

CHAPTER EIGHTEEN

Janeway sat in the shuttle's aft compartment alone, waiting for Decan to inform her that they had received clearance to depart from Proxima Station.

Her evening with Chakotay had gone longer than she'd planned, but it had been well worth the trip to meet with him while *Voyager* was undergoing some routine repairs so near to Earth. She found herself smiling frequently since she'd left Chakotay's quarters and a little unnerved by a newfound lightness in her step and the pleasant warmth that washed through her when she cast her thoughts back to the previous night. *Giddy as a schoolgirl.*

All evidence to the contrary.

The admiral was, however, anxious to depart. Her mission successfully accomplished, she only worried that it might have cost her one last chance to connect with someone most dear to her.

"*Admiral Janeway?*" Decan called from the cockpit.

"Are we on our way?"

"*Just a few more minutes.*"

"If we don't make it back to Earth by noon tomorrow, I'm going to find a new aide, Decan."

"*I will bear that in mind, Admiral.*"

It was a sign of how much she'd come to depend upon him that neither of them ever took her threat seriously, no matter how many times she'd made it.

As there was nothing more to do, Janeway considered settling in for a nap during the return trip. Heaven knew she could use the rest, as there was no end of work waiting for her back in San Francisco. Instead, she found herself pulling out the small travel case she'd packed for the trip and always had on hand in case of an emergency. Beneath the personal padds, clean uniform, and toiletries, she found the item she was looking for. It lay in a small compartment, next to a beautiful silver watch.

She retrieved it and placed it in the palm of her hand, smiling at the remembrances it brought back. The item was a small wooden box with intricate symbols carved on its face and sides.

Looks like I'm going to have to find those original designs, she mused.

"Admiral?" Decan's voice interrupted her reverie.

"What is it?"

"Incoming transmission from Commander Tuvok."

"Damn it," Janeway muttered. "Put it through."

Seconds later, Tuvok's face appeared on the viewscreen before her.

"Good evening, Admiral," he greeted her.

"When are you leaving Earth?" she asked immediately.

"Within the hour," he replied.

"Damn it," she said again. "I'm so sorry, Tuvok. I really wanted to see you before you left."

"I appreciate the sentiment, Admiral, but there is no need. Although seeing you once again in person would have been gratifying, I can as easily bid you farewell in this manner."

Janeway didn't bother trying to explain her completely irrational sense that she *should* meet with Tuvok before he departed for Vulcan. His family was reuniting there for an extended vacation, an event it had taken months to schedule, despite the fact that three of Tuvok's four children, Sek, Varith, and Asil, still made their home there. Tuvok had mentioned that his third son was not coming. Elieth had relocated to Deneva after *Voyager* was lost and married a woman, Ione, whom Tuvok had yet to meet. While *she* knew he was hurt, her Vulcan friend would deny it. It was going to be a long summer without him.

"Promise me you'll pass along my regards to T'Pel and the rest of your family," she requested.

"Of course, Admiral."

"Did you speak to Seven?"

"I did. She is quite amenable to the idea of joining the faculty at the Academy for the summer session. If all goes well, I believe she may choose to stay on."

"She's not happy at the Institute any longer, is she?" Janeway asked.

"She did not advise me of any particular dissatisfaction. However, since the Doctor altered his schedule with the group last year, and given the enthusiasm with which she responded to my inquiry, logic suggests that she no longer found her work at the Institute as satisfying as in the past."

"She was enthusiastic?"

"She said yes."

Janeway shrugged. For Seven, that probably was as close to enthusiasm as one could hope for.

"And did you advise the Academy of your future plans?" she asked.

"I intend to discuss the matter further with my family before I make a final decision."

The decision Tuvok was wrestling with, a return to active duty with Starfleet Intelligence, set Janeway's nerves on edge, but she did her best to hide her qualms. It wasn't that she doubted his abilities, but the potential dangers of such an assignment gave her pause. It seemed that her need to continue to watch over those she had commanded wasn't fading with time.

"Did you speak with Captain Chakotay about Starfleet's plans for Voyager?" Tuvok asked. As this had been the reason for her hurried departure from Earth, it was a reasonable question.

"It turns out I didn't have to," she replied. "While we were en route I received word that Command, in their infinite wisdom, has once again chosen to deny Admiral Batiste's request to send *Voyager* back to the Delta quadrant. I have to say," she went on, "I was more surprised than anyone that he had the nerve to bring it up again, after the reception he received last year."

"You had indicated that he made a most compelling case," Tuvok acknowledged.

"He did," Janeway agreed. "Just saying the word *Borg* elicits a predictable defensive response in most people. And I have to admit that part of me understands Starfleet's perceived need to learn as much as we can about them."

"Then your position on the subject has softened?" Tuvok inquired.

"Oh, no." She shook her head. "*Voyager* will only return to the Delta quadrant over my dead body."

"I am sure it will not come to that, Admiral," Tuvok said.

"Let's hope not."

Janeway couldn't help but smile sadly, certain that Tuvok had others he would wish to speak with before he departed.

"Safe travels, Tuvok."

Tuvok nodded. *"Live long and prosper, Admiral."*

"You too, old friend," she managed before he terminated the communication.

Forcing aside the unease that nagged at her when she thought of Tuvok's new path, she looked again at the box. The symbol on its lid stood for *hope* in an ancient Native American language.

Despite her many concerns and well-grounded fears for the future, she was actually filled with that emotion for the first time in a long while.

JUNE 2380

CHAPTER NINETEEN

Phoebe Janeway knew grief.

She knew that one moment, life was a manageable routine of work and play, things scheduled and things forgotten, appointments to be kept, goals to be strived for, brief flashes of insight followed by days, weeks, and years of groping in the darkness toward another chunk of truth that might make a little more sense of the universe. And always the certainty that what one didn't achieve today might be done tomorrow. Most of the time, tomorrow felt like it had promised you something, and if you just waited a little longer, that promise would be made real.

Then death would arrive. The world would tilt on its axis in a shocking roar and in an instant every single thing you thought you knew was ripped away from you. Suddenly you were alone and there were huge pieces of flesh and bone missing from the center of your being. Your thoughts refused to run in an orderly fashion. Time passed and you crawled through it in a somnambulant stupor. The living reached out with warm hands to offer what comfort they could, but the noise of one's own mind made it difficult to hear, let alone respond to their kindness.

Thoughts for the dead would burst through the miasma like weeds. *Where are you now? What was it like? Did you know it was coming? If only you'd turned left instead of right . . .*

But those thoughts, however interesting to follow idly until they trickled into the vast unknown, were nothing compared to their insistent companions: the thoughts for oneself.

Death might have been hard on those who died, but at its worst it couldn't possibly be as hard as what remained for the living.

Inevitably, one day you awoke from the shock of sudden death to find one impossible truth staring you coldly in the face. From this day forward, you must relearn living. You must create for yourself a new life in which the person who has died is no longer present.

You must make peace with the unthinkable.

You must accept loss.

That was the beginning of grief.

Phoebe already knew that for many days to come, grief would dog her waking hours and transform her dreams into terrors. The nightmares her mind would conjure, monsters who would chase her up never-ending staircases, horrific creatures who would use her body for target practice, and all the while she would cry out for the dead to come and save her.

The reality was, grief felt altogether too much like fear.

Phoebe wanted nothing to do with it.

The first person Starfleet had taken from her had been her father. Always on the anniversary of his death, she found herself wondering how she had lived another year without him. Though he and Kathryn had shared many interests, he had been the first and really only person who made Phoebe feel known. All things were possible as long as he lived, because whenever the questions were too hard or the darkness too impenetrable, he was there to shed a little light.

The only consolation his death had ever offered was the new closeness it created with her sister. Kathryn could never replace him, nor had she tried to. But for the first time, Phoebe had seen her sister, not as the dominant force of nature who pursued her dreams with a fury, but as a person, every bit as fragile as Phoebe herself. She had learned to look past the face Kathryn showed the world. She had seen her broken by the only enemy that could never be conquered, and then watched in awe as Kathryn had risen from the ashes and reclaimed what life was left to her. She had found new dreams, new purposes, and through sheer determination, a new life in which their father's memory became a beacon to guide them, even in his absence.

Phoebe had been among the handful of people who had never truly given Kathryn or *Voyager* up for dead. There had been a seismic shift in her body at the moment of her father's death, though he had died on a remote moon thousands of light-years away from her. For a moment it had felt as if there wasn't enough air to breathe, as if her limbs had been leeched of their strength and as if her feet had been transformed into lead weights. Several days later she learned that this feeling had coincided precisely with the moment her father's shuttle had hit the icy sea on that distant moon.

When *Voyager* was first lost, and in the years of fruitless wondering that followed, Phoebe had searched herself for a similar sensation. This and only this would convince her that Kathryn was dead.

Her faith had been rewarded four years after her sister had disappeared, and their reunion on Earth only three years after that had solidified Phoebe's belief that there was simply nothing Kathryn could not accomplish.

And then, just a few weeks ago, while sitting at her easel working on her latest commission, she had suddenly found herself unable to breathe.

An anguished cry, *no, no, no, no, no,* had risen unbidden to her lips.

Staring up now at the gleaming white pillar topped with an eternal flame, which Starfleet had erected in honor of her sister's memory, Phoebe could find only two coherent thoughts. The first was that the pillar itself seemed a little phallic to commemorate one of Starfleet's most venerated female officers. It looked like a damned torpedo. The second was that Kathryn would have hated all this fuss.

Hundreds had gathered at Federation Park for the memorial service, and though summer had only just begun, it was already much too hot. To Phoebe's annoyance, none of the uniformed personnel in attendance were even sweating. Phoebe didn't think there was a regulation on the books that ordered them not to perspire at a time like this, but then again, it was Starfleet, so one never knew.

Admirals had followed ambassadors in a seemingly never-ending train of speakers, all droning on and on about Kathryn's most generic virtues: her sense of duty, her willingness to sacrifice herself in service to the Federation, and how honored they had been to know her and to work beside her.

As Phoebe glanced about her and studied the crowd, she felt certain that if there was a heaven and Kathryn was there now looking down on them, she would have been hard pressed not to order these windbags to shut up and get this crowd a little shade and something cold to drink. This thought brought a conspiratorial smile to Phoebe's lips.

Finally the moment came for Phoebe to rise and take her place at the podium. As the family's representative at the service, she had been given the honor of speaking last. She had tried in vain to prepare some brief remarks, but had settled on nothing. As she mounted the steps to the platform, she felt a brief surge of anger at Kathryn for putting her in this situation. Kathryn was the public speaker. Kathryn would have known what to say.

But she wasn't here.

And for all the pretty words about her legacy living on in the lives of those she'd touched, the only truth Phoebe could find in this moment was the most bitter to swallow.

I will never see my sister again.

She was momentarily awed by the sight of the crowd, now that she was finally facing them. She had always secretly suspected that there were very few people in the Federation that her sister didn't know. Obviously she had underestimated.

Her mother, Gretchen, sat in the front row, trying valiantly to hold back her tears. Their old family friends, Mark and Carla Johnson with their young son, Kevin, were beside her, their faces masks of shock.

Members of Starfleet stood behind the first row of chairs at attention, or parade rest, or whatever stupid thing they called it.

Captain Chakotay looked like a broken stone. He stared at some fixed point near the base of the pillar, oblivious of his surroundings. The always breathtaking figure of Seven of Nine was beside him, and despite the fact that he was a bit taller, Seven appeared to be the only thing preventing him from falling in a heap to the ground.

Next to them were Tom Paris and Harry Kim. These four, along with the holographic Doctor and Commander Tuvok, had been Kathryn's most frequent visitors after everyone had assumed new roles and assignments following the ship's return to the Alpha quadrant. Phoebe had met them only a handful of times, but knew that Kathryn had thought of them as family, and that the ties that bound them surpassed those of blood. She felt Tuvok's absence from the ceremony today most keenly.

The Doctor stood next to three other men: one who could have been his twin in about ten years, a Trill Phoebe knew she'd met but couldn't place dressed in the blue and black of a Starfleet physician, and the man Phoebe would always credit with returning Kathryn to her long before *Voyager* had arrived on Earth, Reg Barclay.

Staring out at the throngs of patient listeners, Phoebe finally knew what she wanted to say to them. Taking a deep breath, she began to speak.

"Kathryn Janeway was my sister. In some ways, you had more of her than I did. You shared her working days and nights and grand adventures in distant parts of the galaxy. You know, as I do, that Kathryn dedicated her life to service, and that she would not have minded, in the least, dying in the course of that service."

Phoebe paused to clear her throat before continuing.

"But I mind very much.

"Kathryn would have accepted death. She would have thought it was her duty. At best, I can only see her death as a necessary evil. She died so that the rest of us can go on living. But let us not mistake that necessary evil for good.

"I can stand here and celebrate her life. But I cannot celebrate her death. It should not have happened—not this way. We have known for years that we have made an enemy of the Borg. Kathryn fought and conquered them many times. Today, they seem to triumph over us. They have taken her from us.

"You are the soldiers of the Federation. It is your duty to make certain that her death was not in vain, nor was it the final chapter in this story. Only you can avenge her, and because she can no longer stand here before us and cry out for justice, I will do it for her.

"For the love I bear her, and for the love each of you still carry with you, I call upon you not to rest until those who are responsible for my sister's death are made to answer for what they have done. If you truly honor what she lived for, if you truly wish to memorialize the contributions she made to this Federation, do not forget how she lived, or how she died. Do not seek to heal this wound. Keep it open. And let it give you the strength you need to find and destroy the monsters who took her from us.

"Do not take 'no' for an answer.

"She wouldn't have."

―――――――――

Phoebe's words took Naomi Wildman by surprise. After so many speeches praising Admiral Janeway, reaffirming her contributions to Starfleet and admiring the nobility of her sacrifice, the admiral's sister's words seemed out of place. Obviously, Miss Janeway was angry, but as Naomi searched her heart, she could not find a kindred feeling.

She was only terribly saddened by the thought that she would never again be near the captain she had idolized for as long as she could remember.

Naomi wanted to speak with Seven of Nine. Seven usually contacted her at least once a week, and occasionally dropped by for a game of kadis-kot, which Naomi had long ago outgrown but would never acknowledge to Seven. They hadn't spoken since her mother had greeted her at breakfast one morning a few weeks earlier with puffy, red eyes and told her of Janeway's death.

More than anything, Naomi wanted to make sure that Seven was okay. Seven wasn't really good at feeling things. She was smarter than anyone Naomi knew, even the father she had come to love so much in the past three years. But Naomi could never remember seeing Seven cry. And tears were part of healing. At least that's what her mother had always told her.

Naomi had brought along a small wreath of white mums for her to leave at the memorial. As soon as the service ended, she had quietly excused her way through the throngs of people standing near it and only managed to come within three meters of the base, as it was already piled with similar offerings.

Apart from the flowers, there was only one thing Naomi wished to say to Admiral Janeway. Maybe since she was dead, she already knew, but Naomi wanted to say it anyway.

Kneeling before the monument and carving out a small space to set the flowers, Naomi whispered softly, "I'm sure Neelix would send his love. Mom has promised to tell him what happened. It may take a while to reach him, but she'll do it. Don't worry. I'll remind her."

Julia held Owen's hand as he spoke softly to Admiral Montgomery. But even as she smiled and nodded and inserted the occasional appropriate comment, she found it nearly impossible to tear her eyes away from her son.

Tom stood with Harry, speaking with an Academy cadet Julia thought might be one of the other Borg *Voyager* had rescued. His name escaped her at the moment.

Tom had wept openly throughout the service, and Julia had longed to go to him. Only Owen's stiff, cold arm linked in hers had restrained her.

For the thousandth time in the last few months Julia thought, *This is ridiculous.*

If anything, she had hoped that their shared grief at Kathryn's untimely passing might have brought father and son close enough to begin to bridge the distance that had grown between them. She had lived in the wasteland of this bitterness before and honestly believed they were long past it. It was both a blessing and a curse that one could never see too far down the road ahead. Had she known they would find themselves here again, Julia would have done everything in her power to prevent it.

The saddest truth of all was that no power she possessed would have been sufficient.

Montgomery stepped away and in the brief interim, Julia whispered to her husband, "Why don't we go and say hello to our son?"

Owen turned his weary face to hers and replied softly, "If our son wishes to speak to me, he knows where I am."

Julia's eyes brimmed with fresh tears, not for Kathryn, who was now beyond them, but for Tom, whose pain was all too fresh.

The moment the ceremony had ended, Eden hurried through the crowd toward the park's western gate. For weeks she had been torn between shock and rage at the news of Janeway's death. The shock was easy to understand. Eden had never truly believed that Janeway could not survive another encounter with the Borg.

The rage was more difficult. She wasn't sure who she blamed more for this horrific turn of events: herself, or Willem. As he hadn't bothered to attend the ceremony, at the moment she was more inclined to weigh his guilt a bit heavier than hers.

A small group of familiar faces was gathering around Seven and Chakotay. Tom, Harry, the Doctor, Jarem, Reg, Vorik, and Icheb had already exchanged many hugs and polite comments about the beauty of the service.

For her part, Seven couldn't really see the beauty. It had been an uncomfortable several hours in which nothing remarkable had been said—nothing that gave any deeper meaning or shed any light of understanding upon Kathryn's death.

In a way, Seven still did not understand why she had been spared the same fate. She had been ready to meet it, as there seemed to be no alternative. But she had been granted a reprieve, and in the countless difficult hours since then had begun to make some sense of the chaos that churned inside her.

She alone truly understood that Kathryn's death had been far preferable to the alternative, a life among the

Borg. She alone had shared Kathryn's brief victory and the resultant destruction of the cube that had enslaved her. The Doctor had suggested gently that this should comfort Seven.

It did not.

But frightened as she was for herself, she believed that ultimately she would adapt. Staring at the lost faces around her, particularly Chakotay's, she was not certain that her friends possessed sufficient resilience and wondered what she might do to aid them. Had Kathryn been among them, this task would have fallen to her. As she was not, Seven decided that she must summon the strength to help them begin.

Icheb moved from her side to make way for Naomi and Samantha Wildman to join their small circle.

"Hello, Seven," Naomi said almost shyly.

"Naomi Wildman, you are looking well," Seven replied politely.

Concern flashed across the child's horned forehead.

"I am not well, Seven. How could I be?"

"Naomi," her mother admonished her softly.

Seven stepped toward Naomi, surprised by how much she seemed to have grown in the few months which had passed since the last time they laid eyes upon each other. Too soon, Naomi would be as tall as Seven. Though she was only nine years old, the top of her head already reached Seven's shoulder.

"I am certain you are experiencing feelings of distress, Naomi," Seven said. "But we must all do our best to be brave. Admiral Janeway would expect nothing less of us."

"I guess." Naomi shrugged. "I just don't know how."

"None of us do," Tom said gently, tugging at Naomi's long braid.

Naomi turned to Tom and asked, "Where are B'Elanna and Miral? I was looking forward to seeing them. I bet Miral doesn't even remember me."

Seven caught the loaded glance between Tom and Harry that followed this innocent remark. Inside she wished to chide Lieutenant Wildman for not telling Naomi in advance that B'Elanna and Miral would not be in attendance. Then again, she rationalized that Naomi should not be burdened with adult concerns.

"I'm sure she does," Harry assured Naomi kindly. "Tom and B'Elanna tell her about you all the time. How well you're doing in school. All of it." He then turned to the group and said, "I don't know about the rest of you, but I think the last thing Admiral Janeway would have wanted would be for us to stand around with these long faces. We should find somewhere to go, and raise a glass to her memory."

Everyone seemed to concur. Seven had no immediate objections, but turning to Chakotay, she doubted he had even heard Harry's words.

Seven moved to face him and said softly, "Lieutenant Kim is right. We should adjourn to a more private place."

Chakotay briefly raised his eyes to hers. He looked at her as if she had just spoken to him in a language the universal translator was unable to parse.

The others immediately seemed to sense the tension and began to shuffle away in twos and threes.

"Chakotay?" Seven demanded.

"What?"

"Our friends are waiting."

"Let them wait."

Wordlessly Chakotay lifted her hand from his arm and began to walk toward the white pillar. The few guests who remained near the base drifted off to allow him a moment of solitude.

After a brief internal debate, Seven followed. She understood the depth of Chakotay's pain. She shared it. But she did not recognize the anger that flared from him unprovoked so often since Kathryn's passing, any more than she had understood Phoebe Janeway's absurd call for vengeance.

Vengeance was irrelevant.

Chakotay waded carefully into the sea of flowers adorning the base of the pillar. When he was close enough, he raised his hands and placed them at the sides of the pillar, almost caressing the monument's cold white surface.

For the first time, Seven realized that something had been engraved there. Searching her eidetic memory, she discovered the quote's source, an American poet. It read: *When a great person dies, for years the light they leave behind them lies on the paths of men.* Beneath these words were carved Kathryn's name, rank, and dates of birth and death.

Chakotay stared at the words, but Seven did not believe he was processing their meaning, which she found appropriate. Finally she said, "Kathryn died a valiant death, Chakotay. She saved us all from the scourge of the evolved Borg cube, and when she died, she was herself, and free of the Collective."

"There is nothing valiant about it," Chakotay replied harshly. "She should never have gone out to investigate that cube with only a science vessel for backup. Starfleet shouldn't have allowed it. You shouldn't have allowed it. I shouldn't have allowed it."

Seven wanted to argue that it had been none of these parties' choice to make, least of all his. Instead, stung by his tone, she turned on her heel and walked away.

Chakotay had never experienced anything like the emptiness that now consumed him. He had lost family and dear friends before. But this was different.

There had been times in the past when he had come close to losing Kathryn. But never in these brushes with death had he felt this crushing weight. And never had he imagined that rage could burn so deeply or constantly.

He knew why this was different. For the first time he had honestly believed that he and Kathryn were about to build a future together, and he had welcomed that possibility the way a man walking in the desert welcomes water. Instead of an oasis, he had found a mirage.

He couldn't blame Kathryn. She had taken more fool-hardy risks in the past.

But there was plenty of blame to go elsewhere.

A soft hand grazed his arm. Startled, he looked up to see a pair of clear blue eyes so like those he had loved in silence for too long.

Phoebe Janeway stood beside him.

"Captain," she greeted him softly.

Chakotay had heard little of the speeches made during the service. In fact, he remembered nothing until Kathryn's sister had begun to speak and had given voice to his own dark thoughts.

"Don't worry," he assured her with an icy calm. "I will see that the Borg pay for what they've done to us."

<hr />

UNREGISTERED VESSEL 47658: BETA QUADRANT: JULY 2380

B'Elanna stared at the message on the viewscreen in the cockpit of her shuttle, waiting for the words to rearrange themselves into something possible, something vaguely resembling a reality that she could accept.

She waited until her mind finally sensed that there was now an abyss where her heart had been beating only moments before.

Her heart was human.

It was weak.

It wanted to cry bitter tears.

But tears were useless in the face of death.

And Kathryn Janeway had died as she had lived.

She had died fighting an honorable battle.

B'Elanna would have given anything to have died at her side, or better, in her place. B'Elanna had become more than she ever dreamed imaginable under Janeway's watchful eyes, and this was a debt she could now never repay.

All she could do was cry out with fury that shook the shuttle's frame.

B'Elanna fell to her knees and began to wail.

She raged at the silent heavens surrounding her so that the living and the dead would hear her call.

A warrior was on her way to Sto-Vo-Kor.

After only a few moments, Miral's frightened cries were added to those of her mother.

U.S.S. TITAN: BETA QUADRANT: AUGUST 2380

No matter how many times Counselor Deanna Troi had performed this particular duty, it never got easier. There was nothing for it. The harder work would begin only once it was done.

Steeling herself, she tapped the chime at Tuvok's door. When it hissed open, his stately wife, T'Pel, stood before her.

"Good evening, Counselor," she said in a voice much warmer than Deanna usually found among Vulcans.

"Good evening, T'Pel. Is Tuvok available?"

"My husband is meditating, as is his custom before retiring for the night."

"May I speak with him?"

"Is it urgent?"

"I'm afraid so," Deanna replied.

T'Pel stepped aside with a nod and gestured toward the small room in their quarters which Tuvok regularly used as an office during his off-duty hours.

Deanna moved briskly toward the room and soon caught sight of Tuvok, dressed in a long blue robe, kneeling before a lamp lit by a single flickering flame.

"Tuvok," Deanna said softly. She knew intimately how traumatic it could be to rouse anyone from deep meditation abruptly.

After a moment, Tuvok rose from his serene pose and turned to face her.

"How may I help you, Counselor?" he asked evenly.

Deanna took a deep breath.

"We've just received our latest communication from Starfleet Command," she began. "Several months ago, a Borg cube entered Federation space. Captain Picard was able to eliminate the immediate threat. The cube, which showed no further signs of life, was quarantined. Admiral Janeway went with a team of scientists to investigate the cube and to ensure that it posed no further danger to the Alpha quadrant. Once on board, she was assimilated. The cube was ultimately destroyed. However, Admiral Janeway was not recovered. I'm so sorry, Tuvok, but Kathryn Janeway has died."

Tuvok did not even blink. After a brief pause during which she presumed he waited to learn if there was anything more she had to say on the subject, he replied, "Thank you for informing me, Counselor. If you will excuse me, I will return to my meditation."

Part of Deanna bristled. If someone had come to her to say that Captain Picard had suffered Janeway's fate, she would have been inconsolable. She knew it was irrational, but part of her had honestly believed that news of this magnitude must elicit some kind of obvious response, even from Tuvok. He and Janeway had served together for more than twenty years.

"Would you like to discuss it, Tuvok?" she asked.

"I would prefer to be left alone," he replied calmly.

Deanna turned and started toward the door to his quarters. Her first thought was that she must now compose a note of condolence to Reg. She knew too well of his special relationship to *Voyager*'s crew and presumed he had been terribly upset by this event.

Troi had almost reached the door frame when a rush of agony rolled through her. She paused, wondering whose turmoil she was sensing, and, after a moment, realized that it was Tuvok's.

More than once since they had begun to serve together aboard *Titan*, she had shared telepathic connections with the Vulcan. She knew that beneath his carefully tended walls there were vulnerable wells of deep emotion where he buried the feelings his mental disciplines would not allow him to express. She was caught off guard, not only by what had to be an unintentional lapse on Tuvok's part, but also the intensity of the pain she had tasted.

Almost as quickly as it had come, the feeling passed, leaving Deanna a little dizzy. She refused to prod, even with her empathic abilities, into her crewmate's private discomfort. She did turn back, however, to see Tuvok still standing where she had left him, his face revealing nothing of what they had just shared.

"If you wish to speak with me further, I will be available to you at any time," she assured him.

Once the counselor had left, Tuvok turned again to his meditation lamp. He knelt, joined his hands at his heart and made a steeple of his forefingers in preparation to resume his deep and cleansing ritual. Clearly he had not engaged in this practice as often or as rigorously as was required. He, too, had felt the brief connection to Counselor Troi, and was appropriately disconcerted by the event.

It would not happen again.

Tuvok closed his eyes and took several long, slow breaths. He then opened them and focused on the flame.

It danced and darted above the wooden vessel that housed its fuel. It was a focal point that provided the doorway to the calm place at his core where he would begin to integrate the knowledge of Kathryn's passing and reinforce the discipline that sustained his mind and body through such trials.

Tuvok stared at the flame.

He kneeled silently for several minutes, awaiting the inevitable descent into the serenity it promised.

Death was a part of life. It was inevitable. It was not to be feared. Kathryn would remain alive in his thoughts until his eventual passing. She would never truly be lost to him.

Tuvok again closed his eyes.

The flame still danced in his mind, but he could go no deeper.

Finally, he reached his hand out and held it just above the flame. Its heat was intense and would soon cause damage to his palm if he maintained the position.

In a brief motion, he dropped his hand over the flame and extinguished it.

He remained kneeling in the darkness for several hours, searching for a peace he was unable to find.

PART TWO

WHAT MEN ABIDE

MAY 2381

CHAPTER TWENTY

Admiral Montgomery found it hard to believe that the man standing before him now had once been, in his estimation and that of many others, an exceptional Starfleet captain.

Though Chakotay stood at attention and his uniform and grooming were well within regulations, the man inside the uniform was a shadow of his former self. He had always been in excellent physical condition. Now he was a good twenty kilos underweight. Visible cheekbones set beneath his strong brow gave him an almost gaunt appearance. He looked years older than the fifty-one Montgomery knew he'd lived.

Most shocking of all, however, were his eyes. The deep shadows beneath them could have been credited to loss of sleep if Montgomery hadn't personally granted him a leave of absence over two months earlier.

But his eyes.

Once they had been lively, alert with frequent displays of good-natured mischief, and sometimes given to deep, reflective pause that testified to the balance he had long ago achieved between his spiritual heritage and passionate scientific curiosity about the universe and its many mysteries.

Now, the black stones that were fixed unsettlingly at a point on the wall behind Montgomery's head bespoke nothing of the man's soul—only its absence. They looked as if death had arrived long ago, without bothering to notify the rest of his body.

In a way, of course, it had.

For all of us.

From the moment the Borg had reared their monstrous heads in the Alpha quadrant almost a year earlier, when the *Enterprise* had engaged what Montgomery had prayed was a lone renegade cube, many of those tasked with protecting the Federation and her citizens had worn a similar haunted expression. As the body count had risen exponentially in the Borg's final assault, most could calculate in double digits the number of friends they'd buried, or more often, been denied the closure of burying. Sixty-three billion had been lost in a matter of days.

After the Federation's protracted war with the Dominion, Montgomery had honestly believed that he had seen the worst the universe had to offer.

He had learned in the most brutal way possible that *worst* could be a frighteningly relative term.

But against the longest odds imaginable, the Federation had survived. No, it had done better than that; it had actually clutched victory from the gaping maw of annihilation. Grief would linger, but all around him people were starting to move past the horrors they had witnessed and, one day at a time, begin the painstaking process of rebuilding.

Montgomery was not indifferent to the particular tragedies Chakotay had suffered, but he did not believe that they were greater than anyone else's. Nor did he think it would be helpful for anyone if he was allowed to continue to wallow in them.

The saddest truth of all was that Montgomery needed Chakotay's experience and expertise, now more than ever. Starfleet needed them. It seemed that they might have been buried, along with his heart, beneath a white pillar at Federation Park eleven months earlier.

"Thank you for responding to my request so promptly, Captain Chakotay," Montgomery said kindly.

"Yes, sir," Chakotay murmured.

Montgomery wanted to inquire about his leave. He had to believe that after two months spent glorying in the beauty of the San Juan Islands, Chakotay would have found some of his old enthusiasm, or at the very least, a little perspective. It seemed clear enough that any such expectation had been foolish.

"Are you aware that Starfleet has issued new orders for *Voyager*?"

Chakotay's gaze remained distantly fixed as he replied, "Commander Paris mentioned it."

"I wanted to extend your leave as long as possible, Captain, but duty often requires us to make compromises."

When Chakotay did not respond, Montgomery went on, "However, before we allow you to resume your former command, Starfleet is requesting that you undergo a psychological evaluation."

Montgomery had been dreading this disclosure. He had yet to meet anyone who didn't find the prospect of such an evaluation offensive. Chakotay, however, betrayed nothing beyond a hint of resignation as he replied, "I'm sure I can handle whatever milk run Command has in mind for my crew."

"Damn it, Chakotay, I'm not talking about a routine assignment," Montgomery fired back, surprising himself with the vehemence of his tone.

Chakotay had the good sense to at least appear curious. Meeting Montgomery's eyes, he said, "Then what are you talking about, Admiral?"

Montgomery was actually surprised Chakotay didn't know. He assumed at the very least that Commander Paris would have let something slip to his old friend and captain, despite the fact that he had been ordered to keep the mission's specs classified. It was strange to think that of the two of them, Tom Paris was living up to his Starfleet oath while Chakotay seemed ready to toss his out the nearest airlock.

I would never have seen that one coming, Montgomery thought ruefully.

"Once you have completed what I am hoping will be the *formality* of your evaluation, I will brief you in detail on your new mission," Montgomery finally responded.

"Can you at least tell me why I've been singled out for the distinguished honor of this evaluation?" Chakotay asked without a trace of mirth.

"In reviewing your record, a number of incidents in the past year have called your judgment into question," Montgomery replied as dispassionately as possible. "I'm certain that after walking our evaluator through your thought process, it will be clear that your actions were warranted or, at the very least, defensible."

Dark fire began to burn behind Chakotay's eyes. It was almost a relief to see that something could still touch the man, even if it was only anger.

"Once you're done, I'm sure you'll be cleared for duty,"

Montgomery added, attempting to convey his strenuous hope that this would, in fact, be the case.

"And if I refuse?" Chakotay asked.

"You will be reassigned."

Montgomery didn't know what he would have been thinking or feeling in Chakotay's place, but he didn't think it would include the serious consideration of refusing a Starfleet directive . . . which was exactly what Chakotay appeared to be doing.

Does he even care if he loses his ship?

Finally the embers lost the fierceness of their glow, and Chakotay lifted his eyes from Montgomery's and fixed them once again on the distance beyond him.

"Then let's get this over with, sir," he said coldly.

Annika.

Seven of Nine refused to answer. Usually, if she ignored the voice, it would eventually subside.

You are Annika.

Of course Seven knew this. Prior to her assimilation by the Borg at the age of eight, she had been the human girl Annika Hansen. Beyond acknowledging this simple fact, she did not yet understand what the voice required of her. She found its unfamiliar presence disturbing, but refused to yield to her fear that if she did not find a way to satisfy the voice, it might never go away.

The voice had been the first thing she'd been aware of once the painful and terrifying process of what she could only think of as "transformation" had occurred. One moment she had been a human woman, sustained by the existence of several Borg implants, who still thought of herself more often than not as Borg. The next, she had felt fire consuming her body. Her mind, which had been a comforting, solitary place for years, had once again been momentarily linked with billions of others, many of whom, like her, were crying out in anguish, confusion, and horror, followed swiftly by an overwhelming, cleansing joy that bordered on ecstasy.

When the transformation was complete, Seven had once again found herself alone in her mind. The Borg implants that had kept her body's systems functioning properly since her severing from the Collective had quite literally dissolved and been replaced by something else, something utterly indistinguishable from flesh and bone, yet she was miraculously still alive.

And the maddening, patient, gentle, totally unnerving voice had begun its constant mantra: *You are Annika Hansen.*

The *Enterprise*, *Titan*, and *Aventine* had witnessed the liberation of the Borg by the Caeliar. But Seven knew long before their reports had begun to trickle into the Palais de la Concorde, the office of the Federation President, that the Borg and the multiple threats they had posed to the Federation were absolutely and irrevocably gone. The Caeliar, an incredibly advanced and xenophobic species, had unwittingly spawned the Borg and in an extraordinary act of compassion had welcomed their aberrant children home, folding them into the Caeliar gestalt where each individual retained their unique identity while still being part of the Caeliar collective.

In many ways, it was the perfection that the Borg had relentlessly sought. The Caeliar had long ago mastered the omega molecule and harnessed its power. Their technological prowess far outstripped any other sentient species the Borg or the Federation had encountered, short of the Q. For the briefest moment, Seven had sensed—no, she had actually been one with—the new gestalt, and had glimpsed perfection, along with the combined relief of billions of minds freed from the oppression and insatiable hunger of the Borg.

Had Seven possessed a spiritual context in which to frame the experience, she might have considered it sacred, perhaps even holy.

As it was, she could only describe the moment as intensely powerful, transcendent, and mysterious. The moment had been fleeting for her, and once the transformation was complete, Seven had been left outside the bounds of this glorious new existence. Having tasted perfection and known briefly the answers to the questions that had driven her as a drone, and having it all ripped away, was now a source of constant and unutterable pain.

Most days, the only thing separating her from complete despair was the pressing needs of those around her. Despite their salvation at the hands of the Caeliar, the Borg had practically destroyed the Federation. All able hands had been immediately called to constant duty, and once Starfleet Medical had determined that Seven had survived the transformation relatively unscathed, she was no exception. Her days were divided now between lengthy meetings and debriefings, her course work as an instructor at the Academy, and her responsibility to her aunt, Irene Hansen.

"Annika."

Seven tore her gaze from the view of the San Francisco Bay afforded from the hillside of Federation Park to see her aunt gesturing her forward imperiously.

Irene had called her Annika from the moment they had been reunited on Earth three years earlier. This had become cause for confusion only in the last several weeks.

Her aunt stood at the base of the white pillar that had been erected to honor Kathryn Janeway. Seven walked dutifully forward, forbearing to let her eyes linger for long on the gleaming monument. Apart from her many duties, the only other sustaining force in her life was a sense of self-righteous anger, and this feeling was only intensified when she looked at Kathryn's memorial.

When Seven reached her side, Irene grasped her hand, which still felt naked without the implants that had once surrounded it. Irene's grip was unnecessarily tight, but Seven had become accustomed to it.

"Who the hell is Kathryn Janeway?" Irene demanded.

Seven bowed her head for a few seconds to compose herself before replying as patiently as possible, "Kathryn Janeway was a Federation officer, the *Starship Voyager*'s captain, and the individual responsible for freeing me from the Borg collective."

"The *what* collective?" Irene asked.

"The Borg," Seven answered.

It had been like this for eighteen months.

Seven had never heard of Irumodic Syndrome, an incurable neurological disorder that caused irreversible deterioration of multiple synaptic pathways in the human brain, until her aunt had been diagnosed with it. The disorder's most prevalent symptoms were temporary loss of memory, confusion, disorientation, and as it progressed, delusions. Ultimately it would prove fatal, but the Federation's best medical minds were unable to give her any real sense of when her aunt would succumb to its ravages. In the interim, regular injections of peridaxon, which Seven administered, usually calmed the worst of the symptoms, leaving Irene in relative comfort and usually remembering who her niece was and how it was that she had come to share a townhouse with her in San Francisco. Shortly after her diagnosis, Seven had been forced to relocate her aunt to her residence near the Academy in order to provide better care for her only living blood relative.

From time to time, the Doctor would come from his current project at Jupiter Station to check in on Seven and her aunt. These visits were usually brief. The Doctor always assured her that their old friends at the Institute continued to work diligently on her behalf to develop a cure for the syndrome. Despite their brilliance, Seven doubted they would find a cure in time to save Irene. She tried not to resent the fact that her staunchest companion, the Doctor, was also engaged in his own pursuits and therefore unavailable to focus his efforts entirely on relieving her of at least this much of her current agony. He offered his sympathy, but often as not such sentiments seemed irrelevant and did little to ease her suffering or Irene's.

Irene had good days and bad days. She had been enjoying a string of good ones when it had occurred to her that she had never formally paid her respects to Seven's beloved friend Kathryn Janeway. Irene had been hospitalized briefly at the time of Kathryn's memorial and hadn't remembered for days after returning home that Seven had just lost one of those dearest to her. She had insisted this morning on venturing out to Federation Park, and Seven had chosen to oblige her. It seemed clear that now her recent lucidity had been cut mercilessly short.

"We should return home for lunch," Seven suggested to Irene.

"I am hungry," Irene conceded.

Seven tugged gently at her aunt's hand to pull her away from the monument toward the park's exit. Irene turned her head back briefly to the base of the pillar, then, opening her eyes in alarm, said, "Kathryn Janeway died?"

"Yes," Seven replied.

"Annika, I'm so sorry," Irene said, her voice filling with concern. "What happened?"

Seven had told this story so many times in the last year that she simply couldn't bear to do it again.

"She was killed in the line of duty, Aunt Irene. It is common for those who serve in Starfleet."

"Yes, but she was such a good woman, and she loved you so," Irene went on. "You must miss her terribly."

Until the days following the Borg transformation, this had been the simple truth. Seven had missed Kathryn—her company, her insight, even her tendency to mother Seven when she least desired it. Their relationship had always been complicated, but once Kathryn had died, Seven found it harder and harder to think about those traits that sometimes smothered and irritated her. Instead, she had found herself focusing on Kathryn's simpler, kinder gestures—the way she had allowed young Naomi Wildman to become her "captain's assistant" on *Voyager*, the way she had encouraged Seven to bond with and nurture the drone One, the faith she had placed in Seven time and again when her abilities were doubted by others or her motives called into question; and most often, the handful of times the Borg had been determined to recapture Seven and Kathryn had risked her life and the lives of everyone aboard *Voyager* to deny them.

However, since the transformation even these comforting and affirming memories had become a minefield. The first time she had gazed upon the tall white pillar, Seven had felt a mixture of shock and pain. Paralyzing bouts of sadness would come later, followed by a hollow numbness. Now as she looked again at the symbol of Kathryn's life, she felt only anger.

Janeway could not be faulted for her inability to know the future. In severing Seven from the Collective, she had done what she always did, what she thought best under the circumstances, and she had never abandoned Seven during the tumultuous years that followed as Seven struggled to adapt to her new existence.

But Seven could not dismiss the feeling that had Janeway not interfered, the pain and confusion that were now a part of Seven's life would never have troubled her. She would either have died or would now be a part of the Caeliar. She would now know perfection, a state she was confident that, as a human, she would never approach.

But most of all, she would not be plagued constantly by the voice, and the knowledge of what *might* have been. Nor would she have to wonder why she had been left behind.

The day Seven had awakened in *Voyager*'s medical bay and learned that Janeway had severed her from the Borg, Seven would have killed the captain with her bare hands. Several days of painful debate had followed as Janeway had insisted that she knew better than Seven how much she would come to treasure and be defined by the individuality that had been her birthright and that was now restored to her. Seven wondered what Janeway, if she were still alive, would make of Seven's current predicament. Seven would have liked to rage at her again, as she had in those early days. That alone might have dispelled some of the anger that now gripped her.

Seven had lost too much in too short a time. Those that she might have turned to for help were all so mired in their own struggles that none of them even questioned how she was coping. Seven did not blame them, but she did miss them.

But for better and worse, Janeway's loss was cruelest of all.

"Annika?" Irene asked.

"Yes?"

"Does Chakotay know what happened to Kathryn? Is he all right?"

Seven swallowed yet another bitter truth.

"He knows, but I cannot tell you how he is coping with the loss. He and I have not spoken for several months."

"I'm so sorry, Annika."

You are Annika.

"Do not trouble yourself," Seven replied. "I will adapt."

"Can we go home now?" Irene asked wearily.

"This way." Seven nodded, gesturing toward the tree-lined path that led to the park's western gate.

You are Annika.

I was Annika. I am now Seven of Nine, she insisted.

Seven would placate her aunt for as long as necessary. But she refused to accept the will of the voice, which seemed determined to take from her the only thing she could still call her own: the strength and the wisdom and the vast knowledge she had attained as a Borg drone. Even Janeway had known better than to insist that Seven's abilities were irrelevant because they had been gifts of a force for great evil.

The harm Janeway had done to Seven now seemed to far outweigh the good; at least Seven could grant her this much and draw a modicum of resilience from it.

I will never be Annika again, not for you or anyone.

Seven only wished desperately to know whom she was trying to convince.

CHAPTER TWENTY-ONE

The room in which Montgomery instructed Chakotay to wait was a monotony of white walls, a white paneled ceiling, and a white floor broken only by a small silver table and two identical metal chairs.

It's like a damned interrogation chamber.

Which in one sense, Chakotay supposed, it was. In another, it was almost comforting. Starfleet counselors were trained to put their patients at ease. Usually their offices were inviting spaces in terms of design, colored in soft earthtones. The furnishings tended to be softer than Chakotay preferred, designed to force one to relax. Had he found himself in such a room at this moment, he would have been hard pressed not to vomit. The captain could no longer abide pretty lies. At least Montgomery had done him the courtesy of not pretending that this evaluation was routine. Chakotay's career with Starfleet and his command of *Voyager* were hanging in the balance.

All that remained was for Chakotay to determine whether or not he cared, and he definitely preferred the prospect of confronting that decision in a cold, hard room.

Right up to the moment when the room's only door swished open and Counselor Hugh Cambridge entered.

Chakotay was on his feet before it dawned on him that, for the moment, he still outranked the counselor.

"Good morning, Captain," Cambridge said neutrally.

"Counselor." Chakotay nodded.

Despite the thready rhythm his heart had begun to disseminate throughout his body, Chakotay tensed his legs, forcing stillness upon them. There was simply no way that Starfleet had assigned his counselor to evaluate his command abilities. The only explanation for Cambridge's presence had to be that he was sent in advance to prepare Chakotay, or perhaps provide a familiar face to put him at ease.

Even in that regard, Cambridge was the poorest choice imaginable. Chakotay had disliked the man from the moment they had met, and though Cambridge's abilities had earned him a certain amount of respect, Chakotay had never warmed to him. He had learned to tolerate and occasionally make use of him, nothing more. What had always amazed him was that Cambridge never seemed bothered by his captain's feelings. He had never requested transfer from *Voyager*, and Chakotay had been hard pressed to make the case that beyond his personal feelings, Cambridge was in any way unfit for his duties.

Clearly unruffled by Chakotay's stern gaze, Cambridge moved to take a seat across the table. He had a way of sitting, his long legs crossed at the knees, his back resting comfortably and his hands clasped in his lap, which always gave the impression that he was relaxed and in complete control.

At least he didn't have a padd in his hand, or any other recording device. Chakotay decided to take this as a good sign as he sat down and attempted to mimic Cambridge's comfortable poise.

"It's my understanding that you've already spoken with Admiral Montgomery," Cambridge began.

"I have."

"Do you need anything before we begin?"

Chakotay felt acid rising up his esophagus.

"*You* are performing my evaluation?" he asked slowly.

"I am."

"Unacceptable."

"Is it?" Cambridge asked with the barest hint of a smile.

"Do you consider yourself to be a disinterested party in this?" Chakotay asked.

"Not at all," Cambridge replied. "But I'm also not nearly as interested as you might imagine." Before Chakotay could register further complaint, Cambridge went on, "Has it slipped your memory, Captain, that nine weeks ago several billion people, many of them Starfleet personnel, died at the hands of the Borg?"

"Of course not," Chakotay replied through clenched teeth.

"The final Borg attacks made the Dominion War look like a skirmish," Cambridge continued. "Starfleet is currently short of capable officers on all fronts, and for the time being, must make do with what it has. I'm sorry if you don't feel that I'm the best man for the job, but I'm afraid that falls into the category of hard cheese for both of us."

"Have you been transferred off *Voyager* while I've been on leave?" Chakotay continued evenly, refusing to be baited by Cambridge's typically blunt approach.

"No," Cambridge said.

"And yet you still believe you can impartially evaluate events that occurred while you were under my command?

Events that, if memory serves, you counseled against and protested in your formal logs?"

Cambridge didn't even bother to ponder the question.

"Unlike most people, I'm highly skilled at separating my personal feelings from my professional ones." Cambridge shrugged. "I've been asked to evaluate your current psychological status, Captain—a job for which I'm uniquely qualified, since I've observed you in a wide variety of on- and off-duty situations for almost three years. I already know what your mental state *was*. I'm here today to determine whether or not you've made sufficient personal progress since the last time we met to warrant once again placing the lives of a hundred and fifty dedicated members of Starfleet in your hands. If you *are* ready to resume command, fantastic. If not, other arrangements will have to be made."

"But you have a personal stake in the outcome."

"And I guarantee you that if those who have requested this evaluation find so much as a whiff of bias in my report, I'll be the one sitting out *Voyager*'s next mission instead of you," Cambridge replied. "Would it help if I assured you that I've come here today hoping that this goes well for you?"

"Not even a little."

"Be that as it may, we have lots of ground to cover, Captain, and time is very much of the essence."

Chakotay saw himself rising, overturning the table that sat between them, and pummeling Cambridge with his fists. The mental image calmed him somewhat. It also made him realize that, like it or not, as long as he sat in this room, he didn't have the power. If he wanted his command back, he was going to have to play nice. For the first time since he had arrived, the thought occurred to him that he did want to return to *Voyager,* if only to wipe the smugness off Cambridge's face in a slightly more dignified manner than in his fantasy.

Chakotay briefly considered the notion that this evaluation was a mere formality and that Montgomery had already decided he was unfit for duty. Perhaps assigning Cambridge as his evaluator was simply pouring salt into the wound.

The captain couldn't bring himself to go down that road. Montgomery had always been a reasonable and, at times, compassionate man. Chakotay couldn't shake the sense that somewhere, Montgomery was actually rooting for him. While he could never give Cambridge that much credit, the counselor had never lied to him nor to any of his crew. And despite his abrasiveness, he was an excellent counselor, once his patients got used to his style. Though Chakotay had never sought Cambridge's advice when they had served together, it might be interesting to see exactly how Cambridge saw him, and the "incidents" he had no doubt been brought here to discuss.

"Very well," Chakotay finally conceded. "Let's get on with it."

"Excellent," Cambridge said, nodding.

There was a brief pause, during which Chakotay wondered if he was expected to speak. He tried to think back over the most likely ground they would be covering and assumed they would begin with the business of that Orion vessel some ten months prior. He was taken completely off guard by Cambridge's first question.

"When was the last time you met with Kathryn Janeway?"

Chakotay found himself involuntarily digging his fingers into his palms.

"I thought we were here to discuss my performance over the past year," he replied.

"We'll get there," Cambridge assured him. "But as any man with eyes and a reasonable intellect could easily see, your actions of the past year did not spring from the vacuum of space. Let's not waste time dancing around the issue, Captain. We're considering both cause and effect today. You have not performed at your peak since the day Kathryn Janeway died. That event is sitting in our 'cause' column. I'd like to explore it further for the moment. When was the last time you met with Kathryn Janeway?"

"June of 2379," Chakotay answered as agreeably as possible.

Cambridge actually raised his eyebrows in surprise, a gesture Chakotay enjoyed immensely.

"That was almost a year before she died?"

"Yes."

"I'm sorry," Cambridge said, shaking his head, "I just assumed that for two people as close as you and Admiral Janeway, you would have been in touch more often."

"We were," Chakotay replied.

"I don't understand," Cambridge admitted, and Chakotay's pleasure intensified exponentially. He could never remember hearing Cambridge utter those words in all the years that they'd known one another.

"You asked about the last time we met," Chakotay replied, "not the last time we *spoke*."

Cambridge replied with a weary shake of his head.

"It's a little early in the day to be splitting such fine hairs, don't you think, Captain?" he asked.

"You asked a question, Counselor, and I answered it," Chakotay replied tonelessly.

"And what was the reason for your meeting?" Cambridge asked.

"*Voyager* was docked in Proxima's maintenance facilities to undergo routine repairs prior to our departure for the Yaris Nebula. The admiral chose to stop by for a visit. It was purely a social call."

"That would have been almost a year after *Voyager*'s mission to Kerovi and all of that unpleasantness with the Klingons?"

Chakotay nodded.

"What did you and Kathryn discuss during your social call?"

Chakotay bristled internally at Cambridge's use of her name rather than rank, but chose to let it pass. Cambridge wasn't going to get under his skin that easily, though Chakotay knew full well he had never been close enough to Kathryn to call her anything but Admiral.

"There wasn't much news on my end," Chakotay replied. "You might remember that as the year of minor missions. After our time in the Delta quadrant I suppose it's unfair to draw comparisons, but the few diplomatic transfers and colony resettlements we were tasked with overseeing at that time were fairly mundane."

"And how was Kathryn?"

"She was in the eighth circle of hell," Chakotay replied, actually smiling briefly at the recollection.

"I beg your pardon?"

"The one reserved for diplomats," Chakotay explained.

"My remembrance of Dante is that the eighth circle contained the fraudulent," Cambridge said.

Chakotay had actually said the same thing to Kathryn when she'd made the reference. It pained him slightly to be reminded here and now that he had been the only person to whom Kathryn had ever loaned her personal copy of *Inferno,* the copy given to her by Mark Johnson as an engagement gift.

"At the time, she was having some difficulty seeing the distinction," Chakotay finally replied.

Cambridge nodded.

"And apart from the witty repartee, was there anything significant about this meeting?" he asked.

Chakotay felt his face hardening.

There was, but he would be damned if he would share it with Cambridge. The memory of that night had been his most constant companion every day that had followed. At times it was a soothing balm, but more often it was the sword's tip that goaded him. Often Chakotay found himself wishing Kathryn had never come to Proxima. It would have made what was to come so much easier to bear. But she had. And because she had, reality was now unbearable.

"Why do you ask?" Chakotay inquired. He had never shared the details of that night with anyone, even his closest friends. Before, he worried that such a revelation might actually jinx the future it promised. And once Kathryn had died, it no longer mattered.

"Because it's my job, Chakotay," Cambridge replied.

He knows, Chakotay realized—perhaps not the substance of that evening, but enough to hazard a reasonable guess. Cambridge had always possessed uncanny observational skills, and Chakotay had to allow that for months following his night with Kathryn on Proxima, his spirits had been high. *Voyager*'s mission to survey a stellar nursery could not account for them.

Chakotay wanted desperately to avoid such personal territory with Cambridge, but he also knew that even the appearance of withholding at this point would damn him.

As objectively as possible, Chakotay returned to that night.

────────

STARDATE 56494: JUNE 2379

"And what was the ambassador's response?" Chakotay asked.

"That *if* the Federation Council was serious about establishing trade with the Syngtara, they would have sent a telepath," Kathryn replied, smiling broadly. "I must admit, he had me there," she added with a chuckle.

Throughout dinner they had covered similar territory. It seemed that both of them were languishing under assignments that, while certainly vital to the Federation, left a great deal to be desired in terms of excitement. Neither was anxious to return to the days when every moment might bring the threat of destruction to their ship and crew, but somewhere in the universe there had to be a happy medium. Chakotay couldn't shake the sense that both of them were being tested for their tolerance for boredom. Both were rising admirably to the challenge, but it was unsettling.

However, Chakotay also knew that Kathryn hadn't come all the way to Proxima to discuss the Syngtara, or the Peeth, or the Children of Fawlwath. When they'd arranged for dinner, Chakotay had felt sure that Kathryn was troubled about something, most likely to do with *Voyager*. He had first sensed it when they had returned from Kerovi. Every time they had spoken in the last year it seemed she ended their conversations buoyed but definitely not relieved of her burdens. These few subtle hints had turned that sense into a disquieting certainty. He had been surprised when she arrived in good spirits, and forced his concerns to the back of his mind, the better to enjoy the few hours they'd managed to steal in one another's company.

"Whatever happened with Captain Leona?" she asked, clearly directing the conversation toward more personal matters as she poured herself another glass of wine.

"Nothing," Chakotay replied. *Voyager* had briefly rendez-voused with the *U.S.S. Osiris* while it was under Leona's command, and he had mentioned in passing to Kathryn how intriguing he found the Betazoid captain. Normally she wasn't the jealous type, but immediately after they'd completed the supply transport to the first of Boreal's six colonies, the *Osiris* had received an abrupt order to return to Earth, and Chakotay had always secretly wondered if Kathryn had a hand in it. Of course, that would have meant admitting that Kathryn might be concerned by a potential romantic entanglement on his part, and he never let himself really believe that was possible.

"What about you and Admiral Harlow?" he teased good-naturedly.

Kathryn heaved a weary sigh. "Let's just say I think there's a good reason he's been divorced twice. He didn't strike me as one who did well in captivity."

Chakotay nodded, refusing to pay too much attention to the relief he felt when he heard this. Both of them had tried, unsuccessfully, to find a romantic interest worth pursuing, and both, it seemed, might be destined to re-main single.

"Any new prospects on the horizon?" Chakotay asked.

"Not really," she acknowledged somewhat wistfully.

"Good," he replied before realizing that the word had escaped his lips.

Kathryn paused, staring at Chakotay intently. It had been an innocent enough remark, but still it sent a tangible charge through the air between them.

"Why good?" she asked lightly.

A familiar tension caused his heart to accelerate, though he kept his expression neutral.

It would have been a simple matter to shrug the comment off. Chakotay had danced this particular dance with Kathryn for years, and there was no reason tonight should be any different.

But she held his eyes with a soft, lustrous gaze. There was something challenging shining forth from the tumultuous depths, something both curious and guarded at the same time.

Chakotay found himself suddenly wondering whether or not he had misread the substance of her unspoken concerns for so long.

Part of him wanted to answer her honestly. It was good because the thought of Kathryn giving herself completely to another man had always felt wrong to Chakotay.

He had long ago accepted the reality that he loved her. Over the years that love had become a safe, predictable place, the quiet companionship of two people who have shared unique experiences and could sense without words the other's moods, needs, and fears.

Duty that had once made anything else between them impossible was not an issue anymore. Since their return to the Alpha quadrant, they had both continued to sit in seeming contentedness by the side of the pool, occasionally dipping a flirtatious toe, but steering well clear of anything resembling a swim.

As to what Kathryn was thinking, he couldn't say. But for his part, Chakotay had always worried that to push her toward anything else would be to lose her forever, and that he could not abide. Since they were no longer stranded together on the far side of the galaxy, the potential was always there that they might simply drift apart. He would always want more, but could certainly live with what he had of her.

When Chakotay didn't answer her directly, she dropped her eyes and studiously began to rearrange the remnants of her dinner. The plate was pushed toward the center of the table, the napkin in her lap folded neatly atop it, and the wineglass to its right nudged a few millimeters closer to the plate.

Chakotay was seized with a sudden urge to put her at ease. He leaned forward and reached for the hand that was still fretting about the stem of the glass.

The moment their fingers met, a familiar electric charge coursed through him.

It was a simple, friendly gesture, he told himself, until she looked up at him again, squeezing his hand in return, ever so gently.

She took a shallow breath and said softly, "You know, there's something I've been meaning to ask you."

"What's that?" he asked as his throat ran suddenly dry.

Kathryn paused, seeming to consider her words carefully.

"We've been home for over a year and a half, and never once in that time have you offered to take me to Venice."

A tense pit formed instantly in Chakotay's stomach.

Of course he'd wanted to ask. As *Voyager's* routine assignments of the last several months had become increasingly mundane, he often found himself thinking back to their years together in the Delta quadrant and their brief reunion to recover B'Elanna and Miral. The longer they were apart, the more he missed her. But he'd been burned once, and wasn't going to willingly tempt the flames again without some indication from her that she shared his feelings. Seeing the cautious hope suffusing her face, he actually wanted to kick himself for missing the signs that in retrospect had been fairly obvious to one who supposedly knew her so well.

Instead, he dropped his eyes to focus on their hands. His thumb began to play softly over her fingers. Without looking up he replied, "I didn't think you wanted me to, Kathryn."

Stealing a quick glance, he noted that her eyes were also firmly set on their conjoined hands.

Her voice deepening a bit, she said, "I thought I made myself perfectly clear back in the Delta quadrant; I never said *never*."

Chakotay nodded. "That's true. But then again, you're still keeping everyone, me included, at a safe distance. To be honest, I always hoped my feelings would change. I tried to make them change."

"And have you succeeded?" she asked calmly.

"Of course not," he replied. "Have you?"

She shook her head slowly.

"Then why didn't you say something?" he demanded.

Shrugging slightly, she answered, "I don't know. I guess I always thought there would be some perfect time, some moment where the truth would become so obvious to both of us that we wouldn't need words. But the more I think about it, the more it seems clear that I might live the rest of my life alone, wondering just how much I've sacrificed on the altar of duty."

"All you ever had to do was say the word, Kathryn," he replied.

"I thought I just did."

Chakotay allowed the moment to breathe and settle.

He had always expected that if Kathryn were ever to actually open this door, he would rush headlong through it. Maybe it was the years of experience, or his knowledge of her mercurial nature, that made him hesitate now. Or maybe it was the reality that once this bridge was crossed, there would never be any going back. Kathryn wasn't suggesting a fling. She wasn't looking for a way to pass the time. As a rule, she threw herself into her choices with her entire being, and would accept nothing less from him.

He looked up to study her face. He saw trepidation there, but also a hint of relief coupled with a compelling tinge of mischief.

Searching his heart, he realized that nothing in the universe would make him feel as complete as walking into the future with her by his side. It was a simple truth, arrived at with little fanfare. Chakotay only wished they had reached it sooner.

"Then how do you, I mean . . ." Chakotay found himself fumbling for words as the choice he had just made sank in, flushing his cheeks and sending a pleasant anticipatory rush through his body.

"I'll make you a deal," she said with a smile.

"I'm listening."

"You're going to be slogging through the Yaris Nebula for the next ten months, and I don't imagine you'll be encountering many fascinating women while you're there."

"Many?"

"All right, *any*," she corrected herself. "But then again, one never knows what fate has in store."

"Fair enough."

"And I have yet to meet anyone in the Alpha quadrant I really enjoy having lunch with, much less anything else," she admitted. "When you get back, assuming nothing has changed for either of us," she said softly, "we'll meet in Venice."

Chakotay considered the proposal. It was sensible and practical.

Rising from the table, he moved to stand beside her, still holding her hand. She hesitated for a heartbeat, then stood to face him.

Dropping any pretense, he allowed himself to fall freely into her eyes. He was a patient man, but knowing what he did now, waiting for another ten months was completely out of the question.

In the last few years, she'd begun to allow her fine auburn hair to grow long and had fallen once again into the habit of pulling it up into an efficient bun while on duty. Gently he reached up and removed the comb that held it neatly in place and watched with pleasure as she shook her head softly, freeing herself in a gesture from the symbol of her years of self-imposed confinement.

"I let you go once, Kathryn," he said, his voice low. "Please don't ask me to do it again."

"Come to think of it . . ." she whispered.

He silenced her with a kiss.

Their lips met, tentatively at first. Soon enough, however, they moved beyond timid exploration and succumbed to the promise that had always lived between them.

The next few hours were the most satisfying of Chakotay's life. They parted with the assurance that as soon as *Voyager* returned, a new chapter would begin for them, duty be damned.

They would meet again in Venice, and Chakotay no longer doubted what the future would hold beyond that.

When Chakotay finished describing the evening for Cambridge, the counselor was good enough to reply with a compassionate nod.

Chakotay stared hard, searching for any trace of his typical nonchalance, but found none.

Finally Cambridge said, "You said that was the last time you met. Why didn't she join you in Venice?"

Chakotay felt certain that at any moment, the anguish which had accompanied every previous visitation of this memory would resurface, but to his surprise, under Cambridge's unflinching stare he felt only cold and terribly alone.

"She was detained," Chakotay replied, "by her death."

CHAPTER TWENTY-TWO

Eden looked up abruptly as Willem entered her office without announcement, followed quickly by her clearly flustered aide, Tamarras.

"Captain, I'm sorry to interrupt, but Admiral Batiste wishes to see you," Tamarras said unnecessarily.

"So I see," Eden replied.

"Get out," Willem barked at Tamarras.

The frightened aide threw a pleading glance at Eden, who simply nodded apologetically, saying, "Thank you, Tamarras, that will be all."

Willem stalked to and fro before her desk, clearly agitated. Torn between anger—at both his gall and his rough handling of her aide—and curiosity as to what had riled him so, she rose and rounded her desk, halting his steps by standing before him and crossing her arms indignantly.

"The day you signed our divorce decree, you forfeited the right to behave like an ass in my presence," she said. "Whatever's troubling you, we're on duty, and I expect you to remember that when dealing with me and my staff."

Willem dismissed her complaint with a huff and replied, "Damn it, Afsarah, he's not going to pass."

Eden was well aware that Captain Chakotay's evaluation had been scheduled for this morning, but found it hard to believe it had been completed in less than an hour.

Which could only mean . . .

"Willem, are you actually monitoring the captain's session?" she asked incredulously.

"Of course," he replied. "The fleet launches in a week. The mission briefing for all department heads takes place tomorrow morning. Until a few minutes ago, I assumed Captain Chakotay would be standing beside me during that meeting, but I'm no longer confident that's going to be the case."

"Willem." Eden shook her head, truly at a loss to prioritize the vast number of things wrong with that statement.

Taking a deep breath, she continued, "In the first place, who authorized you to watch a confidential counseling session?"

"He didn't come to us asking for help, Afsarah," Willem retorted sharply. "He's been ordered to undergo this evaluation, and its results don't fall under the purview of doctor/patient privilege."

"Its *results*," Eden said with emphasis, "but the actual contents of the session?" she asked in disbelief.

"Time is a luxury none of us has right now," Willem replied.

"You think I don't know that?" she said. "I've been supervising six hundred officers and crewmen working around the clock for the last ten weeks to get this mission launched. Right now nobody can say for sure that all traces of the Borg are gone, or the Caeliar for that matter, and no one is more anxious than I to start getting some answers to those questions. But there are lines we don't cross, Willem."

Willem paused, his jaw tensing. "If Captain Chakotay isn't up to sitting in *Voyager*'s center seat—"

"We'll find a suitable replacement," Eden finished for him. "It may take a few more weeks—"

"We don't have a few more weeks."

Eden shook her head. "Command isn't going to scrap the mission, Willem. I know it was a long road getting here, but there is simply no longer an argument to be made that this proposal isn't vital to the ongoing security of the Federation."

"There never was," he interjected, "but that didn't stop them in the past."

"Of course there was," she corrected him. "This is a massive reallocation of resources which has been approved at a time when a lot of Federation citizens aren't sure where their next meal is coming from. Sixty-three billion people just died, and still, Command and Operations have thrown everything they have at these nine ships to get them ready in one-quarter the time such an undertaking should warrant. This, even after we learned about the damn Typhon Pact! Our old adversaries have banded together when we're at our most vulnerable, and still, *still*, Starfleet is going forward with this mission. No one could have foreseen these cataclysms, and you can't fault Command for treading lightly in the past."

"It was never Command," Willem retorted sharply. "It was only that damned Kathryn Janeway."

At this, Eden was forced to turn away. She crossed to the windows behind her desk, unable to revel in the glorious late spring morning she beheld, the sun glistening off the bay as the city of San Francisco buzzed with life. Such a stark contrast with the devastated reality of so many other Federation worlds brought a lump to her throat.

While she, too, had been frustrated by Janeway's resistance to Willem's proposal, she had never resented the woman as Willem had. Unlike Willem, she had actually gotten to know Admiral Janeway, at first through her logs and reports, and ultimately through the lengthy debriefing session they had shared once *Voyager* had returned from its aborted mission to Kerovi. Eden had found the admiral to be unflinching in her honesty and ability to look objectively at her work over the seven years *Voyager* had spent in the Delta quadrant. She hadn't needed to meet Janeway to know that her devotion to duty was a sacred thing. The logs of her senior officers and crew testified to her resolve to adhere to Starfleet principles throughout their journey, even when it was most inconvenient to do so.

All Eden had to do was consider the fate of the *Equinox*, the first known Federation vessel pulled into the Delta quadrant by the Caretaker, to fully grasp the reality that not every Starfleet officer would have been capable of Janeway's accomplishments. Nor had she been overly surprised by the depths of the admiral's disappointment in Captain Ransom and his crew, and the lengths to which she had gone to bring them to justice.

When they had reached that point in *Voyager*'s narrative, Janeway had stated clearly that this was the incident during her command that she felt the least pride and satisfaction in. The admiral knew she had crossed a personal and professional line in her determination to right the abhorrent wrongs of the *Equinox*'s crew, and felt that her actions had tarnished her reputation both personally and in the eyes of her crew. She had been most grateful that during those dark days, the constant if unheeded voice of Commanders Chakotay and Tuvok had helped her to maintain her perspective.

Janeway had been much harder on herself throughout the course of their meetings than Eden would ever have been on her or anyone faced with *Voyager*'s unique circumstances. When they were done, Eden had been left in awe of the admiral.

Eden had not been present the first time Batiste had proposed to Starfleet that *Voyager* should return to the Delta quadrant. She had, however, been so disconcerted by Willem's fears about the potential for another Borg attack that she had completely revised her analysis, giving her full-throated support to the Delta quadrant mission. They would never know how many lives might have been saved had Willem's proposal to send a fleet of exploratory vessels back to the Delta quadrant in June 2379 been approved.

In light of Janeway's ultimate fate, Eden found it impossible to consider this with any objectivity. Secretly, she always believed that Willem had felt vindicated by her assimilation and death. He had been arguing for years that a return to the Delta quadrant was needed, and Janeway had shouted him down at every opportunity. Her death at the hands of the Borg, no doubt, seemed like poetic justice to him.

But Eden was among only a handful of people who knew that Janeway hadn't gone to investigate the cube that killed her simply because her curiosity got the better of her. The moment Captain Picard had successfully rendered the cube inert, Batiste had brought his proposal to Command for a third time. Given recent events, they were hard pressed to ignore the Borg threat and were clearly ready to approve his proposal. Admiral Janeway had stepped up and volunteered to investigate the cube herself, and Command had agreed to table discussion of *Voyager*'s pending return to the Delta quadrant until her analysis was complete.

Eden had never been able to shake the sense that she and Willem had sent a great woman to her death. She knew that everyone had been doing what they thought best at the time. She had actually been moved by the lengths Janeway was willing to go to protect the lives of her former crew. And no one could say for certain whether or not sending *Voyager* back to the Delta quadrant would have made a difference.

But Afsarah couldn't help but hate Willem a little every time he spoke of Janeway with such disdain. All Eden knew for sure was that she deserved better.

Willem pulled her from these thoughts with a question. "Did you know they were intimately involved?"

Eden's stomach fell as she turned to face Willem.

"Admiral Janeway and Captain Chakotay?"

Willem rolled his eyes and nodded.

Cold and trembling, Eden sought out the edge of her desk and took a seat.

"Since when?"

"Just before *Voyager*'s mission to the Yaris Nebula," he replied.

Eden struggled through the math to place the timing in some kind of context. Just before that mission, Willem had approached Command for the second time to propose the Delta quadrant mission. Janeway had made an impassioned speech, calling for Starfleet to focus their efforts on defensive rather than offensive action when it came to the Borg. Starfleet had again come down on her side, and *Voyager* had been spared. Now Eden was forced to wonder if this knowledge on Janeway's part had in any way impacted her decision to enter into a deeper relationship with her former first officer, to risk happiness by reaching out for a more fulfilling personal life.

Nothing in their logs had even hinted that such a relationship had ever been present. But Eden had rarely met two officers who had served together as long as Janeway and Chakotay had and spoke in such glowing terms about the other. She knew that Janeway had been engaged to be married and that her intended had married another when she was pronounced dead. To the best of her knowledge, neither Janeway nor Chakotay had ever been romantically linked with anyone else, either during or after their return from the Delta quadrant, though Eden rarely paid attention to gossip about her co-workers' personal lives, as she knew all too well what it was to be on the receiving end of such speculations.

Eden found her heart pounding. *They had loved one another, probably for years, and once they chose to consummate their relationship, they had been torn apart forever by the Borg.*

"Dear gods," she murmured.

"My sentiments exactly," Willem said.

"What do you mean?" she asked, certain he wasn't sharing the same regrets now tormenting her.

"I mean, Captain Chakotay's problem has less to do with posttraumatic stress following the debacle at the

Azure Nebula and more to do with a broken heart than either of us suspected up to this point. He's not grieving the loss of a dear friend and comrade. His behavior since her death makes a lot more sense now, and I'm guessing won't improve a whit if we put him back on active duty. Of course, Montgomery will make the final call, but I've been watching the man talk for the last hour, and believe me when I tell you, he's not ready."

Eden found it harder to care about that right now. Her many regrets over Janeway's death had just been increased by an order of magnitude.

"I'll start making a list of potential replacements," she said dutifully.

In the long pause that followed, Eden actually believed Willem had left the room without bidding her farewell, but a minute later looked up to find him still standing where she'd left him, staring at her.

"What?" she demanded.

"Nothing," he said with a look of surprise.

To Eden's consternation, he seemed positively relieved.

"Then if you wouldn't mind, Admiral," she said, "you've just added another huge task to a list that's already too long."

"Of course," he replied thoughtfully, then turned and exited looking considerably better than he had when he'd entered.

As Eden could guess that whatever new idea he was chewing on would become clear eventually, she dismissed any further reflections.

Turning to her computer interface, she called up a list of active-duty captains who might be free for reassignment, but after a few moments, found her eyes glazing over.

"Computer," she called, "display transcript of closed session, Starfleet Command stardate 56467.3."

In response, the visual record of the meeting in June 2379 during which Admiral Janeway had taken the floor to refute Batiste's proposal for the second time appeared on the screen. Eden hadn't been in attendance at that meeting either, but had been granted access to its transcript by Willem when he had once again been bettered by Admiral Janeway. Eden had watched it for the first time after learning of Janeway's death.

Settling in, she forwarded the visual record to the frame that contained an image of the admiral rising to address her colleagues and began the playback.

"I would never attempt to minimize the threat posed to the Federation by the Borg," Janeway had begun. *"They are driven by the purest of instincts and a biological and sociological imperative to achieve what they perceive as perfection. But thanks in large part to the efforts of my former crew, we now have a vast repository of information about the Borg and their weaknesses, as well as the knowledge of a former Borg drone, Seven of Nine, which we can and must use to continue to bolster our defenses.*

"I understand that Admiral Batiste is not proposing to send Voyager *back to the Delta quadrant under the same circumstances which prevailed during our first unexpected mission there. He has spoken eloquently about the vast strides made in our quantum slipstream technology over the past year and its ability to send an entire fleet of vessels to the far reaches of the galaxy without cutting them off from the support and resources of the Federation.*

"However, neither he, nor anyone here, can assure us that this technology is ready for such ambitious deployment. We

tested slipstream technology. We worked for months to integrate it into our systems, and believe me when I tell you that no one was more committed than my crew to making it work. It would have ended our exile in a matter of days. I cannot tell you how disappointed we were when we ultimately concluded that it was not safe.

"What I can tell you is that no crew should be forced to face that disappointment again. Until such time as slipstream technology has been thoroughly tested, the mission Admiral Batiste is proposing remains untenable.

"Further, to return to the Delta quadrant solely for the purpose of gathering more intelligence about the Borg will most likely only antagonize them. We're not talking about a show of force, which might convince the Borg to respect our borders. As Voyager's logs indicate, their territory in the Delta quadrant is vast, and they have ships and resources at their disposal we cannot hope to match. To seek out a confrontation with them again, even with the purpose of 'investigating' their capabilities, might only hasten the eventuality that we are all seeking to avert.

"Could the Borg be convinced to coexist peacefully with the rest of the galaxy, we would not be having this discussion. But they cannot. As far as they are concerned, there will be no reason to rest until the entirety of the Milky Way has been assimilated. Our only reasonable course of action is to stop them before they have the opportunity to achieve their stated goals.

"The most unfortunate reality, however, is that genocide, even of a species like the Borg, runs counter to every principle upon which our Federation is founded. We're not talking about sending a fleet of ships with the capability to face and defeat the Borg. We're not going to attack them. That's not what we do.

"So what are our options?

"As Admiral Batiste has suggested, we will likely one day find ourselves facing the Borg again in the Alpha quadrant, when they have mustered sufficient numbers and resources to mount an invasion and discovered another route from their space to ours. We must begin to prepare for that day. But I believe he is wrong to suggest that we do not already possess the knowledge and the determination to face that threat.

"We know more about the Borg today than we have ever known. We have detailed schematics of their vessels and armaments, and several encounters under our belts which will enable us to predict their tactics. We possess weapons, both offensive and defensive, which we know to be effective, and we must dedicate every available resource to enhancing them and building upon them.

"I do not doubt that any Starfleet crew assigned to a mission in the Delta quadrant would accept the challenge. We are trained to seek out such adventures. But I remain unconvinced that such a mission would most effectively utilize our current resources, and might only lull us further into a sense of complacency. What are we doing right now to avert catastrophe at the hands of the Borg? We're investigating them further, we might say to ourselves.

"And while we investigate, they are building ships and weapons and, quite possibly, looking for another way to send them to the Alpha quadrant.

"We know the Borg are a serious threat. But we should consider realistically the best way to counter that threat, and sending one or a handful of vessels with untested and unreliable technology on what might be a one-way suicide mission hardly qualifies in my mind as rising to the level of serious action. We must begin here at home, preparing for an even-

tuality which may be inevitable, but hopefully is still many years in the future."

When Eden ended the playback, she found herself brushing tears from her eyes. She had continued to believe in the rightness of their cause, even after Starfleet's second refusal, Eden had to admit that Janeway had made a compelling case. If Willem was to be believed, she had left that session and rendezvoused shortly after with Chakotay, where their relationship had changed forever. Eden did not believe that Janeway's intentions toward Chakotay had clouded her judgment on the issue or even factored into the equation. No one who hadn't lived those seven years in the Delta quadrant could possibly speak to the hardships her crew had endured, and Janeway's unwillingness to send them back on what must have seemed like a dangerous whim was perfectly understandable.

Eden had always believed that if one wanted to make the gods laugh, all one had to do was make a plan. But rarely, even in the aftermath of recent events, had she considered the gods cruel. Nor had she ever been so cognizant that the road to the hell in which she now found herself had been paved with such good intentions.

Chakotay sat unflinching under Cambridge's stern gaze. To his credit, the counselor hadn't even attempted a witty retort to Chakotay's last statement.

Instead, he sighed, uncrossed his legs, and moved forward to place his elbows on the table between them, bringing his face to rest in his hands.

"All right," he said simply, "let's move on for now."

Chakotay only nodded in reply.

"Let's go to stardate 57585," Cambridge offered.

"The Orion ship?" Chakotay asked by way of confirmation.

"In fairness, I'll advise you that for several weeks prior to this incident, your crew was already expressing concerns about your mental and emotional state," Cambridge said.

"In fairness, at the time, I shared their concerns," Chakotay replied.

"Let's talk about that day," Cambridge suggested, "and then we'll continue on with the series of events that culminated in your request nine weeks ago for an extended leave."

"I'm sure you remember it all as well as I do," Chakotay countered. "You were there and serving under my command at the time."

"Still, I'd like to hear the story from your point of view."

"Fine." Chakotay nodded. "Stardate 57585 . . ."

AUGUST 2380

CHAPTER TWENTY-THREE

Chakotay rounded the corner to find the entrance to the turbolift blocked by Lieutenant Harry Kim and one of Vorik's new engineers, Ensign . . . Ensign . . .

Damn it. What is her name?

His head was still throbbing dully, and despite the fact that his tongue felt like a huge lump of sandpaper and his stomach was rumbling, the thought of actually ingesting anything made his gorge rise. While updating his personal log the night before, he had polished off a full decanter of spiced Bolian ale—a mistake he didn't plan on making again any time soon. He needed to ease off for a few days at least, but synthehol never managed to help him find sleep the way the real thing did.

Maybe it's time to crack that case of Château St. Michelle I've been saving, he thought briefly.

Still, it troubled him that he couldn't put a name to the face of the petite blonde woman Harry had backed against the wall. She didn't seem to mind. Propping himself up with one hand resting on the wall just to the right of her head, Harry was leaning in and whispering something that made her simultaneously blush and giggle.

Chakotay refused to admit that the ire stoked by this

little scene had as much to do with his hangover as its impropriety.

"Aren't you supposed to be on the bridge, Lieutenant?" he said sharply.

Both Kim and the ensign jumped to attention at the sound of his voice.

"I'm sorry, sir," Harry stammered, abashed. "We were just waiting for the turbolift."

The captain stepped past them, and the moment he came within range of the proximity sensors, the doors whisked open.

Her face a bright shade of red, the ensign hurried away as Kim stepped in behind his captain.

They rode for a few moments in silence until Harry asked, "Any word this morning on the Orion ship?"

"If you were at your post where you were supposed to be, you wouldn't need to ask that question, Lieutenant," Chakotay replied.

Harry said nothing further, and allowed Chakotay to step onto the bridge before hurrying to relieve Cappiello, the gamma shift officer, at tactical.

Tom Paris rose to greet Chakotay with a "Good morning, Captain."

"That remains to be seen," Chakotay replied as he settled himself into his chair and began to review the prior shift's reports.

All around him, his officers were all studiously engaged in their duties. A tense hush had descended upon the bridge the moment he entered, broken only by the occasional beep or blurt of a console.

"Captain, long-range scanners have detected a vessel," Lasren called out from ops.

"Is it them?" Chakotay asked.

"A moment, sir," Lasren requested.

The initial scan results were already being rerouted to Paris's interface, and after a moment he said, "The power signatures and hull configuration are a match. I think we've got them, Captain."

"Red Alert," Chakotay ordered. "Adjust course and speed to intercept."

After only a few blares Kim muted the klaxon, for which Chakotay was silently grateful, but the bridge was bathed in pulsing crimson light.

"There's no way to mask our approach, Captain," Tom advised him.

"So we go in hard and fast," Chakotay replied.

Within moments their quarry had detected the danger and had moved into attack position.

"They can't possibly believe they outgun us," Paris noted. The ship's primary function was transport, though a few nasty-looking disruptor cannons had been cobbled onto the hull. And given that they were members of the Orion Syndicate, it was fair to assume they had a handful of other destructive aces in the hole.

"Their port engine is offline, and I'm detecting a coolant leak in their starboard engine," Lasren added.

"Looks like they're done running. Scan their cargo hold," Chakotay ordered.

"They're still carrying the half kiloton of kemocite they stole from Deep Space 5, sir."

"Hail them, Ensign."

After a few seconds Lasren replied, "No response, Captain."

"Open the channel."

"They can hear you, sir."

"Orion vessel, this is Captain Chakotay of the Federation *Starship Voyager*. Power down your weapons, drop shields, and prepare to be boarded."

"They're still not responding, sir," Lasren advised.

"Life signs?" Chakotay asked.

"Six confirmed," Lasren replied.

"Orion vessel," Chakotay called out again, "we have scanned your ship and confirmed that you are illegally in possession of kemocite ore. Don't make this harder than it has to be."

In response, the Orion ship fired several quick disruptor bursts and began evasive maneuvers.

Voyager shuddered slightly under the barrage.

"Shields are holding," Kim reported from tactical. "Attack pattern, sir?"

"At your discretion," Chakotay replied.

"Thank you, sir," Harry said, then added, "Helm, prepare to execute attack pattern delta six."

Under Tare's confident hands the ship rolled to starboard, easily evading another volley, simultaneously firing a steady stream of phasers from their ventral array.

"They just lost twenty-eight percent of their shields," Kim reported, clearly pleased.

"Bring us around," Chakotay ordered.

A few minutes later, the Orion vessel had been completely stripped of its cannons and most of its shields, and was running on maneuvering thrusters only.

"Are they ready to talk yet, Ensign Lasren?" Chakotay inquired.

"No response to repeated hails," Lasren replied.

"Harry, is your security team ready?"

"Yes, sir."

"Tractor them into the shuttlebay, and let's make sure we give them a nice, warm welcome."

A pale blue beam struck the Orion vessel and began drawing it toward *Voyager*.

Suddenly, a massive jolt shook the bowels of the ship, and the beam blinked out of existence.

"What the hell was that?" Chakotay demanded.

Paris was the first to assess the situation. "It's an optronic pulse. They modified their remaining disruptor bank to emit it."

"Our tractor beam is disabled. We can't bring them in or tow them," Harry advised.

"Then we board them," Chakotay resolved. "Assemble a security team for transport. And if they so much as twitch again, open fire."

"Captain," Paris said, clearly dismayed.

"Problem, Commander?"

"That pulse was the bottom of their bag of tricks. Their shields are failing and they're not going anywhere. If we fire on them now, they'll be destroyed."

"They're transporting kemocite ore they stole from a Federation starbase, killing fifteen people that we know of in the process. That was their first mistake. Their second was firing on this ship. They've been warned, and they understand the consequences of their actions, Commander," Chakotay replied coldly. "This isn't a game."

"The boarding party is ready for transport," Kim reported.

"Captain," Lasren interrupted, "I'm detecting a plasma leak in their warp core."

"Is their core about to breach?" Tom asked.

"Can't tell. All of their systems have sustained heavy damage. It could just be a malfunction."

"Tare, let's put some distance between us," Tom ordered, rising to stand behind the helm station.

"Arm photon torpedoes," Chakotay added.

"Sir?" Paris asked, turning abruptly to face Chakotay. Chakotay stood and squared off with his first officer.

"It's not a malfunction. When the warp plasma hits that kemocite it will create a temporal disruption. They're still trying to evade capture, Commander, and that's not going to happen today."

"Torpedoes armed," Kim said.

"Lasren, is that channel still open?" Paris asked.

"Yes, sir."

"Orion vessel, we are detecting a leak in your warp core. Do you require assistance?" Paris said.

An unintelligible burst of static blared over the comm system.

"Can you clean that up, Ensign?" Tom asked.

"There's too much interference on their end," Lasren replied.

"Harry, take out the last of their shields and have the transporter rooms lock onto the crew and beam them aboard," Paris said.

"Belay that," Chakotay said immediately.

"What?" Paris asked, incredulous.

"There's no time. Lieutenant Kim, fire photon torpedoes," Chakotay ordered, his eyes fixed defiantly on his first officer's.

"Belay that!" Paris ordered.

"Commander Paris, you are relieved," Chakotay barked. "Mr. Kim, destroy that ship."

There was a moment of stunned silence in which no one on the bridge seemed willing or able to move.

"Harry—" Tom began.

"Lieutenant Kim, follow my orders or stand aside," Chakotay said, turning to face Harry.

Kim hesitated for only another second, and then fired the torpedoes.

Simultaneously, Lasren called out to Chakotay from ops, but his words were drowned out by the obliteration of the Orion ship.

"Get off my bridge," Chakotay growled at Tom. "Stand down from Red Alert."

"Captain—" Lasren began.

"What?" Chakotay snapped.

Only after Paris had reached the turbolift did Lasren continue, his voice shaken, "Just before the torpedoes hit, they managed to lock down the warp plasma leak. I think they were trying to comply, sir."

Paris turned to look at Chakotay. The captain met his eyes without flinching.

"They brought it on themselves," Chakotay answered. "Lieutenant Kim, you have the bridge. I'll be in my ready room."

He could feel the eyes of everyone upon him as he turned away from his crew and retreated into his private sanctuary.

Only when he was safely ensconced did he begin to shake. Chakotay kept telling himself it had all happened too fast for him to make another choice. The ship they had just destroyed had been responsible for the deaths of four Starfleet officers and eleven civilians when it had blown its way out of Deep Space 5. It was carrying the dangerous ore that, when refined, was a key component in weapons of mass destruction.

They didn't deserve the benefit of the doubt, he assured himself, and no one was going to mourn their passing.

The captain stepped toward the replicator, debating whether he should order the water his body desperately needed or something a little more bracing, when a chime sounded at his door.

"Come in," Chakotay called.

Counselor Cambridge entered.

"What do you need, Counselor?" Chakotay asked.

"I just had a very interesting conversation with Commander Paris," Cambridge said evenly. "Would you like to give me your version, or shall I wait for your report?"

"I've already relieved one of my senior officers from duty, and it's not even time for lunch yet," Chakotay replied. "If your services are required, I'll let you know. Until then . . ." Chakotay gestured toward the door.

Cambridge considered him for a moment before saying, "Then may I at least make a suggestion, sir?"

"If you must."

"Unless you want to end up alone on that bridge, you might try directing your obvious anger at the person for whom it is meant rather than your crew."

"And who might that be?" Chakotay asked.

"Kathryn Janeway, sir," Cambridge replied, then exited the room before Chakotay could order him out.

Several hours later, Harry entered holodeck three to find Tom waiting for him in the cold gray room.

"He didn't confine you to quarters?" Harry asked.

"He's giving me a few days to think about my behavior," Tom replied, "and a few extra duty shifts in waste reclamation."

Harry nodded. "Then we'd better get started. A little time with Chaotica should cheer both of us up."

Tom nodded and moved toward the holodeck control panel, but before activating the program he turned to Harry and asked softly, "Are you as worried about him as I am?"

"You have to ask?"

"What are we going to do?" Tom said.

"What can we do?" Harry asked. "He's the captain."

"I talked to Doctor Kaz this afternoon," Tom said. "He's going to review Chakotay's report of the incident, but given the circumstances, he doesn't think he can relieve him of duty based on this alone. There's a case to be made that they intended to allow the warp plasma to hit the ore. The captain could have been right."

"But he wasn't," Harry replied grimly. "And he never used to err on the side of violence."

"Why did you fire?" Tom wanted to know.

"They were the enemy, Tom. And it wasn't an illegal order, just a merciless one."

"I just don't understand," Tom went on. "What happened?"

"She died," Harry replied.

"So he's the only one who misses her or who's having trouble dealing with her death? I mean, we all loved her. If anything, I expected that he'd be the one helping *us* to move on," Tom said.

"Me too," Harry agreed.

"I swear there was a moment this morning when I thought he was going to take a swing at me," Tom admitted.

"Maybe we should try to talk to him. You, me, Doctor Kaz. Hell, we could contact Jupiter Station and get the Doc in on it," Harry suggested. "I'm pretty sure Seven is back at the Academy by now. She might be able to take a short leave. He's still stuck in the anger stage of his grief. It actually reminds me of that time B'Elanna . . ." Harry trailed off.

Tom turned away, and Harry quickly added, "Sorry."

"It's okay." Tom shrugged. "And you're probably right. B'Elanna might be the only person left who could get through to him."

"Is that an option?"

"No." Tom shook his head.

Harry stood, dejected, staring at the holodeck grid. "It'll pass," he finally said, clearly trying to convince himself more than anyone. "He's hurting now. It hasn't even been six weeks. But sooner or later he's going to bounce back, and until then, we just have to support him the best way we can. We owe him that much."

"So we should just stay out of his way and pretend he isn't becoming more erratic every day?" Tom asked.

"We'll think of something," Harry assured him.

Tom turned again to the holodeck controls, and again hesitated to activate them.

"I'm sorry, Harry, I'm just not up for Captain Proton right now," he finally admitted.

"How about some velocity?" Harry suggested.

Tom thought about it before replying, "I think I'd better save myself for those waste processors."

Harry nodded, resigned.

"If she was still here, what do you think she would do?" Harry asked.

"Admiral Janeway?"

"Yeah."

"If she could see him like this," Tom said sadly, "she'd be kicking his former Maquis ass."

FEBRUARY 2381

CHAPTER TWENTY-FOUR

Jarem Kaz found his captain alone in astrometrics in the small hours of the morning. He looked like he hadn't slept in a week. The puffiness under his eyes had recently resolved itself into deep circles the color of a bruise. His shoulders were stooped and his hands trembled slightly as he worked the control interface. In some ways this was better than the alternative of the last several months. The shakes were symptomatic of the detoxification process his body was undergoing. Chakotay had stopped drinking the day word had arrived of the Borg attacks on Acamar and Barolia. The doctor had discreetly offered him a drug therapy that would make the process easier on his body, but accepting treatment would have meant acknowledging he had a problem, and Chakotay would never do that. His mood hadn't improved dramatically, but at least Kaz was comforted by the knowledge that he had to be more clear-headed now that he was no longer intent on numbing his obvious pain.

Instead, he had become focused with laserlike intensity upon one idea: destroying the Borg. No other topic had been up for discussion among the senior staff for weeks, and though several innovative strategies had been proposed, they had yet to locate even one cube on which

Chakotay could vent his too-long-pent-up rage. Kaz believed it was only a matter of time. He was actually surprised to find that Chakotay was the only occupant of the astrometrics lab, even at this hour, as it was the most efficient tool at their disposal for detecting Borg activity. Likely as not, Chakotay had grown impatient with the officer on duty and simply dismissed him so as to better do the job himself.

"Captain?" Kaz asked deferentially.

Chakotay jumped, startled by the interruption.

"What is it, Doctor?"

"I couldn't sleep," Kaz admitted.

"Join the club," Chakotay muttered.

"Actually, I've had a thought I wanted to run by you."

Chakotay paused to rub his eyes vigorously and squeeze his head between his hands to forcibly remove the grogginess that held him.

"I'm listening."

"In the past, we've always focused our efforts on developing nanotech-based weapons targeting the Collective's interlink, to render the Borg incapable of taking action, hostile or otherwise."

"You're talking about the various neurolytic pathogens we've used before?"

"Yes. Doctor Beverly Crusher has been working closely with Seven of Nine and several others to modify the latest effective pathogens, since we know the Borg have already adapted to and will be able to counter everything we've thrown at them so far."

"Right."

"And as for conventional weapons, we know that randomly rotating shield and phaser frequencies is effective only up to a point."

"True."

"And you're sure we can't get clearance to allow Vorik to try his hand at re-creating those transphasic torpedoes?"

"I've asked Admiral Montgomery about it daily, and he keeps telling me Command is saving them as a weapon of last resort."

"Saving them for when?" Kaz demanded.

"I wish I knew," Chakotay replied bitterly. "Vorik is working on duplicating the shield and phaser frequencies first used in the Delta quadrant by the advanced drone, One, and with some serious power rerouting I think we're going to have that up and running soon."

"But sheer firepower isn't going to get the job done, is it?"

"I doubt it."

"So we need something else."

"What did you have in mind?"

Kaz took a deep breath, collecting his thoughts.

"The first time the Federation battled the Borg, the *Enterprise* subdued them by giving the drones a very simple command: sleep."

"But that was only effective because Captain Picard was still linked to the hive mind and his crew were able to give the command through him," said Chakotay. "The Borg aren't assimilating anymore. They are simply destroying anything and everything in their path. Even if we could develop a new pathogen to disrupt their functions, there's no easy way to get it assimilated into the Collective."

"Setting the delivery system issue aside for the moment,

rather than trying to develop a new and complicated pathogen to sever their link, what if we were able to design a program which when assimilated would simply make the Borg
believe that all affected technology had been catastrophi-
cally damaged—a 'critical failure' message, if you will."

Chakotay paused.

"But all they'd have to do is look around to know that
they weren't damaged. How does that help us?"

"The Borg believe what their nanoprobes tell them to
believe. They don't seek secondary confirmation for orders
or assessments. They don't think outside the Collective.
And somewhere in Seven's voluminous files on the subject
she reported that when Borg systems are critically damaged, they automatically self-destruct to avoid the possibility of capture."

Chakotay's face brightened. "You think we can fool
them into blowing up their own vessel?"

"I think if we can get properly modified nanoprobes
into the central plexus of a Borg ship so that the signal will
be carried beyond one cube, we can fool them into blowing up all of their vessels."

"Any questions?" Chakotay asked.

Standing at the head of the conference table, his hands
resting on the back of the tall chair in which he was much
too restless to sit, *Voyager*'s captain met each of his senior
officers' eyes with what he hoped was reassurance.

Harry Kim was the first to look nervously around the
table before clearing his throat.

"It's a pretty ambitious plan, sir," he said quietly.

"Is that a problem, Lieutenant?" Chakotay shot back.

"No, sir," Kim replied immediately.

"Five drones will be hard to neutralize, assuming we're able to capture them," Jarem Kaz piped up.

"I believe five is the *most* we can hope to subdue and infect," Chakotay replied. "And since it's essential that at least one of them reach the central plexus to disseminate the modified nanoprobes, I want us playing with the best hand we can possibly build."

"Playing, sir?" Cambridge asked.

Chakotay had never had much patience for his counselor's semantic games.

"If you have an objection, Counselor, out with it," Chakotay replied. "Once we leave this room, the subject will be closed to debate."

"Fine," Cambridge said, checking his fellow officers' faces before continuing. "Every single time Starfleet has confronted the possibility of infecting the Borg with a software virus or pathogen capable of destroying them, we have hit the same ethical wall. We will protect ourselves, with deadly force if necessary, but we will not use tactics that are tantamount to genocide. Previous pathogens that have proved effective were designed to disrupt the Borg's ability to function collectively. While it is clear that in some instances the results were more destructive, that was not necessarily the weapon's intent. The possibility always existed that the Borg would lose their ability to attack us, without suffering complete annihilation."

"It's highly unlikely that the modified nanoprobes Doctor Kaz has developed will do more than destroy one cube at a time," Chakotay replied. "And we'll be lucky if they don't adapt after our first attack. But if they don't, and we're lucky enough to infect all of the cubes that have infiltrated the Alpha quadrant, then I won't lose any sleep over it."

"That's precisely my objection, Captain," Cambridge said evenly.

Chakotay took a moment to see if anyone else seemed inclined to share the counselor's point of view. All eyes but his were studying the table.

"In the past few weeks, the Borg have made their intentions toward the Federation crystal clear," Chakotay said simply. "Command has authorized every Federation and allied vessel to use any and all means necessary to destroy the Borg. If we don't end them, they're going to end us. This is war, Counselor. Billions have already died. We're now fighting for our right to exist. And we might not be in this position if at some point in the past someone had realized that principles are nice until you're facing an enemy who doesn't have any. If we must sink to their level in order to beat them, so be it."

"It's a compelling argument, Captain," Cambridge conceded. "There's only one problem."

"Only one?" Chakotay almost laughed.

"We may succeed, but if we lose what is best in us in the process, what have we won? Does a Federation willing to forgo the beliefs upon which it was founded in order to defeat its enemies deserve to exist?"

"Of course it does," Jarem Kaz replied.

"Doctor Kaz—"

But Kaz continued on, rolling right over Cambridge's interruption. "The Federation doesn't engage in inhumane practices because they are historically ineffective. We don't torture sentient beings for information and we don't execute them, even for the worst offenses. We don't do these things, not because of their effect on our enemies, but because of their effect upon *us*. It's wrong for a state to turn its people into monsters, even to secure ourselves, because we draw the line at becoming what we behold. But the Borg *are* different."

"So was the Dominion, if I recall correctly," Cambridge argued.

"Counselor, your objection is noted," Chakotay said. "For the record, I agree with Doctor Kaz. We find ourselves in extraordinary circumstances. The principles that we all swore to uphold will die with us if the Borg have their way, and I'll die before I allow that to happen."

After a brief pause during which no one else seemed inclined to speak, Chakotay continued. "Lieutenant Vorik, how much longer will it take to implement the shield and phaser modifications we've discussed?"

"At least two days," the Vulcan replied.

"You have thirty hours, no more," Chakotay said. "Tom, adjust the duty shifts to twelve-hour rotations until further notice. Harry, begin drilling your teams to subdue our anticipated guests. Patel, get busy constructing those interlink nodes, and Doctor Kaz, get to work on the modified nanoprobes. Ensign Lasren, continue to monitor the tactical scout and be ready to intercept."

Nods all around the table confirmed that his orders would be followed.

"Dismissed."

<hr>

Twenty-eight hours later, *Voyager* set a course for the small tactical vessel their sensors had detected four days earlier.

As the ship grew larger on the main viewscreen, Kim hoped that their preparations would be sufficient. He would have been reassured immensely by the presence of Seven of Nine, but she was serving as a special adviser to Federation President Bacco during the crisis. *Voyager* still retained data from every Borg encounter they had experienced while in the Delta quadrant, and that data was about to be put to a brutal test.

"Helm, what's our distance?" Chakotay asked.

"Five hundred thousand kilometers," Tare replied.

"Commander Paris, your shuttles are clear to launch," Chakotay called over the comm.

Within moments Harry watched as the *Delta Flyer* with Tom at the helm and four of *Voyager's* Type-9 shuttles streaked out of the bay and entered formation ahead of *Voyager*.

"They'll be in weapons range in ten seconds, Captain," Harry advised, careful to keep his voice calm and steady.

"All weapons, target their shields. Doctor Kaz, is your team ready in cargo bay two?"

"*Affirmative, Captain.*"

Kim watched his chronometer count down, and when it reached zero called out, "The Borg vessel is now in range."

"All ships, open fire," Chakotay ordered.

At his command, the shuttles broke formation and commenced hammering the tactical vessel's shield generators with a barrage of augmented phaser fire, each ship cycling through different frequencies at any given instant. Every time the Borg ship compensated for one of them, it became vulnerable to another, and its shield generators fell like dominoes.

The Borg returned fire, but the Starfleet ships' redesigned shields were proving as effective as their enhanced phasers. The power required to sustain these modifications was massive and would blow out the power relays in minutes, but Harry was confident that this battle was not going to last that long.

"Prepare to drop shields," Chakotay ordered. "Transporter room one, get a lock on five of the Borg and beam them directly to the cargo bay. Tom, bring our shuttles home."

"We're on our way, Captain," Tom's voice replied.

A few tense seconds later, Kaz called over the comm, *"Cargo bay two to the captain. The drones have been captured and subdued."*

"Good work, Doctor. Transfer them to sickbay at once."

"Captain, the Borg vessel's shields are beginning to regenerate," Lasren advised.

"Harry, launch quantum torpedo barrage while there's still time," Chakotay said.

Seconds later, a bright burst of green and orange filled the viewscreen, and Harry, along with everyone else on the bridge, breathed an audible sigh of relief.

Chakotay rose from his chair, smiling for the first time Kim could remember in a long time.

"Take us down to Yellow Alert. All hands, this is the captain. Job well done. We are now moving into phase two."

Turning to Ensign Lasren, he said, "Begin continuous long-range scans. Find us a Borg cube."

Fourteen hours later, Chakotay entered sickbay to find Kaz and his staff monitoring the five drones they had captured from the Borg vessel, each of whom lay unconscious on a biobed behind a level-ten force field.

"Report," he said crisply.

"The procedure was a success, Captain," Kaz informed him. "The drones now all carry the modified nanoprobes."

"Which version of the code did you finally settle on?" Chakotay asked.

"The crudest but also the most effective. The nanoprobes will propagate an alert indicating catastrophic damage. Once that message reaches enough of the cube's systems, the ship will automatically initiate its self-destruct protocol. There's always a chance that the queen, wherever she is, might step in and stop it, but the time delay is set just long enough to allow for maximum dispersal before they emit the 'catastrophic' message. Heck, the queen might just destroy the ships herself before she realizes there wasn't anything wrong with them."

"From your mouth to her ears," Chakotay replied. "And how about the interlink nodes?"

"Thanks to your former EMH's extensive work in the area, it was easy enough to sever these drones from the hive mind, but it was a little trickier to establish a stable link between them. Two of them almost died in the process. But the link appears to be active. You are now the proud owner of your own little collective, Captain. Their orders are simple. 'Go immediately to the central plexus and inject the nanoprobes.'"

"What are the chances the other drones will attack them when they realize that the ones we're returning aren't connected to the rest of the Collective anymore?"

"Excellent," Kaz replied bitterly. "But by transporting

them to five separate locations, we're doing all we can to maximize their potential for success."

"It's the best we can do for now, isn't it?" Chakotay mused.

"I wasn't sure we'd get this far," Kaz admitted. "I'd say it's better than we could have hoped for."

"Once we've detected a cube, we'll need to be ready to deploy the drones at a moment's notice."

"Just give the word, Captain." Kaz nodded. "We'll be ready."

Paris had broken into a cold sweat the instant a cube had showed up on long-range sensors and altered course to intercept them. The tense silence on the bridge suggested that everyone around him shared his fear, but as expected, they were doing an admirable job of focusing on the task at hand. Only Chakotay, seated next to him, appeared both confident and somewhat relaxed.

"Two minutes to intercept," Kim called from tactical.

"Distance from the Rattlesnake Flats?" Chakotay asked.

"Point zero one light-years," Lasren reported

"Helm, maintain course and speed," Chakotay ordered.

"Aye, sir," Tare replied.

"What if they don't follow us?" Paris asked.

"One problem at a time, Commander," Chakotay said.

Seconds later, Harry reported, "One minute to intercept."

"Hold us steady, Tare," Chakotay said.

The face of Tom's father rose unbidden to his mind. His countenance was calm and collected, seemingly at peace. Tom found himself thinking of all the things he suddenly knew he needed to tell him.

"They're charging weapons," Lasren's voice cut through the image, bringing Paris back to the present moment.

"Attack pattern gamma nine," Chakotay called.

A bright green beam blossomed from the cube, and seconds later, the bridge shuddered under the impact.

"Return fire!" Chakotay ordered.

A few volleys were exchanged in which neither ship suffered serious damage.

"I think we have their attention," Chakotay said. "Helm, bring us about. Heading one four one mark eight."

Tom actually envied the grace with which Tare swiftly executed the maneuver. He and Chakotay had briefly discussed the option of Tom taking her place for the mission, but both had agreed she was up to the challenge, and she was calmly proving them right.

"New heading entered," Tare reported.

"Take us to warp nine-point-five," Chakotay said.

"Warp nine-point-five confirmed," Tare replied.

"They are pursuing," Harry added.

"At our present course we will enter the Rattlesnake Flats in less than three minutes," Paris said.

"Steady as she goes," Chakotay said. "Transporter room one, what's your status?"

"*The* Voyager *collective is ready for transport on your order, sir,*" the officer replied.

"Stand by."

"*Acknowledged.*"

Minutes later, bright pink and orange flares began to sprout in the distance. There was nothing flat about the Rattlesnake Flats, a designation given by a stellar cartographer for a stretch of plasma storms and gravimetric eddies not unlike the Badlands, and just as hazardous. Tom could only guess that the shape and swiftness of attack of the whirling strings of plasma had inspired the designation. Warning buoys alerted travelers to avoid the area, but *Voyager* was now headed straight for it.

Several thousand kilometers before reaching the edge of the Flats, Tare dropped out of warp and went to impulse. *Voyager* entered the Flats, and soon it was hard to tell whether the forces pushing the limits of the ship's inertial dampers and artificial gravity were coming from the plasma flares or the Borg.

Tare managed to clear the most destructive flares before guiding the ship into a region near the center of the storms that Patel had mapped earlier. This area contained fewer eruptions, but those that did develop here were of greater intensity. Vorik and Patel had adjusted the ship's sensors to search for trace particle densities, which spiked just before an eruption, in this zone.

"What do you see, Tom?" Chakotay asked.

Studying his armrest display, Paris called to Tare, "Adjust course to heading one three six mark eight. Harry, prepare to drop the pulse mine."

Both officers acknowledged their orders, and though the aft section was struck hard by a volley from the cube, Tare firmly guided the ship into the path of the eruption.

"Release the mine," Tom shouted. "Helm, adjust course to heading one one seven mark two and get us clear."

"Reroute all available power to shields and brace for impact," Chakotay added.

The Borg cube detected the mine the instant it was dropped and moved to avoid it. As it did so, the mine exploded simultaneously in the path of a major plasma flare.

Voyager was far enough from the blast to avoid destruction, but was still battered about by the explosion and failed to avoid a smaller plasma burst directly in front of them. Overloaded relays sent sparks flying throughout the bridge and threw Kim, Lasren, and Oden to the deck.

"Report!" Chakotay called as those who had fallen picked themselves up.

"Hull breach on decks ten and eleven. Emergency force fields are holding," Harry replied. "Shields are down to twenty-eight percent. Power to deck two sections five through nine is offline."

"Evacuate those sections," Paris ordered.

"What about the cube?" Chakotay demanded.

"Their shields are down," Lasren confirmed.

"Chakotay to transporter room one. Send our collective home."

After a few seconds the transport officer's voice came over the comm, *"Transport complete."*

"Tare, get us out of here," Chakotay ordered.

Tare brought the ship around and maneuvered deftly past the cube and headed for open space.

"The cube is still pursuing," Harry said, as a confirming bone-rattling charge shook the bridge. "Our shields are at fifteen percent."

"Reroute power from all nonessential systems," Tom ordered, certain that Lasren was already in the process of doing so.

Another blast struck *Voyager,* harder than any of its predecessors. "Damage to decks three and four," Harry reported. Moments later, "Direct hit to our port nacelle. We're venting plasma."

"What's happening on the cube?" Chakotay asked.

"Their shields have almost regenerated," Lasren said.

"Chakotay to Doctor Kaz. Where are our drones?"

"Three, Four, and Five of Five have almost reached the central plexus. They are encountering resistance. One is no longer active, and Two injected the modified nanoprobes into the main regeneration sequencer."

"We are clear of the Flats," Tare announced.

"Evasive maneuvers," Chakotay said. "Continuous fire, phasers and torpedoes."

Voyager began its final steps in the deadly dance with the cube. After only a few minutes, her shields were at less than ten percent and her phasers were offline.

The cube was having difficulty maneuvering, testament to the damage *Voyager* had already inflicted, but was not yet down for the count.

"Doctor Kaz, report!" Chakotay ordered.

"Five was the only one to reach the central plexus, but scanners cannot confirm whether or not the nanoprobes were injected."

"Should it have worked by now?" Chakotay asked.

"Give it a few more seconds."

All on the bridge held their breath, waiting for the explosive spectacle they had worked so hard to create. Ten seconds later, the cube was still intact and in pursuit.

"I'm sorry, sir," Kaz reported. *"It looks like the* Voyager *collective failed."*

Paris turned to Chakotay, whose face was set in a determined scowl. He didn't have to guess what the captain's next order would be.

"Helm, bring us about. Set collision course," he said.

To her credit, Tare didn't hesitate to carry out the order.

"All hands, this is the captain. We've done what we can, and now we are going to do what we must. It has been my honor to serve with each and every one of you."

Tom returned his gaze to the viewscreen, where the Borg cube was growing larger by the second. He didn't really wonder at Chakotay's order. Other ships had made suicide runs in the last few weeks in similar confrontations, and *Voyager* would not shrink in *her* duty. He did wonder if Chakotay would have been as quick to give that order a year ago, but it didn't matter. *Voyager*'s first captain had given her life to stop the Borg, and surely the crew she had led could do no less.

As the view of the cube began to dominate the screen, all he could think of were B'Elanna and Miral. He knew they would understand, but that wasn't going to make it any easier to accept. Turning back, he glanced at Harry, whose eyes were lowered to his interface.

"Captain!" Harry called out suddenly. "I think it—"

But he didn't need to say more. Bright orange plumes were billowing up from multiple locations within the cube.

"Veer off!" Chakotay shouted. "Veer—"

Voyager groaned in protest as Tare reversed thrusters, and before Tom was thrown from his seat he had a brief but spectacular view of the death of the Borg cube.

CHAPTER TWENTY-FIVE

Jarem Kaz entered the charred remnants of *Voyager*'s conference room to find Tom Paris standing before the room's expansive windows, staring out at the barren star field.

What remained of the oblong table sat at an odd angle to the floor. Fragments of a few chairs peeked out from beneath it. An armrest was now a permanent part of the bulkhead near the door, and every surface remained coated in detritus and dust, the result of an explosion that had ripped through the deck a week earlier during their bloody encounter with the Borg.

Kaz had been up to his elbows in wounded since then, and though all of his patients were now stable, he remained agitated. The minute he had them patched up, it seemed, there were more to fill sickbay's biobeds and the temporary recovery ward they had created in cargo bay three. He hadn't slept for more than an hour in the past six days, but he honestly believed that his inability to relax was less a result of what had recently transpired than of his well-grounded fears that something worse was just around the next corner.

"Am I early or late, Commander?" Kaz asked as kindly as possible.

Paris turned toward him slowly, his face bearing the flat aspect common to victims of shock. "I'm sorry?"

"I thought the captain had called all senior officers to the conference room," Kaz said.

There was a long pause during which Kaz had to wonder whether or not Paris had heard him or was simply struggling to remember the definitions of the words he had just spoken.

"Commander . . ." Kaz began.

"He did," Paris finally answered.

Kaz crossed to face the first officer and was hard-pressed not to unholster his medical tricorder. He had known Paris for almost three years now, but he had never seen the man look so lost.

"What's wrong, Tom?" he asked gently. Though whatever was troubling Paris might be more appropriate to Counselor Cambridge's specialty, Kaz couldn't bear to see the officer who had become the most stable and reasonable command presence *Voyager* had these days beginning to unravel without lending whatever help he could.

"My father's dead," Paris said softly.

Kaz winced, shaking his head in mute acknowledgment of Paris's terrible loss.

"I'm sorry. What happened?"

"When the invasion started, he was assigned to Starbase 234. The Borg destroyed it."

The eyes Tom lifted to Kaz's were damn near vacant. Kaz realized in an instant that the most damaged thing in the room wasn't the furniture. He had been hoping that their recent success against the cube would have reinvigorated everyone. Now it seemed likely that the universe had decided to make the last moments of life he and his friends might have left as excruciatingly painful as possible before granting them the release of oblivion.

Gradak—the former host of the Kaz symbiont—was a Maquis. He had witnessed repeatedly the ravages of war. It had taken Jarem a long time to come to terms with that past. But he had never expected to witness anything approaching the devastation that had almost driven Gradak insane. Now he wondered if integrating those experiences into himself could actually help him navigate through their current crisis. There was really only one way to find out.

Kaz raised his right hand and slapped Paris hard across the face. When Tom recovered, he looked at Kaz with more anger than confusion.

That's a little better.

"Grieve later, Commander," Kaz said. "I imagine when all this is done, if we are still around to count and mourn the dead, the list is going to get substantially longer. But if you don't pull yourself together now, *Voyager* and her crew will most certainly be on it."

Paris took a few quick, revitalizing breaths.

"You're right," he replied more firmly.

"How is the captain?" Kaz asked.

"He's riding everybody pretty hard," Paris answered, "but nowhere near as hard as he's pushing himself. I can't say for sure, but I haven't seen him eat a thing in the last two days."

Kaz nodded. He hadn't expected their victory to slake Chakotay's appetite for revenge for long. But that victory had come at a price the ship couldn't long continue to pay.

"So what is this meeting about?" Kaz asked.

"I honestly don't know," Paris replied.

A breathless Harry Kim was the next to push his way through the room's permanently half-open doors, followed quickly by Counselor Cambridge, Lieutenants Tare and Vorik, and Ensign Lasren. Once he was inside, Cambridge looked desperately for a place to sit and, finding none, perched himself on the edge of the faltering table while he struggled to catch his breath.

"What kept you?" Paris asked.

Kaz was relieved to see that Paris was maintaining his poise and once again doing what he could to keep the mood light. This proclivity of their first officer had done more than anything else of late to keep the crew's morale as high as possible.

"We were in engineering," Harry said between breaths. "Turbolifts are down."

"Say no more." Paris nodded.

Everyone turned as the captain stepped in behind Harry, slapping him on the back good-naturedly. It would have been a comforting sight, the sort of friendly gesture Chakotay would have made in years past, had Kaz not clearly seen its manic origins.

"The good news is, Starfleet has finally managed to construct a cohesive strategy for confronting the Borg," Chakotay said as he moved to the center of the group. "Based on intelligence collected by the *Starships Enterprise* and *Aventine,* Command believes they have found the Borg's gateway to the Alpha quadrant. All available ships have been ordered to regroup at the Azure Nebula, where we will end this invasion once and for all. *Voyager* has been given the honor of leading this fleet."

These last words were spoken with such confidence, Kaz suspected that Chakotay was surprised when everyone in the room didn't break into applause when he finished his announcement.

Instead, wary, troubled eyes focused en masse on the captain.

"Why isn't the *Enterprise* leading the fleet, sir?" Kim asked dubiously.

"The nebula contains multiple subspace apertures, one or more of which, it is believed, leads to the Delta quadrant and has been compromised by the Borg. The *Enterprise* and the *Aventine* will be investigating those apertures, and if possible closing them down. *Voyager* will remain in the Alpha quadrant to hold the line should they fail."

When this was met with somber trepidation, Chakotay asked, "What's our current status, Lieutenant Vorik?"

"Warp drive has been restored, though I do not believe it would be wise to push the engines beyond warp 6 for now. The antimatter injectors are running at borderline efficiency. Repairs to decks eight and nine are proceeding, but it is likely sections ten through fifteen will not be restored to normal operational capacity for at least another twenty hours."

"All personnel have been relocated from those sections and reassigned quarters," Paris added.

"Structural integrity and power distribution remain our primary focus and should be operating at maximum within the next three hours, assuming we are not attacked again between now and then," Vorik concluded.

"Just get us there at best possible speed." Chakotay nodded. "What about weapons, Harry?" Chakotay asked.

"The enhanced phasers have been restored, but we're down to five quantum torpedoes."

"Priority one when we rendezvous with the fleet will be to resupply those stocks, Lieutenant," Chakotay advised.

With a nod, Harry continued, "The shields should be functioning again within the hour, but we're still getting some intermittent energy spikes whenever we attempt to initiate the enhancement protocols."

"I have a team working on that now," Vorik advised Harry.

"Keep up the good work," Chakotay said heartily. "Doctor Kaz?"

"Eighteen crew members remain in critical condition. Four have been returned to duty, and six more should be in the next twenty-four hours. I'd like to suggest we allocate cargo bay two as an additional overflow facility for wounded, as bay three is almost at maximum capacity."

"Do it." Chakotay nodded before adding, "I don't have to tell you that the fate of the Federation may well now lie in our hands. We know how to beat the Borg. We've done it time and time again. We're not going to let the billions of people who are counting on us down. This is one of those times when all of us have to look deep inside for the strength and the will to beat the odds. But that is one thing at which this crew has always excelled. Make me proud."

Everyone but Cambridge appeared visibly heartened by Chakotay's words.

With a crisp nod, Chakotay dismissed his officers, and Kaz watched with a heavy heart as Paris followed his captain to the bridge.

"We few, we happy few," Cambridge said softly to Kaz.

"I beg your pardon, Counselor?"

"Several hundred years ago, King Henry V of England

led a small but determined band of soldiers against a French army that greatly outnumbered his, and through the sheer force of his will conquered that army and won the field at Agincourt."

"Then you think we will succeed?" Kaz asked.

"Oh, no." Cambridge shook his head. "I think we're buggered eight ways to Sunday."

"But . . ." Kaz began.

"This is the battle Chakotay has been seeking for months," Cambridge said. "His ship is being held together right now with spit and a prayer, but he's managed to convince Starfleet Command that he and his crew are ready to lead a fleet. He's encouraging people again, trying to rally the troops. It's just a pity he doesn't understand that he can kill every Borg in the galaxy and that still won't solve his problem."

"No, it won't," Kaz agreed. "But it would solve the Federation's."

"For now, perhaps," Cambridge said.

"You think that somewhere out there, there is something worse than the Borg?"

"Don't you?"

Kaz considered Cambridge carefully. "How do you sleep at night, Counselor?" he asked.

Cambridge actually chuckled.

"Lately, I just try to remind myself that it's probably better to die a man than to live a drone."

"Probably?"

"Civilizations rise and fall, Doctor Kaz. History has taught us well that this is the way of things."

"The Borg are not a civilization. They're a pestilence . . . a force of nature."

"Precisely," Cambridge replied. "And nature always gets the last word."

───────────

Three days later, Chakotay sat expectantly in his command chair waiting for aperture twenty-six alpha of the Azure Nebula to open so that he could unleash hell upon what he knew in his gut would emerge from it. He had a promise to keep, and he'd never been more certain that destiny was about to grant him redemption.

The aperture began to glow faintly, vivid sparks dotting the nebula's bluish swarm of gases like blinking distant stars. Then, as if that multitude of stars had simultaneously gone supernova, the aperture erupted in a blaze of white.

A singe Borg cube blotted out the brightness of the spectacle.

Followed by a second.

And a third.

Tom Paris had already ordered the fleet to open fire when Chakotay lost count of the number of cubes tearing through the brilliance before him and time slowed to a crawl.

Over three hundred and forty Federation and Allied vessels were arrayed in battle formation inside the nebula. The first cube to emerge opened fire upon *Voyager* while the second and third targeted the two ships closest to them, the Romulan *Warbird Loviatar* and the Imperial Klingon vessel *Ya'Vang*. As the bridge rattled thunderously under the initial impact of the barrage, the cube held its course. Its compatriots hurled themselves directly at the flanking ships, and what the Borg's directed energy weapons failed to pulverize, the cubes themselves completely eradicated, charging headlong toward them through the ships that had all too briefly stood in their way.

Chakotay found his eyes moving to the conn, where his helmsman, Akolo Tare, immediately corrected course to avoid the oncoming cube. The wailing of overstressed tritanium echoed briefly through the bridge as Tom's voice called out, "Brace for impact!" And then there was silence as Chakotay's eardrums were shredded by the concussive force of *Voyager*'s port nacelle being sheared from the ship. Tare had managed to avoid the collision, for the most part.

In a violent lurch Chakotay was thrown by a force several times that of normal gravity against the console between his chair and Tom's. With a sharp crack, his left arm snapped and a blinding rush of pain shot through his body. Simultaneously his nose briefly burned, then numbed, and he tasted the tang of blood pouring over his lips.

Voyager's inertial dampers were miraculous things, but clearly even they had their limits.

Shrapnel hit the back of Chakotay's neck, but it was little more than a stinging nuisance. Turning to assess the damage, he saw the tactical station in flames. Seconds later, the blaze grew brighter and hotter, indicating that the fire suppression systems were offline.

The shadow of Tom Paris flashed briefly through his peripheral vision, moving toward the conn. Another explosion sent Tare flying from her seat before she fell in a tangled heap to the deck.

The now rudderless ship rolled precariously to the right. Chakotay felt the beginnings of the sensation of free fall, a lurching in his gut as his body anticipated descent.

A final explosion caught the left side of Chakotay's face, but he barely registered the pain as dark pinpoints began to squeeze his head.

Through streaks of static the viewscreen registered the fate of the rest of Chakotay's fleet. There were no vessels in sight, only charred hulls and chunks of twisted metal glowing and flaming to their deaths.

And still, more cubes were coming.

All of this the Borg had wrought in less than thirty seconds.

For the first time, Chakotay glimpsed in all its horror the truth Kathryn might have known in the seconds before she was lost to the Borg. Two words pummeled Chakotay's mind but failed to reach his lips before the blackness swallowed him.

I'm sorry.

Tom Paris was certain he had been upright the last time he checked. Now, he was lying flat on his back beneath a heavy piece of bulkhead. His eyes stung as fine particulate matter cascaded into them from above. Without a free hand to dislodge it, he was forced to blink through the tears attempting to do that job for him. Apart from a dull ringing in his ears, the bridge was shrouded in silence. Tom gingerly rolled to his right, shifting the bulkhead debris and freeing his left arm, but came to an abrupt stop when he found himself staring into the lifeless eyes of Akolo Tare. Death had clearly taken her by surprise.

The bulkhead still weighing down upon him, Tom began to crawl from beneath it, using his elbows for leverage. Inhaling deeply, he tasted the bitter stench of burning plasma.

A million miles away, from the sound of it, Chakotay's voice was murmuring, *"Smashed the whole fleet . . ."*

Tom finally reached his hands and knees and dragged himself over the helm console, which was now a couple of feet closer to the floor than it used to be, to briefly see the grainy image of Captain Jean-Luc Picard staring grimly at what was left of *Voyager*'s bridge before blinking out of frame.

The first thought that came to Tom's mind was that if, after what he had just witnessed, Captain Picard and Captain Chakotay were somehow still alive, there might yet be hope for the Federation. Tom turned back over his left shoulder and received a jolt of pain shooting up his spine for his trouble. Chakotay was slumped over in his chair. The left side of his face was blackened and the front of his uniform was covered in fresh blood, which, as best Tom could tell, had originated from his clearly broken nose.

But the sight that caused Tom's heart to momentarily still was his captain's eyes.

Paris managed to pull himself upright with effort and after a quick check determined that, amazingly, aside from a few tender spots and more complaints from his lower back, he was relatively unscathed. Crossing to Chakotay, Tom brought his face level to his.

"Chakotay?"

A low gurgling suggested that the captain might be trying to answer, but might just as easily mean that he had sustained internal injuries that included the entrance of fluid into his lungs.

Tom looked about him for the emergency medical kit

standard to the bridge, but amid the wreckage surrounding him was quickly disabused of the notion that he had that kind of time. Instead, he turned back to Chakotay and began to gently palpate the captain's chest and abdomen. When this crude examination failed to elicit a visible pain response, Tom decided that Chakotay's injuries, while serious, were not going to result in immediate death.

Chakotay's eyes remained open, their gaze fixed on the viewscreen. Tom took a moment to wave his hand back and forth before Chakotay's eyes and registered no response.

He's gone. Not dead, but definitely in shock, Tom realized in an instant. The grief Chakotay had carried for so long, coupled with his anger and fear, had just culminated in a moment so scarring to the soul that finally the captain's spirit had buckled under the weight. Tom couldn't really blame Chakotay, though given the fact that Tom had his own demons to battle right now, he spared a moment to accept that while Chakotay's condition might also have been one possible end for Tom, he wasn't going to embrace that option right now. There was nothing more Tom could do for Chakotay at this instant, but there might be others he could help.

Paris moved to the ops console, where Ensign Lasren sat upright on the floor.

"Lasren, are you all right?" Tom asked.

"I don't know," Lasren replied. "Where am I?"

Hell, Tom almost replied, but caught the word before it could escape his lips.

"If you can stand your post, I could really use a report right now," Tom said.

Lasren nodded slightly, then with Tom's help pulled himself toward his console, which had taken less damage than the rest of the bridge.

Rather than wait for him to get his bearings, Tom moved to the rear bridge stations, where wisps of smoke flickered up from what once had been the tactical station.

"Harry!" Tom called, suddenly fearful.

A tangle of conduit had fallen from the ceiling and Tom maneuvered carefully through it, worried that he might hit the end of a severed wire that still had power running through it. It wasn't all that likely, but at this moment it would be Tom's luck.

"Harry!" Tom called out again, when he failed to locate him immediately on the other side.

"We've lost primary power and are running on forty-two percent of backups," Lasren called out from ops.

"Can you raise engineering?" Tom asked. *Harry, where are you?*

"Negative. Communications are down through the ship."

"What about navigation?"

"Are we going somewhere?" Lasren asked.

Tom almost smiled at the gallows humor.

"Emergency force fields are in place on decks eight through fifteen, but they're taking a lot of power," Lasren said. "Shall I reroute—" he began, but Tom cut him off.

"Take whatever you need from everywhere but life support," Tom said as his foot impacted something soft but unflinching.

Kneeling, Tom finally found Harry rolled on his right side, practically hidden under what remained of his former station.

Paris gently rolled him onto his back and had to swallow deeply to keep his churning stomach acids where they belonged.

Harry's face and torso were covered in plasma burns.

Tom checked immediately for a pulse, and though what he found was neither strong nor constant, it was at least there.

Tom knew it wouldn't be for long unless Harry received medical care immediately.

"Is the *Enterprise* still out there?" Tom asked.

"No, sir," Lasren replied, "but it looks like they sent emergency personnel over before they left."

"Where are they?" Tom asked.

"Engineering and sickbay," Lasren replied.

"I don't suppose we've got transporters?" Tom asked.

"No, sir."

Tom's mind began to race around the dozens of brick walls that were separating him from his only priority at the moment: saving Harry's life.

"How much damage did the shuttlebay take?" Tom asked.

"All shuttles are undamaged," Lasren replied after a moment, clearly surprised.

"Can you tap into the *Delta Flyer's* transporter system?" Tom asked.

"I think so," Lasren said almost enthusiastically.

"Do it," Tom said, "and transport me and Harry to sickbay immediately."

While he waited for Lasren to execute his request, Tom grasped Harry's hand.

Hang in there, Tom thought. *That's an order.*

A few moments later, Tom felt the tingle of the transporter effect. When his vision cleared, he found himself in the corridor outside sickbay among dead and dying crew who were being evaluated by two harried-looking medical officers Tom had never seen.

"I've got an emergency here!" Tom shouted.

One of the medics glanced his way but failed to move toward him.

Sensing that no amount of screaming and yelling was going to get him what he needed right now, Tom began to tread carefully through the ship's new triage area toward the doors of sickbay.

As soon as he reached them one of the medics barked, "You can't go in there, sir. The damage was too heavy."

Tom had no interest in arguing the point. As long as the damage wasn't complete, there might still be something behind those doors that could save Harry's life.

Grabbing a loose wedge of metal, Tom hurriedly set about prying the doors, which were uncomfortably warm to the touch, open.

With a heavy groan, Tom managed to wedge the doors wide enough to slip through. What he found was a black space, filled with smoke and littered with debris and carnage.

Taking a deep breath of cleaner air from the hall, Tom entered. The first body he stepped over was that of Jarem Kaz. His once gentle face was now a mask of shock. Deep, black, smoking burns covered much of his body. Tom knew he was past help but couldn't stop himself from pausing over yet another friend lost in a matter of moments. Steeling himself, Tom realized that two lives had been taken in Jarem Kaz. The burns left no doubt that both host and symbiont were dead.

Refusing to give in to the shock and accompanying wave of dizziness, Tom moved on to search what was left of *Voyager*'s sickbay. He managed to find a few intact hypos and one shelf of medication that had tumbled onto the floor without shattering.

Gathering these few precious discoveries along with a working medical tricorder, a laser scalpel, and a dermal regenerator, Tom hurried back out into the hall and returned to Harry's side.

Scanning him, he detected numerous internal injuries to accompany his external ones. Still, the vibrant young man's heart refused to stop.

That's right, Paris thought. *Stay with me.*

Hurriedly Tom searched through his small cache of drugs and found both tri-ox and kelotane. It wasn't much, but it was a start and should be enough to keep Harry alive until the full extent of his injuries could be evaluated.

Tom injected Harry with the medications and sat back on his heels. He knew he needed to get up and move on.

Soon, he promised himself, he would.

After a few selfish seconds of dull immobility, Paris picked himself up and moved to the next nearest injured member of his crew.

MARCH 2381

CHAPTER TWENTY-SIX

Two weeks after the slaughter at the Azure Nebula, as Tom Paris had privately taken to calling it, he was sitting a weary vigil outside Harry's room at Starfleet Medical on Earth. The *Enterprise* medics had succeeded in stabilizing Harry. The surgeries he required had been postponed until Harry had been shipped out with the rest of the grievously injured to Earth thirty-six hours later.

It had taken Paris another week to get back home. With Chakotay confined to quarters under the care of Counselor Cambridge, the task of supervising *Voyager*'s recovery efforts had fallen to him. Cambridge had suggested more than once that they abandon ship, but Tom had found that unacceptable. Instead, he, Vorik, and *Voyager*'s eighty-nine other survivors had focused on beginning repairs that would at least make the ship space-worthy again. Using their shuttles, they and a handful of other vessels that avoided complete destruction had managed to scavenge parts from the ship graveyard that rung the Azure Nebula, supplementing their supplies with what the *Enterprise* had been able to spare when they had returned for the final confrontation against the Borg. Miraculously, that confrontation had ended both quickly and in the Alpha quadrant's favor. To this day Tom still found it hard to believe that anyone had survived. But to his credit, and that of the crew, *Voyager* had been spared the indignity of being towed back to Earth, though more than one vessel, heartened by *Voyager*'s survival and determination, had assured Tom they would consider it an honor to do so. Vorik had managed to get their warp drive working, and Paris had never been so proud in his life than he was the moment he had sat in the stripped-down bridge's command chair and ordered Ensign T.J. Sydney, a gamma-shift conn officer, to set a course for home.

The latest reports Tom had received from Harry's doctors indicated that he would make a complete recovery— eventually. For the moment, he was lying in a medically induced coma to minimize the strain on his body as it continued to heal.

For the last several hours, strains of delicate music had been wafting gently from Harry's room. It was the most melancholy sound Tom had ever heard and made him physically ache for B'Elanna and Miral.

He knew they were safe for now, if completely beyond his reach. Painful as it was to remember, he found himself thinking back to the last time they had been together and there had still been hope in his heart.

STARDATE 57312: APRIL 24, 2380

At B'Elanna's insistence, Tom had first contacted his old Academy buddy, Dil Moore, just before *Voyager* had shipped out following the rescue of B'Elanna and Miral and liberty on Earth. After weeks of arguing, B'Elanna had awakened one morning more at peace than Tom could remember in some time. Unfortunately, she had also awakened with a plan, and Tom had been unable to talk her out of it.

Dil had completed the Academy specializing in the most esoteric of engineering theories, but had resigned his commission after the required years of active service following graduation. He had established a civilian research facility in the wilds of Montana and happily spent his days theorizing technology Tom could rarely pronounce, let alone understand the applications for.

B'Elanna had insisted that he find a place for her with appropriate facilities for herself and Miral that did not fall under Starfleet's purview, so Dil's had been at the top of a very short list.

Eighteen months later Tom had received an urgent message from B'Elanna. He'd requested permission to return to Earth several weeks before *Voyager* had completed their exhaustive analysis of the Yaris Nebula. Even before Tom had finished making the request, Chakotay had given him his blessing and an extended leave to take the *Delta Flyer* to Earth. Tom didn't think he'd succeed in talking some sense into B'Elanna, but buoyed by Chakotay's encouragement, he had set off, determined to do what he could.

Dil was the first to greet him when he arrived in the warehouse that had become his family's home.

"Can't wait to see her, huh?" Dil said, slapping Tom on the back cheerfully.

"You've got that right." Tom smiled.

"It's a shame, really," Dil said.

"What is?" Tom asked, dismayed.

"She's much too beautiful a ship to go under the name *Unregistered Vessel 47658.*"

"You think?" Tom asked, realizing that of course Dil was more interested in the fantastic new toy B'Elanna had built than the woman herself. As Dil's tastes ran toward more exotic and classically buxom women, and even in his darkest hours Tom had never questioned B'Elanna's love for or devotion to him, Tom hadn't lost a night's sleep worrying that in spending so much time together, B'Elanna and Dil would have done anything that would have forced Tom to murder his old friend. Unfortunately, he'd had plenty of other fears to keep him up at night.

"I have to admit, I never thought B would be able to re-create that crazy slipstream drive from scratch without Starfleet, the tech being classified and all, but damn if she didn't. Guess the work she did with it in the DQ really sank in."

"She solved the phase variance problem?" Tom asked, his heart sinking. Frankly, he'd been hoping that this, the most difficult part of slipstream technology, might never be overcome and would force B'Elanna to reconsider.

"She found a way around. A couple of algorithms I've never seen. She says they're Borg inspired, which scares the crap out of me, but they sure seem to do the trick for the little UV. I don't think they'd be as effective at compensating on a larger scale, but then again . . ."

"Did she finish the defensive systems?"

"Hell, yes. I wouldn't want to meet B'Elanna in a dark corner of space if she was pissed at me with the phasers and torpedoes she's loaded the ship with. Do you have any idea where she came up with the idea for a transphasic torpedo?"

"Nope," Tom lied.

"They're a hell of a thing, at least what little I understand of the theory of them. Of course, she'd eat the schematics before she'd let me look at 'em."

With good reason, Tom mused, as Starfleet had classified that device the moment *Voyager* had returned to the Alpha quadrant, right after B'Elanna had personally handed the schematics and the remaining ordnance to Starfleet.

"But just wait until you see the holodeck," Dil went on. "My girlfriend's closet is bigger, but it'll do the trick for little Miral."

Tears rose unbidden to Tom's eyes at the casual ease with which Dil referred to his daughter. Oblivious, Dil continued, "I swear if there was an amount of latinum or Risan bath salts that would keep B'Elanna here, I'd gladly pay it. I've never in my life seen anyone as resourceful."

"If latinum was all it would take, my friend, I'd have stolen it long ago," Tom replied.

They navigated several rows of shelving loaded down with unknown containers before they entered into the open space at the end of the warehouse containing one of the most beautiful ships Tom had ever seen. Of necessity, she was a little larger than the *Delta Flyer*, but her lines were every bit as graceful and sleek.

Part of Tom wanted to take a turn at the helm.

The rest of him wanted to drop a photon torpedo on it.

The aft hatch was open, and, bidding Dil farewell, Tom slid quietly inside.

"*B is for banana,*" Tom heard B'Elanna's voice say. "*Banana. You love bananas. Can you say banana?*"

Tom hesitated to enter the forward compartment, as he was suddenly dying to know if Miral could.

"*Guh,*" Miral's halting voice stammered.

"*Banana,*" B'Elanna repeated patiently.

"*Gunana,*" Miral tried.

"*Almost. Try again. Banana,*" B'Elanna said, enunciating each syllable. "*Ba-na-na.*"

"*Buh-ganana,*" Miral finally said jubilantly.

Tom stepped forward.

"Buganana—that's close enough," he said, his heart torn to shreds at the sight of his wife seated on the floor of the cockpit with Miral in her lap sharing a banana.

The instant she saw him B'Elanna's face was filled with joy as she set down Miral and pulled Tom into a fierce hug. Several passionate kisses later she said, "I was terrified you weren't going to get back here in time."

"In time for what?" Tom demanded. "You weren't going to leave, were you?"

"We're ready, Tom," she said, her eyes alight. "A few more tweaks and we can launch—before the week is out, I'm sure of it."

"You say that like it's a good thing," Tom replied.

"Isn't it?" she asked, her face clouding over. "The sooner we get out there the sooner—"

"I know," Tom cut her off. "I just . . ."

Miral had lost all interest in the banana and had teetered over to her parents, but instead of jumping into her father's arms, as her mother had, she firmly grabbed B'Elanna's right leg and held on, staring up at Tom warily.

She doesn't remember me anymore, Tom thought, alarmed.

Of course, given how little he'd seen of her in the last eighteen months, that was almost to be expected. Still, it rent his heart anew.

Kneeling down to her level, Tom said softly, "Hi, beautiful. I've missed you so much. Do you have a hug for Daddy?"

"Miral, go to your daddy," B'Elanna encouraged her.

Instead, Miral stayed put and managed to bury her face in B'Elanna's leg.

"Miral," Tom gently coaxed again.

A single eye poked out, toying with Tom.

"Daddy?" she asked.

"Come here, baby," Tom said, reaching out for her.

She didn't unglue herself easily, but finally allowed Tom to pick her up. She continued to stare at him uncertainly, but at least she wasn't pitching the fit Tom had feared. When it came to tempers, Tom didn't think Miral would consider herself blessed to inherit either her mother's or her father's.

"Do you want some more buganana?" Tom asked, nuzzling her forehead.

"Don't encourage her," B'Elanna chided him.

"Buganana," Miral repeated, reaching toward the deck where the uneaten portion remained.

Tom retrieved it for her, replying, "You parent your way, I'll parent mine."

B'Elanna sighed deeply but let it pass.

"How's everyone?" she asked, obviously trying to change the subject.

"On *Voyager*?"

"Yes."

"According to Harry, we've gone from the Ship of Death to the Ship of the Bored to Death. He sends his love, by the way. And he picked up a couple of Taborian Puzzlemanias for Miral. I have them in my bag."

"I'm sure she'll love them," B'Elanna replied. "Last I heard, though, Starfleet found a Borg cube in the Alpha quadrant."

Tom didn't really want to know how B'Elanna knew that. He'd heard about the cube the moment he'd arrived on Earth, about the *Enterprise*'s recent encounter with a vessel that had somehow gotten separated from the rest of the Collective and ended up in Federation space.

"Chakotay says Admiral Janeway wanted to send Seven to investigate, but Captain Picard managed to solve the problem before she could get there."

"Why didn't they send *Voyager*?" B'Elanna asked, as if that would have been the obvious thing for Starfleet to do.

"We were in the middle of a mission at the Yaris Nebula, where I'm sure we were much more useful counting baby stars and scanning uninhabited systems," Tom replied with disdain. When B'Elanna said nothing more, Tom went on, "So if you're worried about *Voyager*'s duties becoming too hazardous for you to return, you really can put those fears to rest."

"You know that's not what I'm worried about," B'Elanna said a little more forcefully. "Kahless says the Warriors of Gre'thor are just biding their time, waiting for the right moment."

"The Warriors of Gre'thor don't have the slightest idea where you are right now. And even if they found you one day on *Voyager*, we'd take them. You know that. Oh, and while we're on the subject, when exactly did Kahless's wishes become more important than your husband's?"

"Please, Tom, let's not do this again."

"You're getting ready to leave the quadrant, and you're

taking our daughter with you. I'd say we have at least one more discussion in us before that happens."

"It's not forever, Tom," B'Elanna fired back. "If I could return to *Voyager* without putting the lives of those I love most in terrible danger, don't you think I'd do it?"

"We're all in danger every day we serve in Starfleet," Tom countered. "Hell, I'd take the Warriors of Gre'thor over Species 8472 or the Swarm or the Voth any day."

"That was different. We didn't have a choice when we were in the Delta quadrant. We do now."

"I'm pretty sure at several points in our lives together you've reminded me that running away from my problems was nothing but a temporary solution."

"I'm not running away," B'Elanna insisted. "I'm going out there for a reason. And once I've done what I need to do, you and I and Miral will be a real family again and we won't have to run from anyone. You agreed to stick to the plan. It's the only way."

Tom knew a B'Elanna wall when he saw one.

"Swear it," he said softly.

"I'll do better than that," she replied.

After a bit of private time back in B'Elanna's quarters, with Dil happily watching over Miral, they returned to the warehouse and Tom found himself going over his wife's launch preparations with a fine-tooth comb. He had to admit, she'd thought of everything, right down to a holographic nanny, a Klingon who bore an uncanny resemblance to Kularg.

At the end of that day, just when Miral had finally

warmed up to him, Tom bid them both farewell. He went first to San Francisco to tell his parents a necessary, painful lie: that he and B'Elanna had decided to separate. This had also been at B'Elanna's insistence. If the Warriors of Gre'thor were going to accept the big lie, which was still several carefully plotted months away, they had to believe first that B'Elanna and Miral were on their own, separated from anyone who might come to their aid. Tom's parents were the first, but eventually, Tom would have to make this known more publicly for it to reach T'Krek's ears.

In doing so, Tom had shattered irrevocably the peace he had established with his father. Owen had harangued his son mercilessly for failing in his duty as a husband and a father, and Tom had been so stung by his remarks that he had responded in kind.

Tom had then returned to *Voyager*, and literally begun to count the days until the heart he had left behind in a warehouse in Montana would once again be returned to him.

Julia hadn't thought her son could look worse than the night he had come home and told her and Owen that his marriage was over. Seated in the hospital corridor, hunched over in a terribly uncomfortable chair, his head resting in his hands, she could actually see the weight of the universe dragging Tom down. He looked smaller than she could ever remember.

She had been moving through a fog of grief and shock for the last two weeks. As she approached Tom, part of her worried that if she got too close, he might evaporate before her eyes.

She was grateful when he looked up to see her standing a few meters away and immediately rose to take her in his arms.

Julia had promised herself that she was done with crying. She had always believed the day would come when a couple of clean-cut ensigns would arrive at her door to tell her that her husband had been killed in the line of duty. It hadn't happened exactly that way. There had been too much chaos on high for such niceties at the peak of the Borg invasion. She had been alone, watching the Federation News Service, when she learned of the destruction of Starbase 234, and she had been forced to wade through hours of uncertainty before confirmation finally arrived that Owen was dead.

Her first thought had been to try and reach Tom. That had proved impossible until the threat had passed days later. This was the first time they had laid eyes on each other, let alone spoken, since Owen's death. In what had felt like the endless interim, she had survived on his swiftly worded communiqués updating her on *Voyager*'s progress and expected return to Earth.

The moment she felt Tom's strong arms around her, the tears began to pour forth again. He allowed her to sob until she had exhausted herself, then gently drew her toward the chair where he had been sitting.

She was suddenly aware of the most strange and ethereal music and actually wondered if she might not be imagining it.

"Do you hear that?" Julia asked her son.

"The music?"

Julia nodded.

Tom knelt before his mother, taking both her hands in

his, and replied, "Do you remember Harry's former fiancée, Libby Webber?"

Lately Julia was hard-pressed to remember what she'd had for breakfast, but the name almost rang a bell.

"She's a concert musician, specializing in a Ktarian stringed instrument called the *lal-shak*. She's actually kind of famous. Anyway, I don't know how she found out about Harry, but his parents told me that ever since he arrived, she's been here. She rarely leaves his side, and most of the time she plays for him. He's in a coma, but the doctor still thinks it might be comforting. Mr. and Mrs. Kim were adamant that she be allowed to stay. I don't think she's left his side for a week."

"That's lovely," Julia said.

"I guess." Tom shrugged. "She broke his heart, a couple of times now. And she told me the other day she's actually getting married in a couple of weeks."

"To whom?"

"I don't know, Mom. I think she said his name was Aidan . . . Fletcher maybe."

"Darling, he's a director of Starfleet Intelligence, isn't he?"

Tom paused, clearly taking this in.

"Hmm," he finally murmured.

"What?"

"Maybe that's why she turned poor Harry down," Tom said ungenerously. "Guess she thought she could do better."

Julia considered this for a moment before realizing that it was nowhere near as important as what she had meant to say to her son the moment she saw him.

"Tom, your father never meant what he said to you that night."

"I know—" Tom began, but she went on, as the words she'd been holding back for Owen's sake finally came pouring forth.

"He loved you and B'Elanna and Miral so. He was terribly disappointed, of course. But he shouldn't have blamed you. He knew there was more to it than that. He just—"

"Mom," Tom cut her off. "*I know.*"

Julia was bewildered. Even at Admiral Janeway's funeral her husband and son, united in their grief, hadn't been able to find a civil word to say to one another.

"How?" she asked.

"He told me," Tom said, clutching her hands tighter. "He sent a message, just before . . ." Tom swallowed hard. "He said he was sorry. He said . . . everything I needed to hear."

Tom trailed off before his own grief reasserted its stranglehold upon him.

Julia, whose gratitude to her husband for this final gesture was now beyond words, gently pulled Tom's head toward her heart and held him there as she had so often when he was a boy. Back then there was no problem so big that her arms and a few comforting words couldn't solve. These days it seemed woefully inadequate, but was truly all she had to offer.

Finally, Tom pulled away and rose.

"How are you holding up?" he asked.

Julia smiled faintly. "The universe all but came to an end a few days ago. But we're still here. I don't understand why we were spared."

"It has to be enough that we were," Tom replied. "We're never going to know the reasons why. But as long as we are still here, we owe it to ourselves and to those who didn't survive to make the best of it."

Julia gazed up at Tom, fierce pride welling inside her. Rising, she placed her hands on either side of his face and replied, "You're so like him, do you know that?"

"Like Dad?" Tom asked, almost incredulously.

Julia nodded firmly.

"He would have been so proud of what you've done, leading your crew through this savagery. It's what he would have done."

"Thanks, Mom," Tom replied softly.

A soft hiss of the door behind them sounded, and Julia ended their embrace and attempted to collect herself. A lovely young woman emerged, her long black hair caught up in a disheveled ponytail and her face betraying deep-set lines of worry.

"Don't mind me," she said quickly, and started down the hall.

"Wait," Tom insisted. "Libby, this is my mother, Julia Paris."

Libby extended her hand, and Julia took it graciously, saying, "What a tremendous gift you have. Your music is enchanting."

Libby blushed under the compliment. "Thank you. It's a pleasure to meet you, ma'am. I'm so sorry for your loss."

Julia nodded and replied, "Thank you. But my son tells me congratulations are in order for you. You are engaged to be married?"

Libby looked lost for only a moment, then said, "Oh, yes. I guess I am."

"In the shadow of these dark days, any ray of hope is welcome, my dear. Embrace the happiness that is before you, for it is upon such simple joys that the rest of us will have to begin to rebuild."

"Thank you," Libby replied, her voice thick. "I will."

"Are you going home?" Tom asked.

"No," Libby replied. "They're not going to wake him up until tomorrow morning. I just needed to get some coffee."

"Allow me, dear," Julia said. "I could use some myself."

"Mom . . ."

"I'll be right back," Julia insisted, and strode away, her head held high.

As Tom and Libby looked after her, Libby said, "You didn't want to tell her the lounge is the other way?"

"She's trying to make an exit," Tom replied. "She wouldn't want me to mess that up for her. It's too important that you and I believe she is just fine."

"Amazing," Libby said.

"That she is."

"I don't know how I'd survive what she's . . ."

There was an uncomfortable pause in which neither of them seemed to know how best to continue. Finally Tom said, "You know, it's really nice, you being here and all. I know it means a lot to Harry's folks. But if Harry wakes up and sees you, he's just going to think—"

"I know," Libby cut him off. "Don't worry. I'll leave before he knows I was ever here. And Mr. and Mrs. Kim have promised not to tell him either."

"But why did you come in the first place?"

"How could I not?" Libby asked.

"Pretty easily, I'd say."

Libby had always known how close Tom and Harry were. The rule of best friends required that Tom hate Libby now even more than Harry did, as she had been the one to refuse Harry's proposal. True, Harry had actually ended their relationship, but Libby didn't think that would matter much to Tom. She had broken what was between them. Harry had just finally decided to stop trying to glue it back together.

A lot of time had passed since then, and Libby truly hoped it had lessened the sting. In case it hadn't, she said, "It's okay to still be angry at me, Tom, for Harry's sake. I don't expect these past few days to change anything."

"Good," Tom replied. "It's not that I don't appreciate the gesture and all. I just don't want you opening old wounds."

"Harry was my first love," Libby said sincerely. "There will always be a place in my heart with his name on it. I regret that things didn't work out, but the moment I learned that he might die, I had to come. I had to tell him—" She caught herself before finishing the thought.

"Had to tell him what?"

Libby took a moment to choose her words carefully.

"That it wasn't his fault."

"What wasn't?"

"It doesn't matter," Libby replied. "He's going to be fine. That's all that's important now."

Tom studied her face, as if he could force the answer to his question from it. With practiced ease she kept her countenance maddeningly neutral.

Finally Tom said, "Would you mind if I spend a few minutes with him? I'm going to have to check in with *Voyager* soon, and Harry's parents are due back in an hour."

"Please, take as much time as you want," Libby replied.

Tom nodded and moved past her to enter Harry's room. Once he was inside and the door closed behind him, she bowed her head and exhaled slowly, allowing the tension that had flared between them to dissipate.

Placing her hand on the closed door, she chided herself for her little lapse. What she hadn't been able to tell Harry before they separated, she wasn't about to tell Tom. He would undoubtedly tell Harry, and Libby couldn't bear the thought of Harry hearing the truth from anyone but her. When she had accepted Aidan's proposal, she had resigned her commission with Starfleet Intelligence. She could marry Aidan or she could work for him. She could never do both. So now the secret that had kept her from marrying Harry no longer needed to be kept.

She had come here half hoping that she could finally share this with Harry. Libby knew that what she had withheld had damned their relationship. But as she had sat by Harry's side, day after day, allowing her music to offer the only solace she could provide, she'd come to the conclusion that after so long, the truth might not do Harry any good at all. Harry had moved on, just as she had. Though unburdening herself to Harry would have relieved her regrets, it would probably only add to his. At a time when Harry needed all of his strength to get better, she refused to add to his physical and mental pain just so she could assuage her guilty conscience.

She hadn't been willing to sacrifice her work as a covert operative for Harry. When Harry had proposed, she honestly believed she had been doing good work with SI. As much as her musical abilities, that work had begun to define her. To marry Harry would have been to resign both of them to half a life and a marriage built on a foundation of ever-shifting sands. She could never share herself with Harry completely. But with Aidan, this would never be an issue. That had been the first reason she had finally agreed to marry him.

The second was that even before Aidan proposed, just after the Borg attack at Acamar, Libby had been overwhelmed by the futility of her choice to be an operative. She and hundreds of bright, capable, and dedicated officers just like her had spent the vast majority of their waking hours trying to detect and prevent attacks upon the Federation. What the Borg had done in a week proved beyond a doubt that either the Federation was wasting their resources, or the term *military intelligence* truly was an oxymoron.

Now she only wanted Harry healthy and one day as happy as he had made her when both of their lives had been much less complicated. And she wanted to find her own peace, far from the realm of secrets and subterfuge.

In the meantime, she knew Tom would continue to look after Harry, and that brought her a modicum of happiness. More importantly, Harry would also still be around to look after Tom.

"Take good care, both of you," she said softly, before squaring her shoulders and walking away—an exit of which she felt even Julia Paris might have approved.

APRIL 2381

CHAPTER TWENTY-SEVEN

The Doctor emerged from Irene's bedroom to find Seven sitting on the floor in the hall outside the door. Her back was straight, and both of her arms hugged her knees into her chest. Her eyes held a wistful, faraway expression. There was something both childlike and dejected in the pose.

"Seven," he said softly, "are you all right?"

Instantly pushing herself up off the floor and once again towering over him, she replied, "My well-being is not the issue. Were you able to help her?"

"I have increased her dosage of peridaxon, and I'm also ordering daily doses of xanatopropoline. It's a new formulation, it should allow her to rest more comfortably. I'm truly sorry that there isn't more I can do for her right now."

"Her condition seemed to have stabilized," Seven said. "I did not expect the delusions to begin so soon."

"Irumodic syndrome attacks every brain differently. Clearly hers is an aggressive form. At the very least, I can assure you that her suffering from this point on will not be extended, and she will, from time to time, continue to enjoy periods of lucidity."

Seven looked briefly as if he had struck her across the face. The Doctor instantly regretted the bluntness of his approach. Usually with Seven he was dealing with an individual whose clinical temperament made his look positively warm. Seeing her now, for the first time freed completely of the Borg technology that had once sustained her, she appeared more fragile than ever. In a way, it was to be expected. She had lost her first mother figure only ten months earlier, and had never, as far as the Doctor could tell, truly grieved Admiral Janeway's death. Of course she had been upset. But the process of actually beginning to come to terms with the emotional devastation of such deep loss was the work of time, and Seven hadn't had enough, between her rigorous schedule at the Academy, her aunt's deterioration, and the imminent destruction of the Federation.

Now, he had just told her that she was soon to add to the list of those lost the second woman Seven had ever looked to for strength and emotional support and her only blood relative on Earth. He was briefly overwhelmed with a desire to take her in his arms and comfort her. But she remained, as ever, completely untouchable.

"Why don't we go downstairs and sit for a while?" he suggested.

"You must return to your duties at Jupiter Station," Seven replied.

"They'll still be there whenever I get back," he countered, heading toward the stairs and hoping she would follow him down.

When they had served together, the Doctor had made a point of taking Seven under his wing and offering her instruction as to how best to begin to integrate herself socially with the crew. He was well aware that many of the senior officers felt this was a little like the blind leading the deaf, but over time he had been terribly pleased with Seven's progress. She had not shared with him or anyone, as far as he knew, exactly what had happened to her when the Caeliar had transformed the Borg. He had hoped that this transition might bring her that much closer to the humanity that she had studied but rarely fully embraced. Watching her perch herself gingerly on the edge of Irene's favorite and very worn sofa, and looking much paler than usual, he began to worry that whatever had happened to her had actually somehow managed to force her in the opposite direction.

"How are your classes going?" he asked, choosing the most innocuous ground he could think of to begin to bridge the palpable distance between them.

"My students wish to speak of nothing but the Caeliar," Seven replied coldly. "And since, for the moment, what little intelligence Starfleet has gathered about them remains classified, I find it most tiresome to deflect their questions."

"And how are *you* dealing with the experience?" the Doctor asked cautiously.

She refused to meet his eyes.

"I will adapt."

"Of course you will, but how?" the Doctor tried again.

"I do not know," she faltered.

"Is there anything I can do to help?"

"No," she replied firmly. Changing the subject too abruptly, she asked, "What is the status of your work with Doctor Zimmerman and Lieutenant Barclay?"

Normally this would have been his cue to launch into a lengthy discourse on their progress, which was actually quite thrilling at the moment. As it was, it seemed too much like willful deflection.

"Seven, we don't have to talk about me right now," he assured her.

"Social lesson number four," Seven countered. "Collegial Conversation. When interacting with your peers, put them at ease by inquiring about their work. You taught me that."

"I did." The Doctor smiled. "It seems so long ago, I can't believe you actually remember."

"Of course I remember," she said tonelessly. "I am . . ." but she halted again before finishing the phrase with the standard "Borg." Instead, correcting herself, she muttered more softly, "I was Borg."

"Very well," the Doctor decided to oblige her. "Since you were kind enough to ask, the Emergency Medical Vessel has been approved for a test mission."

"You must be pleased."

"I am." The Doctor nodded, unable to suppress a wide grin. "I don't yet know the mission's specs, but I am sure it will be fascinating. I've requested to join the crew in the capacity of both Emergency Medical and Emergency Command Hologram. A hearing will be convened at Starfleet Command to discuss this request in a few weeks. I was actually hoping you might be available to attend it with me. I am understandably quite filled with trepidation at the prospect."

"Why would Command convene a hearing to discuss a routine crew assignment?" Seven asked with actual interest.

Sensing that he was finally engaging her, he went on, "Actually, I was the one to demand the hearing. Starfleet declined my initial request, stating that I was much too valuable in my work at Jupiter Station to be spared for the mission."

"And you do not agree?"

"Seven, we designed this ship so that a wide variety of holograms like myself would be able to play an active role in service to Starfleet. Who better to lead such a group?"

"Do you need to be reminded again, Doctor, that there are very few other holograms like you?" Seven asked, almost warmly.

He accepted the compliment before continuing, "In any event, I want very much to participate in this mission. I've thought for some time that much as I enjoy research and development, part of me truly misses the action of starship duty. Do you ever feel the same?"

She considered the question briefly.

"At times. Although to hear our former comrades talk, the vast majority of their missions over the last few years have been routine in the extreme. I do not believe such an assignment would be nearly as satisfying as my current work at the Academy."

"Not to mention serving as the official Borg expert to the president of the Federation. I must say, I find President Bacco to be a most intriguing woman. I can't think of anyone better suited to lead us through this difficult time."

"Nor can I," Seven agreed before asking, "Is there further word on Lieutenant Kim's recovery?"

"He will return to active duty next week. I looked in on him several times during his recuperation at Starfleet Medical and consulted constantly with his attending physicians. His survival is nothing short of miraculous."

"If memory serves, Lieutenant Kim has something of a history of defying imminent death," Seven said.

"For which I am most grateful," the Doctor added. "Oh, and I heard Naomi Wildman has been accepted into the Academy for next year's class."

Seven smiled with pride. "She performed quite well on her entrance exams. And I have already asked Icheb to monitor her progress when she arrives."

"She'll love that," the Doctor retorted sarcastically.

"You object?"

"Icheb is as close to an older brother as she could have, so I don't doubt that he would keep a close eye on her whether you asked him to or not. But she's a young girl on the verge of becoming a young woman. She's going to want to test her limits and find herself. I hope he gives her the space to do that."

"I will advise Icheb accordingly," Seven agreed with obvious reluctance.

"I saw Commander Paris a few times at the hospital," the Doctor went on. "He seems to be holding up, but I must confess I still can't believe he and B'Elanna have separated."

"Nor can I," Seven offered. "I did not sense that either of them took their marriage vows lightly."

"I'm sure they didn't. And I, for one, still hope that one day they might reconcile."

"As neither B'Elanna nor Miral has been heard from for several months, I seriously doubt your wish will be fulfilled," Seven said.

The Doctor hesitated to ask after Chakotay. He knew that the captain and Seven had remained quite close until Admiral Janeway's death. At the memorial service, the tension between them had been obvious, and the conversation was going so well, he didn't want to remind her of such a potentially painful topic.

After a pause, Seven surprised him by bringing it up.

"Have you heard any word of Captain Chakotay?" Her hands, which had been comfortably clasped throughout, suddenly began to fret about the edge of the sofa, almost of their own accord.

"Commander Paris indicated that he had requested and been granted an extended leave after their return from the Azure Nebula. I do not believe he has been in contact with anyone since then," the Doctor replied, watching carefully for her reception of this information.

"I see," she said, clearly agitated.

"Seven—"

"If you'll excuse me, Doctor, I really should check on my aunt," she said, rising briskly.

"Of course." The Doctor nodded as he came to his feet.

She was up the stairs and out of sight before the Doctor realized that he had just been dismissed as surely as if someone had instructed *Voyager's* old computer to deactivate his program.

The Doctor left the house more concerned than he had been when he arrived. He had already resolved to send Seven a message as soon as he returned to Jupiter Station, reminding her of his upcoming hearing at Starfleet Command. He had wanted her there initially for purely selfish reasons. But the last half hour had convinced him that she was quite desperately in need of help for which no preceding social lesson would have prepared her to ask.

It had rained day and night for the first six weeks Chakotay lived on Orcas Island. As it was still technically winter when he arrived and only now spring, on the fifty-seven-square-mile retreat located in the Pacific Northwest, that was to be expected. Unexpected was the ease with which Chakotay found himself adapting to the bitter morning and evening cold, the inability to ever get completely warm or dry, and the scarcity of daily comforts to which he had become accustomed on a starship.

His ancestors had thrived in the wilds of their native lands, though admittedly in more temperate climates. Chakotay had chosen to find refuge in a terrain that would provide a heartier challenge to his survival skills or, failing that, would kill him more quickly.

Orcas, and the chain's other large islands, San Juan and Lopez, had once been tourist attractions for boating enthusiasts. Famed for dramatic resorts like Rosario and quaint towns like Friday Harbor, they offered relative comfort in one of nature's most spectacularly beautiful settings. The three-hundred-sixty-degree view of glistening blue water dotted with lush green oases from the peak of Mount Constitution, which Chakotay had climbed during the third and fourth weeks of his self-imposed solitude, had been truly awe-inspiring.

Now that April had finally begun, the madrone trees lining the island's lower elevations were once again in bloom, their delicate, bell-shaped flowers bursting forth in a riotous annual ritual celebrating the renewal of life. But the trees had proved more than picturesque. The delicate, almost paper-thin, reddish orange bark that peeled easily from the trunks made excellent kindling when dried, and the smooth, almost satiny wood beneath burned long and hot once it had been chopped.

In the early days, Chakotay had managed to survive by scrounging in the cold, wet dirt for a few remaining berries the trees had dropped in autumn. Bitterly astringent, they had barely satisfied his stomach, but he found that chewing them throughout the day at least eased the hunger pangs until he had managed to hunt and kill his first deer.

For most of his life, Chakotay had observed a strict vegetarian diet. He'd learned only after he arrived that the island provided little beyond the madrone berries in the way of edible plants. His instinct to survive had finally asserted itself over his personal preferences, and he had chosen to take what the Earth did provide without complaint. He took great care when killing any animal to thank it for its sacrifice and to put every bit of its flesh and bone to good use.

Once, the deer of Orcas Island had been all but domesticated by the tourists who flocked to the islands in summer. As the islands had returned to their more natural, wild state in the absence of human habitation in the early part of the twenty-second century, those deer who had forgotten what it was to forage for the necessities had died off, replaced by a sturdier and much craftier strain.

Chakotay had been pleased by the ease with which his body had adjusted to the rigors he now demanded of it. He remembered little of the week following the attack at the Azure Nebula beyond Cambridge's constant presence. Distant visions of tossing and turning on sweat-soaked sheets between nightmares still plagued him.

Once that had passed, he had emerged from the painful fugue and awakened feeling more himself than he had for some time, though terribly empty. With a heretofore unknown clarity, Chakotay realized that he barely recognized the man he had become. His grief was destroying him. But even this knowledge did nothing immediately to relieve the anger he still felt every time he thought of Kathryn's death.

He had requested an open-ended leave, which after *Voyager*'s performance, no one in Starfleet would have dared deny. His only coherent thought at the time was that he must put as much distance as possible between himself and the man who had become *Voyager*'s captain in the last nine months. That man, the one who had been so devastated by Kathryn's death, was not who he wanted to be. He walked beside Chakotay now, magnifying every twinge in his stomach and every ache of muscle tissue grown soft through disuse.

Usually, Chakotay managed to ignore him. Today, as the morning cloud cover had given way to a sun-streaked afternoon sky and light drizzle, that man had fallen sullen and silent. Chakotay almost found himself smiling at the man's inability to find at least a little joy in the simple beauties in which he was now immersed.

Chakotay's mind had lost track of the days; his body had awakened to a more natural rhythm, rising with first light and resting in its retreat. His senses had been reinvigorated by the plethora of fragrance, visual splendor, and faint rustlings of the natural world. His mind, which had been a whirl of tormented duty for months, was once again a clear and calm space in which he could begin to examine his past and search for the various forks in the road that had led him into darkness.

Despite this—as often as he had tried to walk the path

he had begun—the anger would not leave him be. As the demands of his body were both constant and great, Chakotay had found it easier to focus upon them and had done so with vigor, even as his spirit continued to languish untended.

As he gathered wood for his evening fire, breathing easier now with the exertion of hiking over a kilometer from his most recent campsite in a thicket of evergreens, he was startled into stillness by a sharp crack.

Instinct drove him to bend low and slowly drop the few branches he carried while reaching for the short spear he'd lashed to his back. He had carved dozens of sharp heads for it from wood and bone, and depending upon the size of whatever was tracking him, it should prove effective for defensive purposes. Part of him hoped the buck he had been stalking for days might be foraging nearby. Though he still had a week's worth of dried venison, his stomach rumbled appreciatively at the thought of fresh meat.

The next sound that met his ears simultaneously shattered that hope and his peace. It was more shocking than his dips into the waters off the beach at Massacre Bay every few days.

"Chakotay!"

He recognized the voice at once.

Tom.

Torn between the appropriateness of moving toward the sound and a more subtle desire to evade it, Chakotay remained still. A few moments later, the cry was repeated, closer, and Chakotay could clearly make out Tom's form traipsing through the woods, followed by a smaller figure with white hair.

Sveta?

At the sight of his old Maquis comrade, Chakotay's heart began to pound. She was one of his oldest and dearest friends, and wouldn't have dared disturb his solitude without good cause.

Accepting the inevitable—if Sveta was there, he was as good as found already—Chakotay rose and began to walk toward those who had sought him out.

"His life signs are strong," Tom was saying.

"Probably because I'm right here," Chakotay replied, stepping through a pair of young trees.

Tom's face was instantly alight with relief. Sveta merely eyed him evenly, as was her wont.

"Thank God," Tom said, dropping his hands to his knees to catch his breath as Sveta stepped past him to offer Chakotay an embrace.

"You look like shit," were the first words she spoke when they had separated.

"Nice to see you too," he replied. "What are you doing here?"

"Freezing our asses off," Tom replied. Though in uniform under a heavy field jacket, his lips were a little blue and the hand he extended to Chakotay was hard and cold as ice.

Chakotay was quite comfortable in the light cotton pants and the layers of shirts beneath a makeshift jacket he had wrought from his first deerskin.

"You should have checked the weather before you transported in," Chakotay said, suddenly quite cognizant of the graveled edge to his voice. As he hadn't used it often in the last several weeks, it was a little strange to hear.

"We transported to Obstruction Pass Park," Tom corrected him. "That's how many kilometers from here?" he demanded of Sveta.

"Seven, maybe eight," she said, smirking.

Something in Chakotay liked the fact that she hadn't made this little trip easy for Tom. Noting the combadge Tom wore, a piece of technology Chakotay had left behind in San Francisco, he said, "Well, transporting out from here shouldn't be a problem. Just make the call."

Tom's face hardened.

"Come on, Chakotay," he goaded, "haven't you missed me just a little?"

Chakotay kept his face as neutral as possible. The truth was he hadn't missed Tom, or any other part of his past life, at all, and this intrusion into the only peace he had felt for what seemed like forever was most unwelcome.

"What do you need, Commander?"

Tom paused, obviously stung.

Finally he replied, "Sveta was good enough to help me track you, since you didn't happen to tell anyone where you were going. We've been at it for almost a week."

"Then Sveta is obviously getting rusty. Usually she's much better at finding people who don't want to be found," Chakotay deadpanned.

Tom shook his head, obviously frustrated.

"Okay, fine. That's the way you want to play this, great. I just thought you should know that Starfleet has new orders for *Voyager*. I don't have the details yet, but based on the intensity of the preparations and the number of people involved, they're big. I'd hoped that all this time doing your rubber tree thing might help you find a little clarity, but even if it hasn't, you need to put whatever demons are driving you someplace dark and quiet and get back to your ship while it's still yours."

Chakotay took a moment to shudder under the impact of Tom's words. More than their subject, the thought of once again being bound by duty and ordered around by an admiralty with the barest shred of a clue chafed.

"Does that complete your report, Commander?" Chakotay asked stonily.

"Yes, sir," Tom replied coldly.

"I'm sorry, but for now, I can't accommodate you. My demons and I still have a few things to work out. My presence should not be a factor in determining your level of participation in whatever mission is on the drawing board."

Given the damage *Voyager* had sustained and what had to be the seriously depleted reserves of Starfleet's materials and personnel, he doubted that whatever mission they were contemplating would become a reality for at least another couple of months.

Tom raised his hand to tap his combadge as Sveta stepped toward Chakotay, causing Tom to pause.

"Who are you?" she demanded fiercely.

"Sveta . . ."

"Don't even try," she warned. "I thought you came here to bury your past, not wallow in it. The ancient Lumni people have a spot just over that hill for the sanctified dead. As long as you're not interested in living anymore, it would be easy enough to lie down and join them."

"You don't understand."

"I don't have to. I only have to know who you were to see that who you are now does no justice to him, or those who once loved him. You're not even worthy of my pity anymore."

With that, she turned abruptly and hurried past Tom into the dense woodlands. Chakotay watched a moment of panic flicker across Tom's face, followed by acceptance that even alone, she was better equipped to handle their surroundings than he would ever be.

"Will you at least do one thing for me?" Tom asked.

"What?"

Tom reached into a pocket in his jacket and pulled out a combadge. "Catch," he said, tossing it toward Chakotay, who caught it instantly.

"I left mine at home for a reason," Chakotay said.

"I don't care," Tom replied. "The time may come when you feel differently, and I don't have another week to spend hunting you down."

Chakotay nodded slightly and placed the badge in the small leather pack he carried around his waist. As Tom turned to follow Sveta, Chakotay called after him.

"I'm sorry, Tom."

Tom stopped but did not turn around.

"I'm just not ready yet," Chakotay said to Tom's back.

"Then I suggest you hurry up and get ready," Tom replied. Without a backward glance, he disappeared into the forest.

As soon as he had lost sight of them, Chakotay returned to gathering his firewood. A lazy creek trickled through the brush a few meters away and Chakotay directed his steps toward it, pausing to run his hands through the icy current before leaning over to splash a little into his mouth.

He was taken aback by his reflection. He'd already grown accustomed to the rough beard that covered his jawline but hadn't realized how, in combination with his unruly mane, it gave him the appearance of what his mother would have called a *shantlor*.

Wild man.

The other version of himself seemed to have awakened from his stupor and now sat beside Chakotay, his face clean shaven and his proud tattoo unsullied by days of dirt and grime.

They don't understand, the other assured him.

No, Chakotay agreed. *They don't.*

The rage again began to bubble up inside, turning his stomach to a mass of writhing snakes. For an instant, another face appeared before him, blotting out his own.

Her hair was pulled back, but a few loose wisps betrayed her tension and stress. Her eyes were grimly set, though she did her best to hide her obvious fears.

"Can't you at least tell me where you're going?" Chakotay found himself thinking.

"It's classified. Believe me, I'm not looking forward to it, but it's something I have to do. More important lives than mine are at stake. Do you understand?" she pleaded.

"You know it scares the hell out of me when you talk that way, Kathryn."

"The only thing you should fear right now is my wrath if you don't show up in Venice in three weeks."

Chakotay sat back on his heels, willing her face to disappear. He could feel the cold and gleeful joy of the man beside him and could sense the strength he continued to draw from Chakotay's pain.

It was no longer just Kathryn's death on which he fed. Spectral shadows closed in upon him: Tare, Kaz, Beekman, Hillhurst, T'Reni, Curtis, Campbell . . .

The list of those who had died on his watch grew longer every day he served with Starfleet.

He had spent more than six weeks convincing himself that he was, no matter what Sveta thought, learning to live again in the world, rediscovering who he was and what he was meant to do.

The other man began to laugh, and Chakotay felt the flesh at the back of his neck begin to tingle and rise.

Suddenly he knew that whatever this was, it wasn't life. The thought made him tremble with fear.

———————

Paris stormed into his temporary quarters in San Francisco and threw himself down onto the low sofa in the apartment's small living room. He'd left Chakotay over an hour ago and still had no feeling in his hands or feet.

Frankly, he preferred it to the parts of his body he could still feel, as they were a riot of frustration.

"Computer, increase room temperature by five degrees," he ordered.

With a sonorous chirp the computer complied.

I should have told him.

This thought had been torturing Tom since he'd felt the transporter free him from Chakotay's icy domain.

"Damn it all, I should have told him," Tom said aloud to the empty room.

Tom hadn't actually spent much time in the apartment since he'd been called to a meeting at Project Full Circle six weeks ago with Admirals Montgomery and Batiste, Captain Eden, and a handful of other officers he now knew much better than he cared to. The quarters were similar to the temporary housing Starfleet had provided to all of *Voyager*'s crew when they first returned to Earth. Tom refused to allow himself to remember the hours he'd spent in that first suite imagining the life he and B'Elanna were going to build there with Miral. This time around, he hadn't made the mistake of beginning to personalize any of the space, apart from a few pictures of his wife and child that sat on the small dresser by his bed.

That meeting had been enough to make Tom seriously question how soon he would be ending his career. *Voyager* and a fleet of eight other vessels were being fitted with slipstream drives and sent back to the Delta quadrant. Only after the mission's objectives had been clearly enunciated by the admirals had Tom actually seen the wisdom in Starfleet's plan and how nicely the objectives would dovetail with his and B'Elanna's. And much as he hated to see so many of his old friends tossed back into the wilds of the galaxy, part of him understood that *Voyager*'s crew was being given a mission of the caliber and importance they deserved, and were best qualified to fulfill.

And at least this time we know it's not a one-way trip.

Captain Eden had assured Paris privately that Chakotay was still *Voyager*'s commanding officer under fleet commander Admiral Batiste. Every officer in the room had been advised that until the crew briefing, still several weeks away, the mission specifics were considered classified and no one was at liberty to speak of them with anyone outside the room.

Tom hadn't counted on Chakotay's hostile reception. Part of him had honestly believed that after all this time he would find his commanding officer restored to health and sanity. Had that been the case, Tom would have shared the whole truth about the mission with Chakotay. The man whose wisdom and compassion he had come to respect and rely upon so thoroughly in the Delta quadrant and in the years that followed would have never revealed to anyone that Tom had broken his oath with the admirals.

But Chakotay hadn't been kidding when he said he wasn't ready. Tom had sensed that the moment he'd first laid eyes on him. Even Sveta, who had known and loved Chakotay longer than any of *Voyager*'s crew, had confided to Tom that Chakotay might never be ready to resume his former life.

"What happened?" Tom demanded of the silence around him.

He and Harry had dissected Chakotay's behavior for months, and neither of them had ever come to a satisfactory conclusion as to what exactly had pushed their captain so far over the edge.

Clearly it was connected to Admiral Janeway. But all of them had lost friends and loved ones before, during and after the Delta quadrant. No one but Chakotay had allowed such losses to cripple him so thoroughly.

Tom knew that the only thing that might have pushed him that far would have been the death of B'Elanna or Miral. He had flirted with that fate two years earlier and in the darkest of those days knew he had almost lost himself completely.

But Chakotay and the admiral were just fellow officers. They were close, but they weren't . . .

A memory brushed past Tom's mind so quickly he actually had to stop breathing to coax it into returning. When it finally did, Tom felt a heaviness descending upon his chest even as a shot of adrenaline burst through his stomach.

But that was years ago . . .

Over five years earlier, Chakotay had spent a few days wound tighter than a Vulcan logic thread, and Tom had finally confronted him about his odd behavior. Chakotay had reluctantly admitted that it had to do with a woman. At the time Tom couldn't imagine who he was talking about. He had accidentally learned the truth when he'd loaned Chakotay some of his holodeck time and seen him entering his Venice simulation with Admiral Janeway.

Nothing had come of it, as best Tom could tell, and compassion for his friend had forced him to file it away in the least traveled portions of his mind along with a promise he had made to Chakotay that their conversation would remain between the two of them.

But Chakotay and Janeway had been in regular contact and met frequently in the years since *Voyager*'s return, and who was to say that at some point . . .

Oh, no. Please tell me you didn't.

Like a puzzle piece you thought you'd lost and suddenly discovered under a sofa, Tom saw the action and its consequences and for the first time, a complete and perfectly horrible picture.

It was the only thing that could account for Chakotay's behavior.

"Why didn't you say something, you idiot!" Tom shouted, rising to throw off his heavy coat, which was, at long last, now stifling in the tropical heat he had ordered for his quarters.

Tom didn't know what he or anyone else might have been able to provide Chakotay to make her loss easier to bear, but they could have taken a shot.

Instead, Chakotay's grief had festered until it had actually transformed him into the worst possible version of himself. And if this afternoon was any indication, that version might be here to stay.

He wanted to contact Harry, who would probably accuse him of having an overactive imagination. To this day Harry was so uncomfortable with subterfuge that he would find the scenario impossible to believe of two people he thought he had known as well as Chakotay and Admiral Janeway.

Tom knew he was right.

And he also knew that being right made absolutely no difference now.

But it might, in the very near future. At some point Chakotay was going to return to *Voyager*, and then they were going to have a very long captain/first officer conversation. After all they'd been through together, Chakotay would have to acknowledge the truth, and that alone might be a good start.

Suddenly abashed, Tom realized that for months, he too had been guilty of some serious withholding. Many people, Chakotay among them, had been devastated when he told them that he and B'Elanna had separated. Because Tom always believed that he would have a chance to make it up to them and that when they learned the whole truth, they would forgive him, he had refused to delve too deeply into the temporary pain he was causing them.

His father would never know the truth. But even after his death Tom hadn't hurried to lighten the burden of his mother or other friends.

That was largely because the time had finally come to put the final phase of B'Elanna's plan into effect. Tom had known it as surely as his name the moment he had been briefed on *Voyager*'s new mission.

Earlier that week, Eden had provided him with the fleet's final launch schedule. Calculating out a few weeks from there, Tom had arrived at a date.

All that remained was for him to send a simple message.

Tom hurried out of his apartment to the nearest public communications terminal and, using a draconian series of encryptions, sent the transmission that had been agreed upon months before.

"Now" was the only pertinent word in the message.

Tom knew that Kahless would understand.

MAY 2381

CHAPTER TWENTY-EIGHT

Seven had been surprised, upon entering the small conference room, to see the room filled beyond capacity. She recognized no one present apart from the Doctor, though clearly she was not moving among the room anonymously. The moment she entered, Seven was conscious of whispers and murmurs even as the crowd was good enough to clear a space for her to walk to the table where the EMH was seated.

"Seven, you made it," he said with obvious pleasure, rising to greet her.

"You did indicate that it was important to you," she replied simply.

"We should be getting started any minute," the Doctor went on, clearly anxious. "I've saved a seat for you."

Seven would have preferred to stand. She was not in attendance in any official capacity and did not want to presume upon, or interfere with, the deliberations at hand. However, having been denied the restorative powers of regeneration in favor of the far less efficient restorative powers of sleep, she was physically more tired than usual these days and accepted the chair with silent gratitude. Dealing with the constant voice added to her burden, but Seven had grown accustomed to its presence.

A trio of officers entered and were momentarily taken aback by the size of the crowd.

The captain in charge, a Bolian female, addressed them briefly.

"While I understand that these proceedings may have a broader interest than a simple personnel assignment would warrant, this is a closed session. Anyone not here in an official capacity, please avail the exits in an orderly fashion."

A few grumbles were met with a fierce and unbending stare by the captain, and the crowd began to disperse. Seven imagined that the Doctor's physical parameters visibly shrunk as what had surely been his "supporters" filed out. Seven started to rise, but a firm hand was placed over hers by the Doctor, and she kept her seat.

As the captain and her aides took their own places opposite the Doctor, the captain turned a dismayed eye on Seven.

"Professor Hansen, isn't it?" she asked.

"I prefer to be called Seven of Nine, or Seven," she replied.

"Very well, Seven. If you'd be so kind as to—"

"I invited Seven to this meeting, Captain," the Doctor interjected, "and would consider it a personal favor if you would allow her to remain."

The aides exchanged a nervous glance, but the captain merely sighed. "Fine. But I will advise you on the record, Miss Seven, that this meeting is confidential, and your discretion will be appreciated."

"Of course." Seven nodded.

"Then let's get on with it, shall we?"

"Please," the Doctor said, smiling expectantly.

"I have reviewed your written objection to our previous

finding as well as the letters you provided on your behalf from Doctor Louis Zimmerman, Lieutenant Reginald Barclay, Commander Thomas Paris, and Doctor Bruce Maddox. To my mind, they only confirm our initial conclusion that your work on advanced holographic design is far more important to the Federation at this time—"

Before the captain could finish her thought, the room's main door swished open.

"I thought I made it clear—" she began, but stopped mid-sentence when Captain Eden hurried into the room.

"I'm sorry," Eden said, clearly flustered. "I'm late, aren't I?"

"Captain Eden," the Bolian said, rising.

"Captain Ferchew," Eden responded, shaking her hand. "I'm sorry to interrupt, but I have just received the final approval for the Emergency Medical Vessel's inclusion in the fleet that is being assembled under Admiral Batiste in conjunction with Project Full Circle."

"I wasn't aware—" Ferchew bristled.

"And for that I apologize. We're all working long days and nights to prepare the fleet, and I was not certain until this morning of its final complement."

"Understandable. However, our offices have already assigned all relevant personnel to the vessel. Are you here to request changes?"

"I am." Eden nodded, slipping into a vacant chair at the head of the table and bridging the distance between the Doctor and Ferchew. "As you know, I am the officer in charge of operations and logistics for the fleet, and wish to state unequivocally that it is my belief that the fleet's upcoming mission will be aided tremendously by the presence of the EMH Mark 1 we've come to call the Doctor."

Seven noted that Eden hadn't so much as glanced at

her or the Doctor since she entered the room. At her announcement, the Doctor sat up a little straighter.

"Upon what do you base this assertion?" Ferchew asked.

Eden continued authoritatively, "I am not at liberty to discuss the specifics of the fleet's upcoming mission in the presence of anyone but yourself, Captain. In general, however, we believe that the Doctor's past experience will prove invaluable to the fleet's work. I have personally interviewed the Doctor a number of times in my work with Project Full Circle, and even outside the auspices of the fleet's mission I believe that he has proven himself to be a unique asset in his previous starship assignment."

"Not to put too fine a point on it, Captain," Ferchew interrupted, "but he's a hologram, and all of the fleet vessels, particularly the Emergency Medical Vessel, are being equipped with our most recent and most advanced versions of his original program. Aren't we up to the Mark 11 now?"

Eden actually sat back and considered Ferchew with what Seven sensed was disdain.

"He's a sentient hologram, Captain," she replied.

"We're not here to debate that prickly issue," Ferchew said wearily.

"Good," Eden replied, "as I don't think anyone who actually knows the Doctor or has served with him would question it."

Ferchew withered slightly under Eden's reproof.

"If I may, in support of my position, I would like to read to you from the final letter then Captain Kathryn Janeway placed in the Doctor's permanent record upon *Voyager's* return to the Alpha quadrant. As you are undoubtedly aware, she placed similar letters and commendations in the files of all of her crewmen."

"We are aware of Admiral Janeway's recommendations, and they have always been taken into account when considering assignments for her former crew."

"If that's the case, I don't understand why your office would have denied the Doctor's request to return to active duty."

"Captain, the EMH Mark 1 is a unique creation and was a valuable asset to *Voyager* while they were lost in the Delta quadrant. Beyond that, I'm not sure what one might find of relevance in Admiral Janeway's recommendation."

Clearing her throat, Eden began to read aloud from a padd she held before her.

" 'Initially, like most of my crew, I was inclined to dismiss the EMH as nothing more than a very useful tool provided to us by Starfleet engineers. However, over time, and thanks in large part to the insights of the crew members serving consistently with him, including the Ocampan, Kes, and Lieutenant Thomas Paris, I began to see the shortsightedness of my own prejudices. As the Doctor's program was forced to run almost continuously over the seven years he served aboard *Voyager*, it became clear that over time and primarily through his own efforts, he far exceeded even the most optimistic expectations of his designers. He learned to adjust his behavioral subroutines to offer a more compassionate presence to his patients. He engaged regularly in activities for which he was never programmed in order to better understand the crew under his care. He developed deep and intense personal relationships with the crew and a number of aliens we encountered. And in an incident that forever banished any question I might have had about his sentience, he struggled valiantly through an imminent cascade failure when his ethical subroutines encountered a situation which, as a commanding officer, I have often faced: the choice between saving the life of one crew member with whom he had interacted regularly over another whom he did not know well. As a human, I am forced to accept my limitations and grieve for the reality that often is situational ethics. To the best of my knowledge, no advanced computer programming could possibly resolve that crisis for him, but he managed to overcome it through patience, reasoned debate, and most importantly, the comfort he was offered and accepted from his friends aboard *Voyager*.

" 'Unique individuals like the Doctor are often misunderstood, especially by their creators. Time and again he demonstrated the capacity to learn and to grow, and it is my belief that he would continue to do so most effectively if he were allowed the opportunity to continue to serve actively aboard a starship. I realize that several new generations of Emergency Medical Holograms have been designed and implemented while *Voyager* was away. I would never trade the Doctor for any of them, as none of them have demonstrated the humanity I came to treasure in our chief medical officer. In closing, I doubt seriously that my ship or crew would have survived our long journey without him.' "

As Eden finished reading, Seven found her eyes welling up. Hearing Janeway's words was an unpleasant reminder of the loss and her own current internal battle as to what had been best and worst in the admiral. Much of her anger had begun to subside, but Seven was struck again by an intense desire to discuss the challenges she was now facing with her former captain and friend. She was equally curious to know if Janeway had placed a similar letter in her file, and if so, the nature of its contents.

Glancing toward the Doctor, she could see that he had been both moved and uplifted by Kathryn's words.

Eden's final remark on the subject was brief. "I can't say it better myself, Captain, and given what the fleet's crew is about to face, I can only recommend that we provide them with those among us with the most experience and ability to meet the challenges ahead. I don't know about you, but Kathryn Janeway's recommendation is good enough for me."

Ferchew took a moment to stare at the Doctor, who returned her gaze firmly. Finally she made a note on her own padd and said, "Your request to add the EMH Mark 1, also known as the Doctor, to the crew complement of the Emergency Medical Vessel is hereby approved. His program will be added to those already installed aboard the vessel, and he will serve in the capacity of chief medical officer. If there is nothing else, we are adjourned."

"Thank you, Captain," Eden said graciously.

Ferchew responded with a brisk nod and left quickly, followed by her staff.

The Doctor turned immediately to Seven and enveloped her in a tight, joyful hug. As Eden rose, he hurried to her to shake her hand and profess his undying gratitude.

"I'm just doing my job, Doctor," Eden assured him. "I know it isn't everything you wanted, but I fully expect that your command abilities will also be enhanced in your upcoming assignment, and I look forward to reading your new commander's reports."

"What can you tell me about our mission, Captain?" the Doctor asked.

"Unfortunately, nothing more at the moment. You'll be briefed along with the rest of the crew in a few weeks. Until then, keep up the good work."

"Thank you, Captain. I will."

Turning to Seven, Eden said, "I'm surprised to see you here today."

"The Doctor was in need of moral support," Seven replied.

"Do you have a moment to speak with me in private?" Eden asked.

Somewhat discomfited, Seven nodded and with the Doctor's blessing allowed Eden to usher her from the room.

Eden led Seven out of the building into a lushly landscaped courtyard. Several other tall white edifices comprised the complex; the parklike setting was clearly designed to provide a convenient location for lunches or peaceful reflection outside the confines of their cubicles.

A few officers walked the manicured paths, and atop a small knoll a group of several administrative personnel were enjoying a makeshift picnic lunch.

Eden had been naturally drawn here. She hadn't breathed enough nonrecycled air for months.

Seven's long strides easily matched her own. Stealing a glance at her, Eden was struck again by her fine, strong features. There was definitely something softer about her now that Borg implants no longer marred her face. But there was also something sadder about her. The captain could only imagine the toll the last ten months had taken on Seven; Eden had been called upon time and again during each escalating crisis to provide counsel to those in command.

And here I am, about to do it again, Eden thought ruefully.

"Have you ever been offered an official position within Starfleet?" Eden asked.

"I am a professor at the Academy, as you undoubtedly are aware," Seven replied in a tone that suggested her inability to suffer fools.

"But you aren't an officer?"

"No," Seven said.

"Any reason why not?"

"I have never been offered a commission, nor would I accept one were it to be offered," Seven replied. "My current obligations are sufficiently strenuous."

"And yet the Federation hasn't failed to add to those obligations on a regular basis by asking you to consult on a variety of matters relating to the Borg?"

"No." Seven shook her head. "They have not."

Eden paused her steps and turned to face Seven. "I find myself in the unenviable position of trespassing upon your generosity once again on behalf of the Federation."

Seven's head cocked to the right. "Explain," she requested.

"Before I do, I must advise you that you are not at liberty to discuss this conversation with anyone."

Eden thought Seven was about to roll her eyes, but she settled for a deep sigh.

"I believe I possess sufficient discretion to rise to the challenge, Captain," she replied icily.

"I don't doubt it for a moment," Eden hurried to add. "I just needed to make sure you were aware of the sensitivity of what I am about to reveal to you."

"Explain," Seven said.

"Starfleet is currently preparing to send nine ships, including *Voyager,* back to the Delta quadrant."

Seven did her the credit of at least appearing shocked to hear this.

"May I ask why?" she demanded.

"The fleet's primary mission is exploratory and diplomatic. *Voyager*'s circumstances permitted it to chart only what lay in the path it took to get home. Even then, tens of thousands of light-years were skipped as it found shortcuts along the way. On the diplomatic side . . . well, let's just say there are a few fences we'd like to mend, if we can. More importantly, however, Starfleet is seeking confirmation that the Borg are truly gone and also investigating the possibility that the Caeliar might still be out there."

Seven's face flushed slightly.

"I believe I have indicated on a number of occasions my position on that question," she said.

"And I don't doubt you have expressed those beliefs honestly," Eden agreed. "But we can't just take the word of a handful of people as proof positive that the Borg have miraculously vanished and that the Caeliar now pose no further threat to us."

"Why not?"

"Because . . ." Eden found herself faltering. "Because we can't," she finally insisted. "And even if the Caeliar and the Borg really are gone, it's going to leave a disproportionately large power vacuum, particularly in the Delta quadrant."

"Does the Federation intend to fill that vacuum?" Seven asked warily.

"No," Eden replied. "But we need to understand what's out there now and what, if any, impact it might have on the Federation in the long term."

"Might I suggest that for the foreseeable future, the Federation busy itself with tending to its own territories?" Seven said, clearly irked.

"You may. But Starfleet is still going, and I think you would be an invaluable asset to the fleet."

Seven shook her head in obvious frustration.

"Are you ordering me to accompany the fleet?"

Eden corrected her. "None of us, least of all me, are in any position to do that. I'm *asking* you to once again lend your expertise and vast knowledge to a very challenging undertaking. Many of your old crewmates have been assigned to the fleet, and I do not doubt they would be very pleased to have you among them once again."

"*Voyager* and the Emergency Medical Vessel," Seven said softly as the weight of all she was about to lose settled upon her.

"The EMV was actually designed for just such a mission, to provide medical support to numerous vessels in situations when there might be a high risk of casualties in deep space, where there are no Federation starbases, and where advanced medical facilities are few and far between."

"The Doctor, Chakotay, Commander Paris, Lieutenant Kim . . ." Seven began to list.

Eden nodded. "Are all going. And the fleet is being equipped with slipstream drives so there is no risk of once again becoming stranded far from home." Taking a deep breath, Eden asked, "May I tell them you will join them?"

Seven didn't even pause to consider it.

"You may not," she replied.

"Do you mind if I ask why?"

Seven struggled briefly to formulate an appropriate response. "I believe it is too soon to mount such an expedition," she began. "I believe Starfleet would be better served by focusing all of its efforts on rebuilding its forces and considering what role it is meant to play in the Alpha quadrant, particularly in light of the recent emergence of the Typhon Pact. Further, I am needed here, both at the Academy and to look after my aunt, who is gravely ill."

"I'm sorry to hear about your aunt," she said sincerely. "And I understand your other reservations. I can assure you that this decision has not been reached quickly nor made lightly. The mission the fleet is about to undertake has been on the drawing board for almost three years. If this is your final word on the subject, I understand, but I will tell you that should you change your mind, the door will be open up until the moment the fleet launches."

"Thank you, Captain," Seven replied dismissively, "but I suggest you not hold your breath."

Eden nodded, accepting this as graciously as possible.

"Thank you for your time, Seven," she said, and walked quickly away.

Eden knew it had been a long shot, but she had felt compelled to ask. There were still a few weeks remaining until the fleet was to launch. The optimist in her hoped that Seven might give the matter a little more thought.

The realist believed she had already heard Seven's final word on the subject.

As Captain Eden hurried off, Seven found herself trembling. It had never entered her mind that Starfleet would mount an expedition to the Delta quadrant any time in the near future. The fact that they were asking many of *Voyager*'s former crew to lead this mission only added insult to injury. Despite the promise of slipstream technology to make the journey practical, any such relatively untested system was fraught with potential problems. These might be mitigated by the fleet's large number of ships, but still, it seemed a huge risk.

Further, Seven could not help but feel it was an insult to the memory of Kathryn Janeway. She had risked everything to bring her crew home, and Seven could only imagine the ferocity with which the admiral, were she still alive, would have battled anyone who dared propose such a mission.

In every respect but one, it seemed a waste of resources. That one—determining if anything, Borg or Caeliar, still existed in the vast region of space once dominated by the Collective. Such a possibility gave Seven pause.

The question that had plagued her for months and brought her conflict with the voice to its sharpest pitch was why she had not been asked to join the Caeliar gestalt at the moment of the Borg's transformation. Her memory of that process had grown vaguer with each passing day, but at no time since she had first awakened could she recall actually having been given a choice in the matter. The report of Captain Picard was that the Caeliar had left the galaxy. Seven would have been inclined to accept this completely were it not for the presence of the voice and her unsubstantiated certainty that it actually came from the Caeliar. If any yet remained, the Delta quadrant would logically be the first place she would look for them. And if she could find them, they might be able to help her resolve her current dilemma.

Intriguing as the possibility was, she could not weigh it above her obligation to her aunt. To leave Irene in a Starfleet Medical facility while she went off to pursue what might very well be a fruitless quest, would be the height of inhumanity, and unworthy of the love and generosity Irene had shown Seven since the day she returned to Earth. The Caeliar had already judged her as such, and she would do nothing now to prove them right.

More troubling, however, was the thought that in a matter of weeks, all of those she thought of as friends would be beyond her reach. Seven had believed she had come to fully understand the concept of the word *alone* when she was first severed from the Collective. As she contemplated her near future, she realized that there were nuances to the concept she had never anticipated and did not relish exploring.

Her attention was abruptly drawn to the sight of the Doctor hurrying up the path toward her, accompanied by Lieutenant Kim. Seven had stopped in to see Harry during his recuperation, but had not enjoyed the pleasure of his company since he had been fully restored to health. His grim and troubled countenance suggested that though his body might have healed, his mind might still have some distance to go.

"What's wrong?" Seven asked without preamble the moment they reached her side.

Kim shared a questioning glance with the Doctor before speaking, which ratcheted up Seven's discontent another notch.

"I'm sorry. I don't know how to tell you this," Harry began. "I still can't believe it myself."

Seven looked to the Doctor, who was usually better at delivering bad news, to see that he too was stunned into silence.

"Every morning, first thing, I review casualty reports from the Federation."

"A grim hobby, Lieutenant," Seven offered.

"It's part of my job," Harry replied. "Almost two months later we still haven't been able to confirm all of those killed during the invasion." Harry paused to take a deep, steadying breath.

"This morning, there was a report of shuttle debris found in sector 22093, an unregistered shuttle."

"I'm sorry, Lieutenant, but I still do not understand the relevance," Seven said as calmly as possible.

"It's B'Elanna and Miral. It was their shuttle. That sector saw heavy fighting, and they must have gotten caught in the cross fire."

Seven's heart turned to cold and heavy ice.

"B'Elanna and Miral are dead?" she said softly.

Harry nodded.

"And you're sure it's them?" the Doctor asked. "Someone might have made a mistake."

"Their names are on the list," Harry confirmed. "That means someone identified whatever was left . . ." he trailed off.

Silence hung heavy between them as the vivid natural hues of the courtyard turned suddenly bleak.

"I have to . . ." Harry began, his breath coming quicker. "I have to tell Tom. Will you both come with me? I don't know where Chakotay is right now, and there isn't anyone else."

"Of course," the Doctor said, placing a comforting arm around Harry's shoulders.

Seven followed them numbly to the nearest transporter station, adding a new item to the list of the Caeliar's sins against her. Several years earlier she had asked the Doctor to disengage the fail-safe Borg system within her which prevented her from experiencing human emotions at too high a level of sensitivity, and she believed she had adapted well to the new extremes that were the result of this choice. If she had still possessed her Borg implants, Seven would have requested that the Doctor reverse the procedure. Right now, she would have given anything to avoid the pain she knew would follow too quickly on the heels of the disorienting shock she was now experiencing.

Unfortunately, the Caeliar had not even left her this option.

CHAPTER TWENTY-NINE

Eden's first order of business after attending the EMH's hearing was to report to *Voyager* for her daily briefing on the fleet's status. These meetings consisted of the commanding officers of each vessel or, in *Voyager's* case, the acting commander, Tom Paris, and the few engineering specialists who had been, of necessity, included in the outlining of the fleet's mission at the beginning of March.

Eden materialized in the transporter room to find Tom waiting for her, as usual. In the short time they had worked closely together, Eden had come to rely upon and, more important, truly like *Voyager's* first officer. The irreverent young man who had found a new life in the Delta quadrant had been replaced by a more temperate version of his former self. Like his father, he now possessed a shell of tritanium around him and did his work efficiently and with professional enthusiasm. For those who were close to him—and much of the ship's current staff fell into that category—he always had a ready smile or good-natured barb, and many of the new faces seemed already to sense that in him they would find a firm hand, but also a patient mentor.

Paris always greeted Eden respectfully, and always maintained a professional distance in their dealings. He had never confided in her any misgivings he might have about the upcoming mission, though Eden believed he must have reservations. Still, if the rest of the crew accepted their new mission with Tom Paris's equanimity, Eden believed that the fleet would find great success in facing the challenges ahead.

"Good morning, Captain," Tom greeted her.

Eden forced her disappointment at failing to secure Seven's services for the fleet to the back of her mind.

"The ship commanders are assembled in the mess hall this morning," he informed her. "The new table is being installed in the conference room. I took the liberty of assuming you would prefer not to be briefed while battling the noise of the engineers."

"Thank you, Commander," she replied sincerely.

When she did not immediately move to lead him from the room as usual, Tom asked, "Are we waiting for someone?"

"Actually, yes," Eden replied. "An old friend I haven't seen in a while is coming aboard this morning."

"Will they be joining the meeting?"

"No."

"Shall I wait for you in the mess hall?"

"This won't take a minute," Eden replied as Counselor Cambridge shimmered into existence on the transporter pad.

The moment their eyes met, Cambridge shook his head in disdain.

"Are you here to gloat, Captain?" Cambridge asked as he stepped down to give her a brief hug.

"Not at all, Hugh," she replied with a wide smile. "Why do you ask?"

"You've managed to retain that lovely office in San Francisco while I've been banished to these dreary halls for almost three years. Should I have divorced an admiral too?"

Eden accepted his ribbing as par for the course. She knew that despite his protestations, Cambridge must be enjoying his work on *Voyager* a great deal or he would have demanded transfer long ago.

"This crew has performed exceedingly well, despite your presence, Hugh," she teased, "and since the rest of us can barely tolerate you, I'd suggest you make the best of it."

Cambridge nodded sagely. "Charming, as ever."

"I have a meeting, but I wanted to make sure you received those files I sent over," Eden said.

Cambridge's face lit up appreciatively. "I did. And you were right. They're quite lovely. Though I'm not quite sure . . ."

"Just put them in the back of that terribly large brain of yours and let me know if you find any interesting comparative images," Eden requested.

"Glad to. Now if you'll excuse me, I'm off to meet with our new chief medical officer. Why a Tamarian would bother to learn Federation Standard, let alone join Starfleet, is a mystery to me, but I'm intrigued nonetheless. I've always wanted to know more about Shaka and those bloody walls."

Eden dismissed him with a nod and turned back to Tom, who was trying hard to hide his surprise.

"Question, Commander?"

"No." He shook his head. "I just didn't realize you were acquainted with Counselor Cambridge."

"We've known one another for years," she assured him. "Have you enjoyed having him aboard?"

Tom paused, obviously choosing his words carefully. "He's an excellent counselor, by which I mean he is usually dead-on in his assessments, but he does take some getting used to," he finally said.

"He thinks highly of you too, Commander," Eden replied, then asked, "Is there any chance we're going to finish this meeting before lunch?"

"Only if we'd started an hour ago, ma'am," Tom replied.

"Then let's get to it."

Three hours later Paris emerged from *Voyager*'s mess hall to find Harry, Seven, and the Doctor waiting for him. All three had worn similar, gloomy expressions before they had noted his presence, and all three tried much too hard to mask them the moment they saw him.

"Hi, guys," Tom said with forced cheer. "What's going on?"

Harry, who had apparently been elected the trio's leader for the moment, stepped forward and said softly, "We need to go to your quarters."

"Do I need to bring a phaser with me?" Tom joked.

"No," Harry replied as he turned his steps toward the turbolift and refused to meet Tom's eyes.

A few minutes later all of them entered Tom's darkened quarters. They had recently been refurnished and had a fabricated, "new" smell, which reminded Tom, much to his regret, of the *Delta Flyer*; both times he'd helped build it.

Tom activated the cabin's lights on arrival and turned to see his friends staring at him with great concern.

"Okay, somebody needs to tell me what's happening," he said as lightly as possible under their heavy gazes. The room felt uncomfortably warm, though Tom knew full well that the climate controls were one of the few things on *Voyager* that were functioning perfectly at the moment.

"Tom, I . . ." Harry began.

"Lieutenant Kim, if you'd prefer . . ." the Doctor said.

"No." Harry shook his head, collecting himself.

Suddenly, the room was not only too hot; it also seemed to lack sufficient oxygen for Tom's needs.

"Maybe we should sit down," Seven offered.

"Damn it, somebody say something," Tom demanded.

Finally Harry took a deep breath and blurted out, "B'Elanna and Miral are dead."

"What?" Tom heard himself asking, even as most of his mind untethered itself from the rest of his body and the room began to tip on its axis.

Immediately his friends were around him, their firm hands guiding him to the sofa. Soon he was seated between Harry and Seven, with the Doctor kneeling before him. All three of them were still holding on to him, but their presence, though immediate, was somehow disconnected from the rest of him.

Harry continued, soft and controlled. "We received the latest casualty reports this morning, and debris from B'Elanna's shuttle was discovered. Both of their names were on the list. Tom, I'm so very sorry."

In a flash of comprehension, Tom was off the sofa and on the far side of the room. It was almost as if putting space between them would somehow make the message they carried equally distant.

Hang on, part of him thought.

"Tom?" Harry said, approaching him with the care one would give a terrified and wounded animal.

"It's not . . . I mean . . . that's it, right?" Tom asked.

"I don't understand," Harry said.

"He's in shock," the Doctor added unnecessarily.

"No. What I'm saying is," Tom went on, "that's the only proof you have? Their names on a list?"

"I contacted the duty officer in charge, and he confirmed the remnants of the shuttle and positively identified it as B'Elanna's."

"It was unregistered," Tom argued.

"Every single ship in the combat zones during the invasion, Starfleet or civilian, was forced to identify itself and its occupants. I'm sorry, Tom, but it's not a mistake."

"Tom, please tell us if there is anything at all we can do," the Doctor said gently.

"Perhaps we could contact your mother?" Seven suggested.

"No," Tom replied softly, shaking his head. "No."

"I'll try and find Captain Chakotay," Harry assured them.

"Don't bother," Tom said coldly.

"What?" Harry asked.

"Get out, all of you," Tom replied.

"Tom," Harry pleaded.

"Just get out!" Tom shouted.

Seven and the Doctor moved toward the door, but Harry stood his ground.

"I'm not leaving you alone right now," he insisted kindly but firmly.

"Harry, I love you like a brother. You know that. But right now, I need a few minutes by myself."

Harry eyed Tom warily.

"A few minutes," Harry finally conceded. "But I'm standing outside that door and I'm counting."

Tom nodded, and all three moved out the door.

The moment they were gone, Tom rushed to his comm station and pulled up a list of his most recent messages. Among them was an official, unencrypted notice from Emperor Kahless. It read simply, "Commander Paris, please accept the condolences of the Klingon Empire on your recent loss. B'Elanna and Miral brought honor to us all, and they will be missed."

Tom read and reread the message, counted the words, then read them one final time.

Though he had guessed the moment he had seen Harry's face what news he carried with him, he had been unprepared for the visceral response to Harry's words. In his immediate shock he had actually feared that somehow something had gone terribly wrong.

Kahless's message, however, put those fears completely to rest. Tears welled in Tom's eyes, but they were not tears of grief. After more than two years he was finally almost free to live the life he had always wanted.

Tom sighed through his tears with complete relief.

⸻

In the days following Tom and Sveta's brief visit, the traces of peace Chakotay had achieved prior to their arrival had dissipated completely. Now, he found himself wondering if that brief respite had been as illusory as his angry companion.

Instead, the fear Chakotay had first felt when his counterpart had begun to laugh at him had coiled itself around his heart and stubbornly refused to be dislodged. In place of his daily hikes to take in the grandeur of the island and cleanse his mind and body, he had taken to spending long hours staring into his small campfire. His body was still, but his mind raced with furious determination.

He had studiously avoided the thoughts that were now tormenting him: Kathryn, the many fine officers and crew he had lost while in command, the dreams of the life they would have shared after Venice, and most painfully, the persistent certainty that his life was now over.

The only piece of technology he had brought with him was wrapped inside the medicine bundle he hadn't opened since Kathryn's death. The *akoonah* had been created by his people to facilitate the spiritual exploration of a vision quest, replacing the hallucinogenic plants used by his ancestors. He had sought the comfort of his spirit guide regularly throughout his life, but after Venice had felt no desire whatsoever to seek its counsel. He was as angry with the spirits as he was with the Borg, and frankly didn't want to hear whatever they might have to say.

In his long hours of quiet contemplation, however, the thought had finally occurred to him that even when one didn't want the spirits, they never truly left you. Some would say that in the darkest times, the spirits existed to carry you through them. Chakotay didn't really know what he was seeking in contacting them. He only knew that he had tried every other means at his disposal to make sense of his confusion and fear, and thus far found nothing.

Chakotay unwrapped the medicine bundle and laid it out before him. Embracing his fear, he placed his fingers on the *akoonah*, closed his eyes, and said aloud, "Akoochimoya. Gods of my fathers, I am far from the lands of my home. I walk in darkness, alone and frightened. I ask you to find me in the darkness. I ask you to explain yourselves."

Chakotay's mind began to hum. It was a common effect of the *akoonah*, the last physical sensation experienced before entering the spirit world.

As he opened his eyes, the hum receded, and he found himself staring at the fire he had built that afternoon. Though it seemed to have grown lower with the passage of time, he had no memory of having walked with his spirit guide.

Chakotay closed his eyes again, determined to force a connection.

Blackness surrounded him.

He floated in it, frightened and alone.

What have I done, he cried out to the darkness, *that even you have abandoned me?*

With a disarming jolt, Chakotay found himself trembling with cold.

The fire had died.

He was as alone in the forest as he had been in the emptiness of his vision. Hours had clearly passed, but had brought him no closer to the clarity he sought.

Chakotay had never wished so desperately to speak with the spirits. And they had never before failed to heed his call.

A word rose unbidden to his lips.

"Why?" he asked aloud.

Why what? the familiar needling voice of his usurper asked.

"Why did she go out there alone?" Chakotay asked.

What does it matter? She was never really yours. Perhaps she never meant to meet you in Venice at all. Perhaps she was afraid she had made a mistake.

"I don't believe that."

No. But you fear it. Who are you, Chakotay? At what point did you stop charting the course of your own life and hand it to others? To her? To Starfleet? Was that the life you wanted, or was it the life you lived with because you couldn't think of anything better to do?

"I made my choices."

Did you? Or did you run from choice? Did you want to remain in the Delta quadrant? Did you want to join Voyager's crew? Did you want to become a captain? Or did you abide the whims of destiny, the cruelest of all mistresses?

"I don't know anymore."

Who does?

"Leave me alone!" Chakotay shouted, warmed by familiar anger.

You are alone. You've been alone for longer than you care to believe. You abandoned yourself, Chakotay. You hid behind pretty words like duty, honor, and love, and then you cloaked yourself in ugly ones: pain, anger, regret. But they mean nothing. They do not define you. Only you can do that. Only you can claim your own life. Why do you hesitate? Why do you fear?

"I knew what I wanted and it was taken from me."

Then it was never yours.

"Why?"

With that word hanging unanswered in the cold night air, Chakotay heard a distant chirp.

Startled, he looked about for its source and found it in the pouch he carried at his waist. The combadge Tom had left him was demanding an answer.

Hands shaking, Chakotay activated it.

"This is Chakotay."

"*Captain, I'm sorry to disturb you.*"

Chakotay immediately recognized the voice and answered automatically.

"It's no trouble, Admiral Montgomery. What do you need?"

"*I need you to report to Command in two days.*"

Chakotay paused briefly.

"May I ask why?"

"*I'll explain when I see you. Good travels, Captain. Montgomery out.*"

The communication terminated, Chakotay replaced the badge in his pouch and listened to the stillness around him. Finally, he rose and began to clear his campsite.

CHAPTER THIRTY

Cambridge rose from his chair when Chakotay's retelling of the events of August 2380 to the present had concluded. He did so not because his work with the captain was at an end, but because his lower back was shooting spasms up and down his spine after sitting in one position for over four hours.

Chakotay abruptly mimicked his action and began to pace the small room, shaking his legs alternately with every few steps.

"What do they usually use this room for?" he asked.

"I don't know." Cambridge shrugged as he stretched his arms overhead in an effort to give the disks of his lumbar spine some desperately needed breathing room. "But I'd sell my soul right now for a really good massage therapist. Or failing that, a mediocre *dabo* girl might suffice."

Chakotay cracked a perplexed smile.

"So what now, Counselor?" he asked.

Cambridge returned to the table, but rather than take his seat, perched himself on its edge.

"The obvious question, I suppose," he replied. "How do you feel now?"

"About what?"

"About resuming your command?"

Chakotay came to a halt and turned to face Cambridge, almost at attention.

"I serve at the pleasure of my commanding officers," he said a little too ironically.

"That's true," Cambridge acknowledged, "but it's not an answer."

"What do you want me to say, Counselor?" Chakotay asked with a little more heat.

"Do I regret destroying the Orion ship? No. Was my pursuit of the Borg during their invasion of our sovereign space too aggressive? I think not. Do I recognize that since Admiral Janeway's death many of those closest to me have been concerned about my behavior? I'm not an idiot, Counselor. We all face these things as best we can, and that's what I did at the time and that's what I will continue to do when *Voyager* ships out again."

"The last time we spoke, Captain, you were just beginning to recover from sinking into a deep state of shock brought about by acute trauma and further complicated by untreated chronic depression characterized by personality changes, self-medication through the inappropriate use of alcohol, manic outbursts, denial, and barely controlled aggression. You've had over two months to begin to heal. How's it coming?"

Chakotay paused to consider his analysis.

"I'm all better now?"

"Your sense of humor is returning, and that's a step in the right direction," Cambridge replied.

"But is it enough?" Chakotay asked.

"Enough for what?"

"Enough to get you and Admiral Montgomery off my back?" Chakotay bristled.

"I think you've missed the point," Cambridge replied.

"Then please, explain it to me," Chakotay countered. "And be sure and use lots of small words," he added icily.

"Why do you think Command requested this evaluation?" Cambridge asked.

"Because calling my judgment into question has become a habit around here."

"Really? Why would that be?"

"Why?" Chakotay paused, as if struck by the word. "Why?" he said again.

Instinct drove Cambridge to straighten his posture. For the first time since their conversation had begun, he felt Chakotay was close to discovering something that had been eluding him.

"I'm here because from the day *Voyager* returned from the Delta quadrant, no one in the upper echelons of Command has really trusted me or the rest of my crew."

Cambridge's eyebrows shot up at this revelation.

"I left Starfleet years ago to join the Maquis. I betrayed them. And even though the Dominion war might have opened some eyes to the rightness of our cause against the Cardassians, my fellow Maquis and I weren't welcomed back into the fold because Starfleet understood or had forgiven us. We were accepted back because we had done our penance, seen the error of our ways, and demonstrated that we could toe the Starfleet line for seven years. After the war Starfleet needed all the able hands it could get, so at Admiral Janeway's insistence they decided to give me a shot, but they never really trusted that they were doing the right thing. They never really trusted any of us."

"Upon what do you base that assumption?" Cambridge asked.

"Right after we got home, a new Borg threat emerged: a virus conceived by a warped woman at the heart of Starfleet Intelligence. At that point we were the best qualified officers around to investigate and conquer that threat, but we were all pushed to the sidelines, suspected of actually causing the problem. Three of my people were actually put in prison. We only succeeded in stopping Covington because we did what had to be done over Command's protests instead of with their blessing.

"Of course, we were right. We solved the problem. And the next one at Loran II. And because it would have been bad form for Starfleet to do any different, they finally decided to give me the first officer I deserved, another officer they have serious 'trust' issues with, Commander Tom Paris. But I don't imagine they were happy about it.

"A few months later, after saving the lives of B'Elanna and Miral Paris and revealing a serious threat to the health and welfare of the Klingon species in the bargain, I was once again called on the carpet to explain my behavior. Yes, the mission to Kerovi had failed, but I have a hard time mourning the loss of our ability to interrogate a Changeling who was going to lie to us with his last breath when we were able to save countless others by our efforts.

"The chancellor of the Klingon Empire saw fit to honor me and my crew with commendations, but Starfleet decided to reward us for taking the initiative by giving us for the next two years the most mundane assignments imaginable. Frankly, I'm surprised they didn't throw all of us into the bowels of a warehouse to count self-sealing stem bolts, for all the use we were ferrying around diplomats and escorting supply vessels."

"You think you were being punished?" Cambridge asked.

"I think no one here really understands me or my crew. I think because we didn't serve in the Dominion war, we have always been considered somehow 'less' than those who did. I think they use us when it seems convenient, but no one has ever really given proper weight to the service we did in the Delta quadrant, not just by surviving it, but by gathering enough data to keep every one of your analysts busy until the end of time, had anyone bothered to actually look at it before they classified it or filed it away.

"And I think that the disrespect we have suffered is nothing compared to the unconscionable decision to send Admiral Janeway out to investigate a Borg cube with only a science vessel for backup. They sent her out alone. She died alone.

"No, I don't think we were being punished. I think we have been and continue to be the victims of negligence on the part of our commanding officers that some might define as criminal.

"Despite that, my crew and I have done everything Starfleet has ever asked of us. We have routinely gone above and beyond the call of duty, right up to leading that doomed task force to the Azure Nebula, and because we had the unmitigated gall to survive it, we must once again account for our actions."

Cambridge actually flinched as Chakotay crossed to stare directly into his eyes.

"You know what? I'm sick of it. I'm sick of having my every action questioned by those who are only alive because we continually throw ourselves between them and danger. Who the hell are you to ask me to justify myself? My actions speak for me, and if they aren't enough to convince you that I belong in *Voyager*'s center seat, then I have nothing more to say."

After a long pause, Cambridge replied with a deep sigh, "I see."

"You do?"

"Yes."

"And?"

Chakotay's question hung in the air unanswered.

"Turn it off," Batiste said. "We've heard enough."

Montgomery had been struck not only by Chakotay's words, but by the intensity behind them. And for the moment, he was inclined to agree with Batiste. His heart heavy, he switched off the monitor they had used to oversee the evaluation, rose to his feet, and ambled over to examine the view from his large office window.

Montgomery understood Chakotay's frustration. Command had been occupied by so many pressing matters when *Voyager* had made its unexpected return, and at the time it had been hard to determine how best to put the ship and its crew to use. His instinct had been to keep as many of the crew members who still wished to serve together. Naturally, those who requested transfer or extended leave were obliged. Among many there was a sense that Janeway's crew had done more than enough already and at the very least deserved some well-earned rest.

As the admiral in charge of *Voyager*'s deployment, Montgomery had conscientiously searched for assignments that would challenge the crew's abilities. Between Kerovi and the Borg invasion, he could admit that he hadn't done much to make *Voyager*'s crew feel useful. Of course, for much of that time he'd had Admiral Janeway to contend with at every turn. She had always respectfully deferred to his choices, but she also never hesitated to express her feelings about the assignments *Voyager* received, and she usually erred on the side of caution. Perhaps subconsciously she hadn't been willing to see her people thrown into the deep end after all they had endured. Montgomery didn't think he'd given *Voyager* any special treatment, but perhaps he hadn't pushed them enough.

And if he was going to be completely honest, Montgomery had wondered whether or not Chakotay was up to his assignment. All he had to base that decision upon was Janeway's word and Chakotay's record in the Delta quadrant. That record had been sterling, but it had also been the product of a unique set of circumstances. Montgomery had chosen to reserve judgment initially but had worried that once removed from the limited scope afforded them in the Delta quadrant, Chakotay and many of his crew might find it difficult to adjust to more routine assignments. The "initiative" Chakotay had taken during the Kerovi mission would have been understandable in a more seasoned officer. In a new captain, it walked right up to the line of refusing a direct order, something Montgomery would not tolerate in a Starfleet captain.

He understood Chakotay's anger, especially in the wake of his personal tragedy. He sympathized. But all of that had to be set aside when answering the only question on the table at the moment.

"We can't send him back to the Delta quadrant right now," Batiste said, giving voice to Montgomery's unspoken thoughts.

"No, we can't," Montgomery agreed.

"Someday, maybe. But right now—"

"I know, Willem," Montgomery cut him off. "At the very least he has anger issues. We may have needed a few loose cannons when the Borg attacked, but we can't send someone who is not in complete control into the dicey diplomatic waters of the Delta quadrant."

"And I'm not going out there as admiral of the fleet to spend all of my time debating command decisions with a hothead who's got a grudge a mile long."

"So whom do we send?" Montgomery asked, not really expecting an immediate answer. The truth was, he had wanted Chakotay to be ready to take on this new assignment that he hadn't seriously considered any alternatives.

"I have a suggestion," Willem replied.

"Who?"

Batiste's choice took Montgomery by surprise.

"You don't think that's just trading one set of problems for another?" Montgomery asked.

"At least it's a set of problems I'm comfortable with," Batiste replied. "And nobody else I can think of knows as much about the ship, the people, or the Delta quadrant. We won't lose any time."

"True," Montgomery conceded. "I guess we should wait for Cambridge's final report before making the formal assignment," he added.

"Do you really think we need to? You know what he'll say."

Montgomery nodded. "I do."

"Then I'd suggest we get on with it."

Chakotay studied Cambridge's face. The righteous indignation that had sustained his tirade had evaporated as quickly as it had come, and a weary calm settled over him.

"And, Counselor?" he asked again.

He was utterly shocked by Cambridge's response.

"And I couldn't possibly agree more," the counselor said.

Chakotay found himself struggling to remember the number of times prior to this when Cambridge had so readily agreed with him.

None came to mind.

"You couldn't?"

"Absolutely." Cambridge nodded. "I just can't believe it's taken you this long to come out and say it."

Chakotay thought about it.

"Neither can I," he replied with a faint smile.

"Captain, I meant it when I said that I hoped this session would go well. Most of the time I've known you, I've found you to be thoughtful, compassionate, balanced, and wise. Even after our first conversation, I never made the time to locate *Voyager*'s escape pods, because you are the only starship captain I've ever served under who didn't make me worry constantly that I'd need to use one. And that didn't change when Kathryn Janeway died. Grief humbles the best of us. And while you walked terribly close to the line, you never really crossed it. At times I may have disagreed with your choices or wanted to make certain you were considering all of their implications, but I never lost respect for you or your position. I watched you battle your demons into submission until they struck with such crippling force that any sane man in your situation would have needed to find an island and spend some time regrouping.

"My only concern then, and now, is that the healing process is not complete. And for reasons that elude me, you continue to stubbornly refuse help from those around you who are most anxious to offer it. It's not serving you to try and do this alone. It's not like you."

"No," Chakotay replied honestly. "It's more like her."

"Admiral Janeway?"

"I can't tell you the number of times we had that discussion during those seven years," Chakotay went on. "I never understood it until the job was mine. I always thought it was one of her only weaknesses."

"So you think this is learned behavior?"

"I think the job forces a certain amount of distance. And I think my particular circumstances fooled me into believing that the rest of the distance was necessary."

"You weren't ready to confront your pain."

"I've done nothing but confront it every day since she died. I can't get away from it."

"But you can't make peace with it either. What's stopping you?" Cambridge asked kindly.

Chakotay pulled out the chair closest to him and straddled it, resting his arms on its back.

"Not knowing why."

"Why? Why what? Why she died? Why our best laid plans are the playthings of the gods?"

"No. Why she went out there in the first place. Why she would risk so much, my happiness and hers, for the sake of curiosity."

Cambridge pushed himself off the table and stood before Chakotay, his arms crossed.

"Is that what you really believe, Captain?"

"I don't know what else to think. She told me more important things were at stake than her life, and in a way, hindsight proved her right. But it still seems the dumbest way possible to assess a potential threat."

"Captain, are you aware of *Voyager*'s new orders?" Cambridge asked.

Chakotay was startled by what seemed like an abrupt course change in the conversation, but replied, "No. Admiral Montgomery wouldn't tell me until this evaluation was complete. Are you?"

"*Voyager* is about to lead a fleet of nine vessels on a long-term assignment to the Delta quadrant."

Chakotay felt certain that someone had just sucker punched him in the gut.

"What?"

"The mission was only finally approved in light of recent events. But Starfleet has been considering it ever since you returned. For almost three years, Admiral Janeway was the plan's most vocal opponent."

A rush of images bombarded Chakotay's mind. Kathryn's admonishment to be careful how much excitement he wished for, her silent preoccupations, his certainty time and again that she was worried about something she could not or would not share with him. And finally, the look on her face the last time he had spoken with her via subspace, her headstrong determination trumping her fear.

"She knew," Chakotay said, as the pieces fell into place. "She knew and she wouldn't tell me because she never intended to let it happen. Did she go out to investigate that cube so that we wouldn't have to?"

"She went out to investigate that cube in hopes of convincing Starfleet Command that there was no need for you or your ship to return to the Delta quadrant."

Chakotay took this in, his heart breaking anew at the only weakness Kathryn possessed that had been greater than her capacity for self-reliance: her capacity for self-sacrifice.

"How do you know all this?" Chakotay finally asked. "If Kathryn couldn't tell me, why are you free to do so?"

"For the moment you're my patient, and to deny you this information would be cruel. Doctor-patient confidentiality prevents me from telling you how I know this, but suffice it to say, I know that what I am saying, while common knowledge to only a few in the uppermost echelons of Command, is true. You have labored too long under a serious misconception. And that misconception has colored every action you have taken since her death. You assumed Kathryn made a foolish choice. You assumed it because you had seen her make similar choices in the past but had always been there to put a stop to them. You haven't been blaming her, as you should have. You haven't even been blaming the Borg, though they became the target of your rage. You've been blaming yourself. You weren't there for her when she needed you most. And so she died alone. Had she died in any other way, you would have come to accept it long before now. And you would have been spared the need to transfer your anger. You've been beating the hell out of yourself for months and in the process beating the hell out of everyone around you who wanted to see you stop your own foolishness. It's created a crisis you have been unable to resolve because your pain has been in charge instead of your mind."

Chakotay nodded. Usually he hated it when Cambridge was right.

Usually, but not today.

"You tried to tell me this a long time ago," Chakotay acknowledged wearily. "That she was the one I was really angry with."

"You weren't ready to hear it. But it's right for you to be angry with her. She made a choice, without consulting you, which shattered your hopes for the future. But it's also right, and absolutely necessary, that you forgive her for that choice. Understanding why she did it should make that possible in time. She did it not because you meant too little to her. She did it because you and all of those she led through the Delta quadrant meant infinitely more to her than her own life."

Chakotay pushed himself up off the chair and began to wander a bit aimlessly around the room.

"We're really going back to the Delta quadrant," he mused, finding the concept difficult to accept.

"With slipstream drives," Cambridge added. "It's not like anyone intends for the fleet to become stranded out there."

"It actually makes sense," Chakotay conceded, "now, more than ever."

"So I must ask you again the question I asked a few minutes ago. Are you ready to lead that mission, Captain? Are you ready to go back to the Delta quadrant?"

"What do you think?"

"What I think isn't nearly as important as what you think," Cambridge countered. "You've obviously found the path, but you're still going to have to walk it, and I don't believe it will be easy. But I do believe it will be *easier* in the presence of the men and women you have come to think of as family. If you don't want to do this, you shouldn't."

"She'd never forgive me if I didn't," Chakotay said.

"That's not a good enough reason to accept the mission. You're going to have to get used to not doing things for her. You cannot continue to define yourself by her expectations. I think that's why you found yourself floating in the darkness when you attempted that vision quest. You've lived so long in the shadows of her accomplishments, hopes, and dreams that you've lost the ability to decide anything outside of that context. It's one of the ways you've kept her close to you. But it's time to let her go."

"I don't know if I'm ready to do that," Chakotay admitted.

"Fair enough. But every day you don't is one more day you're wasting."

Chakotay stopped pacing and turned to look at Cambridge for what felt like the first time. They had begun, years ago, on the wrong foot, and Chakotay had never really given the man a fair chance after that. Taking a deep breath and pulling himself up straight, he crossed to the counselor and extended his hand.

"Hello, Hugh," he said simply. "I'm Chakotay. It's nice to finally meet you."

"The pleasure is mine, Chakotay."

"With your permission, I think I'd like to return to my ship now."

"Permission is not mine to grant," Cambridge replied. "But I can give you my recommendation."

"Thank you."

"Not at all, Captain."

CHAPTER THIRTY-ONE

Eden wasn't surprised when Tamarras ushered Willem into her office a few hours after his visit that morning. But she rose automatically to her feet at the sight of Admiral Montgomery trailing behind him.

"Good afternoon, sir," she said respectfully.

"As you were, Captain," Montgomery replied, gesturing for her to resume her seat as he and Willem took the two vacant ones opposite her desk.

"I'm pleased to report that Utopia Planitia's engineers have confirmed that all of the new slipstream drives are now ready for their test runs. We're still waiting on personnel for final assignments to the *Demeter* and the *Achilles*, but we should have them by the end of the day. All senior staff have received notice of tomorrow morning's briefing."

"Excellent work, as usual, Afsarah," Montgomery replied.

"Thank you, sir."

"I'm afraid, however, that there is going to be one last change to our senior crew assignments for the fleet."

Eden stole a glance at Willem, who was at his most inscrutable, folding her hands on the desk before her and replying, "What change is that, Admiral?"

"Captain Chakotay will not be resuming command of *Voyager* for this mission."

Eden nodded, grateful in a way that Willem's earlier visit had left her prepared for this unfortunate eventuality.

"I'm sorry to hear that, Admiral."

"Not as sorry as I am to say it," Montgomery countered.

"If you'd like to review a list of alternatives—" she began, but Montgomery cut her off.

"That won't be necessary. Willem and I have already conferred on the matter, and we have made our selection."

"Oh," Eden said, truly surprised. "Very well. Who is the lucky captain?"

"You are," Montgomery replied.

"I beg your pardon, sir?" Eden said automatically, certain she hadn't heard him correctly.

"Apart from *Voyager*'s old crew, no one here knows more about their past or the new fleet than you, Captain," Montgomery said calmly. "I realize it's been a few years since you served on a starship, but your record in that capacity as well as in your more recent assignments is exemplary. In addition, you have spent the last several months establishing a rapport with the fleet's officers and crew. Neither of us believes there is a better candidate for the post. Congratulations, Afsarah."

With that Admiral Montgomery rose and extended his hand to Eden.

Eden stood and shook it firmly, even as her heart tried to pound its way out of her chest.

"Thank you, sir," she said with forced restraint.

"You're to report to *Voyager* first thing in the morning for the senior staff briefing and continue your preparations for launch from there. I realize this is sudden, and hope it will not be too much of a personal inconvenience to you."

"Not at all, Admiral," Eden replied.

"Then we'll leave you to it," Montgomery said with a nod as Willem rose to follow him out.

"Admiral Batiste, a word?" Eden requested.

"Of course." He smiled.

Montgomery did them both the courtesy of continuing on his way without comment.

Once the door had slid shut, Eden practically launched herself around her desk to confront Willem.

"Are you out of your mind?" she demanded.

"May I remind you, Captain, that you are addressing a superior officer, and your new fleet commander?" he said without a trace of amusement.

Eden stopped short, shaking with impotent shock. Their mutual tendency to casually disregard their respective positions had just come to an abrupt end, but it was going to take some getting used to.

"Permission to speak freely, sir?" she asked with a look that dared him to deny her.

"Granted," he said congenially.

"While I am honored by the confidence you and Admiral Montgomery are willing to place in me, I have reservations about accepting this position."

"Such as?"

Eden spent a moment mentally prioritizing her objections, but the greatest wasn't hard to enunciate.

"You and I don't do well in the same room together most of the time. We haven't worked closely since our divorce, and sometimes I believe the only reason we're both still alive is because we've steered clear of each other as much as possible since then. I was willing to go out on a limb with you to get this mission approved because I truly believe in it, but if you've got concerns about Captain Chakotay's baggage I'd love to see how they stack up next to ours."

"You underestimate both of us, Afsarah," Willem said gently.

"Please don't do that," she replied forcefully.

"Don't do what?"

"Don't pretend that this is easy for you. And if it really is, don't insult me by making it so obvious."

"I'm dead serious," Willem said. "I can't believe the idea didn't occur to me sooner than this morning. You have immersed yourself in Project Full Circle since its inception and have dispassionately analyzed every facet of *Voyager*'s time in the Delta quadrant. You are an outstanding commanding officer. You are professional, discreet, courageous, and adventurous. You can't tell me that the part of you that isn't pissed at me right now isn't thrilled by the opportunity."

Eden shook her head, "Part of me . . . maybe . . ." she admitted, "but the rest of me isn't going to like serving under you one bit."

"All I ask is that you give me a little time to prove you wrong," Willem said. "I have unwavering faith in your ability and mine to set aside our personal issues. It is our duty, and nothing is more important to either of us than that. And frankly, there's no one I would trust more to stand beside me when things get tough. You want me to say it? Fine. I need you on this mission, Afsarah. The fleet needs you. You're not serving me. You're serving the Federation. And if, in time, we both realize that this was a colossal mistake, other arrangements can be made."

Eden considered Willem cautiously. He was saying all of the right things. And while it was asking a lot, it was nothing compared to what many Federation citizens and Starfleet officers were grappling with at the moment.

She was suddenly conscious of a new thought. Kathryn Janeway had faced death to protect many on board *Voyager* who were once again being sent into the belly of the beast. She had set aside personal and professional concerns to do her duty and had always placed the needs of her people above her own. Eden's sense of guilt and remorse could never persuade her to accept this challenge, but her heart stirred at the thought that dedicating herself to Janeway's cause might, in time, grant her absolution.

She didn't really trust Willem anymore. She hadn't since the day he had asked her to leave their home. But she had learned to trust herself again. And she could not refuse to do for *Voyager,* or the rest of the fleet, less than she was asking of them.

"Very well, Admiral," she finally said. "I'll see you in the morning."

"Thank you, Captain," Willem replied.

***

Counselor Cambridge had been waiting for several minutes in Admiral Montgomery's office for him to return. His session with Chakotay had been intense and exhausting, but its successful resolution had filled

Cambridge with new purpose. *Voyager* and the fleet were about to face a daunting task, but he no longer believed that Chakotay's presence would make that task more difficult. *Voyager* would once again soon be in the hands of its most capable leader.

"Sorry to keep you waiting, Counselor," Montgomery said briskly as he entered his office.

"Not at all, Admiral," Cambridge said as he stood to make his report. "I have completed my evaluation as ordered and wish to present my findings."

"Aren't they going to be presented in writing?"

"Eventually, but don't you want to hear the short version?" Cambridge asked.

"Actually, that won't be necessary, Counselor," Montgomery said, taking a seat at his office's small conference table.

Cambridge joined him, asking, "Why not?"

"I witnessed your session with the captain and am certain that we have already come to the same conclusion. We've selected a replacement for Captain Chakotay, and for now he will remain on leave, pending future reassignment."

Cambridge blinked several times as he stared open-mouthed at the admiral. "I'm sorry, you *witnessed my session?*" he asked.

"Time is of the essence in this matter, Counselor."

Cambridge was annoyed but not surprised by Montgomery's actions. He chose to let the breach of his patient's confidentiality pass. Instead he asked, "Did you witness *all* of it?"

"I saw enough."

"I rather doubt that."

"Counselor?"

"It is my professional opinion that Captain Chakotay is not only ready to resume his post, he is absolutely critical to the mission's success."

"I don't agree," Montgomery replied, unruffled. "My impressions of Captain Chakotay were that he was argumentative, hostile, and in no way fit for command at the present time. We need a diplomat out there, not a warrior with a short fuse and unresolved personal issues."

Cambridge rose and circled the table, determined to choose his next words carefully.

"And that's your professional opinion?" Cambridge asked.

"What else would it be?"

"Well, I'm a trained physician and counselor. Which is why, I'm assuming, I was asked to perform the evaluation."

"And I'm a Starfleet admiral with over forty years of experience. I know a problem when I see one."

"Apparently not," Cambridge replied coolly.

"You'll want to watch your tone, Counselor," Montgomery said, rising to face him.

"You didn't expect him to succeed, did you?" Cambridge asked.

"No, but I hoped he would."

"Then I don't understand," Cambridge said softly.

"That will be all, Counselor," Montgomery replied. "If you will advise Captain Chakotay that I am ready to see him, I'll take it from here."

Cambridge strode toward the door. He had observed more than his fair share of absurdity in his professional life, but rarely was it so blatant. He paused and turned back to the admiral.

"May I make a request, sir?" he asked.

"Go ahead."

"The next time you concoct an exercise in futility, I'd appreciate it if you would use another officer. I don't appreciate having my time wasted so egregiously."

Montgomery returned his frigid gaze.

"Dismissed," he replied ominously.

Chakotay sat at ease in the white room. Remembering his misgivings of only a few hours before, he was relieved that they had come to naught. He was further amazed that it had taken him so long to finally accept the help he had needed for too long. He knew that the road before him was still long and arduous, but he no longer feared it. Kathryn had once suggested to him that he and Cambridge were very much alike. On the surface the suggestion had seemed absurd. But now he wished it hadn't taken so long for him to see that she had been right. He found himself looking forward to returning to *Voyager*, almost more so than when he had first assumed command. There were so many things to be done differently and so many people he had missed and longed to see again.

His enthused spirits held until Cambridge reentered the room. He'd seen bitter disappointment on the counselor's face too many times in the past to misread it. A flood of heat rushed to his head as he realized that the counselor had not returned bearing good news.

"A word to the wise, Counselor," Chakotay said, rising to meet Cambridge halfway to the table. "Poker is never going to be your game."

"A fact I am all too well acquainted with," Cambridge replied. After a long pause, he said simply, "I'm so sorry, Captain."

Chakotay was too, but to his surprise, he didn't find any anger to accompany that regret.

"I understand."

"That makes one of us."

"Given the past eight months, it was always going to be a long shot," Chakotay conceded. "I don't blame you—or me, for that matter. I take full responsibility for my actions."

"You deserve this mission, Captain. And I did make that clear."

"I believe you. But maybe it was never meant to be mine."

Cambridge replied quizzically, "You give your higher powers a lot more credit than I ever could."

Chakotay nodded with a wistful smile. "That's only because I believe that they see, as we do not, the whole story. I brought myself to this place. There were lessons to be learned. As long as I live, there will be more to learn, and it is my job now to seek them out. We never really lose the path, Counselor, even when we are floundering in the darkness. We are always exactly where we are supposed to be at any given time and possess every resource that we need. I'd forgotten that by living in the past and fearing the future. From now on, I must live fully in the present. Thank you for reminding me of that today."

Cambridge nodded.

"Watch over our people," Chakotay requested. "They will push you and they will disappoint you and they will surprise you daily with their capacity for greatness."

"I will," Cambridge agreed.

"And promise me that whoever Command has chosen to replace me, you serve them as faithfully as you have served me."

"Of course."

"Dismissed," Chakotay said calmly.

"Yes, sir," Cambridge replied.

CHAPTER THIRTY-TWO

Harry hardly recognized *Voyager*'s former mess hall. In lieu of smaller tables and chairs that provided a casual dining environment, a single podium had been set up in the center of the far wall, and dozens of chairs rested in neat formation facing it. Near the podium, Tom was conferring with Captain Eden, a woman Harry knew only by reputation. He understood from Tom that she had coordinated operations and logistics for *Voyager* over the past several weeks, and to hear Tom tell it, she was demanding and a stickler for details. Counselor Cambridge soon entered and pulled Captain Eden away from Tom. What Harry could see of their exchange appeared to be heated, at least on Cambridge's part.

Kim recognized a few familiar faces scattered about the room. Vorik stood in a corner near the windows, listening attentively to a slight, gray-haired Vulcan. Lasren and Patel were already seated next to a petite human woman bearing lieutenant's pips whose long brunette hair had been swept up into a neat ponytail. As Lasren and Patel studied the same padd, she looked about, as if she might soon be asked to take a test, evaluating all those present. The Doctor stood between a stout alien male who appeared to be Tamarian and a lithe human female with long, straight, strawberry blonde hair. The Tamarian wore a sciences uniform, which Harry found interesting. He was not aware that any member of this species served actively with Starfleet, given what he believed was an unbridgeable communications gap between them and most of the Federation.

As several more people, most of whom Harry could not place, entered the mess and either took seats among the gallery or moved to the front to greet Captain Eden, Harry took a moment to study Tom's face. He was now exchanging pleasantries with a very young woman whose short, spiked blue hair testified to either a mixed heritage or a need to stand out in a crowd.

Both Tom and Harry had been too busy over the last few weeks to speak in depth about B'Elanna and Miral, but Tom seemed to be holding up well. All Tom had almost grudgingly shared with Harry was the fact that there would be no public memorial service for his family. John Torres and Julia Paris had both agreed with Tom to keep the proceedings within the immediate family. To Harry, this indicated that his best friend was holed up behind a thick wall of denial. He knew that B'Elanna and Tom had been formally separated for months and hadn't spent much time together in two years, but he never believed that Tom had truly gotten over her. The loss of Miral should have devastated him. To Harry's amazement, Tom hadn't even requested a day off since hearing the news. Harry had considered contacting B'Elanna's father. He knew they'd had a strained relationship but also believed he had tried to reconnect with his daughter when *Voyager* had returned. Harry's duties had been so pressing, however, that he hadn't yet found time to track down John Torres.

The only person not yet present was Chakotay.

A robust officer in his mid-fifties with short, full dark hair strode into the room and immediately Captain Eden called out, "Admiral on deck."

All present were instantly on their feet and facing the podium, where he quickly took his place.

"Please take your seats," the admiral said officiously, and everyone hurried to comply. Captain Eden, along with the older Vulcan, the woman the Doctor had been speaking with, and six other officers Harry did not know arranged themselves facing the crowd on either side of the podium, as Tom and Vorik took seats in the front row. Harry quickly grabbed a seat next to the Doctor and found the chair next to him filled by Lieutenant Reg Barclay. Harry was pleased to see the garrulous engineer but knew he'd have to wait until the briefing ended to express that sentiment.

"Good morning," the admiral began. "For those of you who may not know, I am Admiral Willem Batiste, and I will be commanding the fleet's upcoming mission. I know that all of you have been working long hours over the past several months to prepare for this mission and I would like to thank you now for your efforts and to advise you that I don't expect your jobs will get any easier in the days and months to come.

"You have all been selected from among Starfleet's finest to take part in an unprecedented exploratory effort. The U.S.S. Voyager, a ship which has served with distinction for almost ten years, has now been tasked with leading the most advanced fleet Starfleet has ever assembled on a vital expedition to the far reaches of known space. In three days' time, this fleet will launch and begin a journey to the Delta quadrant."

This news was met with absolute silence, as expected of senior officers, but Harry had to swallow hard to hold down his instinctive response to the announcement.

Are you kidding me?

Harry wished desperately at that moment that he could see Tom's face, but he was suddenly certain that he had known for some time what Starfleet was planning.

"As the fleet's respective engineering staffs are aware, all of our vessels have been fitted with Starfleet's next-generation FTL propulsion breakthrough, the quantum slipstream drive," Admiral Batiste went on. Harry noticed that the blue-haired woman seated behind Tom seemed to sit up a little straighter in her chair at this. "Each vessel will have the ability to use these drives independently as needed, but we will spend our first several days in open space coordinating flight patterns so that for our longest journeys, all fleet vessels will travel in a single slipstream corridor. It will be an exciting challenge for our pilots and one I'm sure they are all looking forward to mastering.

"Once that task is complete, we will set our course for the demarcation of the terminus between the Beta and Delta quadrants. At that point, three of our ships will be tasked with dropping and testing advanced communications relays which will enable the fleet to remain in time-delayed contact with the Command for the duration of our mission.

"That mission has several priorities; the most important will be to assess political and geographical changes to the quadrant in the absence of the Borg. As some of you may know, the Borg are believed to have been completely transformed by the Caeliar, an incredibly advanced species that has also apparently left our galaxy for parts unknown. We are going to make sure that this is the case, and we are also going to make our best efforts to establish new and lasting diplomatic relations with the Delta quadrant's warp-capable species.

"The experience and expertise of those of you who have already visited the Delta quadrant will be invaluable to our efforts. We go in peace, but we are prepared to face those who might be hostile to our presence. The Federation has no intention of expanding beyond the worlds we already encompass. We will, of course, extend the hand of friendship to any who wish to form alliances with us. Most importantly, we go to chart the unexplored and to seek out new life and civilizations. We do not expect to encounter or antagonize another race as opposed to the principles of the Federation as the Borg, but if they are out there, and if they pose a potential threat to the Federation, our efforts will enable Starfleet to prepare and meet any such threat.

"We will remain in regular contact with the Command and from time to time will be able to refresh personnel with replacements. You should expect your part in this mission to take no less than three years.

"These are the officers who will be commanding each of the fleet's vessels. We will adjourn so that each of you can meet directly with your senior staffs.

"*Voyager* will be accompanied by two of our newest vessels: the *Vesta*-class *Esquiline*—under Captain Parimon Dasht—and the *Quirinal*—under Captain Regina Farkas. These three ships have been assigned a dedicated science vessel: the *Hawking*, under Captain Bal Itak; the *Planck*, under Captain Hosc T'Mar; and the *Curie*, under Captain Xin Chan. Rounding out the fleet are three vessels with unique specialties. The *Galen*, under Commander Clarissa Glenn, which will be staffed by advanced holograms and which will serve as our primary medical resource. The *Achilles*, under Commander Tillum Drafar, which will carry vital backup components for our technology along with industrial replicators. And the *Demeter*, under Commander Liam O'Donnell, which will house a vast airponics bay to provide homegrown produce to supplement our replicators, as well as storage facilities for biological resources we may find along our way."

Kim's head was spinning as each captain Batiste introduced stepped forward briefly when their name was mentioned. In time he assumed he would get to know all of them better, but what struck Harry was the conspicuous absence of *his* captain.

"*Voyager* will be led by Captain Afsarah Eden, and as the fleet's flagship, it will also be my home for the duration," the admiral finally announced, ending Harry's confusion but adding to his consternation.

"If you will all now regroup under your respective commanding officers, they will provide you with detailed reports of remaining tasks prior to our launch. But before you go, let me to say this: I look forward to working with each and every one of you. I realize that this mission may appear to be daunting, but I assure you it is vital to the Federation. Let us move into the unknown confident in our abilities to preserve the Federation's highest principles and determined to do credit as ambassadors to the Delta quadrant."

The admiral's concluding remarks were met with polite applause. He stepped down with a nod and quickly left the mess, as Harry rose on leaden feet to approach his new captain. Tom was already at her side, along with

Counselor Cambridge. Lasren and Patel filed in behind him, along with the Tamarian doctor, the blue-haired pilot, Harry assumed, and the bright-eyed brunette he had noticed earlier. As they mingled through the crowd the brunette tapped his shoulder and said, "Lieutenant Kim?"

"Yes?" he replied.

"I'm Nancy Conlon, formerly of the *da Vinci*."

"It's nice to meet you, Lieutenant," Harry said absently.

"I know you're our security chief, but Vorik tells me you're also quite the engineer," she said cheerfully.

"I guess." Harry nodded.

"It's good to hear. I'm taking over *Voyager*'s engine room for this trip, and . . ."

"You're our chief engineer?" Harry interrupted, less kindly than he'd intended.

"That's right," she said with a little more reserve.

"What about Vorik?"

"He asked to be transferred to the *Hawking*. I think he and Captain Itak are old friends," Conlon replied.

Harry looked past her to see Vorik standing beside his new captain and wished suddenly he had a little Vulcan equanimity.

"I'm sorry," Harry said quickly. "It's just a lot to take in all at once."

"This is Starfleet," Conlon replied. "When isn't that the case?"

"Ladies and gentlemen," Captain Eden said over the din filling the room. "If you'll follow me, we will move to *Voyager*'s main conference room to continue the briefing."

Harry began filing out behind the others even as his heart protested loudly that he really didn't want to follow her anywhere. He knew it was unfair, but he couldn't shake the sentiment. He had faced the Delta quadrant once, but under the steady hand of a captain he would have gone to the ends of the universe to please. Serving under Chakotay had felt like a natural transition. He knew Chakotay hadn't been at his best for a while, but still could not believe that anyone who hadn't been to the Delta quadrant before had any business leading *Voyager*. With a deep sigh, he struggled to banish these thoughts.

Unfortunately, over the next few hours he found that increasingly difficult to do.

Chakotay had been knocking at Seven's door repeatedly for several minutes before faint footfalls could be heard approaching from the other side. When she finally opened the door, Chakotay was taken aback by her appearance. Sweat had plastered tendrils of long blonde hair to the sides of her flushed face. Her chest rose and fell rapidly as she struggled to compose her breathing, and her eyes skittered over his face and beyond until she seemed to register who was standing before her.

Once she did, she seemed every bit as disturbed by the sight of him as he had been by her.

"Seven, are you all right?" Chakotay asked immediately. He had actually tried to prepare a few words in advance of his arrival that might break the ice that had no doubt frozen between them in the last several months. The moment he saw her, his concern for her mental and physical health became priority number one.

"What are you doing here?" Seven demanded as her breathing began to mercifully slow.

"Right this second I'm worried about you," Chakotay replied honestly. When she remained rooted to the ground rather than asking him to enter, he added, "May I come in?"

Seven turned her head swiftly, as if responding to a sound that Chakotay had not heard. After a moment she looked back at him warily, and with a barely perceptible nod stepped aside.

He entered a dim hall. There was still plenty of late afternoon sun hitting the townhouse's west-facing front windows, but heavy curtains had been drawn to block the light, and his eyes took a few minutes to adjust to the disarray of the living room to his right.

Embroidered pillows, which Irene Hansen had lovingly stitched by hand and which normally cushioned the sofa and love seat, were strewn about the floor. The small cocktail table was littered with padds and half-filled glasses of rank nutritional supplements. A potted fern, which had once been the table's centerpiece, was now tipped on its side on the floor beside the table, loose soil littering the rug. It looked and smelled more like an Academy student's dorm room at the end of term than the gracious, comforting, and welcoming space Chakotay had visited since Seven had relocated Irene to San Francisco.

Seven remained standing in the small atrium, watching Chakotay's quick survey of the room, her eyes defying him to remark upon what he saw. Chakotay stared at her for a moment. In place of the aloof, guarded presence he was accustomed to, he saw raw pain coupled with fright.

She seemed equally prepared to fight or flee at whatever move he might make. Remaining still, he said softly,
"Please tell me what's wrong, Seven."

"Don't pretend you care," Seven shot back.

Chakotay lowered his head slightly, allowing her to retain the illusion of dominance, and replied, "Of course you
are angry with me. I haven't been much of a friend to you
or anyone for a very long time. I came here to apologize to
you and to ask your forgiveness."

Confusion wrinkled Seven's brow. For the first time
Chakotay realized that the implants that had circled her
left eye were no longer present. He had always found her
beauty intimidating, but now there was a gentle quality to
her features, marred only by her evident hostility.

"Take my forgiveness, then," Seven said coldly, "and
get out."

"How is Irene?" Chakotay asked, ignoring her request.
Wild dogs couldn't have driven him from the house.

"She is dying," Seven replied almost clinically.

"I'm sorry," Chakotay said. "I had no idea her condition
had grown so bad."

"Only because you have not cared to inquire as to her
condition for far too long," Seven replied, then twisted the
knife by adding, "She continues to ask about you often."

Chakotay was appropriately shamed by this remark.

"May I see her?"

"She is resting right now," Seven replied more softly.
"The Doctor has provided medication to alleviate her suffering. It has proven somewhat effective, but she is unconscious now for long periods of time."

"Does the Doctor have any idea how long she can survive like this?" Chakotay asked kindly.

"Days, perhaps weeks," Seven replied.

Chakotay stepped gingerly toward her. Every instinct in his body cried out for him to offer her the comfort of an embrace, but she moved back toward the foot of the staircase.

"Seven, I am truly sorry," Chakotay said, lifting his hands before him to dispel any concern she might have that he would dare breach her personal space without her consent. "This must be awful for you. Do you at least have help in dealing with her?"

"I do not require help," Seven retorted sharply. "I am . . . I am . . . I am Seven of Nine, Tertiary Adjunct to Unimatrix . . . I am Seven of Nine . . . I am Seven . . ."

Chakotay witnessed her strength failing her. Before she could fall to the floor, he caught her and gently lowered her until they were sitting on the lowest steps. Seven fought against him for a few seconds, but finally released herself to the strength and comfort of his embrace. Her body began to choke with sobs, and Chakotay wrapped her in a protective hug, gently caressing her soft, golden hair and murmuring soothing words until the worst of the tremors passed.

Finally Seven pulled herself away to look up at him, her face wet with tears.

"Don't help me," she pleaded.

"Try and stop me." He smiled.

"No." She shook her head, attempting to pull away from him. "Your presence is temporary. You cannot be relied upon."

Chakotay held her firmly by her upper arms. "Listen to me," he said. "I'm not going anywhere. We can sit here like this for minutes or days—however long it takes for you to tell me what the hell is happening to you."

Seven's eyes registered surprise. With childlike grace-lessness she wiped her nose on the sleeve of her arm and inhaled quickly with a loud snuffle.

"But you have to return to *Voyager*."

"Not right now I don't," he assured her.

"You are leaving," she insisted almost petulantly. "You, the Doctor, Commander Paris, Lieutenant Kim, you are all leaving me. Soon my aunt will be gone too and I will be alone. I must adapt."

"Hang on," Chakotay said. "*Voyager* is leaving, but I'm not going with them. Starfleet has assigned another captain to the ship. I'm still on leave. I promise you, you aren't alone, and you're never going to be alone again."

Seven considered his words and replied, "Starfleet has made an error. You should lead the mission to the Delta quadrant."

"No," Chakotay corrected her. "I am more certain now than ever that this is exactly where I am supposed to be."

Seven winced with pain and momentarily lifted her left hand to massage the side of her forehead.

"What is it?" he asked.

"It will pass," she assured him.

Chakotay raised his hand and gently caressed the cres-cent from the center of her forehead to just beneath her left eye. He then delicately placed her left hand flat on his palm and searched it for traces of the technology that had once sustained her.

"When did you have the last of your implants removed?" he asked.

"I didn't," she replied. "The Caeliar did this to me."

"When they transformed the Borg," Chakotay realized. *Of course.*

"Was it painful?" he asked.

"Yes." She nodded. "And no. It was . . . it is difficult to describe."

"Did you have any idea it was coming? Were you able to prepare yourself?"

"No."

Chakotay sighed compassionately.

"It's no wonder you're frightened," he said.

"You do not understand," Seven insisted.

"Then explain it to me."

Seven's wide eyes studied his fearfully. Finally she answered, "There was a moment, during the transformation, when I was part of the Caeliar."

"The way you were once part of the Borg?"

"No. The gestalt was more than the Collective. There was no unifying force or will, but there was still perfect harmony. Countless individuals were joined together, but they retained their unique identity."

"Are you still part of the Caeliar?" Chakotay asked, his own dubiousness at the prospect quite clear in his tone.

"No," Seven replied. "They severed my link to the whole. They abandoned me."

Chakotay nodded.

"So you glimpsed paradise, only to have it ripped away," he said kindly.

Seven nodded mutely.

"And now you feel more alone than ever?"

"If only," Seven said ruefully.

"What do you mean?"

"Something remains," she admitted. "A voice."

"That doesn't sound good."

"It insists over and over that I am Annika Hansen. That I am no longer Borg."

"But you are Annika," Chakotay said.

"Annika Hansen was assimilated as a child. Her identity disappeared into the Borg collective. All that I am now, I learned as a Borg. All that is best in me was their gift."

"What about your individuality?" Chakotay asked. "You didn't reclaim that until you were severed from the Collective."

"My individuality is irrelevant without my identity, and I refuse to deny the part of that identity that was once Borg," Seven said, her voice rising.

"Okay," Chakotay said soothingly. "I understand. Seven, have you seen a doctor since this transformation?"

Seven's chin jutted out defiantly. "I was examined by several physicians," she replied. "All agreed that I am now in perfect health."

"Did you tell them about the voice?"

"No."

"Why not?"

"The Federation is desperate to learn all they can about the Caeliar. If they knew of my condition, they would restrain me. They would study me. I would become more of a curiosity to them than I already am. I will not allow it."

Chakotay had to admit that there was a certain amount of sense in what she was saying. But he still wasn't sure that going it alone was a wise choice either.

"It's getting worse, isn't it?" Chakotay asked.

"At first it was very difficult to separate my own thoughts from the intentions of the voice. But I thought I had learned to adapt."

"When did that change?"

"I recently learned that my aunt's condition will never improve. Before I could begin to accept it I was told that the rest of my family is about to return to the Delta quadrant."

"Seven, your family is bigger than Tom and Harry and the Doctor."

"Who else is there?" Seven demanded. "Tuvok is on a deep-space assignment. You haven't been available for months. Icheb and Naomi are only children. B'Elanna and Miral . . ." she choked out.

"What about B'Elanna and Miral?" he asked.

Seven paused. "You don't know?" she replied in wonder.

Fear gripped Chakotay's chest.

"What about B'Elanna and Miral?" he asked again.

"They were killed during the Borg invasion," Seven replied through fresh tears.

Chakotay focused on his breath, which was now heaving in his chest.

"No . . . no . . ." he gasped, unable to find another word.

Seven took Chakotay in her arms. For the moment, she sustained them both as grief once again bared its ugly face in the center of Chakotay's being.

They held one another for what felt like hours. Once the worst had passed, Seven told Chakotay what little she knew of the specifics of their deaths. Chakotay listened patiently, waiting for his constant rage-filled companion to return to shatter the short-lived peace he had only begun to taste. But as time continued to pass in the darkened room, Chakotay felt only empty and inexpressibly sad. Seven shared his pain, and between the two of them, the burden became a bit lighter. As much as Chakotay knew he would need to nurse his own sorrow, he found himself much more concerned with Seven's all-consuming pain.

It was well past midnight when he finally left her home. He would return early the next morning, and the morning after that. They would work together, Chakotay assured her, to find a way to make sense of their recent losses and those which dimmed on the horizon.

At least now he was certain he would not again make the same mistake he had made when he lost Kathryn. Shining through his broken heart were rays of determination and strength.

He returned to his temporary quarters, seated himself on his living room floor, and began to meditate. Even without his medicine bundle he was soon sitting in a lush and verdant forest, staring into the eyes of his animal guide.

CHAPTER THIRTY-THREE

Harry stood on a rocky precipice, overlooking the Atlantic Ocean as it violently assaulted the small cove below. He'd transported to this spot over twenty minutes ago and still hadn't worked up the nerve to approach the small cabin nestled beneath a dense canopy of white pines.

He still didn't know exactly why he'd come. He only knew that he had precious few days left in the Alpha quadrant and he needed to see more than the inside of *Voyager* during those days or he would lose his mind. When he thought of pristine beauty and bracing air, only one spot had come to mind. He no longer had a claim to it, but he had to see it, just one more time.

Actually, he had to see her. But he wasn't ready to admit that, even to himself.

Harry had dutifully pushed Libby from his heart and mind years earlier. He'd made new friends, pursued new relationships, and come to believe that she was forever banished to his past.

Ever since he had awakened in Starfleet Medical months earlier, he'd been thinking of her—dreaming of her. Everywhere he went in his dreams, no matter how realistic or bizarre, she was there, always in the next room, just out of sight, and always playing her *lal-shak* for him.

And every time he reached for his clarinet, he found himself playing the tunes they had once shared as duets.

You're being stupid, he chided himself. *She's married. You haven't spoken to her in years. She doesn't want to see you.*

Still, he had come and now stood only meters from her door, with no idea at all what he wanted to say or hear.

"*Indigo!*" her familiar voice called out. Turning toward her front door, he saw her emerge from it, searching the twilight for one of her beloved cats.

"Indigo!" she called again. "Where did you run off to?"

Taking a deep breath, Harry took a halting step forward and she turned, instantly on her guard.

"Who's there?" she demanded.

Given the remoteness of her home, her sense of alarm was understandable. The isolation of the little cabin had been one of the things both of them had loved most about this quiet piece of North America.

"It's me," Harry said, hoping to put her at ease.

Libby stepped forward, squinting into the gloom.

"Harry?"

"Yeah," he replied, continuing forward.

"Oh my God," she said once she was certain her eyes weren't playing tricks on her.

"I didn't mean to frighten you," he began, but was quickly silenced by a hug so firm it bordered on violence.

"Oh my God, I'm so happy to see you," Libby said. Releasing him and stepping back to get a better view, she added, "You look perfect."

"I wouldn't go that far," he found himself joking.

"I would," she countered. "What are you doing here?"

Harry didn't really know how to begin, so he opted for honesty.

"I don't know."

Libby suddenly grew quite still. The joy her face had proclaimed in seeing him transmuted itself into a more complicated emotion Harry could not place. After what seemed like an endless silence, she said, "You want to take a walk?"

"That would be great."

Libby took the lead and began directing their steps down a small rocky path that led to the shoreline. They had hiked this little trail many times in the last six months of their relationship. It led to a favorite large rock from which a truly spectacular view of the ocean could be enjoyed, especially now, so near sunset.

They reached the rock in comfortable silence, and Libby climbed onto its scarred surface, settling in a nook that allowed her to rest her back against the high cliff wall behind them. Harry took his own familiar spot nearer the rock's edge, with his feet hanging over the side.

After a few moments, Harry said, "I really don't know what I'm doing here."

"I'm not complaining," Libby replied. "It really is wonderful just to see you."

"You too," Harry said. "You've been on my mind a lot more than usual. It's weird. I can't seem to make sense of anything right now. But part of me kept thinking that I should come here."

"It's okay. I'll help you any way I can. You know that, or you wouldn't be here."

"I guess I should congratulate you," he continued. "I heard you got married."

Libby nodded a little shyly. "Last month."

"And he makes you happy?"

"He does."

"Good," Harry said, not terribly convincingly.

"You understand, Harry, that just because, I mean, I know I . . ." she stammered. Finally she exhaled sharply in frustration. "Why is this so hard?"

"Everything's hard right now," Harry replied.

"It is, isn't it?" She frowned. "Everything has changed. Whatever illusions we used to have about our happy, peaceful little part of the galaxy are just gone. It feels like no place is ever going to be safe again."

"Exactly," Harry agreed. "Nothing has turned out the way it was supposed to."

Libby looked up at him sharply.

"Harry," she began warily.

"I don't mean *us*," Harry added quickly. "I mean everything else." He paused briefly to collect his thoughts and went on. "The whole time we were lost in the Delta quadrant, I would imagine what it would be like if we ever got home. There were days when my idea of that future was the only thing that kept me going. I just knew that whatever happened, as long as we all made it home in one piece, everything would work out. If we could take the Delta quadrant, we could take anything, you know?"

Libby nodded patiently, allowing him to continue.

"The people I shared that journey with, we became a family. And now, three years later, that family has been scattered to the winds. Admiral Janeway beat the Borg I don't know how many times on their turf, and then they show up here and kill her. Tom and B'Elanna loved each other more than anyone I've ever known, and even they couldn't make it work. Right now they should be raising that beautiful little girl and instead, B'Elanna and Miral are dead and Tom is pushing all of us away. I don't know where Chakotay is. Seven's torn between taking calls from the president of the Federation and looking after her poor aunt. It's not right. And no matter how I try to look at it, it's never going to be right again. It doesn't make any sense. It's like I had this life, and then I somehow wandered down the wrong path and ended up in some alternate reality."

"It wouldn't be the first time, would it?" Libby teased gently.

"I guess not." Harry smiled faintly. "But this time I have a feeling that there isn't going to be a helpful alien with a vast knowledge of subspace anomalies, or a duplicate version of *Voyager* for me to find my way back to."

"You're probably right about that," she agreed.

"And get this," Harry added. "After all we did to get home, Starfleet has decided to send us back to the Delta quadrant."

"I know," Libby said softly.

Harry turned on her, stung. "I didn't even know until this morning. How the hell could you possibly . . . ?"

"Harry, I'm married to a director of Starfleet Intelligence," Libby said gently. "I'm not saying he tells me everything, but he's pretty good at keeping me up to date if it has anything at all to do with *Voyager.*"

"Oh," Harry replied. "I guess that makes sense. But why would you care?"

She shrugged. "Old habits die hard."

Harry didn't know why, but he liked the idea that she was still keeping tabs on him.

"Are you worried about going back?" she asked.

"Not really," Harry admitted. "It was a bit of a shock, but the mission actually makes sense. We need to know what's out there now that the Borg are gone. And they're giving us all the newest technological toys, so I don't really see us getting stranded again."

"I guess that's comforting."

Harry picked up a handful of loose rocks and began to toss them one at a time into the ocean below. It was too dark now to see where they might have hit, and the sound of crashing waves made listening for them fruitless, but just the activity was relaxing.

"I guess I just feel like somewhere along the line, I made a mistake. I turned right when I should have turned left. I did something wrong and maybe if I hadn't, things would be better now," Harry said, punctuating it with a hard throw.

Libby tried not to smile. "Harry, I know your parents raised you to believe otherwise, but the universe actually doesn't revolve around you."

Harry felt his cheeks begin to burn.

"I know that," he replied weakly.

"You couldn't control or change anything that's happened. None of us could. We just do the best we can at any given time, make the best choices possible, and then learn to live with the rest."

"I can accept that," Harry said, "but what about the things I could control?"

"Like what?"

"Like us."

Libby looked away for a long moment, obviously struggling with herself. Finally she turned back and said simply, "Harry, what happened between you and me was not your fault."

"I was there," he countered. "I have to take some responsibility for it."

"No, you really don't," she replied. "If anyone is to blame, it's me."

Her words released something in him, something that had been wound too tight for too long. But part of him didn't really believe it.

"I don't blame you, Libby," he said.

"You should."

"Come on. You asked me for more time, and I didn't think I could give it to you. What if I had? Wouldn't things be different?"

"No."

Libby rose from where she had rested and stepped gingerly toward him. He held out a hand to help her keep her balance. She looked up at him, her eyes misting, and said, "I should have told you this a long time ago. But I didn't. And I'm sorry."

"Told me what?" he asked, suddenly a little nervous.

"When you asked me to marry you, I couldn't, not because I didn't love you, but because I hadn't been completely honest with you. I couldn't tell you who I really was, what I had become, because it was classified. Five months ago, I formally resigned from Starfleet Intelligence. I'd been serving as a covert agent there for almost ten years."

Harry felt certain she had suddenly begun to speak an alien language.

"Now that I'm no longer an operative, I'm not compromising anything by telling you. I'd appreciate it if you wouldn't broadcast it, but it's finally no longer a matter of Starfleet security."

Harry struggled to wrap his brain around the timing. "Ten years?"

"I joined up six months after your ship disappeared. I needed to know what really happened to you. I thought Starfleet Intelligence might know the answer, even if they weren't going to share it with the public. They took me on because my touring schedule created a perfect cover for my work. And it turned out I was pretty good at it. More importantly, I liked it. You always used to talk so much about being of service. I didn't think I had that in me, but it turned out I did. Somehow, following in your footsteps even in a different branch of Starfleet made me feel a little closer to you."

Harry's mind was reeling, but he refrained from saying anything that might stop her from speaking.

"When you got back, I promised myself I would leave you be. I knew I couldn't tell you who I was, and I justified it to myself by assuming you'd forgotten about me long ago. But you became my new assignment. I tried to keep it professional, but I couldn't. I fell in love with you all over again, or maybe I just realized that I'd never really stopped. But that didn't change the fact that you and I just couldn't work anymore. I was lying to you every time I saw you, and I'd have to continue lying to you every day we were married. It wasn't right."

Harry began to shake as the magnitude of her betrayal sank in.

"So why didn't you just resign then?"

Libby stepped back and turned away. "You'll think it's stupid," she said softly.

"I have no idea what to think right now," Harry replied.

"As an agent, I was actually in a position to help keep you safe."

"How did you come to that conclusion?"

Libby smiled faintly. "Do you remember Peregrine?"

Harry felt as if she had physically struck him. Peregrine had been the code name for someone he had never identified, someone who consistently fed him and his crew vital information at critical moments during the Borg virus crisis and their mission to Loran II.

"That was you?" he asked in disbelief.

"Yep. I needed to know you were safe, and I couldn't do that as your wife and a concert musician. But from the inside, I had options. I couldn't walk away from that."

"So, what changed? Why did you finally resign?"

"The last year has been really tough on those in my line of work. It's your job to fight the Federation's battles, but it was mine to try and make sure those battles never had to be fought. Then the Borg showed up and billions of people died. It broke something in me. I needed something to hold on to. And to be honest, I've loved Aiden for a long time. He put me back together when I thought I'd lost you forever, and he's been the one constant in my life since then. He already knew all of my deep, dark secrets. I'd never been forced to lie to him. But I also couldn't continue to work for him. I thought about just requesting a transfer, but at the end of the day, after everything the Federation has been through, I just needed a clean break, a new beginning, and maybe some peace."

"I understand that," Harry said.

"I wasn't ever going to tell you, Harry. You were right to end our relationship when you did because I'd never have had the strength to. I could never think less of you for that choice, and I've always been afraid that if you knew, you would think less of me."

Harry stood silently for several moments. The strangest thing was, difficult as it was to accept, knowing at least this much of the truth did help.

"You're not at all who I thought you were," he finally said.

"No."

"And you're right. It never would have worked under those conditions."

"No."

"And if you'd told me when I proposed to you, I would have . . ."

"Hated me?"

"No. But I would have felt betrayed. I don't think I would have taken it well."

Harry felt something of the weight he'd been carrying for too long begin to lift from his shoulders.

"And now?"

Harry sighed.

"Now, it's the past, and it's not so hard to understand. It makes sense. I can let it go," he said with a smile of relief. "I'm glad you told me. It helps."

"Good."

Harry stepped back to put some distance between them and inhaled deeply. His mind felt suddenly clearer than it had in weeks.

"You were a secret agent?"

"I was."

"That's actually kind of hot."

Libby laughed, and soon Harry joined her.

"I can't remember the last time I heard you do that," she said.

"Me either," he replied. "Don't tell your husband I said that, though. He could probably have me assassinated, right?"

"Officially, no," Libby said. "Unofficially . . ."

"Right." Harry nodded.

"So what now?"

Harry turned to stare out into the darkness.

"Once again into the great unknown, I suppose."

"You're going to be fine, Harry," Libby said gently. "Just worry about the things you can do something about. The rest will take care of itself."

Harry nodded. He didn't know if he really believed her, but that thought was more comforting than any of those he'd brought with him when he arrived.

"I will." After a moment he said, "Just promise me something?"

"Anything."

"Promise me that you'll take care of yourself."

"I will if you will. I meant what I said to you the night we broke up. I can't imagine a world in which you and I won't always be friends."

"Neither can I," Harry said.

Only this time, he meant it.

Chakotay stared at his comm panel. Though it was the middle of the night in San Francisco, it was early morning at Utopia Planitia, where *Voyager* was docked. Much of his time over the past few days had been spent with Seven, but he'd promised himself he would make this call before *Voyager* launched. In a way he dreaded the prospect, but then no one ever said that making amends was easy. Whatever response he received, it would be no less than he deserved.

Finally resolved, he activated the terminal and waited

for the connection to establish itself. Soon enough, Tom's harried face appeared before him.

"*Captain?*" he said, at something of a loss.

"Hello, Tom," Chakotay replied.

"*I don't really . . . I mean things are . . .*" Tom began.

"You're getting ready to launch," Chakotay interjected. "You've had dozens of last-minute requests for accommodation changes and half the crew hasn't reported in for their medical evaluations and your final cargo shipments haven't been cleared for transport."

"*How did you know?*" Tom asked.

"I used to do your job, remember?" Chakotay smiled. "The last thing you have time for right now is a conversation."

"*That pretty much covers it,*" Tom agreed.

"So I'll keep this brief," Chakotay said.

Tom tightened his jaw but nodded for Chakotay to continue.

"I've had a lot of time to think about the last several months, and a couple of things have become very clear to me. I'm not proud of my behavior, especially toward you, but no matter how bad things got, you never failed to support me. I want you to know how much I appreciate that."

Tom's face softened, but he remained silent.

"And I also want you to know that I heard about B'Elanna and Miral. I'm so sorry, Tom. I know there's nothing I can do to make it better. It's going to hurt like hell for a long time. I miss them terribly. They were extraordinary women, your wife and daughter. Irreplaceable. But if you let it, time will help you heal. And if there is anything you need from me, please ask."

Tom swallowed hard before replying, "*Thank you, sir.*"

"You're a fine officer, Tom. You've always made me proud, and I don't expect that to change. I know that *Voyager* is in good hands, and I wish you a safe journey."

Tom nodded. After a moment he said, *"I'm sorry you're not going with us."*

"Everything happens for a reason, Tom," Chakotay replied. "You don't need to worry about me. Just do your job. Take care of your captain and your crew. I'll still be around when you get back, and I expect you to return with lots of good stories to tell."

"I will."

"Now get back to work, Commander."

"Aye, Captain," Tom said, his voice thick.

Chakotay replied with a tight smile. As he reached toward the panel to terminate the call, Tom said, *"You look better than you have in a while."*

"That might be because I am better."

"You were in love with her, weren't you?" Tom asked.

To hear this simple truth expressed with such compassion by an old friend touched Chakotay's heart deeply.

"I was," he finally acknowledged.

"You could have told me," Tom said.

"I know," Chakotay replied. "I'm sorry I didn't. I should have remembered that you are one of only a handful of friends I absolutely trust."

Tom appeared stricken by this comment Chakotay had meant to be a compliment.

"Are you sure that under the circumstances you really want to take this trip, Tom?" Chakotay asked.

"At this point, I don't have much of a choice," Tom answered quickly.

"We always have choices," Chakotay reminded him. "Some are just harder to make than others."

"*I know what I'm doing,*" Tom insisted.

"That's all I'll ever need to hear from you," Chakotay replied.

"*I have to get going,*" Tom said.

"I understand. Keep your friends close right now. They won't let you down. And if you get a chance, have a talk with Counselor Cambridge. I know he can help, if you're willing to let him."

Tom nodded with a faint smile and terminated the connection. Only once Tom's face had vanished did Chakotay realize how much of his heart was going with *Voyager*.

They'll be fine, he assured himself.

Rising from the station, he went to his replicator and ordered a cup of hot tea. He only had a few hours of sleep to look forward to and he needed every one of them.

He reached the doorway to his bedroom before it dawned on him that his work for this day was not yet done.

There was one more call he needed to make.

Captain Eden was still having trouble adjusting to the idea that *Voyager's* ready room was now hers. She'd spent many hours in the inviting space and personally supervised its reconstruction, along with the rest of the ship, but never in all that time had she felt connected to it so personally.

Though her stomach turned with a fair share of prelaunch jitters, Eden had already checked and rechecked every item on her list several hours earlier, and until *Voy-*

ager received clearance to depart, there really wasn't much else for her to do. Paris had the last-minute matters well in hand, and her crew seemed to be performing already like a well-oiled machine.

Willem had yet to make an appearance this morning. He'd spent most of the last few days in his quarters and had received her hourly updates with a minimum of conversation. When she'd signed off around two that morning to attempt to get a few hours of sleep, he'd looked a little pale. Doctor Sharak, her new CMO, had advised her more than once that the admiral was among only a small contingent of crewmen who had failed to report for their standard medical evaluation, and she had promised to drag Willem down there herself if need be. He had every right to be as exhausted as the rest of them, but even the fleet's commander was required to submit to regulations, a fact she would remind him of none too gently as soon as they spoke this morning. If he was coming down with something, he'd be less inclined to humor her, but she'd at least make the attempt.

The captain considered taking her station on the bridge. She expected that some of her officers—Paris, Kim, Lasren, and Patel, in particular—would have a little difficulty seeing her in the center seat, and the sooner they became accustomed to her presence, the better. They were all well suited for their respective positions, and she truly felt grateful to be serving with them. Their expectations of her would undoubtedly be high, considering the shoes she was filling, but Eden did not doubt her ability to exceed them.

In time.

Her misgivings, however, were ultimately overwhelmed by her excitement. She had studied *Voyager*'s logs so thoroughly, there were times it almost felt like she'd already been there. She'd marveled at their discoveries even as she understood that they had barely scratched the surface of what was out there. This time, with peaceful exploration at the top of their agenda, Eden was thrilled with the prospect of digging deeper into those mysteries, old and new.

Now that the command was hers, she had every intention of giving it everything she had to offer.

And maybe . . . just maybe . . .

Her thoughts were interrupted by an incoming transmission. Turning to her companel, she opened the communication and saw Captain Chakotay's face before her.

"Good morning, Captain," she said automatically.

"Hello," he said with more warmth than she'd imagined she could have mustered had their positions been reversed.

"What can I do for you?"

"I'm sorry to intrude, Captain," he said most cordially. *"I know how busy you must be."*

"It's no trouble."

"Congratulations on your new assignment," Chakotay said sincerely. His tone and demeanor were so composed that Eden found herself wondering exactly what the admirals had seen to convince them that he was not ready to resume his command.

"Thank you," she replied.

"You've been given the finest vessel in all of Starfleet, Captain."

"I couldn't agree more."

"If I may, I would like to ask one favor of you."

"Please." Eden nodded.

"*I know there are a lot of new faces on board, but part of me will always think of* Voyager's *crew as mine.*"

Eden felt her face settling into harder lines.

Chakotay went on, unruffled. "*You are about to depart on what will certainly be a wondrous but equally dangerous new mission. When that mission is over, I'd only ask one thing of you.*"

"What's that, Captain?"

"*Bring them home.*"

Eden felt the brief tension that had shrouded her fall away. With an understanding nod, she said, "You have my word."

"*Thank you,*" Chakotay replied.

Once his face had disappeared, Eden bowed her head as the weight and heft of the responsibility she had accepted landed squarely upon her shoulders. Until this moment the true nature of the challenge before her had been an idea.

Suddenly, it was real.

She took a few shallow breaths, then called out, "Computer, bring up personal file Eden Delta Mikhal."

The moment the first image of the ancient carving that had been discovered by *Voyager* on a remote planet in the Delta quadrant appeared before her, its deep colored lines dotted with bright specks of reflected moonlight, her heart jumped, just as it had the first time she had seen the image.

What no one had realized, not the Mikhal who admired the carvings, or Kes, who had been intrigued by them, was that they were not just art left by an ancient civilization.

They were a map.

Or part of a map, at any rate.

How Eden knew this, she couldn't say because much of her own past was shrouded in mystery. She knew she was not a native of the Alpha quadrant. The brothers who had raised her, an eclectic pair of scientists and explorers who had never been a part of Starfleet, had told her comforting lies about her past: how they had found her on an uninhabited planet as a young girl and nursed her back to health. She had no memory of her life before that time, or most of her early years with her "uncles."

All she knew for certain was that her true history, whatever it was, wasn't nearly as simple as they would have had her believe. Once she had reached adolescence, and she had learned all they had to teach her, they had agreed that theirs was no life for anyone with Afsarah's potential. They had brought her to Earth, and she had been accepted by an elite preparatory school before gaining entrance to Starfleet Academy. She corresponded with them regularly throughout her years of study, but once she began her active duties as an ensign, their communications had become sporadic at best. Twenty-three years ago, they had been lost in a doomed attempt to try and reach the Gamma quadrant.

Eden had mourned their loss and gradually come to accept it. Her life in Starfleet was everything they had promised it would be when she had expressed childish misgivings about leaving them to attend school. Ultimately, she had resigned herself to the fact that she would probably never really know who she was or where she had come from. And given all that her life had become, she wasn't sure she cared.

And then Eden had seen a single image in *Voyager*'s logs and read it as plainly as if it had been written in Federation Standard.

She had decided then and there that someday she would be forced to leave her comfortable and predictable life behind to seek out the people who had made the carvings thousands of years earlier and learn more about them.

Of this much, she was certain: whoever they were, they were *her people*. And if she was still alive, odds were, other descendants of theirs had probably survived as well.

When Willem had first suggested assigning *Voyager* to the Delta quadrant, Eden had been thrilled with the notion that Hugh Cambridge could be relied upon to examine the carvings firsthand on her behalf. His passion for an archeological mystery had been piqued when she had transmitted them to him, just as she had expected, even without understanding the full extent of her personal interest in them.

Tantalizing as this mystery was, it alone would never have compelled her to support Willem's plan, especially over Kathryn Janeway's strenuous and repeated objections. The specter of the Borg had been more than enough fuel for that fire. But it had been all she had needed to overcome her many concerns about serving so closely with Willem and to accept the position as *Voyager*'s captain for this mission.

She would keep her promise to Chakotay. She would see to it that when their work was done, *Voyager*'s crew, along with the rest of the fleet, was returned safely to Earth.

They were all leaving their home for a time.

But maybe, just maybe . . .

Afsarah Eden was on her way back to hers.

"Bridge to the captain."

"Go ahead, Mister Paris."

"We have clearance to launch."

"I'm on my way."

Eden closed her private database, rose from her desk, and walked with her head held high onto the bridge.

One of the few aesthetic changes to the bridge for this mission had been the addition of a third seat to the two command chairs originally designed for *Voyager*. Admiral Batiste was already seated in the one to the right of center, though it would usually be reserved for Counselor Cambridge from this point forward. Paris rose from the one to the left as she entered, calling out, "Captain on the bridge."

Eden took a moment as she strode purposefully to her place to acknowledge the faces of her crew. Lasren, Kim, and Patel nodded with brisk determination. Aytar Gwyn, her short cerulean hair freshly spiked for the occasion, sat at the conn with the pent-up energy of a Thoroughbred racehorse champing at its bit. Tom Paris stood with the reserve of a seasoned veteran, clearly hoping for the best but ready for the worst. And Willem actually looked happier than she could remember at any time since their honeymoon, though he did his best to hide it behind a mask of condescending composure.

"Alert the fleet to stand by," Eden said as she took her place in the center seat.

"Aye, Captain," Lasren replied.

"Helm?"

"Yes, Captain?"

"Let's not keep the Delta quadrant waiting."

"No, sir," Gwyn said with anticipation.

"Take us out."

CHAPTER THIRTY-FOUR

B'Elanna sat in the cockpit of the ship she had privately christened the *Home Free*. Miral had spent the last hour and a half fighting her mid-morning nap but finally worked herself into a frenzied exhaustion and curled up on her bunk in the rear compartment.

It was hard to believe that after the years of fear, planning, building the most advanced shuttle ever imagined, and worst of all, the torture of being separated daily from Tom, it was nearly over. Her life since the moment Miral had first been taken from her on Boreth had become purgatory. Her work and the joys, large and small, Miral brought daily to her had made it bearable. But B'Elanna had never lost sight of the real prize: a life with Tom and Miral in some distant part of the galaxy where the Warriors of Gre'thor would never find her.

Once her shuttle had launched, she had spent months perfecting the use of her slipstream drive, charting a random course through largely unexplored areas of the Beta quadrant. In all that time she had not laid eyes on her husband and had received precious few but vital reports from Kahless. She had managed to keep abreast of the happenings in the Alpha quadrant, most importantly the Borg invasion, but easily avoided the strategic centers that had been targeted. Once the worst was past and she was assured that Tom had survived, B'Elanna had realized that the devastation inflicted upon the Federation might provide the precise circumstances she required to end her private nightmare. She was tired of hiding and tired of running and more than ready to use whatever might be at hand to bring this part of her life to a close.

Tom would have to see this opportunity as well, and given his circumstances, the destruction of so many Starfleet ships, the chaos the Federation had to be experiencing in the aftermath, and the death of his father, she wasn't actually expecting to hear from him as soon as she had.

Several weeks earlier the day had finally arrived. Kahless had sent an encoded message indicating that she should dump her cargo—the fragmented remains of a decoy shuttle that matched hers precisely, coated with DNA samples from her and Miral—in a sector that had suffered heavy damage. Carefully maneuvering through the charred hulls and debris of a battle so massive she couldn't bear to think of the casualties, B'Elanna sowed her cargo and then set her course for a distant nebula, where she would await her final communiqué from Tom. That message would provide the rendezvous coordinates where she would finally be reunited with Tom, and from there, the rest of their lives could begin.

The only thing she knew for sure at this point was that the reunion would not take place in the Alpha quadrant. B'Elanna wondered how Tom had managed to secure leave and the transportation that would make this possible, but trusted that she would learn these details soon enough. She also wondered how Tom would feel about leaving his home and, most important, his mother behind for the rest of his life. But she could only assume that he had made peace with this necessity and that given the alternative of placing his mother's life or his daughter's at greater risk, Tom would stay true to the course they had laid out together.

For her, there was little to regret leaving behind in the Alpha quadrant. Before departing she had slipped away from her base in Montana for a brief reunion with her father. He had fussed over little Miral with the same affection Owen and Julia had always displayed. But he had also understood her choice, once she had explained her intentions to him in strokes broad enough to ensure his safety, should he be questioned, but detailed enough to put his mind at ease. She knew that when the time came, Tom would do the same for Julia and would simultaneously pass along B'Elanna's apologies, respect, and love for the woman who had given her the greatest gift she had ever received, her son. Leaving behind these two people, and the love they would shower upon her and Miral, was her greatest regret. But there had simply been no other way to protect them and the life of her daughter and ultimately provide Miral with something resembling normalcy.

A quiet chime from her operations panel alerted B'Elanna to the time. It was midday by her ship's chronometer and, by Klingon custom, time to honor the dead.

For most of her life, B'Elanna had failed to observe these rituals. But once she had found herself alone and adrift in unfamiliar space, she had drawn comfort and strength from this daily practice. The list of those to honor had grown unacceptably long in the past few years, but this simple remembrance brought with it an unexpected measure of peace. She often thought back to the many hours she had spent with Tuvok on *Voyager*, attempting to rein in her aggression through the use of Vulcan meditation techniques he had patiently explained and demonstrated. She still wondered to this day that it had taken her so long to come to understand that running from her heritage, particularly her Klingon nature, would never provide her the serenity she desperately sought. The time she had spent on Boreth, searching for her mother, and then seeking the truth about her daughter, had been a mixed blessing, but it had taught her that there was more wisdom in her Klingon blood than she had ever credited.

Dimming the cabin's interior lights, B'Elanna took a moment to release all thought of the past and future and bring herself fully into the present. Once she had achieved a pleasantly empty tranquillity, she began to speak softly.

"Kahless, we implore you to remember those warriors who have fallen in your name. Lift them out of the cavern of despair and reveal yourself to them in all your glory. Remember those who fought valiantly to secure the empire and those who died to protect their allies within the Federation; remember Kularg, son of Grav, remember L'Naan, daughter of Krelik; remember Miral, daughter of L'Naan; remember Owen, son of Michael; remember Kathryn, daughter of Gretchen . . ."

With each name, a vivid image would form in B'Elanna's mind. Usually they were moments in time she hadn't realized she would cherish until she had begun to honor the dead in this way: Kularg bending his forehead to touch Miral's as she reached up to tug his beard; her grandmother teaching B'Elanna to sing her first Klingon songs; her mother's face glowing by firelight when B'Elanna had told her that she had named her daughter in her honor;

Owen laughing unrestrained while sharing a story of Tom's misspent youth the night they had first shared a meal as a family; and Admiral Janeway, the last time B'Elanna had ever seen her alive . . .

STARDATE 56265: APRIL 7, 2379

Spring had barely begun, and the nights still remembered winter's chill in the mountains of Montana. B'Elanna had been living at Dil's facility for six months and had made a habit of taking Miral away from the grime and dust and steady work of shuttle construction for more quality and uninterrupted time on the weekends. A small river tumbled through a canyon only a few miles from the warehouse. Saturday morning would begin with a hike into the canyon's rugged heart. Miral would invariably insist on walking beside her mother, but after the first hour would consent to being carried the rest of the way on B'Elanna's back.

As they walked they would discover anew the natural beauty around them. Everything was green and fresh. Miral would pluck wildflowers with her pudgy fingers and glow with delight when she remembered their names from one week to the next: buttercups (buttewrcus), starworts (stawts), and blue-eyed Marys (boo-wy mays). Once they had made camp near the river, they would busy themselves collecting firewood and chasing lizards, a pastime of which Miral never wearied until she actually caught one. After an early dinner, as the sun began to fall below the ridgeline, B'Elanna would entertain Miral with her favorite stories. Invariably they were of Tom, exploring an ocean world, losing a shuttle race in order to propose to her, or wrapping Miral in animal pelts and holding her for hours through the long winter nights on Boreth.

B'Elanna treasured these outings and was unpleasantly surprised when she heard a rustling to the south of their camp one night. Someone was noisily following the river toward them, and her first act had been to reach for the phaser that was always close at hand.

In the fading light B'Elanna had soon made out a slight and feminine form. She had already begun to lower her phaser when Janeway's familiar voice had beseeched, "Don't shoot. I come in peace."

B'Elanna had not hesitated to rise and hurry to meet the admiral, who immediately enveloped her in a firm hug.

"It's so good to see you, B'Elanna," she had said, her eyes alight.

"And you," B'Elanna replied, surprised by the knot that caught in her throat at the unexpected sight of one so dear.

"Where is she?" Janeway teased, peeking around B'Elanna to spy Miral, who had looked up from the ant races she was monitoring the moment her mother had left her side. Once Miral had caught her eye, she had ducked for cover behind the log that was their campfire seat, but Janeway had eventually coaxed her out by approaching the log gingerly and coming to rest several feet from the child before bending to the ground and "discovering" a group of burrowing earthworms, which instantly captivated Miral.

By the time B'Elanna had seated herself again by the fire and offered Janeway some water, which she gratefully accepted, Miral had climbed into the admiral's lap and begun to wipe her filthy hands all over Janeway's otherwise pristine uniform.

"It's beautiful here," Janeway said, then added, "I hope you don't mind a little company?"

"Not when the company is good," B'Elanna replied honestly.

"Tom told me where to find you. *Voyager* is still en route back to Earth from Cestus III or I'm sure he'd have led me here himself."

"We'll see him in a few days," B'Elanna replied, wondering why a note of defensiveness had suddenly crept into her voice.

"Unfortunately, I'm here on business," Janeway admitted.

"Really?" B'Elanna said, truly puzzled.

"The strangest thing has happened." Janeway nodded. "A lunatic attempted to take over the Federation Embassy on Qo'noS and during the brief period in which he held it, he demanded that the High Council reveal that the Federation had actually replaced the Emperor Kahless with a hologram."

B'Elanna swallowed hard but managed to keep her face neutral.

"You're kidding."

"I'm not. Of course, at first we all assumed this was nothing more than further evidence of his insanity. The strange thing was, when the emperor finally appeared, he was, in fact, a hologram."

"Huh." B'Elanna attempted to display surprise.

"And not just any hologram," Janeway went on. "He was actually using a version of a holo-emitter frighteningly similar to the one used by our very own Doctor."

At this B'Elanna couldn't even find a sound to make.

"The good news is, Ambassador Worf was able to re-take the embassy, and for now, the fact that the emperor has gone absent without leave and replaced himself with a hologram is still a closely guarded secret, which I trust you will not repeat."

"Of course not."

"Starfleet is helping in the search for the flesh-and-blood emperor, and I'm hopeful that when he is found he will clear up this little mystery. Meantime it has fallen to me to try and make a little sense of it. The bottom line is, there aren't that many people we know of who could have created a holo-emitter so similar to the Doctor's. I've already spoken with him and with Seven, and both of them are every bit as unnerved as I am."

"I see." B'Elanna nodded.

"I realize, of course, that for the last many months you and Miral have been living here and probably have less than no interest in such political matters, but I have to ask, B'Elanna. Do you have any idea who else might have done such a thing?"

B'Elanna forced herself to return Janeway's even gaze.

"I'm sorry, Admiral, I don't," she said.

Janeway continued to stare into B'Elanna's eyes, and B'Elanna told herself she wasn't seeing disappointment reflected back at her.

Soon enough, Janeway turned to study the fire and said softly, "I see."

Miral had finally relaxed into Janeway's arms and was beginning to fall into a well-earned sleep.

"I'll take her if you like," B'Elanna offered, reaching out.

"It's all right," Janeway replied wistfully. "I don't get to see nearly enough of either of you anymore. I'll hold her a little longer if that's okay."

"Of course."

After a brief and uncomfortable silence Janeway said, "She looks so like you, B'Elanna."

"You can't see them now, but she has her father's eyes," B'Elanna replied. "And his funny crooked smile, especially when she's doing something she knows she's not supposed to."

"Well, that's your job right now, isn't it, little one?" Janeway cooed.

"When it comes to mischief, her future is bright," B'Elanna acknowledged with a grin.

Janeway turned back to face B'Elanna. "Are you well?" she asked. "Are you happy?"

"Most of the time," B'Elanna replied, treading carefully.

"May I ask why you haven't returned to Starfleet?"

"I just can't right now."

"But someday?" Janeway asked. "You're so good at what you do, B'Elanna. And I know that Chakotay would have you back in a second aboard *Voyager*."

"Yes, he's made that more than clear," B'Elanna admitted, "but I know Vorik is doing a wonderful job."

"He is. But Chakotay is worried about Tom. He's clearly missing something and my guess is it's you and this beautiful little girl. He doesn't complain, mind you. He'd never do that. But it's hard to understand why you've chosen to remain apart when both of you clearly need and love one another so very much."

B'Elanna picked up a small stick and began to poke the

fire with it, adjusting a log and sending orange and blue sparks flitting upward.

"We didn't make this decision lightly, Admiral," she finally said. "And we both agree that for now, we are where we have to be."

"If that's the case, then I understand," Janeway replied. "I wish it were different, but I will take you at your word, as always."

"Thank you."

"This isn't forever, though, is it?"

"I can only fight one battle at a time, and right now, I'm fighting the one in front of me," B'Elanna replied.

Janeway nodded thoughtfully.

"Okay. But remember, if you ever need an ally in that battle, you know where to find me."

B'Elanna choked back the tears that were welling in her throat.

"I do."

After settling Miral on her pallet for the night and giving B'Elanna another fierce hug, Janeway had transported out, and B'Elanna had spent the next several hours staring at the fire, her bitter tears falling freely.

Janeway had once again put her utter faith and trust in B'Elanna, and this time, she had let her down. She didn't know if Janeway believed her when she had lied about the holo-emitter, but she had at least refrained from pushing B'Elanna.

A year earlier Kahless had first asked about the Doctor's miraculous emitter, and when B'Elanna had come to understand that the emperor intended to sacrifice his work on Qo'noS to assure the safety of herself and Miral, she agreed to build the device that would make that possible.

Technically it was advanced Starfleet technology and certainly not something Command would approve of sharing, even with an ally, without wading through miles of red tape and political nonsense. B'Elanna had cut to the chase and provided him with a crude copy of the emitter, in addition to programming his holographic replacement. Kahless had then returned to Cygnet IV to watch for the Warriors of Gre'thor and to set up the communications network he would require to serve as a go-between for B'Elanna and Tom.

B'Elanna wanted to believe that if she had known that this would be the last time she would ever see Janeway alive, she might have done something differently. But as she saw Janeway's face again in her mind, her eyes filled with love, respect, and pride, she knew in her heart that there was nothing Janeway wouldn't have forgiven her for.

Perhaps one day, B'Elanna would once again meet the woman whose encouragement and support had brought B'Elanna safely through her own doubts and helped to forge the woman she had become. Janeway's presence and influence at such a critical time in her life had done more than anyone else's to define the qualities B'Elanna now held most dear and would work daily to impart to her own daughter. Most surprising of all was B'Elanna's fervent hope that should they meet again, it would not be in some human version of the afterlife, but instead, in Sto-Vo-Kor.

As B'Elanna allowed her mingled regrets and sadness to dissipate in a vision of the glorious place Kathryn Janeway now held among the honored dead, her communications panel chirped, alerting her to the presence of an incoming message.

Tom, her heart gasped as she quickly traced the transmission's origin.

She decrypted it quickly, but found herself running the algorithms through a dozen diagnostics before she could accept that the coordinates for their rendezvous could be accurate.

Just to be certain, she then double-checked the transmission's point of origin. Within moments all of her systems verified that the message had come from *Voyager*.

Her hands shaking, B'Elanna began the lengthy process of charting her slipstream corridor and compensating for the predictable subspace variances common to slipstream travel.

The coordinates Tom had sent were well within her vessel's range, but they were also in the last place B'Elanna would have expected them to be.

It seemed that *Voyager* was returning to the Delta quadrant.

In a matter of days, B'Elanna and Miral would join them.

JUNE 2381

EPILOGUE

"I'm pretty sure it's the right thing to do," Chakotay said softly. "We're wading into deep and uncharted waters here, but if Seven is right and the Caeliar are still out there somewhere, what other choice is there? I'm not willing to watch her fall into madness. We both know how strong she is, but I've never seen her so frightened. She wasn't this vulnerable in her first few days aboard *Voyager*."

After a brief pause, he added, "What do you think?"

The tall white pillar had no answer.

Not that he had expected one.

He'd long ago lost track of the time he'd spent seated at the base of Kathryn's memorial. In the dark days following her passing he had not allowed himself to indulge in the normal and fairly common practice of speaking aloud to the dead. Before he could permit this, he would first have to acknowledge in every fiber of his being that she was truly gone. Once that bridge had been crossed, many months too late, he had realized how much he still needed to say.

The lengthy, one-sided conversation had actually freed something in Chakotay's psyche he hadn't realized had been caged. He had begun by telling her frankly how angry he was at her for choosing to risk her own life rather than his. Didn't she understand how many would willingly have taken her place? Or spent the rest of their lives in the Delta quadrant rather than see her sacrifice herself to the Borg?

The moment he'd said the words, however, he had seen her face again in his mind's eye: the grimly set eyes, the faintly lifted chin, the absolute unwillingness to accept the notion that the universe would not accommodate itself to her wishes.

"You're the most stubborn woman I've ever met, Kathryn," he'd said. "And I'd give anything to be able to watch you stand here and deny it."

I miss you.

With that thought, the tears he had believed he was past crying had begun to fall. But living in the center of his pain were also the memories that made living without her possible.

Only then had he understood that by denying his grief he had also cut himself off from the happiness she had brought to his life.

Suddenly he saw vividly her delighted and disbelieving smile when he had led her into the woods near their temporary home on New Earth and shown her the wooden tub he had built for her; the soft glow of her face lit by candles in Leonardo's workroom the night they had promised one another never to allow their differences to tear them apart again; the chagrin with which she had announced to him for the tenth time that her replicator had once again burned their pot roast dinner; the drowsy contentment and peace of her face in repose, the one and only night she had belonged body and soul to him alone.

Laughter had burst freely through his tears, and Chakotay had allowed his mind to wander buoyantly through their life together.

"Remember the first time you tasted a leola root? The look on Neelix's face when he thought he'd poisoned his captain? The first time you hustled Tom Paris in a game of pool at Sandrine's? The day Naomi brought you her very first captain's assistant report? The day we walked into the cargo bay wondering which of our crew would stay behind with the 37's and their descendants and found it empty?"

It had taken hours to journey through the past—the good and the bad. But as each memory fell from his lips, it had lessened the weight in his stomach even as featherlight strands of recollection had embedded themselves permanently upon his heart where they would never again be lost to him.

Only once this was done had he brought her up to date with the challenges of his present. Chakotay had been raised to believe in a spirit world that inhabited the same universe as his own, but his brief time in that world had left him little doubt that the dead did not concern themselves overmuch with the affairs of the living. They could be a resource and a source of wisdom, but the journey after death was one's own, and there was little use in clinging desperately to your old existence when a new and glorious one beckoned.

He did not believe that Kathryn was watching over his every move, any more than his father or grandfather had dogged his daily path. It was only polite then, when a spirit was invoked, to provide a proper context for any question you might pose.

He had no one else with whom to share his concerns

for Seven. He believed even before he'd asked that she would probably already have taken the actions he was currently contemplating. Still, he made his case aloud, then listened, hoping against hope that he might sense something tangible that would assure him that she agreed.

The moon had been his only companion in the stillness of Federation Park. It had risen behind the gleaming pillar, bathing it in an almost eerie light and for hours making it the only clear object he could discern. But as it had begun to dip before him, the monument had fallen into shadow and ultimately pale darkness.

Suddenly conscious of the stiffness in his back and legs, Chakotay pushed himself up from the ground and brushed off the light droplets of condensation that had gathered on his uniform during his long vigil. He reached out for the pillar he could barely see, its cold, damp surface convincing him that it would stand as long as the Federation that had constructed it.

"What do you think, Kathryn?" Chakotay said again.

A single ray of light struck the pillar's base, and a long shadow grew from there, stretching over the grassy hillside toward the water of the bay. Chakotay turned to see the dawn breaking, and his heart quickened its pace to greet it.

Within minutes the light began to crawl upward, bathing the white stone in a brilliance whose glare was almost painful.

Chakotay watched its progress until it reached the level of his face and for a split second glimpsed briefly his reflection.

At that moment, five simple words echoed in his mind.

When in doubt, look here.

Without further ado, Chakotay raised steady hands to his collar and, one by one, removed the pips pinned there. He then removed his combadge and kneeled at the base of the monument.

He dug briefly in the soft earth, just enough to create a small indentation, laid the symbols of his service in the hole, and covered them with dirt, packing it down to hide any trace of his final gift to Kathryn.

Rising, he brushed off his hands and turned to leave the park, absolutely confident that he had made the right choice.

Within hours he would advise Admiral Montgomery of his decision.

His career in Starfleet had come to an end.

The *Star Trek: Voyager* saga
continues in

UNWORTHY

coming in
October 2009

ACKNOWLEDGMENTS

My friends and family are my first line of support. Their patience with me as I lock myself away for months at a time to do this work is a gift I can never truly repay.

Marco Palmieri gave me my first shot at professional writing. I consider it an honor that he has yet again demonstrated his confidence in me by entrusting me with the continuation of this story.

Maura Teitelbaum has done more to ensure my ongoing sanity than any agent ought to be required to do.

A number of my fellow authors have given their very valuable time and expertise to this project. Heather Jarman is always the first to offer hers. I am ever humbled by her insight and grace. David Mack, Christopher Bennett, William Leisner, and the marvel of *Trek* minutiae that is Keith DeCandido have made this story better, both by vetting the manuscript and by setting the bar to which I aspire in their own brilliant work. Christie Golden started the relaunch rolling and gave me many wonderful stories upon which to build.

My older brother, Matt, has come rather late to the party, but I'm so excited to be able to introduce him to the world of *Trek* literature in the same way he brought me to the original series. See? I told you there was still good *Star Trek* to be had.

My younger brother, Paul, remains a constant source of inspiration and also has my eternal gratitude.

As the only member of my immediate family apart from my mother who never fails to read my works the moment they are published, Ollie Jane Baker is due a special note of thanks.

And finally, Lynne, who literally makes my life as it is now possible.

I could never have written this story had I not absorbed the life lessons offered to me by my mother, Patricia, my mother-in-law, Vivian, and my father, Fred. I dedicated this work to him because even as our heroes struggle to accept an unacceptable loss, I have worked daily for years to come to terms with his. He remains an example of all that one dedicated person can do. More important, I think he would have liked this book. It is a testament to the many truths he has taught me in life and death.

At the end of the day, however, the greatest sacrifice made in the creation of this work was by my dear husband, David. He not only waits patiently while I sit alone for hours writing, he then listens raptly to every word and offers his wise counsel and unfailing support. He is my life, my heart, and my love.

Too many thanks, to one and all.

ABOUT THE AUTHOR

In addition to *Full Circle*, Kirsten is the author of the last Buffy book ever, *One Thing or Your Mother*, *Star Trek: Voyager—String Theory: Fusion*, and the Alias APO novel *Once Lost*, and contributed the short story "Isabo's Shirt" to the *Distant Shores* anthology. Her next addition to the *Star Trek: Voyager* universe will be released at the end of 2009.

Kirsten appeared in Los Angeles productions of *Johnson over Jordan*, *This Old Planet*, and Harold Pinter's *The Hothouse*, which the *L.A. Times* called "unmissable." She also appeared in the Geffen Playhouse's world premiere of *Quills* and has been seen on *General Hospital* and *Passions*, among others.

Kirsten has undergraduate degrees in English literature and theater arts, and a master of fine arts from UCLA. She is currently working on a feature film screenplay and is within spitting distance of completing her first original novel.

She lives in Los Angeles with her husband, David, and their very fat cat, Owen.